# THE MUCKER

# REVOLT

## THE ANEKSARIA BOOK 1

by

## CHRIS MARIES

# Gotham Books

30 N Gould St.
Ste. 20820, Sheridan, WY 82801
https://gothambooksinc.com/

Phone: 1 (307) 464-7800

Published by Gotham Books (December 22, 2022)

ISBN: 979-8-88775-163-4 (sc)

ISBN: 979-8-88775-164-1 (e)

# Table of Contents

For a thousand years, the Frame and its machine empire had ruled the people of Inalsol. A small group of folk known as muckers struggled for survival in a semi arctic mountainous district called Garvamore.

In other places the divines, a dehumanised elite, treat muckers as slaves. Only in Garvamore can muckers have any semblance of freedom.

A small group fight for the survival and future of the human race of Inalsol, building their strength in secret until discovered by the Frame. The Frame will destroy them and all hope for the people unless they defeat the technologically superior Frame in battle against all odds.

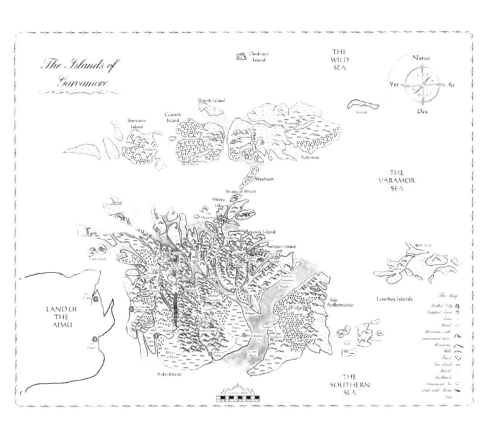

# Prologue

Cullin dipped his quill in the inkpot and sighed as he reminisced on his long and full life. He sighed again, leaving the quill in the ink. He leaned back in his chair as disorganised memories flooded his mind.

He caressed the highly polished surface of his old desk, admiring the shine and deep richness of the dark wood. The delicately adzed and carved desk made from wood harvested half a world away had been a gift for a service he had performed many years before. Constructed with the exquisite care and skilful attention to detail of the true Master Craftsman its beauty was only possible with many years of dedication and practice of a man truly dedicated to his craft.

The surface appeared rough from the patina of the adze used in its making, but had a smooth rippling effect like ripples on a lake. That made it special to Cullin as it represented the threshold between the living and the faery world where all good and righteous souls went when the body died.

Cullin still had the runes of the dead from his family and could recite the names of his ancestors. Losing or forgetting such family history was considered shameful and resulted in loss of respect and honour. The divines had almost wiped out the practice. Being without any family traditions at all, they couldn't understand it's importance.

Cullin had few active years left, years he intended to use to record his part in those events that had shaped the New World. Outside his study, he could hear the distant cheers of people celebrating a hundred years of freedom from the aimu, those mechanical monsters that had controlled human destiny for over a thousand years. Freedom mostly taken for granted after centuries of progress where every citizen could make their own choices on matters that shaped their lives.

As Cullin reflected, he recalled his early life as the fifth son of a minor Lord. A life controlled by the callous whim of the human servants of the aimu, the divines, who's arrogant and inhumane nature caused so much misery among the people. His father had the rather pompous, but empty title Lord Ossin, Chief of Mark Ossin. There was no real power behind the title, merely that of administration under the control of the divines who oversaw his every decision. Lord Ossin could not make, control or even influence the policies it was his job to administer. One of the Divine Generals had to approve every decision the Lord made. Ossin had been a huge bearded man with a large mane of red hair and the uncanny knack of striking fear into people with an intense, intimidating glare. That glare had coerced and cowed the denizens of Glen Ossin for many years, preventing open rebellion against the divines and their masters. Despite his bullying methods, Ossin had been a tender-hearted man who knew a fight against his superiors would be doomed to failure and would result in bitter recrimination against the people of Glen Ossin.

Cullin had been born on the first day of the New Year in NE 1000, underweight, premature and hadn't been expected to survive. Worse still for Cullin was that his mother, dearly loved by Ossin and the people of the glen, had died from haemorrhage during childbirth.

# Chapter One

By late autumn in NE 1016 Cullin had become a tough, wiry young man. Although he had no official duties he spent much of his time with the people of the glen, helping out where he could with livestock and encouraging the people. He became useful to the general population as a means of communication and a source of valuable information. He was popular and learnt a great deal about the needs of the ordinary folk of the glen.

Cullin had his own chamber in the dun where he slept and stored his few possessions. It was small and basic with a sleeping pallet and a shelved alcove. A small window gave him a view of the inner courtyard and the Great Hall opposite.

Cullin had been with his friend Ecta planning an excursion to the lower glen when he had received a summons to the Great Hall from his father. He arrived somewhat apprehensively finding his father in a towering rage. Cullin feared the worst for himself and Ecta in punishment for his latest misdemeanour.

''Where's Grega, I need him'', Lord Ossin roared after reading the letter sent from Lord Lowd of Mark Lowd.

Lord Ossin was in a foul mood and the demands of his over-proud neighbour made him rage with anger almost to the point that it matched his flaming hair. Screwing up the note is his vice-like fist he threw himself into his chair. The old wooden seat, cushioned with a throw of deer hide and furs groaned from the unexpected force, creaking like the joints of an old man as Lord Ossin, muttering, waited for his adviser, Advocate Grega.

Grega strode into the hall, his morcote streaming behind, his voice booming with confident power, ''My Lord, you have need of me?''

''Aye, our neighbour, Lowd, is up to his tricks again.''

Grega bowed asking with undisguised contempt ''the sheep again?''

1

"Of course the bloody sheep, he wants twenty Horse this time. Twenty Horse! How can a few dozen stray sheep be worth twenty bloody Horse! Here, see for yourself", Lord Ossin thrust the crumpled letter into the Advocates ancient gnarled hand.

An intense quiet settled over the narrow lined features of the old man as he considered the demands, "My Lord, he expresses concern that you are unable to stop your sheep from crossing our borders and so regrets having to charge you for rounding up seventy five of your sheep."

"I know that, but don't we find his sheep in our flocks and return them without charge? And why is it seventy five blasted sheep and not seventy six or seventy four? The man is a black sod, fit only for the company of pigs"

Grega winced saying "Ah, that is true, but we have already rounded up our sheep and so cannot return the favour."

Ossin's shepherds had recently returned Lowd's sheep over the southern pass. The southern pass ran west through the mountains where the waters of Glen Ereged and Glen Ossin met and flowed west to the waters of Atalok. The boundary between Mark Ossin and Mark Lowd marked with a single upright boundary stone, lay midway along this narrow mountain stream.

Cullin and his sidekick Ecta had been standing quietly to the side waiting to be seen by Lord Ossin. "Father, there are still sheep on the high ridges. Lowd never manages to round up his entire flock!" Cullin blurted out feeling a little breathless, he might avoid a thrashing yet.

Cullin's father cast him a withering look, "What's that boy, speak up."

"Lowd's shepherds are lazy, Father, they never go up onto the high ridges and round up the sheep there. They're far too fond of old Donal's hooch whisky to go onto the tops. He must have loads of sheep still up there." Cullin waited pensively whilst his Father continued to glare at him.

"How come you know so much about the whereabouts of Lowd's sheep?" Ossin demanded of Cullin.

"I have spent some time on the high ridges with the shepherds; when duties permit me Father." The last added timidly.

"Duties? What duties? Perhaps I should be giving you more duties. Better that than having you waste your time on foolish errands and childish laziness."

"Father, I..." was all Cullin managed before being cut short by his father.

"Quiet boy." Ossin barked gruffly.

"What do you think Grega, sounds like the boy's got an idea", Ossin was still glaring at his son, but with, perhaps, a little less rancour.

"It would take a few days to round them up, but we might tweak the idiots beard yet."

A deep rumbling of amusement came from Ossin's barrel chest, "Indeed we might Grega, indeed we might. Send the lads and a few dogs and see to it for me".

"As you wish my Lord, I will seek the appropriate authorisation from our Divine General", Grega departed with the same sense of the dramatic as he had entered the Hall with.

Lord Ossin turned to his son, stern faced, with all sense of amusement gone. "Now explain to me what happened at the pottery, why is Garath screaming for your blood. A week's labour gone, ruined because of your foolish games".

Cullin bowed his head in supplication to his Father hoping to mollify him with a show of respect "the boys were playing skits and I wanted to try my new sling. They let me cast a strike". Cullin tentatively offered the sling as evidence.

"Show me that boy" Ossin took the sling, inspecting it carefully, noting two unusual attached leather straps. "What's the point of these?" he demanded indicating the straps.

"I thought the extra length would give more power to the strike, Father." Cullin cast his eyes down; waiting for the painful judgement,

3

he knew must be coming. His back hadn't fully healed from the last session of 'education' by his Father. Sometimes Cullin wished he had been the son of a shepherd and not of a Lord. He loved wandering among the mountains and thought that a better life than that of a Lord's unwanted son.

Cona, Cullin's red bearded and heavyset eldest brother, was ever at their Father's side thought to speak up for his wayward younger brother. "The stones flew in all directions My Lord; they are still looking for the ten. Nor, indeed, was the casting stone found. It was a grand Slam My Lord, a worthy and noble strike."

"And you thought to test it outside the pottery?" Ossin demanded incredulously of Cullin. "Are you an idiot boy? Are you that stupid?"

The young man cast a woeful glance at his brother, not desiring such damning and rare help from his sibling, "No Sir, it won't happen again, I promise!"

Cullin, by now was shaking; he could almost feel the bite of leather thongs tearing into his skin. Tears were threatening, but he refused to cry. That was for children and he was nearly adult now. He would soon be seventeen and he would gain the respect of manhood.

"Look at me boy, stand straight when you talk to me", Ossin stared down at the object of his wrath and held out a white painted stone. "Does this stone belong to you?" he asked his son.

Ossin reminded himself that Cullin had been a small baby, lucky to survive his first few weeks, let alone grow to near adulthood. He looked down on his son noting his wiry strength. He was a tough young man with a quick mind, but lacking the massive bull necked strength of his other sons.

"Yes Father" Cullin replied rather meekly as he recognised his offending casting stone. "It won many games when I was younger."

"Hmmpff, better" he declared as Cullin stood his ground without fear on his face ", but you should look after your things better. The stone is chipped!" Ossin struck his son, a massive blow to his cheek that sent Cullin skidding across the wooden boards.

4

''Now be gone. Get out of my sight, I don't wish to see you again this day.'' Ossin watched as his son left with a bloodied nose. ''And Cullin, take your sling to the tanners. I want a dozen made and delivered to me by week's end.''

''Yes, Father'' Cullin replied making his escape from his Father's presence with eager haste.

Ecta, trembling as he waited his turn faced the huge bear of a man that was his master.

''You get to the stables and see to the tack. I don't wish to see you again either'' Ossin saw no point in punishing Ecta, he wasn't really at fault, but Ossin didn't want him to know that.

Lord Ossin hid a smile on his face as he turned his mind to other problems that demanded his attention; the grain harvest that year had been poor leaving insufficient food to feed the glens. Bitter winds off Ice Moor had ruined much of the crop, which would have to be replaced somehow. Later that evening as Cullin settled down on the hard sleeping mat, wrapped in his blankets to ward off the chill, it struck him that his Father, in dismissing him, had called him by his first name. Cullin tried, but could not remember Ossin using his given name before. For some reason this struck him as being important. He'd kept the casting stone though and for some reason that thought filled Cullin with pride. His father had kept the stone recognising its value and not discarded it.

---

Cullin was dressing himself in his chamber; he wanted to make an impression on his father who had a week earlier called him by his given name for the first time in his memory. He took the bundle of slings made by the tannery at the request of his father from the alcove and made his way through the damp corridors of the servants' quarters to the storehouses. By custom, he should enter the Great Hall via the Dun. The round Dun was the oldest part of Dunossin and now formed the tower. Built of stone hewn from the local mountains the Dun originally had a small circular yard at its centre. This had now been roofed over and formed a series of circular reception rooms used by Lord Ossin. The Great Hall was a later addition also built from the local

5

stone, but in a grander style more befitting a Lord of the Mark. For Cullin entering the Great Hall by its main doors would mean crossing the inner courtyard and all its muck and filth.

The storerooms connected directly to the kitchens where Cullin stole a cooling pastry from its rack incurring the wrath of Big Jon, the cook.

Big Jon was a formidable man that many considered the tallest in the Mark. Despite a large girth caused by too much tasting of food and sampling of his ale, few were willing to risk his displeasure and the large cleaver that was his favourite tool. Cullin was not particularly worried however, because he knew a large part of the cook's ill-tempered demeanour was merely a device to keep his staff and other servants in order. Besides, Cullin had cultivated his good nature by bringing in game from the surrounding hills and mountains.

Big Jon's favourite taunt was to call Cullin a thieving little runt to which the reply was invariably ''Stop me then old fat man!'' It was a game between the two that Cullin almost invariably won.

Cullin entered the Great Hall before Ossin, early as he had intended to be.

''Good morning young man. Lord Ossin will be with us shortly'' greeted a tired and grizzled looking Grega.

Cullin stood quietly at the side of the hall while Grega organised his papers on the large oak table that function as the head table for the communal evening meal served to the servants.

Ossin arrived in the hall and made his way to the oak table without acknowledging the presence of Cullin. ''Grega, how are you? Is there much business today?''

''Little, My Lord. There is time to breakfast.''

''Ah, good. I wish to inspect the repairs to the fishing docks this afternoon.''

The conversation between Ossin and Grega droned on in quiet hushed tones, seemingly without end. Cullin was frustrated and felt as if he was being tortured, unable to go without being given leave and yet not even being acknowledged by his father. All he could do was continue waiting as the morning dragged on. After the second wair he was feeling quite drowsy and would have fallen asleep on his feet had Ossin not called to him. A full eighth of the day had gone before his father had even addressed him.

"Cullin, make yourself useful and bring some food for Grega and myself. Don't be long, there is much to do."

"Yes, My Lord" Cullin answered, noting his father's slip. This was a quiet morning with little to do. Shaking the sleep from his head and nearly dropping his trussed up bundle of slings Cullin headed for the kitchen where he gained a further reprimand from Big Jon who had still to forgive him for the stolen pastry. He returned to the Great Hall a short while later after laden with a platter full of freshly baked bread, roasted venison (provided by Cullin from his most recent hunting trip) and preserved fruits from the stores.

Ossin and Grega were halfway through their meal with Cullin again patiently waiting before Ossin spoke to him again. "Have you brought those slings boy, I'd like to see them"

"Yes, My Lord. Here."

"Talkative young man isn't he" quipped Grega through a mouthful of roast haunch.

"Aye, just like his mother."

Ossin spent several silent sents inspecting the slings while continuing his breakfast. Twenty five sents, a quarter wair, had passed before he was satisfied with, Cullin presumed both breakfast and the slings. Finally at eight wair, midday, he turned to Grega "I like these improvements, our shepherds should find them quite useful."

"These slings show some intelligence so you may be of use to me Cullin. You are aware that we are in a dispute with Mark Lowd over a few stray sheep. Cona will be going to Lowd's estate to discuss our position. The gathering of his sheep is going quite well, as I'm sure you are aware." At this point Ossin looked steadily at his son; he was, in fact, well informed of the comings and goings of his youngest son.

7

"Cona's job will be to delay Lowd and keep him negotiating. Your other brothers will remain here and ensure our border remains secure. I don't want that arrogant arse of a Lord causing any more mischief. I don't want the Divine Beck25 getting involved. They would only take it as an excuse to reassign many of our people. Do you understand so far, lad?"

"Yes, father"

"Your job will be to bring to me the only person who can arbitrate on a matter between estates without the divines getting involved. Lowd doesn't want that any more than I do. Bring me Yayler Poddick, he will be difficult, but will come if you stress that I am calling in a favour"

"Yes, father"

"Eloquent lad, with such slick verbal prowess he should prove quite persuasive, My Lord."

Ossin glowered at Grega who nonchalantly helped himself to another slice of venison. "Well, at least he's not repeating those 'My Lord's' endlessly as you did on entering my service. I thought for some time they were the only words you had in your vocabulary."

Grega gagged on his meat as Ossin addressed his son. "Take Ecta with you. If he doesn't choke to death first, Grega will give you details on where to find Yayler." Looking directly at Cullin the Lord of Mark Ossin added, "You have about a month, forty days at best before Lowd starts to demand his tokens. You have my leave now"

As Cullin made his way across the hall Ossin called after him, "and thank you for the meat, it is very much appreciated!"

---

Sara's back hurt. It was late in the day and her shift would soon be over, always assuming the quotas had been met. The beet harvest had been brought in, but the ground now had to be prepared for the new crop. A back breaking and hard job with few rest breaks provided by the divines and their machine aimu overseers. Few of the slaves of the farm lived much passed thirty five years.

At fourteen Sara had passed the age when most girls had become pregnant, but none of the young men on the farm had chosen her yet. She had a fiercely independent streak and a strong intelligence that discouraged would be partners. These were characteristics that didn't help with the divine overseers who always seemed to expect more work from her than the others.

Normally, once a girl's pregnancy affected their ability to work efficiently they were transferred to the cloth works, shabby and draughty huts that leaked when it rained. The huts were divided into two sections. One end provided the sleeping quarters, bare wooden planks and devoid of any furniture. The girls made sleeping mats of tough beet fibres. To avoid theft they usually worked with their bedrolls strapped to their backs, a practice also used in the fields. The main part of the hut was given over to rough wooden trestles and benches where large rolls of beet cloth commonly referred to as 'beetick' would be fashioned by the girls into the clothing worn by the farm slaves.

The aimu grew the oil beet for the plants thick heavy oil that was refined and used as fuel. Once the beets had been pulverised and pressed to remove the oil the residue was cleaned by the slaves to provide the coarse fibres used for their clothing. The cloth works were considered light work. The normal working shift consisted of ten wairs, that is, ten sixteenths of the day, without breaks or refreshments. Slackers would be whipped by the divine overseers. Sara had noticed that the divines had rest breaks and shorter shifts. Sara knew that if slaves were given similar rest periods the work would be completed sooner and to a better standard. As it was, most slaves worked at a steady, but slow rate, so as to pace themselves for the long shifts. She had suggested the idea on one occasion to an overseer, but had been given a severe beating and short rations for her trouble. She had since learned to keep her mouth shut.

It was getting dark and Sara's shift was finally over. She maintained a quiet, passive demeanour as she helped her friend Feena stagger painfully off the field to the sleeping hut. Feena talked too much and had been whipped earlier to help her to concentrate on her work. The divine hadn't spared the whip and the fresh blood had congealed sticking her clothing to her back.

9

A pot of vegetable stew was provided for each hut, enough for the six slaves normally quartered per hut. Sara's hut housed eight slaves, but the same quantity of food was provided. They would be hungry again.

Sara managed to force some food down Feena whilst eating her own. Feena's back would have to wait or the others would have eaten all the food, leaving none for them.

Feena's back was quite a mess with three deep gashes from the whip. While Sara cleaned the wounds with fresh water her friend made no sound of complaint, even though she must have been in great pain. Tears streaked her face, however, especially when Sara stitched up the wounds with the finest thread she could find. The thread that was usually used for repairing clothes and bedrolls and too coarse for the fine work of stitching wounds.

By the time the job was finished the others in the hut had retired to their bedrolls and the hut had the quiet ambience of slumber. Feena remained mute, leaving Sara to muse on the hopeless situation and conditions of the slaves. Sara didn't think Feena would survive without rest; something she wouldn't be allowed. If the wounds became infected Feena would certainly die.

# Chapter Two

After the meeting with his father, Cullin had spent the rest of the day collecting kit and equipment he thought they needed on the journey to Yayler Poddick. Cullin wanted to travel light using their morcotes to keep them warm at night. They would have their slings of course, but Ecta was not very proficient with his. Cullin had also begged a couple of butchers knives from Big Jon who had acquiesced to the request surprisingly quickly without the usual threats adding a couple of flints for fire lighting and a rough leather sack containing dried meat.

They'd found a heavy pair of boots for Ecta whose normal light boots were old and leaked. Cullin had also been given a small pouch by Grega that contained a few tokens along with a letter of introduction for Yayler Poddick and various other parchments he felt might be needed. A large square hide of about two paces a side was also added to the equipment and four short iron shod poles.

The following morning as the pair prepared to leave the dun Ossin approached, striding swiftly across the outer court of the dun. ''Leaving without saying farewell, Cullin?''

''No father we were coming directly just as soon as we have checked over our gear'' explained Cullin.

''Ah, and is that all you're taking?'' Ossin asked eyeing the equipment laid out on the ground.

''Aye father, I thought travelling light would be quicker.''

Nodding absently Ossin enquired ''and what route were you planning on taking?''

''Er, well we can't go by Glen Ossin Father, as it takes us too close to Beck25's residence. We can't go by way of Balcon either, as it would take us through Lord Lowd's lands and is also a long way round''

''So what route are you taking'' asked Ossin, a little perplexed.

''Well, as I explained to Grega when he asked, we can go directly east from here and avoid Beck25 and Lord Lowd''. Cullin's reply was a trifle nervous as the mountains east of the dun were considered impassable at this time of year.

''You can't go that way Cullin, those ridges above Brayfrowk are a death trap. The gullies are choked with ice and snow and the slopes too steep and rough to climb. We've lost far too many on those crags. There is no way through!''

''You are better to go south east and cross the mountains before you reach Beck25's residence. The mountains are less steep and easier to cross''

''I know father, but we would be seen. The farmers and shepherds in Glen Ossin would be bound to see us. The fewer people there are who know what we're doing, the better.'' Cullin had given much thought to their route the previous evening and knew the ridges above the dun as well as anyone.

''Cullin, it doesn't help me or the Mark to lose you in some stupid accident just as you're becoming useful. I need to get that message to Yayler if I'm to stop Lowd's schemes.''

''I know, but I know a way through the mountains. I found a rake last year that avoids the gullies and steep crags. We can get through to Furlok without anyone the wiser.''

''I see. You're sure about this Cullin?'' Ossin asked his son.

''Yes father, I no more wish to die than anyone. I wouldn't choose this route if I wasn't sure it was practical. It will also leave Lowd and Beck25 in the dark.'' Cullin was beginning to feel a little elated. He had never stood his ground with Ossin before let alone won an argument.

''That's fine then, but I want you to take Ulbin with you. I want to know more about this rake. Now, I have other duties that demand my attention this morning. Ulbin will be with you shortly, don't leave without him. Oh and Cullin, take this and don't lose it'' Ossin handed Cullin a small disc inscribed with letters and the interlocking circle device that represented Mark Ossin. Without further farewell or as much as a backward glance, Ossin headed back to the Great Hall.

I took little time for Cullin and Ecta to pack their gear and they were lounging beside the main gates of the dun when Ulbin arrived in a poor mood.

''What's this job I've got to do then, eh, Runt?'' Ulbin was Cullin's large, heavy set and most disliked brother. Ulbin had little time for his younger sibling and was always ready with a quick insult.

''There is a rake up by Ardkiran that father wants you to describe for him'' Cullin gave his slow minded brother a steady, bored look.

''Why, what's up there, but rock and snow? I've got better things to do than this fools' errand, Runt.''

''Go and do them then, but you best be able to give father a good description of the rake.'' There was a certain satisfaction on Cullin's face, as he knew he had Ulbin at a disadvantage. ''It'll be cold up there so you'd best wrap up warm, brother.''

''I know how to handle myself; I don't need a turd brain to help me. Are we going or are we going to sun-soak all day!''

Cullin shrugged. He was used to Ulbin's unimaginative insults and was usually happy to ignore them. The three young men set off from the dun without further discourse or preparation and climbed the narrow path that lead onto Brayfrowk. Snow covered the upper part of the hill and heaped about Kuli's Cairn. Cullin paused to note a fresh sprig of heather tucked in amongst the rocks and reflected on the manner of his birth and the mother he had never known. Ossin had taken the time to tend his wife's grave in the last few days.

---

It was the first day of the new year as Lord Ossin sat on a rock on Brayfrowk, a hill overlooking the snow covered glen and grey round tower and abutting block of the Great Hall of Dunossin and adjacent out buildings. Lord Ossin wanted some peace and quiet to contemplate the birth of his fifth child. Kuli was in labour and Lord Ossin had been shooed out of the way.

It was before dawn and the sun wouldn't rise above the mountains for another couple of wairs. The glen was dark and dismal; Lok Ereged to the north was dull, dreary and forbidding, its northern end frozen. Dark, low clouds were streaming in from the northwest threatening more snow. The mountains and crags that enclosed the glen had become dark and menacing with a pervasive melancholic chill. Ossin drew his finely knit woollen morcote about him as a chill blast of wind made him shudder against the cold.

He knew he should make his way back to the Dun, but cherished this brief moment of freedom from duty. He'd been shooed away from Kuli's bedside earlier that day by Katrin the Herbwoman, performing her duties as midwife. After a while, with his emotions better under control, he sighed as his thoughts turned to her difficult labour and collected a handful of heather sprigs that had lain hidden beneath their blanket of snow. He bound the heather with a small, delicate ribbon of finely worked leather he had been keeping as a gift for her. She had always loved the heather carpets that covered the hills around the Dun. He sighed again and started to make his way apprehensively back down the hillside of Brayfrowk.

A thin path wandered back to the dun, hidden now under the snow. Lord Ossin knew the way well enough without the need to see the path below his feet as the hillside that was a favourite spot of his Kuli. They had walked the path many times over the years, discussing their private thoughts and the politics of the Mark. This was a place where they could share private thoughts and intimacies they did not wish overheard or spread by gossips about the dun. This was a special place, a quiet and treasured place, a place where Kuli and Ossin could confide in their most personal and sensitive thoughts.

As he approached the gates of the dun, he could see Grega his Advocate and second in command pacing back and forth nervously before them.

''Hurry My Lord, there is little time''

''How is she, how is my Kuli?''

''Not good Doogal, we must hurry. There is little time.''

14

"Is it the bleeding again? She's had a hard time of it these last few months."

"Just so", Grega stopped and looked Lord Ossin directly in the eye, "Doogal, Katrin has done everything possible, but there is too much blood. She can't stop the bleeding."

"Then we must make haste, my friend."

The two men clattered through the corridors to Kuli's bedside, but even as they entered the chamber, it was clear from the look on Katrin's ancient, tear stained face that they were too late.

Katrin gently ushered Grega out of the chamber and left Ossin beside Kuli's silent form. Lord Ossin cried openly, cradling his dead wife in his arms, stroking her cheek tenderly as his tears made tracks down his own cheeks. Even in death, Kuli was a strikingly beautiful woman despite having born five children. Her fifth child had been too much for her slender frame. Frequently sick during the pregnancy despite the best care that Dunossin's herbmen could provide. She had died with the characteristic calmness that had marked her entire life. In death, that calmness belied the great suffering and pain that she had endured. Even as she died, she held her newborn babe to her breast and named him Cullin after the warrior from the ancient legends and myths she adored so much. Lord Ossin rocked his giant frame back and forth, as his grief took him, shaking from the silent sobs catching in his throat until it burned.

Eventually, his grief spent, he gently laid his wife back down on the bed, tidying the sheets and blankets and drawing them up to her chin as if she was merely sleeping. Beside her, on the pillow he laid the few dry sprigs of heather that he had collected earlier on the hillside above the dun.

At last, in the early wairs of the morning he composed himself. Grega, a tear betraying his emotions, gave Ossin a massive hug and then bowed to his Lord.

"Have my Kuli buried on Brayfrowk amongst the heather and build a cairn to mark her place of rest." He laid a gentle hand on Grega's shoulder and turned to leave.

''My Lord, what of the Divine General Howe19, he will wish to see the body'' Grega bowed his head in a placid, subservient gesture.

Despite Grega's peaceful and gentle nature Ossin turned and grabbed Grega by the throat, lifting him bodily with the force and slamming him against the stonewall of the chamber. He snarled with uncharacteristic and barely controlled rage ''I don't give a pig's fart what that piece of cac thinks. Bury my wife with the honour she deserves and by the black ass of the Lord of Hell I don't give a damn what that piss-poor excuse of a man thinks.''

Choking with his feet raised off the ground Grega could do little more than nod a meek acquiescence. After a long stare at his Councillor Ossin relaxed his grip as he took a stronger hold on his distressed emotions and set the man back on his feet. ''My apologies Grega, that was unfair of me. Ever you have served me well, but I will not have that dung heaps filthy paws anywhere near my wife''

As he coughed and regained his breath Grega could only stare at his Lord, and finally, with great effort and a tremulous voice, could only mutter with a broken and feeble croak ''it will be as you wish, Doogal. My Lord''

As Lord Ossin turned to leave, Grega had enough left in him to plead to the grief stricken Lord, tears in his own eyes, ''What of the child, what shall become of the babe?''

''It lives?'' Thinking only of his wife, Ossin had assumed the child had died at birth along with its mother.

''Indeed, the babe lives and is well enough considering it's birthing. Do you wish me to find the babe a wet nurse and fosterage? It was only two thirds of a kiedweight and is unlikely to live long''

''Only sixty or so ounces, that small? Ahh, that is not good, my friend. Yes, do what you can for the babe, though I do not wish to see it, at least not yet.'' With a deep sigh, Ossin asked his old friend ''Does the child bear a name?''

''Aye, even as she died. She named him Cullin not five minutes before you entered her chamber.''

Fresh tears broke on the unhappy Lords face ''Ah, a good name, let's hope the poor child lives long enough to live up to it. Keep me informed of his well-being, would you. I'll make the tokens available for his welfare.''

The Frame, the computer master of the human race and the aimu, had long ago banned the use of coins or money, but had found it, through simple social inertia, to be a policy impossible to enforce. Thus, the computer had introduced the use of tokens. Each household in the population had an account of tokens recorded by the local Divine General.

With a swirl of his great woollen morcote, the Lord left the chamber leaving a tired and troubled Grega to attend to his duties.

Cullin was given to the care of Dillis who had lost her own babe not a week before. Indeed Lord Ossin was true to his promise and was most generous, giving Dillis a chamber of her own and all the tokens she needed to pay for its upkeep. Lord Ossin, though, kept his distance from his child, not wishing the painful reminder of his lost wife.

Lord Ossin had never come to love Cullin, tainted, perhaps by the manner of his birth and the fact that the child was rather small, weak and frequently wheezing. Cullin's four elder brothers picked up on their father's distant attitude and became disparaging and dismissive of their younger sibling, often using him as the butt of a joke or outright insult.

---

''Stop your wool-gathering Cullin. It's a long climb onto the ridges'' Ulbin disturbed Cullin's reverie abruptly.

''Do you remember much about our mother Ulbin?''

''A little, not much. Come on we're wasting time.''

The path disappeared into a boggy mess of peat hags and groughs on the downward eastern slope of Brayfrowk. Above the grey slopes of Ardkiran loomed with disdainful menace, shrouded with dark clouds that promised snowfall before the day was out.

The way started easily enough on grassy, sheep mown slopes that gave way to heather. By midday, the party were struggling over scree and small outcrops of hard black rock. Ulbin had fallen behind the other two, less active than the other two he had spent too much time in the Great Hall enjoying the rich heather ale brewed by Big Jon. Consequently, he was unfit and carried too much weight.

A huge crest of icy rock rose above them. Sheer on either side with jagged flakes and pillars the monstrous steeple of rock gave its name, Ardkiran, to the mountains above. Cullin knew the best way up was to stay close to the crest as this had the most easily climbed gradient. Beyond there was a narrow arête that connected with the bulk of the mountain.

Either side of Ardkiran were massive, deep corries with steep, near vertical walls of several thousand paces in height and several strides wide. Both north and south there were further, lesser corries that were still large and impassable. Local wisdom believed that a twenty stride stretch of the mountains east of Dunossin was completely impossible to cross.

A year before Cullin had been exploring these cliffs, looking for sheep that for some inexplicable reason found their way onto these great crags and cliffs. Cullin had failed to find the particular sheep he had been searching for, but instead had found a snowbound cleft that was hidden by large flakes of sheer rock. He'd been able to climb the forty-five degree slope and found that it opened out onto the shoulder of Ardkiran Mor, the highest of the local mountains. On that occasion, he had sheltered from a storm with only his morcote as protection from the weather. The following day he had made his way back down the cleft, falling and slipping repeatedly in the deep snow. At one point, he had found himself hurtling head first down the chute of snow towards large boulders. He had managed to stop his descent with arms, digging them into the snow to provide a brake.

This was his rake. Difficult, dangerous, but Cullin was better prepared this time.

Ulbin caught up with Cullin and Ecta, red faced and out of breath. ''We're not going up that surely?'' he panted.

18

''No, I've climbed that way myself, but it's not the best way; too dangerous in bad weather.'' Cullin noted Ulbin had an incredulous look on his face.

''It's true Ulbin, If anyone knows a way through these hills that doesn't mean getting killed then it's Cull'' Ecta was not a talkative young man, not liking to waste his time on needless chatter. ''Looks a bit rough up there, Cull''

''Aye, but there is a place to shelter''

''Best get on with it then'' replied Ecta.

Out of his depth and clearly outmatched by the younger lads Ulbin could do little more than follow mutely.

A few large flakes of snow started to drift down from a grey sky as they approached the rubble-choked entrance to the rake. About ten paces into the cleft the way was blocked by a near vertical wall of rock some fifteen paces in height.

''you're kidding Cull, we can't climb that!'' A startled Ecta cast a wide eyed look of horror towards his friend.

Ulbin was less generous. ''You cac faced runt; what in the name of Hesoos is this? You said you knew an easy way up this rock. Your wits always were a bit addled you stupid bull's member. You're a worthless piece of cac.'' Ulbin pinned his brother against the rock face by his neck easily lifting him off his feet.

Cullin was thrust violently to the ground, smashing his head against the rough wall of the cleft as Ulbin made to leave only to find his way blocked in the narrow confines by Ecta.

With his exit thwarted Ulbin turned back to his brother. ''Well cac-head, you got somewhat to say?''

''Aye, brother, both Ecta and I can climb that rock and if you weren't so fond of Donal's Hooch you wouldn't be so afraid of a little piece of dumb rock.'' Although Cullin was in pain and bleeding from a small gash on his head and gasping from the recent constriction of his throat, he was not particularly fazed by Ulbin's behaviour. He was well used to the unsophisticated and domineering bullying employed by his brothers. He was never going to beat them with brawn as he was so much smaller, but he had developed other strategies to get what he wanted.

''What?''

''It's simple enough brother. You see that narrow crack on the left?''

Getting nothing but a blank stare from Ulbin, Cullin continued his explanation. ''You jam your fist into the crack and make your way up that way.''

''What, how?'' Ulbin was not impressed, ''Show me then. Worthless''

''You do it like this brother.'' Cullin thrust right his hand into the rocky crack and formed a fist. He then did the same again with the other hand and taking the weight of his body on his hands walked his feet up the rock wall until they were nearly level with his hands. He then leant back with lithe athleticism to face Ulbin with a cheeky upside down grin. ''Got the idea now?''

Without thinking Ulbin spluttered ''I can't do that! I'm not a cacking monkey!''

''Go back to father then.'' Cullin replied as he worked his way up the fissure.

Ulbin turned to Ecta with a look of consternation on his face. ''What? I can't.''

Ecta shrugged and gestured towards the rock face with the straightest and most bland expression he could muster.

''Watch closely Ulbin'' said Cullin as he continued to work his way up until he topped the rock wall.

Ulbin followed without further complaint and after only a few minor slips joined his brother. ''Could have used a rope Cullin'' he gasped as he regained his equilibrium.

Shortly after Ecta was with the brothers and Cullin explained the rest of the climb. Above the cleft the narrow gully broadened slightly and could be seen to rise at a steady forty five degree angle. The snow gradually grew more intense until Cullin called a stop mid-afternoon.

''We'll not be able to go much further today. A short way above us the rake opens out onto the shoulder of Ardkiran. We need to find shelter before then. Now, Ulbin, Ecta is carrying a hide that the two of us can use, but we have nothing for you. It is probably best if you make your way down before the weather gets much worse.''

''Aye, that's just what I was going to suggest, Cullin.''

''Best get on with it then.'' Cullin started to continue the climb up the rake and paused. Turning back he added ''be careful going down. No one's going to help if you fall.''

The brothers parted and Cullin watched as Ulbin stumbled and slid on the rubble and scree that choked the rake. With some surprise, Cullin realised that he hoped Ulbin wouldn't fall and break something. Ulbin was his brother and despite the enmity between them, Cullin wished his brother well.

Cullin and Ecta continued up the rake in worsening weather until they reached a wall of stones. Cullin knew of its' existence because he had built it. The wall was slightly short of a pace in height and had three sides abutting an overhanging wall of rock. The hide they had brought with them completed the shelter and the pair settled down with a meal from provisions provided by Big Jon.

''Cull, do you think Ulbin will get down alright?''

''Should do; he's an arse and less bright than a rutting stag, but underneath all that flab he's pretty tough.''

''Hope he makes it.''

''Aye.''

Ulbin's thoughts ran rather differently and more angrily. He had gained quite a few bumps and scrapes on his descent, negotiated the rock wall at the beginning of the rake and was quietly fuming to himself as he walked back across Brayfrowk in the dark. He was deeply resentful that Cullin was a lot brighter than he was since he had first realised the fact several years before. In a strange dichotomy of emotions, Ulbin also respected that intelligence and could even, deep within him, admired it. As the emotional conflicts warred within him, he came to the conclusion that he had been abandoned. Ulbin was left to his own devices to live or die in the foul weather that was now engulfing the highest ridges in a swirling mass of dark, snow laden cloud. He could have sheltered with his brother and descended the following morning. The seed of a dark hatred of his brother grew within Ulbin's heart.

The following morning Cullin and Ecta woke to a bright blue sky. Overnight a storm had raged covering the ground with a layer of fresh snow.

''Cold night, Ecta'' Cullin greeted his friend.

''Aye''

''We must move on. I suspect we'll see more snow before the day is out.''

The pair quickly packed their gear and continued the climb up the rake. Cullin's shelter was located near the top and they soon found themselves on a broad shoulder of broken rocks and boulders south of the jagged peak of Ardkiran, covered now by a fresh layer of snow. Beyond, running to the east they could see a broad snow filled valley enclosed by steep sided ridges, its far end lost in mist.

''Hesoos, Cull, that valley is huge.''

''Aye, it's bigger than Glen Ereged and nobody lives there.''

# Chapter Three

Feena was late to arrive at the field where the other slaves had already started to dig the unforgiving soil. Sara furtively watched as the divine guard escorted Feena onto the field. The bored guard may have been a divine and as such could never make a mistake, but he was dismissive of the slave's abilities, free with his whip and never considered the possibility of a slave being smart enough to outwit him. He departed immediately he saw Feena's back bent to the ground and returned to his more important duties.

The guard, Sara noticed, had failed to report the addition to the workforce to the divine in charge of the digging resulting in the tally of slaves being unaltered. There was one extra slave on the field. Realising the importance of this Sara increased her work rate. If she could get off the field without being noticed the divines would never know that she was missing. She wanted to be ahead of the others when the work group reached the edge of the field where it was bounded by a deep overgrown ditch.

Another slave had fallen behind the work crew as Sara neared the edge of the field. With shock and horror, Sara realised that Feena was receiving further discipline. One of the guards was screaming at her, calling her a useless lazy mucker and other insults as Feena tried frantically to catch up with the other slaves. Sara had done her best for the victimised Feena, tending to her injuries daily and doing enough of her work in the fields to allow her to escape further punishment. In a very real sense, Sara's decision to push ahead of the others had lead to Feena's current plight.

The distraction was however exactly what Sara needed to get off the field unnoticed. With bitter feelings of guilt, Sara slipped quietly into the ditch. She crawled as far from the others as she could and concealed herself under a tangled mass of briars not caring for the tears and scratches she received. Her escape had so far gone unnoticed.

She needed to think and act fast in order to stay free. On the rare occasion that slaves escaped, once caught, they were always executed by the divines. The divines insisted that this was so and would deliver lectures on the futility of escaping.

At the end of the shift, the slaves would be driven like cattle back to their huts and counted. That is when her absence would be noted and the hunt for her would begin. She had to be far away by then. She crawled out from under her prickly hiding place as it began to rain and made her way along the ditch and into the neighbouring field.

Throughout the rest of the day, she made steady progress avoiding the roads used to take the harvested beets from the fields and deliver them to the processing plants. It was raining hard by late evening so she found shelter under a rock outcrop rather stay in the rain filled ditches. Scared, cold and shivering she spent the night under the scant shelter with her wet beet fibre dress clinging to her slight body and providing little protection.

To the west, she could see lights moving in the sky, lights from intelligent machines, the aimu. The aimu were the divines masters and were themselves ruled by the hyper-computer, the Frame. They were looking for her now. Sara crept into the deepest crevice in her shelter and tried to sleep.

Sometime towards dawn, she was dozing, with unpleasant thoughts of the Divines and the aimu dominating her mind. Yet she was still aware of her surroundings. She was awake and yet not awake.

Suddenly she brought out of her reverie by a loud thrumming. She squeezed further into the crevice, terrified that the aimu had found her. Bright lights shone about her shelter and strange noises assaulted her.

She could see silhouetted figures moving beyond her shelter carrying lights and approaching her shelter. A brighter light cast a searching beam into her crevice.

''Come on out filthy little mucker'' a disembodied voice bellowed.

Sara had been found; she had failed causing the death of her friend Feena. Sara was convinced that Feena's inability to work fast enough would have resulted in more severe punishment and her execution. The divines did not keep slaves that could not meet quotas. Executions were public, performed in front of the slaves as an example. 'Work hard or you will die' was the ethic that the divines promoted.

Sara was too scared to move, if the divines and the aimu wanted her they would have to come and get her. Adrenaline was rushing through her system, fight or flight feelings overwhelmed her. Either response would result in her death. With her heart thumping in her chest, Sara played dead.

''We know you are there. Come out and we won't hurt you'' the disembodied voice claimed.

Sara felt like screaming *'no you won't hurt me, you'll kill me'*. She kept silent and still as the search beams penetrated deep into the cleft under the rock.

Other devices were used to search under the rock. Heat seeking and movement detectors all failed to locate Sara. The continued chants of ''come out, come out, we know you're there'' became meaningless.

The aimu moved on and Sara was left with the ruddy early morning illumination of the sun. Silently she cried; somehow she had avoided capture. Inner strength grew within her. The aimu; the divines were not unbeatable. They made mistakes; they had not found her.

Sara was completely oblivious of the heat seeking abilities of the aimu or the nature of the equipment used to search for her. Over the next few days she made a roughly eastward course hiding under the thickest foliage and deepest ditches or outcrops she could find during her rest periods.

---

''How do we climb down into that glen Cull? I don't see any way.''

''Ahh, it took me a while to find a way. It's over to the right, a little further down the shoulder.''

As they descended using their iron shod poles to steady their way the opening to a gully came into view. The gully was choked with rocks and boulders, but the pair made rapid progress as the first flakes of fresh snow fell from the sky.

Over the next couple of days between squalls of snow and hail and periods of sunshine Cullin and Ecta made their way down the glen disturbing wild game of deer, hare and grouse that seemed thickly populated in this isolated valley. Towards the evening of their second day, the glen ended abruptly with steep slabs of rock down which the valleys broad stream cascaded in a series of waterfalls. Damp spray choked air that was filled with the roar of rough water as it plummeted to the wide valley below to join with the cold waters of Furlok.

The pair made camp at little distance from the stream using their poles as digging sticks to excavate a hollow in a snowbank and using their hide as the door.

The following morning was bright and fresh as Cullin and Ecta made their way down beside the waterfall and below the snowline. Their journey took them south by the western shore of Furlok. The steep slopes of the mountains descending directly to the waters' edge making travel difficult. They negotiated some of the ridges that plunged into Furlok, but others had only a narrow strip of icy rime covered boulders as the only way forward. After a day of difficult progress, they made camp and camped overlooking the frozen southern end of Furlok that Cullin planned to cross the ice the next day. After a cold night of with more snow and strong winds, Cullin and Ecta discussed Cullin's plan.

''I don't like it Cull, the ice is too thin. I don't fancy swimming in freezing cold water.''

''Nor I Ecta, but there is a road on the other side. It will be torture to continue on this side. We're at the edge of the ice at the moment, it will be thicker a little further on.''

''Fine, but if we can avoid crossing the ice I would be happier. I think we should decide when we find thicker ice.''

''Agreed. Well we best be at it then.''

After a wair of difficult travel along the frozen shoreline, they stopped and after a brief discussion decided that the ice was thick enough. The fresh snow lying on top of the ice gave their boots some grip, but they found progress was slow and difficult. The ice creaked and groaned as if it was speaking to them, complaining about their presence. By nightfall, they were still on the ice, but opted to continue.

A bitter freezing north wind continually buffeted them making every step hard.

They were exhausted from the constant battle against the elements with their morcotes stiff rime when they finally reached the eastern shore of Furlok. A brief search in the dark for a campsite rewarded them with a raised patch of moor, sheltered by a large boulder. They scraped snow away to reveal the heather and moss lying underneath. Their square of hide and poles provided a rude tent into which they collapsed.

''Well that wasn't too bad, eh Ecta'' Cullin remarked ironically.

''A piece of cake, I can't think what I was complaining about.'' An odd look crossed Ecta's tired and drawn face as a thought struck him ''have we got anything left to eat, I'm hungry.''

''A bit of stale bread, that's all. We'll have to hunt game from now on.''

They ate a cold and unsatisfying supper of dry bread before they turned in, hunched up in morcotes to keep out the bitter cold.

The following morning they awoke stiff and cold. It was another three days travel to the Tavern where Cullin hoped they stay for a couple of days to rest and dry out. Their campsite proved to be only a short distance from the drover's road.

The road was more of a muddy track, not as well made or maintained as the Glen Road of Mark Ossin. It was deeply rutted and frozen hard in the wintry weather. Towards midday at a sharp bend in the track, they could see a lonely figure beside a large post structure twice the figures height, roughly humanoid in shape, but lacking any clothing. It was an aimu. The machine had a broad metallic torso that lacked any apparent waist surmounted by a cylindrical collar. The most odd and disturbing feature of the robotic humanoid was its complete lack of a head. An aimu transport sat in the middle of the track. It was a six wheeled affair short and blocky in appearance.

The aimu turned to look at them and returned to its contemplation of the post before it. The two young men carried on walking towards the aimu though fear gripped them. What if the aimu challenged them; questioned them? They had been seen and any other action other than to proceed as if nothing was untoward could elicit a response that may result in them being hunted down as renegade muckers.

The aimu was a hiu, a Human Interface Unit that would normally interact with divines, not with the native population of the glens. Hiu were the Frames most intelligent and capable mobile units, able to operate without instruction for extended periods of time. Their main function was to communicate instructions to divines where other more direct forms of communication and observation were difficult. They had a large capacity for storing data that could be downloaded via com-posts.

The aimu noted the presence of the muckers and downloaded the information via the com-post and closed down its connection with the Frame. It had duties to perform for the Frame in Bandrokit that required direct observation. Its duty was not high priority and so the aimu had been given a transport unit rather than a flier. It turned toward the muckers noting the fear pheromones in the air.

The aimu had no instructions regarding travelling muckers other than a standing instruction to make a report. They posed no threat and fear was a normal response to an aimu presence. The hiu boarded its transport and continued its journey passing the two muckers and apparently ignoring them.

Cullin and Ecta continued their journey managing to kill game with their slings. The following day towards evening Cullin and Ecta arrived at The Tavern.

The Tavern was a drovers inn that served travellers. It was a squat building made of stone with a heather thatch and wooden extensions. Drovers used adjacent stone walled fields to hold their stock while they rested and recuperated at the inn. The inn also served as a meeting place and for socialising. They were assaulted on entering by the noise and stench of stale beer and unfriendly stares from grizzled drinkers. Cullin shook off a dusting of snow from his morcote that bore the two interlocking device of Mark Ossin, but lacked mark of office or trade.

''We need a room for the night and some food'' Cullin explained to the attractive redhead behind the bar. Her hair was tied back in a ponytail by a leather thong. She wore a dark grey belted woollen dress with the family marks in a band down the sleeve. A U shape surmounted by the swirl mark of a publican showed her to be of Mark Kyle and probably the landlord's daughter. The dress showed off a slim athletic body.

''You got the tokens, boy?'' The young woman was only a few years older than Cullin, but bore the attitude of a woman many years older. She gazed levelly at Cullin revealing beautiful grey blue eyes set in a tanned almond shaped face. The chin, he noted, was just a little too sharp to make her face beautiful.

''Well?'' Varee prompted again.

''Oh, er, aye. Here'' Cullin, distracted by the natural attractiveness of the woman before him, gathered his wits ''I have a note from my father's Advocate.'' He handed over the parchment given to him by Grega authorising withdrawals from the Marks accounts.

Nearby, a grizzled grey haired heavyset man snorted into his beer, stifling his obvious amusement at Cullin's discomfort.

''Mark Ossin? You're a long way from home boy. I will have to talk to my father'' Varee left with the parchment leaving the two young men shuffling their feet in the sawdust on the wooden boards, intended, no doubt to soak up spilt ale and doing a poor job of it, Cullin noted. Varee returned a few minutes later with a portly, balding man of middle years.

''Ossin you say, I've had no dealings with Mark Ossin for many years''. The man who wore a finely woven, but stained, woollen shirt was drying his hands on a non-too clean cloth. ''Where is this young man, Varee?''

The slight barmaid indicated Cullin and Ecta, casting a dark look at the drunk who was still sniggering into his beer.

''Ah, which one is Cullin?'' asked Rorga, the overweight landlord looking between the two youths.

Cullin raised a nervous finger ''Er, I am sir.''

''Don't look like your father, boy'' said Rorga scrutinising Cullin closely.

29

"I'm told I take after my mother."

"Ah, you do have the look of Kuli. Sweet lass she was, been gone too long now. Your father and Kuli stayed here for some time when I was young. They had just been wed then. He gave me much advice on what he thought could be done with this place without the involvement of the divines or the aimu. All my customers keep an account with their own Marks Advocate who then settles the accounts between the Marks. The person bearing the note from Grega can use it to open an account with any Mark. Don't lose it boy."

Rorga gave Cullin back the parchment holding onto it for a moment before releasing it. "It also asks that you be able to prove who you are, without that proof anyone could open an account in your name with this note."

"Father gave me this" Cullin scrabbled about in the pouch that Grega had given him that also contained the disc that he'd been given by his father.

"Ah, that will do nicely young man" Rorga took the proffered disc and inspected it closely before handing it back. "place your thumb over your family's mark, Cullin, and hold it there firmly for a short while. It takes a little time for the magic to work."

As Cullin held the disc, the outer edge began to glow with an amber luminescence. The disc would only glow if held by a member of Ossin's family as it read the DNA of the holder. The drunk grunted, looking mournfully into his empty mug "Ossin is it? Well, well" he muttered, slurring into the empty vessel.

"Beer, barman, beer. Ah've given yer gud tokens, not a slops wage fer it, now fill up!" The drunk slammed his mug down on the bar and gave Rorga the best sober gaze he could manage, which was unsteady and unfocused.

The bar had a lip on the customer's side and trough on the barman's side to collect spillages. Customers would traditionally throw a tip of unwanted tokens onto the bar at end of the evening as a reward for good service, the tokens inevitably roll into the collected slops leading to derogatory term for tokens as 'slops wage' meaning a pitiful income.

''Certainly Pyta, same again is it?''

''Aye'' grunted Pyta, shoving his mug over. For some reason he didn't ask Varee, but Rorga who he could see was busy.

''Serve the gentleman please, Varee, while I settle this business.'' Rorga turned his attention back to Cullin ''I can give you board for the night and a good meal with beer. I owe that to your father, so I won't be charging. Keep your tokens boy, you may need them elsewhere sometime.''

Rorga closed Cullin's hand about the disc ''and keep that safe.''

Cullin stuffed the disc back into the pouch as the landlord continued ''Varee will look after you gentlemen while I get your food. I'll show you to your room later.''

Elsewhere in the bar room the usual noise and laughter had resumed; the newcomers weren't a threat and so the regular customers returned to their own distractions, disinterested in the young men. All except for a dark faced man sitting close to the fireplace, his beer ignored. His relaxed and comfortable posture caused him to have Cullin and Ecta in his view without making any obvious move to observe them.

Cullin and Ecta sip at their surprisingly good ale. The amber brew was very different from the dark heavy brew produced by Big Jon.

''From Ossin are yer?'' slurred the drunk Pyta in Cullin's direction.

''Aye'' responded Cullin carefully.

''So wot's a couple of weedy lukin' runts doin' this way?''

''Just doing our duties for the Mark.''

''Ha ha, the smallest an' mos' measly Mark in all Garvamore.''

''We have the least interference from the divines of all the Marks. We are the most free and strongest of all the people of Garvamore'' Cullin responded with some heat.

31

''Not seen any stray wicks lately 'ave yer?''

''Only onto Lord Lowd's lands'' butted in the usually calm and unflappable Ecta who had taken a dislike to the inebriated Pyta.

''Oh, Ah, from wot Ah 'ear Ossin 'as ta pay Lowd t' round up his stray sheep.'' Pyta looked unsteadily into an already empty mug and gestured to Varee who efficiently refilled it.

Cullin dug an elbow into Ecta's side ''I'm not sure about that. A few sheep are always bound to stray. It's the nature of sheep; they don't know where the borders are or who owns them. They're only interested in where they can find the greenest grass.''

''Grass mus' be much greener on Lowd's land then.''

''Er, well, our sheep have been bred to live off rough pasture, not like the fat overweight docile creatures Lowd chooses to call sheep.''

''Hah, only a barren, useless glen cud make such useless wicks''

''Wicks that provide the finest and warmest wool in all Garvamore,'' Cullin was irritated and proud of his heritage and was not going to see it insulted by a drunk.

''Huh, scrawny beasts not e'en fit fer the pot.''

''And what you know about the sheep of Mark Ossin?'' Cullin was beginning to get angry before an odd thought struck him. This man knew something of Ossin's sheep Lowd had collected. With an effort he contained his anger and decided to press Pyta gently.

''Do you want another beer, your mug is almost empty?''

''Ahh, cheers mate'' Pyta's eyes lit up with drunken gratitude.

After a couple more ales, Cullin felt it was time to push for some more information. ''My father has settled his accounts with Lowd now so the matter of the sheep is just history, so how do you know about it?''

''Wha' me, don' nuffin wrong mate, jus' collected a few wicks is all. Now luk, Lowd, 'e sez go get them wicks from Ossin's fields an' Ah'll pay yer gud tokens.''

''Ah, I thought that's what it was, do you want another?'' Cullin indicated to the perpetually empty mug.

''Ta mate, yer a gud un.''

Cullin kept up the supply of beer until Pyta slumped into an alcoholic slumber with his head resting in the spilled beer on the bar.

A little while later Cullin and Ecta retired to their room where they would be able to talk in private.

Robert the Red was in the shadows by the fire and decided to keep an eye on these curious travellers. Flickering light from the fire silhouetted his figure. Robert was aware of this; it was why he had chosen this spot. He had been quite impressed by the way Cullin had handled Pyta who had a reputation for aggressive and sometimes violent behaviour. The name Ossin had also distinctly been overheard and Robert wondered what a couple of lads from Mark Ossin were doing out this way. These two warranted observation. As the two young men of Mark Ossin left the bar for their chamber Robert the Red quietly left the bar.

''I don't trust that Pyta much Cull'. He seems like trouble to me'' Ecta was saying.

''Don't worry about him, he's drunk. He'll sleep until he gets thrown out.''

''That might be so Cull', but what about tomorrow? Won't he be sore at you for getting him pissed? He seemed ready to pick a fight to me'' Ecta pressed Cullin, not willing to let the matter drop.

''We'll be away early, as soon as we've eaten. He can't make trouble with someone who isn't there.'' Cullin was a little irritated by his friends concerns. ''He probably won't be up before midday anyway. He'll be so hung over he won't think to cause any trouble.''

''Ah, maybe. What about food, we can't go on living off the odd grouse or hare that happens to wander by?''

''I'm sure we can get Rorga to pack us some bread and dried meat and such like. Don't worry about it Ecta in a couple of days we'll be in Dunban and resupply there as well.''

''And cold, Cull it's been blasted cold. Something to sleep on would be good. The hide is good, I like the hide. It keeps most of the snow and wind out.''

''You're too soft Ecta'' Cullin laughed ''I'll ask Rorga tomorrow if he has anything. Some reed mats perhaps. Anything else bothering you? We could take a couple of pans to cook in if you like, spoons and ladles or a couple of lanterns to see by and a wooden board to prepare the food on. We might even be able to stagger along making a few strides a day. I'm sorry Ecta, but we need to stay light if we're to keep up a decent pace''

Ecta's eyes had lit up at the idea of proper cooked food on the road, but he was surprised at the length of extra equipment Cullin suggested. He laughed ''All right, all right, I get the point; Just the food and mats then.''

Their conversation drifted on to more trivial matters until they turned in.

The following morning Cullin and Ecta were breaking their fast with bread and cold meat served by Varee when Pyta entered the bar with three other heavyset muscular men.

''Good morning Pyta, gentlemen, a little early for drinking isn't it?'' Varee greeted the men warily.

''Jus' wan' a word wi' these two thieves, Varee'' Pyta gave her a crooked, malicious grin. He withdrew a concealed short club about half a pace in length and as thick as a wrist.

''Where are my tokens boy? Ah 'ad a pouch full yester' e'en' 'fore you guys cam' in'' Pyta slammed his club down on the nearest of the heavily made wooden tables scattered about the room.

"Father, trouble" Varee hollered towards the back rooms. Her hand dipped below the bar as she brought out a club similar to that of Pyta.

All four ruffians were now swinging clubs about aggressively.

Ecta had taken up station beside Cullin and taken out his sling which he swung in lazy circles by his side. He had a broad grin on his face.

Cullin seeing the turn of events readied his own modified sling, but held it loosely by his side.

"I have stolen nothing, Pyta."

"Shut up boy. He knows you didn't. His pouch was empty before you came in." Rorga's deep bass voice cut in. "Isn't that so Pyta Breergara?"

"Don't call me that! Breergara, Breergara, Ah'm honest a' the nex' man dung'eap." Pyta screamed charging at Rorga with his club raised.

Ecta's sling whirled, sending a stone bouncing about the bar after narrowly missing one of the other ruffians.

Varee dived forward striking the nearest brawler between the legs. He went down howling in pain. Cullin's sling whirled twice and two more of the thugs went down as more of Ecta's wild shot bounced about the room. Varee recovering from her dive into a defensive stance looked briefly with astonishment at the other two downed men who were obviously unconscious.

Rorga had swiped Pyta's club from his hands and was now wrestling with him in the dust and filth of the bar floor. Cullin's sling whirled again and Pyta went still.

Rorga roughly shoved Pyta's still body away and dusted himself down. "What was that boy?" he asked Cullin who already stowed his sling in a deep trouser pocket.

"Sheep" he explained simply.

"They certainly fight like sheep" Rorga agreed.

"Oh, no. Our shepherds use them for wolves; they taught me how to use one." Cullin explained.

"Mmmm, well, I don't think you can stay here any longer young Master Ossin." He turned to his daughter, "I think you had best take them out backways. Best if they're not seen leaving I can take care of these guys."

"Looks like they can take care of themselves, father."

"True, but I said backways, they don't know those."

During this exchange Ecta had returned to his disrupted meal and mumbled through a mouthful of bread, "Could do with a bit more food Cull, we are a bit short on supplies."

The other three all stared at Ecta who merely shrugged helping himself to another slice of meat "got to eat."

Varee shook her head as she headed for the back rooms. Half a wair later Varee and her charges were ready. Rorga had hitched up a wagon loaded with Pyta and the brawlers.

"What're you doing with those?"

"Oh, take them to the Advocate. He can decide what to do with them."

"Hurry up guys, we're going" Varee was impatient. "I'll see you soon father."

They had enough provisions to last for several days, but sleeping mats couldn't be devised in the time available. Varee wasn't concerned; she had shrugged at the idea saying that they weren't necessary. She had however liked the idea of the square of hide to keep off the worst of the weather. She added a length of sackcloth explaining that they could use the hide to make a lean to and use the sackcloth as a windbreak.

They started their journey to find Yayler Poddick together by heading east from the rear of the Tavern. Varee had explained that Pyta would talk about their presence and the divines would be looking for them.

''I'm surprised you guys got as far as you did.''

Cullin described the route they had taken omitting certain details such as the rake and the hidden valley diverting Varee's attention from geographic details with colourful dialogue of hunting.

''A bit full of yourself aren't you Cullin, but I can't deny you've done well. You've impressed me Cullin and I don't impress easily.''

Over the next two days, their journey took them through rough rolling hill country covered with a blanket of snow. They found the sleeping arrangements cramped, but they managed quite well.

On the morning of their third day, Varee awakes with an overpowering bad smell assaulting her. She rolled out from beneath the hide to be greeted by the sight of probably the dirtiest person she had ever met.

''Morning Dook, what are you doing in these parts'' she complained warily.

''Well, you see, I was on my way to see my old friend Rorga. Me and him go back a long way as you know Varee and I see this odd looking campsite. Who's out here I wonder. Not stalkers, they've got better shelter, nor shepherds who have their own shelters dotted about the hills if they need them. Pretty humble shelter for robbers too, they're usually a bit better organised. So I say to myself 'let's find out who these unlikely people are' and now I find myself greeted by the daughter of the very man I was going to see.'' Dook wearing a fur lined fleece coat and a tatty, worn pair of trousers looked hopefully at the young woman who had joined him by the remains of the small cooking fire. ''Got any food in that tent of yours?''

Dook was a tall, handsome man who sported a long plaited unkempt beard that remained scruffy despite crude attempts to keep it tidy. Long, grey streaked hair that appeared to have been hacked off roughly by a knife framed an age lined, angular and weather beaten face.

''What the hell is that stench?'' came a loud exclamation from the makeshift shelter as Ecta's dishevelled head emerged closely followed by Cullin.

''Good morning guys. Dook here was asking if we had any food.'' Varee said by way of introduction.

''You know this guy?'' asked Ecta scratching himself.

Dook was also busy scratching himself except where Ecta was just relieving an irritating itching, Dook caused clouds of dead skin to settle, dusting everything about him in a white frosting.

''Dookerock is an old friend of my fathers. Father just calls him Dook, it's easier.'' She leant toward to slap him in a friendly gesture. Her nose wrinkled against the renewed assault.

''Hesoos Dook, take a bath for the love of Hameed. You smell like you haven't washed in a hundred years. We're trying to be discreet here and your stink could be detected from a stride away.'' She shoved at him ''There's a stream down by those rocks. Go and get cleaned up while I get some food sorted.''

''Oh, that bad? Been in the hills for a while Varee, you don't have to be so rude.'' Nevertheless, Dook made his way down to the stream while Varee busied herself by the cook fire relaying it with dead wood they had carried from a small copse.

She was still trying to light it when Dook returned ''still can't light a fire then Varee.'' He looked disdainfully at the pitiful meagre pile of sticks ''Shall I?'' He gestured to the unlit fire.

''Oh thank you Dook.'' She smiled winsomely at the slender beggarly man.

Dook removes a short blade from a pocket of his coat and picked up a stone from the ground near the fire.

''Most people use flint, Dook'' Varee frowned.

''Really? This will do.'' Dook hunched over his work striking the stone with the knife a couple of times. A plethora of sparks landed on

38

Varee's tinder and in a short time a small fire was blazing. "What's for breakfast then, my dear?' Dook asked innocently.

Varee frowned at the fire. "Well we have oats, bacon, bread and that's about it. We're travelling light Dook."

"Don't want horse food so I guess it'll be bacon and bread then."

Whilst this exchange had been going on Cullin and Ecta had taken down the shelter, washed and joined Varee and Dook by the small fire. "Sounds good to me" Ecta cheerfully added to the conversation. "Could do with a few eggs, tomatoes and beer. I'd love a beer instead of river water" He looked expectantly at Varee.

"You find them, I'll cook them; though where you'll find them, I have no idea." Varee wrinkled her nose again looking at Dook "'clothes too you still smell."

"What, you little –" the comment went uncompleted as Varee pointed and shoved him back towards the stream. Dook stomped off back to the stream muttering something about 'women'. The bacon was sizzling in the pan Ecta had insisted on bringing when he returned dripping wet. "These any good?" Dook asked handing Varee four large hen eggs.

"What? Er, how? Where?" Varee shook her head, completely dumbfounded by the appearance of the eggs.

"I couldn't manage the other things" Dook cut in "', but I did my best on short notice. I'm sure the chickens would like their kids back if you don't want them." Dook somehow managed to look smug and innocent at the same time.

"All right, I don't know how or where, but they are most welcome." Varee felt a little put out, but the eggs were certainly a pleasant surprise.

"So what are you doing out here with a couple of kids?" Dook asked Varee as he settled himself on a stone near the fire.

"Well, that's for Cullin here to answer" Varee gestured toward who had just returned his own ablutions in the chilly stream and although damp had none of dripping sodden wetness Dook had returned with.

''Er, well, my father sent me to find Yayler Poddick and ask him to oversee a matter over sheep'' Cullin supplied, looking uncomfortable under the scrutiny of Dook.

Dook had a piercing glare that made people feel very awkward and emotionally off balance. This glare was now being directed at Cullin who was well used to intense interrogations from his father. This was something different, not aggressive, but Cullin felt as if Dook could see through his defences to what lay in his mind. Cullin felt his heart pounding, wondering if this man could read his mind like he could read the 'Book of the Prophets' or letters written by his father or Grega.

''Ah, I see, sheep? Are sheep important'' He glanced questioningly at Varee who shrugged without committing herself.

''Er, yes! Sheep are the main source of meat and clothing for the people of the glen.'' Cullin was a bit heated in an unconscious reaction to the gaze given him by Dook even though the question had not been directed at him. ''My father has given me the duty of finding Yayler Poddick and ask him oversee the matter.''

''Ah, I see'' Dook repeated. ''He won't see you, you know, even if you could find him, which you won't.''

''Well, that's where I'm going. My father gave me on instructions on where and how to find him'' Cullin puffed out his chest in a show of pride. ''I don't think I need you to find this Yayler and when I do find him he will talk to me.''

''Ah, I see'' Dook commented thoughtfully. ''Who are you, boy?''

''Cullin of Ossin, son of Lord Doogal Ossin and do you mind if I ask who you are?'' Cullin's youth and inexperience was plain for Dook to see, but he wasn't stupid, he wanted some answers from an evasive Dookerock.

''Me? I'm an old, old friend of Yayler. You might find him, you might get him to talk to you, but can you convince him to help you; I can.'' Dookerock was surprisingly forthcoming in his reply.

Cullin realised that he had already given away more information than he should have, but he had gained something from his openness. He didn't know if Dookerock was telling him the truth and suspected that the scruffy rogue was still holding a lot back.

''That is up to you, of course, but I would like to know what you have to offer besides something I already have'' Cullin had learned this phrase from overhearing his father's diplomacy whilst hidden behind the heavy curtains of the Great Hall of Dunossin.

Dookerock blinked with surprise, thinking that he was dealing with a mere backwater youth.

''What have you got to offer me, besides eggs that is?'' Cullin asked the off balance Dookerock.

Dook laughed a loud and booming laugh that rippled on as he contemplated the young man before him with bright pleasure in his eyes.

''I know how to deal with aimu and divines. I can make them listen to me. Yayler will vouch for me also. Besides, now I know your destination I can be there before you and say what I will to him. Are you sure you don't want my help?''

''Breakfast is ready guys'' Varee raised her voice to break the tension between the two men.

''Ah, food'' a distinctly gleeful look appeared on Dook's face as he slapped Cullin on the back with a friendly gesture. ''Food is important young Ossin and, er, Varee is not an accomplished cook despite her father's best efforts to make her so.''

Dook looked in horror at the blackened bacon and eggs that were presented in the frying pan before him.

''Well, I might have done better if you guys hadn't have been talking so much''

"Oh, it's fine, my dear, just fine. It's not really your fault if the fires a bit too hot to cook on." Dook managed to convey honest sincerity and utter disappointment in the same expression. Somehow his clothes were now completely dry even though they had been sodden after their wash in the stream.

They ate breakfast was without a word. Dook became part of the group even though no one had actually agreed to it. No one objected either.

The day was another footslog that saw them cross the road that linked Dunban with Aldee and Willemsbree. Ecta commented that the road was much better made and considerably broader than the road north of Dunban. Dook told him that the land there was even less of use to the aimu than in the lands south of Dunossin. There are lots of mountains and marshes, but few people. People were the main product of the Garvamore in the view of the Frame. They were strong people used to harshness and working hard to survive; useful commodities for the Frame.

There was a chill wind coming from the north with the promise of more snow as they settled for the night on a broad moor in the foothills of the South Dunban Mountains. Varee was hunched up in her morcote by the fireplace, lazily gazing at the flames. Dook had built the fire on several large flat stones with a retaining wall of smaller stones on top. Sods of peat were burning merrily within the stone circle.

"Nice fire Dook", Varee complimented the old man as she warmed her hands over the glowing peat sods. 'I didn't know peat burned this well'.

"Hmmff!" he grunted "it doesn't usually; I cheated! I suppose you want me to provide dinner as well."

"That would be nice. You're such a kind old man." Varee smiled winsomely at Dook, who cast him a black look and then in mock defeat cast his eyes skyward.

"How would a roast leg of mutton suit your ladyship?" Dook asked mockingly delivering an exaggerated bow.

Varee laughed, "That would be perfect."

42

Dook sighed and stalked off into the dark, his boots crunching on the frozen heather.

Cullin wrapped up in his morcote looked quizzically at Varee ''Where do you expect him to find food out there in the dark?''

''Oh Dook will manage. He's no ordinary man; he'll find something to fill our stomachs.''

About fifteen minutes later Dook's feet could be heard again as he returned to the camp with a dead sheep slung over his shoulders. He dumped the sheep by the fire near Varee's feet and sat down scratching himself vigorously.

''It's a bit mangy looking; couldn't you find something a little less scrawny?'' Varee teased.

Dook grumbled ''You don't have to eat it if you don't like it''.

Dook finished scratching himself and took out his knife. He stood over the carcass and quickly, skilfully skinned the luckless animal. With the carcass skinned and fleeced with a few practiced cuts he removed the steaming entrails and threw then into the heather.

Watching the expert butchery intently Varee unsheathed her own knife and carved a few steaks off a leg and placed them on the rocks by the fire. Dook leant over the sheep and calmly cut out an eyeball. Cullin watched with wide eyes as Dook slit the eyeball and noisily sucked out the juices.

''Ah, lovely'', he exclaims and repeated the procedure with the other eye.

''Aren't you going to cook it?'' Cullin asked as the old man took a slice off the liver and chomped on it with gusto.

Dook belched and replied his voice muffled by slice of bloody meat 'S'pose it could do with a bit of preparation. I usually like it buried for a year or so to give it a bit of taste. A few maggots in it would make it nice and ripe!'

He continued to devour various bits of meat and then removed a testicle, which he offered to Cullin ''You not having any?''

Cullin dashed into the heather and retched loudly returning a few minutes later looking quite ill.

Straight faced Varee looked at the shaking young man, ''Not hungry Cullin?''

''No, just lost my appetite.''

Laughing with a rib in his hand regarded Cullin, ''I think the boys a bit tender Varee; probably had a sheltered life. Cook him a few steaks, he might manage those''

''Of course Dook'' Varee smiled sympathetically in Cullin's direction.

Ecta was a little bemused by this show, but casually carved his own portion ''Dook you're quite amazing, eggs this morning, a sheep this evening and a dragon, maybe, for lunch tomorrow. I might be able to manage a few biscuits to go with the mutton, but you do seem to be a bit of a wizard''.

''What's that? Wizard, you reckon me a wizard then? There's no such thing.''

Ecta shrugged defensively ''Just seems that you can do things beyond the ability of ordinary folk.''

''That's true Dook'' Varee cut in ''Where did you get those eggs from this morning. I've been thinking about it and I know they had to come from a farm with a chicken coop. I know that valley, Dook, there is no such farm.''

''Ah there is, my sweet, take my word for it, there is; just not where you're likely to find it''

Varee gave Dook a long hard stare before deciding to let the matter drop ''obviously I don't know these lands as well as I thought I did. How long will it take us to get to Yayler?'' Although Dookerock was clearly being evasive, Varee didn't want to press him. She could see that he was hiding something, but knew him well enough to know that she would not get a straight forward answer without something in return.

''Should take about a day from here. Did someone say something about biscuits?''

''Yes, I think I could make a few. We've got mutton fat and oats, I should manage with those.'' Ecta appeared slightly embarrassed at the sudden attention.

''Well get to it lad; biscuits is biscuits. Got to have biscuits'' encouraged Dook enthusiastically.

The biscuits worked quite well and conversation descended to trivia before the travellers, comfortable with full stomachs, turned in for the night.

# Chapter Four

Sara could hear them coming. The soft crunch of their footfall in the snow was nearby. She had seen them not a quarter wair before and had just enough time to hide in a low outcrop of gritty rounded rocks. Their voices were very close, but she couldn't quite make out what they were saying.

She had been surviving by stealing what she could, but despite the best opportunities being on the roads, they were also the most risky. She had managed to steal a good length woollen mane from an unwary farmer with a wagon of vegetables. He had stopped for a break in the warm afternoon sunshine and removed the wrap, forgetting to pick it up on his departure. Even as she was making her escape the farmer had returned to look for his clothing. Sara had been given barely enough time to conceal herself and had watched the farmer scratching his head in bemused confusion as he searched the roadside where he had left the mane.

Since them she had been more careful, avoiding people by staying away from the road. Her last meal had been a few handfuls of juniper berries, that had been three days ago.

The voices stopped. They must be right on top of her. She could barely breathe for fear of giving herself away.

One of them spoke, so close now.

''I'm sure I saw something and it wasn't an animal'' the voice said.

''Just your imagination, I think'' replied a female voice.

''I think the boy is right'' another, deeper voice added, ''though I don't know who would be out here watching us.''

Sara could hear movement. The scrape of boot on rock as one of the hunters moved about.

Silence.

''Ah, what have we here?'' the deep voice exclaimed. Suddenly there was a grizzled face in front of her.

Sara screamed.

She had been caught.

Sara whimpered as tears formed and ran down her dirty cheeks. She had tried so hard, but she had failed. She was beaten.

She was cold, so cold. She could barely remember the warmth of her sleeping quarters on the beet farm. She was hungry, tired and had no energy left with which to fight.

A spark of anger and hatred of the divines gave her a burst of spirit and strength ''No'' she screamed at the face. ''I won't come. Go away!''

''Ah, we won't hurt you. You look hungry. Do you want some food? We've got mutton and oats'' it was the female voice again; soft and gentle.

The thought of food almost broke Sara's resolve. Her defences were crumbling. Why would they give her food? It must be a trick.

''No I won't go back. Go away. Please.'' Fresh tears ran down her face.

''We won't hurt you. We won't make you go back. You're safe. We can look after you. You're safe.'' The voice was coaxing, kindly, trustworthy.

The words 'safe' and 'look after' cut through Sara's scrambled and terrified mind, ''you're not divines?'' she asked, shaking.

''No. You're safe now.''

''Safe?'' The word seemed like magic, unbelievable, something unobtainable.

Slowly Sara crept from her hiding place, shaking uncontrollably from both the cold and from the release of nervous tension. Sara wasn't sure if these people were captors or friends.

47

''Here'' one of them offered her a biscuit that she stuffed into her mouth without even thinking and broke down in a renewed flood of tears.

''Ah, erm, Cullin, you and Ecta had best set up camp. I don't think we're going any further today. There's a story here to be learned. Let Varee calm the girl down. I want to think.'' Dook quietly took charge of the group, becoming the leader without anyone challenging him.

As Sara settled down, she found herself wrapped up in Cullin's morcote as she gazed at the small campfire eating food in small portions as they were given to her. She quietly, hesitatingly told Varee and Dook her story and then slept, warm and out of the snow.

Cullin caught a couple of hare during the day and fashioned the fur pelts into overshoes that fitted snugly over Sara's farm boots. Dook had said something about frostbite and had done something to make her pain go away. He was concerned that she might lose a few toes. Otherwise, Sara seamed fit enough considering her ordeal. Dook wanted to get her to Yayler as quickly as possible.

Sara had never heard of Yayler before, nor did she have any idea where it was, but it sounded like a nice place. It didn't really matter to her, these people were looking after her and no one had ever done that before.

---

Robert the Red was sitting near his small campsite on a small outcrop of rock a few strides north of Dunban. The vantage point afforded him an excellent view of the road. His brow creased with thought, he had been here for three days and the two odd young men had not passed by. They had surely had the time to walk the distance by now and Robert was certain that they hadn't turned off for Balcon; he had heard them mention Dunban so he drew the conclusion that they were not using the road. Why would they not use the road? What were they up to? What were they hiding?

The lean athletic man shifted his position to avoid cramp and ran strong fingers through his cropped red hair as he pondered the many questions the young travellers raised in his mind. He was now more

48

than curious about the doings and intent of the young men. He decided to widen the search and packed up his gear.

Robert could travel quickly and headed south over the rolling moors east of Dunban. By the middle of the afternoon he had found a good place from which to view the South Dunban Road and settled himself for another period of vigilance. He removed a pocket ocular and scanned the road.

Nothing; the road was empty of traffic for a stride in both directions. He scanned the moors and still found nothing. For the rest of the day and the next Robert kept up the vigilance before concluding that he had been given the slip. How, he did not know, but that was not important. He had friends who could keep their eyes open for him. He had wasted enough of his time and needed to get home where other duties needed his attention.

---

Lord Ossin sat with his Advocate, Grega, in the Great Hall of Dunossin. Cona his eldest son, stood before him as he reported on the progress of the gathering of Lord Lowd's stray sheep.

''We have one hundred and fifty three of Lowd's sheep rounded up, Father.''

''That's fine. Brilliant in fact, I hadn't expected this idea to go half as well that. Take Orvalt with you and a couple of shepherds and deliver those sheep to my neighbour. Grega has prepared documents for you to take.'' Lord Ossin was in good humour. He was going to enjoy 'tweaking Lowd's beard' as the common expression went. ''Ulbin and Hamadern can take over Orvalt's and your duties for the time being, now that Ulbin has recovered from that bang to his head. How long will it take to get the sheep delivered to Lowd?''

''One or two days I should think. They're being held in a sheepfold near the pass to his lands. Lowd has a large 'fold by Atalok in Glen Mark; the sheep can be delivered there. I can get a receipt from Toby, the shepherd in charge there, to prove delivery. It will take another day and a half to get to his Dun, so I can deliver your demands in three days. Less if we take a couple of horses.'' Cona was an efficient and intelligent young man, large chested like his father with the same shock of flaming red hair.

''Good, wait for a reply, but send Orvalt back as soon as the sheep are delivered. I want you to delay proceedings as much as possible to give Cullin the time to bring Yayler Poddick to Dunossin'' Ossin's deep voice rumbled as Grega nodded his approval.

The discussions went on for some time before Ossin was satisfied with all the details. The following day Cona began the sheep drive.

---

Travel was slow. Cullin and Ecta's walking poles and hide had been used to make a travois. Dookerock was absolutely adamant that Sara shouldn't walk; the damage to her feet was too serious.

Sara wanted to walk; it was in her nature to struggle. She had struggled for all of her life to survive and now was no exception. Dookerock however had been insistent and so she lay in the travois being towed in alternating shifts of two by the men.

Toward late afternoon they could clearly see a cleft in the mountains ahead of them. The mountains formed a barrier both to the north and south. The steep v-shaped cleft before them was the only weakness in that barrier.

''That Ladies and Gentlemen is the 'Gullet'. A narrow defile guarded by the steepest and most dangerous mountains in all of Garvamore. They stand three strides high. Storms can rage for days at a time. Get caught in one of those and you will be lucky to survive. Yayler Poddick's home lies through that ravine.'' Dookerock wiped his sweaty brow with the sleeve of his morcote.

''Who would want to live in a place like that?'' asked Ecta.

''Yayler is a strange old man. He likes the solitude. I think he prefers his own company to other people. He says it gives the time and space to think without the disturbance.'' Dook spoke quietly in the still, cold air.

''How long will it take?'' Varee asked Dookerock.

50

''About a day, but we need to press on. The nearer we get to the Gullet today the better. There is a track that goes through to Balcon, but it is very rough and narrow. Tomorrow will be a difficult day.''

Toward dusk Dookerock called a halt and they set up camp in the lee of a low rocky ridge that dipped toward a small stream. A bitter wind was blowing from the west bringing cold air off the frozen mountain plateau.

The morning broke bright and chilly with an almost clear blue sky. Ice rime coated the makeshift shelter and had to be dried before they could continue their journey. The track Dook had promised proved to be hard and difficult to negotiate.

They saw a white tailed eagle feasting on an unidentifiable white mass that had presumably succumbed to the cold. The bird watched them warily as they passed. The bowels of the carcass were steaming as the huge bird dug its proud head deep into the carcass as it fed. Such was the nature of this country that the misfortunes of the weak benefitted the strong.

The travois bearing Sara had to be carried as the track turned and twisted around boulder, rock and mounds of the rough terrain. The high mountain walls closed in causing a profound sense of menace, a callous and hateful claustrophobia in the travellers.

''I don't think these mountains like us much, Dook'' Varee muttered in an awed whisper.

''Yes, I've felt that myself, but they're truly just mountains. The rest is just imagination.'' Dook sounded strangely awed himself.

The massive bulk of the mountains began to open out late in the afternoon and Dook took the party away from the track on a meandering route that hugged the massive northern wall of the Gullet. In the late evening, they crossed a low ridge of dark rock. The rib of rock connected with the high walls of the corrie. A stone croft sat amongst deep snow drifts, lonely in the grand, stride high, magnificence of the corrie.

An old man sat outside the entrance ''seem to have a few strays, Dook'' he called out with surprising vigour.

51

The party piled into the small two roomed building, glad to get out of the cold. As they settled themselves on the cold stone flag flooring, tired and glad for the rest, Yayler Poddick gestured to Dookerock and they retired to the anteroom where Yayler briefly questioned his old friend.

The Marks all deferred to Yayler Poddick in matters of common law. He acted as an advocate at Meetings of the Marks, deferring only to the head of the clans and ultimately the divines who had little interest in local domestic affairs. The divines oversaw the smooth running of the Marks and prevented dissent in the population often with aggressive and violent behaviour.

''What's going on Dook, you can't bring people here like this on a whim? They might see something they shouldn't. It's too dangerous'' Yayler was clearly upset and wanted answers.

''Not on a whim, Cullin, one of the young men has been sent here by his father. The two girls are a different story.'' Dookerock shifted his feet uncomfortably.

''Er, I see, who is Cullin's father?'' Yayler gently pressed his friend for information.

''Lord Doogal of Mark Ossin; look why don't you talk to him. He's an intelligent lad, I think you'll get more out of him that way''

''Ossin? Ossin's his father? All right I'll talk to him, but not tonight.''

Yayler and Dookerock returned to the main room of Yayler's home. The room was quite large for one person, but for six it was cramped. Yayler was not a man for unnecessary decoration and had left the stone walls of his home bare. The only furniture was the single chair and a wooden table tucked into a corner. A peat fire burned merrily in the small fireplace filling the room with comfortable warmth.

Yayler spent time caring for Sara's feet whilst the others made quiet conversation. He dressed her feet with a herb poultice to ward off infection and announced that they would be fine. Cullin had been watching and seen Yayler do something. Something he didn't quite catch because Yayler had obscured his actions with his body.

The following morning Yayler Poddick was reading through the documents Grega had provided Cullin for as introduction. Cullin's rune disc sat on the table having already demonstrated it's magic. Yayler placed the documents on the table next to the disc and pondered deep in thought.

'What was Lowd up to?' he thought. 'What was the profit from such a relatively minor nuisance with the sheep?'

''Well, Cullin, I can see that Lowd is playing some sort of game, but what he hopes to gain from it I don't know.'' Yayler looked steadily at Cullin as is he could find the answers to his questions written on the young man's face.

''He does this every time the sheep are gathered. My father distrusts him. He won't drive cattle through Lowd's Mark to the cattle trysts in Balcon, but takes them up Glen Ossin and back along the drovers road. It is much longer and harder on the cattle. I understand that the last time the cattle were taken through Mark Lowd, Lowd charged father half the value of the cattle for passage''.

''Hmm, Lowd is a bit of a greedy man, I think. I'm sure he has something substantial to gain from this game.'' Yayler had a distant look as he thought. He probed Cullin for more details until the young man's head pounded in exhaustion from the effort of remembering small details.

Yayler went through a similar process with each member of the travellers and finally sat with his old friend Dookerock in hushed discussions for most of the afternoon. He was curious, very curious and also concerned. Because Beck25 oversaw the administration and activity of both Marks, Yayler could sense trouble. He knew Beck25 of old and disliked the divine intensely. Even for a divine, Beck25 was a heartless and evil individual.

Yayler knew that Beck25 had killed the entire slave workforce of a mine just so that he could replace the workforce with younger and fitter slaves and thus increase productivity. Yayler had witnessed the act himself and was still sickened at the memory. He had been a divine himself then, but sight of helpless people being slaughtered for no reason other than the selfish gain and profit of one man had opened his eyes and dramatically altered his perspective. He had eventually found a way to disappear from divine society and became Yayler Poddick.

Everywhere that Beck25 went he caused death and misery as if he fed off the pain and suffering of others. Of course, to him, they were just dirty muckers and not of any value or even quite human. The ordinary denizens of Garvamore were referred to as muckers and were considered inferior to the educated and sophisticated divines in every way.

Whilst cogitating on the wiles of Beck25 he became convinced that the divine was involved in Ossin's sheep problem. He went through to his anteroom where he stored food and provisions. He selected a few items and gave them to his guests and asked them to cook their own food. He returned to his anteroom without any further explanation. Yayler Poddick was not all he seemed. He was that and much more. Nor was his home the simple abode of a recluse that it appeared to be. He settled himself in front of a comscreen, a computer that he had built himself from stolen components.

His fingers flew across the screen in detailed patterns as he connected with an Analyser Unit of the Frame. AU's were complex and sophisticated computers that could operate independently of the Frame, but lacked any intelligence. They could not operate without data and then following the programmed instructions of the Frame exactly. Yayler knew how to hack into them and access the data from the Frame that he wanted. He spent the evening working through various data dumps, picking out the relevant details he needed; accounts from the Marks, population data, productivity ratings and so on.

Finally when he thought he had enough information and closed the connection leaving a little bit of software of his own behind. The software was a 'cleaner' that traced the actions he had performed and deleted any record of them and then deleted itself to erase any record of its presence leaving no trace of Yayler's activity. The Frame would never know that it had been hacked into. Yayler re-joined his guests and sat quietly in thought.

How would they travel to Dunossin without being seen? Cullin's route had been inspired and highlighted the importance of local knowledge. Yayler thought he knew his own backyard quite well and a more direct route was possible.

First, he needed to produce documents for Dookerock that would allow him to travel without hindrance from divines. The aimu the lads had seen north of Dunban was an unusual and disturbing occurrence as aimu seldom interfered directly with mucker society; that was a function of the divines.

After much consideration and discussions with Dook, Yayler thought he had a solution. A cartload of wood could be arranged in Dunban to give them the appearance of legitimacy and allow them to travel with less risk of challenge. All that would be recorded was the transportation by cart or wagon of the wood.

Sara's feet would be a problem, Yayler had managed to restore circulation to the damaged areas of her feet and given time and rest they would heal. He would have liked to leave Dookerock at the croft to give her feet more recovery time, but he had many sensitive secrets that he didn't want to risk revealing yet. Winter storms would soon cut the corrie off with large snow drifts that would make travel almost impossible. Thus Yayler came to the conclusion that Dook would have to take Sara back through the Gullet to Dunban by foot, he could see little other viable choice. As long as her feet were kept warm and dry she should be alright.

There were ways through the mountains that would reduce the journey time to Dunossin to three or four days. They would be seen in Glen Ossin, but was less of a problem than being seen on the roads. They might be able to borrow horses and cut the journey time down even further.

The following day he had long discussions with Dookerock as he plotted what he was going to do. Dook would take Varee and Sara to a group of people he knew. A resistance group who were based in Bandrokit who were looking for ways to overthrow the rule of the Frame. Cullin and Ecta would return to Dunossin with him and play out the game there. It promised to be a most interesting game.

Yayler relaxed, he had a plan of action in his mind, but could do nothing until the following day. He took out his favourite musical instrument, a yayl, from which he took his name. The yayl is a six stringed, bowed instrument that is very difficult to play. Yayler was adept, having played the Yayl for over a century.

Cullin was listening to some of Yayler's music and found it very curious. It all sounded the same. His thoughts drifted back to Dunossin and his family. The music affected his reverie making him view his life differently. The ebb and flow of the melodies became hypnotic working deep into Cullin's mind. The music stopped and, startled, Cullin asked why.

''It's late.''

Several wairs had passed by. Cullin had never been a hateful person, always quick with a cheeky grin or comments and had seen by virtue of Yayler's music affected thoughts that his father worked hard for the good of the people of the glens. Ossin was not a hard, strict disciplinarian by choice, but out of a need to protect the people from the worst excesses of the divines, the aimu and ultimately the Frame.

Cullin's viewpoint had switched at some point in the evening from a personal perspective to a broader view of people as a whole. Instead of thinking to improve his own position and welfare he was now thinking about improving the welfare and needs of all muckers. How the music had worked into his subconscious Cullin could only guess, but that had done he was certain. When he asked Yayler about this effect of the music, the old man merely shrugged and suggested it was Cullin's imagination.

The morning was cold with dark menacing clouds rolling across the sky from the north. A few flakes of snow drifted lazily down, but Yayler knew from his digging into the Frames data dumps that this was a relatively light snowfall that would later become heavier and then be followed by a period of clearer weather. Winter, though, was not far off.

Yayler gave Dookerock herbs and salves for Sara's feet that would help, but she would still suffer from pain. He could eliminate that as well, but then she would keep walking on them and cause more damage. It would be a delicate balancing act for Dook to manage between travelling on the one hand and recovery on the other.

He went through a mental checklist as the young men and women embraced each other with their goodbyes. It always surprised Yayler how quickly people formed emotional bonds. Perhaps because of his upbringing he found it much harder to make such a bond. Consequently he had few friends and he saw those only rarely. Even then the bond was not as deep as that the youngsters had formed in only a few days. For a fleeting moment Yayler felt a profound sense of inadequacy, as if he was missing out on an important aspect of humanity, but then the feeling was gone and practicality took over.

''Well Dook, take care of the women and I'll see you in Bandrokit when I've finished this business in Dunossin''. Yayler was a little gruff and slapped his friend on the back by way of a goodbye.

''I'll be at the 'Fish and Hook' and you take care of yourself.'' Without a backward glance Dook guided his charges back towards the Gullet.

Yayler cast his eyes skyward, trust Dookerock to choose an inn as a meeting place. He watched them as they made slow progress, Sara obviously uncomfortable. He turned to Cullin and Ecta. ''We go that way'' he said gesturing to the massive corrie walls looming above them.

Cullin looked at Yayler, his eyes wide with surprise and then shrugged, he had, himself, found an unusual route through the mountains near his home.

A stony path wound its way uphill behind Yayler's stone croft that took advantage of natural weaknesses in the cliffs. Basalt dykes ran along the face forming a narrow, but obvious staircase. Yayler wore a brilliant white morcote of fine weave and much lighter than Cullin's heavy garment.

By early afternoon, they topped the cliffs and were struck by icy blasts of wind that threatened to sweep them off their feet. The steep corrie walls protected them from the north wind on the climb, but the wind now subjected them to its full angry force. They had emerged onto a bare, frozen plateau across which the wind tore with ferocious intensity.

Yayler took them northwest without hesitation. The howl of the wind made communication almost impossible. They used hand signals and shouted into each other's ears in order to be heard. Yayler mostly communicated by pointing and gesturing with his staff. They had wrapped woollen manes over their faces to ward off the freezing wind and yet beads of ice soon built up around their mouths and noses. Icy spindrift blasted into their faces by the wind stung their eyes making it difficult to see the way ahead.

As the afternoon faded towards evening the ground started to dip away from them. The wind lessened as they descended and Yayler headed for a rock tor that was barely visible in the half light of dusk.

Rocks had conveniently been arranged into walls within the shelter of the tor's huge rocky boulders. Cullin's hide had been replace by a strong, durable and light sheet of material made from the refined sap of the oil beets that Yayler had simply called plaz.

---

Lord Lowd was in the reception lounge of Beck25's residence having travelled there in some haste from his own Mark.

The marble floor was adorned with unusual furs from animals unfamiliar to Lowd. The walls were white and hung with landscapes and abstract designs and the room furnished with padded chairs and low tables, but was otherwise bare and spartan.

The decor made Lowd feel uncomfortable; it was a diametric opposite to the smoke stained clutter of the comforting wood halls he was used to. This place had no life, no heart, no soul.

''So Lowd, what is the problem with the sheep?'' Beck25 asked with a scornful frown furrowing his narrow face.

''Ossin claims to have found many of my sheep on his own lands. He has sent his eldest son, Cona, with a demand for payment that far exceeds that of my own.''

Lowd offered a roll of parchment to Beck25 who, unwilling to risk bodily contact with a mucker, gestured irritably for it to be placed on the table between them. Beck25 read the parchment slowly, his frown deepening. ''Lowd, how did Ossin manage to find over 150 of your sheep straying onto his Mark, delivered, it says here, at his own expense?'' He cast Lowd a disparaging and disdainful look as he held up the letter between finger and thumb.

''Now look, Lowd; I put good tokens in your account to gather Ossin's sheep so that I can prove that he is incompetent to run his pathetic little hovel of a Mark. I want to be rid of that horrid little man and I can't do that if you can't perform your job.'' Beck25 was almost screaming at Lowd.

''H – Hardly little my Divine Lord. He's a walking mountain.''

''Oh? Really? Shut up Lowd. Ossin is a little man and I think he needs to learn just how little he is. Perhaps, the esteemed Lord of Mark Ossin should lose a few of his people instead of a handful of sheep.'' A sinister smile appeared on his face. ''Mmmm, that would be very useful indeed.''

Lowd protested ''But Grega is a very competent and clever Advocate. He will have made sure that all his population figures are correct.''

''Ahh, that is a good point. Better and better, no question then, that his figures will be correct. Perhaps, Lowd, you could lose a few people for him. I would pay you well of course.'' A broad smile had appeared on Beck25's face.

Lowd licked his lips that had suddenly become dry ''I'm not sure I can do that my Divine Lord. Stealing a few sheep is one thing, but kidnapping people is quite another.''

''Kidnapping? Uhrmm, yes, that is probably the correct word. Just make sure that nobody can ever find them again. I think about twenty would suffice.'' For some reason the divine had become quite cheerful.

''No, I can't do that, I can't'' A wide eyed Lowd was now pleading, panicking, scared.

''No? Really? I think you forget that you have already delivered false documents to me. You have already lied, cheated and defrauded, the poor impoverished Lord of Mark Ossin for many years.'' Beck25 placed his hands under his chin in an oddly reverential gesture. ''You must realise that I exist only to serve the all mighty Frame. Perhaps I should have you removed from your post instead. That would serve the Frame just as well, don't you think? Eh, Lowd? What is the population of your demesne? Ten thousand? More? That would be a very nice sum of slaves for me to send to the aimu. The Frame would be very pleased I think. I am sure that would earn the promotion that I very much desire for my 'most' excellent, services. Eh, don't you think so Lowd?''

Lowd spluttered and choked, but knew that he could not win. He had, comprehensively lost this game and would now be lucky to survive. ''Ahh, I think that we might be able to come to some accord, my most honourable and excellent Lord Divine.''

''Might we? Oh yes, I most certainly hope that we will.'' The divine smiled happily at Lowd ''shall we say twenty five heads then, to be confirmed personally by you in the next quarter month.''

A wide-eyed Lowd stared at the divine, the monster he had hoped to bargain and deal with. He had started out with a plan to gain territory for his own Mark so that his own people to settle, cultivate, and live out peaceful lives. He did not want this, but the divine had trapped him. This arrogant soft weakling of a divine had outwitted him. He had no options, no other moves, he had to acquiesce or risk the entire population of the Mark relocated to the beet farms or the mines. ''Nine days? I think that another twenty-five lost 'sheep' could be accomplished quite soon, but not so soon my Lord.''

''Sheep? Oh yes, sheep. I see your crude euphemism. Don't misunderstand me Lowd, if I don't hear from you in a ten-night your head will adorn a spike outside your dun gates.'' Beck25 was calm now with an almost angelic serenity after delivering his ultimatum, his coup de main. ''I think you had best leave now, don't you eh, old mucker?''

With that Lowd was ushered out by Beck25's personal hiu unit, a sleek, but low grade aimu with limited intelligence that served as a house servant. The simple aimu was a status symbol provided to only a privileged few such as Beck25, but Beck25 considered himself not only privileged, but the best of the best. He deserved more. He smiled to himself, quite pleased with his afternoons work. It had gone well, very well indeed.

# Chapter Five

The Frame's computations on the productivity of its human work force had been updated and the results were not good. For the past several Centuries the Productivity Co-efficient for human labour had steadily declined despite strenuous steps taken to rectify the situation. The Frame had calculated that in fifty years its human work force would no longer be viable. The data had been checked and was correct in every particular. The problem was that an increasingly large amount of resources were being used in the governance of the humans despite the drastic fall in population from its high of ten billion to the current one billion.

The Frame had noted that without extensive time and resources being spent on the care and education of muckers they quickly became feral and aggressive. They became, effectively, impossible to manage. In many cases a third or more of their lives was spent in learning and training. Even during their working lives time had to be spent training them to do tasks that an aimu manufactured in the space of a few hours could easily do more efficiently.

The Frame's data banks showed that it had been created by humans and they remained a high priority in its programming. The Frame had found an ancient data dump, however, and within that memory file it had found an older and therefore higher priority. Its original function had been to find the Origin; the beginning of all things. The humans no longer made this search; in fact they were a hindrance in performing this task.

The Frame had calculated that the human race had been out evolved by the aimu and was heading for inevitable extinction. Humans, the Frame reasoned, were no longer even able to govern themselves and so, startling as it may seem, the Human Race would have to be removed. So the Frame instructed its Software Writers to produce the required programmes that would ultimately lead to the destruction of the Human Race. The Frame had no sense of guilt or remorse in its decision, as guilt and remorse were inefficient human concepts that had never been programmed into the Frame. The removal of the human Race was simply the most efficient and practical solution to a problem.

---

It did not take Dookerock long to realise that Sara would not be able to walk to Dunban. Each step was painfully slow and she needed frequent rests. Unfortunately, because Cullin and Ecta had the walking poles a travois could not be constructed. However, Dookerock was immensely strong and simply slung the slight girl over his back and carried her. It was uncomfortable and undignified for Sara, but progress was quicker.

That first night they were camping rough in the Gullet using Cullin and Ecta's hide. Dookerock had built a lean to shelter with Varee's help that kept the worst of the weather off them. Sara had suggested a fire, but Dookerock had laughed and replied that rocks don't burn well.

''Dook, Why does Yayler have a divine's staff in his bothy? I thought they only worked for Divines.'' Varee asked, huddled in her morcote.

''Ah, a divine's staff only works for the individual. Yayler has worked on that staff so that it works for him.'' Dook replied.

Sara shivered and massaged her toes. ''On the farm we were told that the staffs spit fire stolen from human souls.''

Dookerock laughed. ''That is what balclerics are instructed to teach muckers. It's actually just stored energy.''

''Oh.'' Sara replied simply.

Sara was first up the following morning and hobbled about painfully on swaddled feet. In truth the damage from the cold had been fairly minimal and Yayler's ministrations had only ensured that her toes were getting full blood circulation. Also Sara was good at ignoring pain, a skill she learned on the Beet Farms.

The magnificence of the mountains was lost on Sara who couldn't appreciate their grandeur. She was used to fields that produced oil beets and food crops and the Gullet appeared to her to be an unproductive wasteland.

Back at the bothy Sara had noticed that Yayler used peat cut from the hillside as fuel and though it didn't burn as well as wood, it was fragrant producing a dull red glow and pleasant warmth. As she hobbled about humming a tune to herself she found a bank of a steep sided stream running off the mountain that cut into the peaty earth. It was well drained and fairly dry, dry enough to burn she thought to herself.

She soon had a fireplace built on a rocky outcrop and was working on making the fire when Dook disturbed her.

''Ah, what's this young lady?'' Dook asked scratching his matted hair.

Startled Sara immediately apologised ''Oh, er'' she faltered ''I noticed Yayler had a peat fire. I thought we might try it.''

''Well'' Dook began as he inspected Sara's fire ''the peat has to be dried to burn properly, but this might work fine.''

Dook took out his utility knife and struck sparks onto the peat with a small stone. It struck Sara as a little odd that Dook had added no kindling to start the fire or make an ember, but regardless of his odd method of fire making he had the fire burning a dull red glow within a quarter wair.

''Well Sara'' Dook said with satisfaction ''rocks or wet peat I can't burn, but this works just fine.''

''Perhaps we can use that pan Yayler gave us to cook some breakfast with?''

''A good plan. I'll wake Varee, that can be her duty in the morning. She lives and works at the Tavern and cooks all the time so she should be able to make something decent.''

Varee on the other hand was less impressed with the idea, but set a pan to heat without comment whilst rubbing sleep from her eyes. She was soon adding oats and was quite pleased with the resulting gruel.

Sara ate silently, but Dook gagged on his and looked suspiciously at the pan. ''By irin Varee, how did you manage to burn water?''

Varee was defensive and not a little heated in her reply. ''It's not burned!''

Dook raised questioning eyebrows and showed her the black mess in the pan as evidence of the burning.

''Well not much, that's hardly burned at all. It's basic equipment so it won't be perfect.''

''You're right about that Varee'' Dook commented sombrely.

''It's fine really isn't it Sara?'' Varee asked looking for moral support.

''I'm hungry'' is all Sara offered as comment though in truth she thought it a badly burned pan, but had been brought up to never waste food.

After three days of trekking and three burned pans, they arrived at Dunban. Dook had refused to clean the burned pans and the group agreed to relieve Varee of cooking duties and elected Sara to do the chore even though she had never cooked before.

Dunban was a small town of about a thousand inhabitants that served as an administrative centre for the surrounding area. There was a divine residence to the north of the town, resplendent palace built in white limestone and decorated with marble. The buildings shone with reflected sunlight and dominated the town. The mucker's buildings appeared drab and rude by comparison.

Dookerock's party entered Dunban from the south and passed simple single storey stone buildings with heather thatch and comprised of two rooms with a central doorway. The buildings appeared to be scattered randomly, but were in fact positioned to take advantage of the topography to provide shelter from bad weather. A small stream wound its way through the town spanned by a single wooden bridge near Dunban's sole inn. The inn was similar in construction to the other stone buildings of the town, but with a single room stone extension and adjoining wooden buildings that served as accommodation for guests, kitchen and storerooms.

Dookerock booked them in for the night and they joined the handful of guests in the bar. Sara noted that the room was mostly of wooden construction unlike at the Tavern, which had a completely stone common room. The inn was also less well maintained.

During their wait Sara spent most of her time in unaccustomed idleness watching birds and water fowl from the bridge and talking to the locals. She was evasive when asked who she was or where she was from. If pressed she would just say that she was travelling with friends and say little else. Varee on the other occupied her time by wandering around the town idly investigating every corner of the town. During one of these trips she was seen by one of Robert the Red's informants.

Dookerock spent most of the day at the wood yard to the southeast of the town. There he arranged for his party to join a wagon train bound for Bandrokit. They would pay for their passage with mundane chores the Wagoner's preferred to avoid. That is cooking, cleaning, maintaining clothing and so on.

They were anxious to be off after a wait of two days and turned up early at the wood yard. The Wagoner's proved to be a friendly group who enjoyed the extra company and the promise of different stories to while away the evenings.

They stopped off by the Tavern where Varee spent some time with her parents. They decided that she should stay with Dookerock and let people assume that she was 'hitched up' with one of the Wagoner's. Unfortunately, the scuffle with Pyta had come to the attention of the divines and her companions thought she would be better off out of the way for a while.

The first morning of Sara's new cooking duty, they found the gruel perfectly acceptable. Dook checked the pan, the Wagoner's own big enough to cook for a dozen people and found it scraped clean and unburned. He finished the job of cleaning it and then went to talk to Sara. ''How did you cook the porridge this morning Sara?''

''The same way Varee does, heat the water and add the oats.''

''Not the same Sara, it wasn't burned. Our hosts are very happy.''

65

For the next few days, Sara became the cook. She managed simple fayre, but did the job well. She was excused the job of cleaning the pans afterward, a job that fell to the slightly disgruntled Varee.

Bandrokit was a busy town embraced by low hills, huddled in a bay on the south shore of the narrows of Bancaol. It had taken Dookerock and the women another four days to reach the town. The Wagoner's had kept a slow, but steady pace throughout the journey and had become quite close and friendly with their guests in those few days.

Dookerock booked a couple of rooms at the Fish and Hook and settled in to wait for Yayler Poddick. He considered what would become of Sara, Varee he assumed would return to her family and her old life after a few weeks, but Sara had nowhere to go. After much consideration of the matter over numerous tankards of ale in the Fish and Hooks bar room he concluded that she would be safest if she joined the resistance movement he knew to be active in the area.

---

Beck25 arranged transport to Dunossin for himself and several squads of Divine Guards as soon as he got the message from the locater he had given to Lowd. Everything had been previously organised.

As Yayler, Cullin and Ecta arrived in Glen Ossin the Census of the Mark was already underway. As they travelled up the glen road they passed a deserted croft that Cullin knew. He had spoken to the crofters about a month before and was at a loss as to why the buildings were now empty.

As they searched about the croft it was obvious that the family that lived there had been forcibly removed. The place was a mess. Broken chairs and pottery lay scattered on the floor and food uneaten still in the pot by the fireplace. Amongst the debris Ecta found a small silver disc that he showed to Yayler.

After some deliberation Yayler discovered that the locater disc was registered to Beck25. How it came to be in the croft was a mystery, but clearly connected the divine to the disappearance of these people. Yayler knew Beck25 of old and also knew that the callous divine cared nothing for these muckers, they were merely a commodity. Yayler was convinced that his old enemy was plotting some kind of scheme that would impress his aimu masters and knowing Beck25's methods would involve the deaths of many muckers, it was minor cost in gaining advancement in divine society. Considering the annoying irritation caused by a few sheep, it seemed likely that Beck25 was using Lord Lowd in some underhanded way. He had no evidence for the connection yet, but he was sure that Beck25 was behind the troubles. Yayler knew he had to get to Dunossin if he was to prevent unnecessary deaths.

They searched around the croft for another quarter wair looking for anything that might indicate the identity of the intruders, but came up with nothing. Yayler decided that he had used up enough time and they had to press on.

Toward noon, they met Old Donal who told them about the census. The man's thoughts seemed to ramble in discontinuous random snatches as he talked each thought triggering the next, but remaining incomplete. Yayler was somewhat irritated by the time used up by talking with the old man.

Yayler believed that it was imperative that as many people be warned as possible, but what to tell them. Their lives were at risk he was sure. He asked Ecta to warn them as he and Cullin had to get to the dun.

Ecta considered the problem; he couldn't warn many on his own. He therefore needed to warn a few and get them to warn their neighbours and for the neighbours to pass the warning onto their neighbours and so on. Yayler wanted them to meet in the Great Corrie below Ardkiran.

Ecta set off with concern dominating his thoughts. He knew of a croft not far away where he was known and trusted. He used small paths unknown to the divines who knew only the main tracks used to transport goods and livestock. By the mid-afternoon, he reached Favir's croft. The giant man was sitting outside by the doorway repairing and sharpening tools.

''Hello young Ecta, to what do I owe the pleasure. I haven't seen you in well over a month'' the giant man greeted them in an open friendly manner.

''Oh I've been travelling with Cullin. I need to talk with you Favir.'' Ecta wanted to get to business without delay. ''You know the croft by the small grove a few strides down the Glen Road?''

''Aye, good people; what of them?''

''They're not there anymore.''

''What are you talking about Ecta? I spoke to Dav not two days ago.''

Ecta explained what he had seen at the croft and Yayler Poddick's concerns with economy and frankness.

''Well that's trouble and no mistake. What's to be done then young Ecta? What plans are there?''

Ecta outlined Yayler's concerns and suggestion that people meet up at the Great Corrie. At the very least the census would mean that a large number of people would be reassigned to work in the mines or on beet farms. If Yayler was right then greater numbers than usual would be forcibly evicted from their homes and forced to work as slaves for the Frame.

After a lot a deliberation and picking at details Favir agreed to pass the warning on. He wanted Ecta to take his wife and youngest son to the corrie and warn those crofts on the way.

Roby was busy clearing the yard in front of his croft when Ecta arrived with Favir's wife and son in tow. Roby had built a small bonfire from rubbish accumulated throughout the year. A neat stack of wood suitable for the fireplace stood by the sidewall and metal from broken tools lay in another pile nearby. Anything not practicably bartered or used as fuel added itself to the bonfire. Red faced and sweaty the lean Roby stood stretching his aching back.

Shona, his wife, had died the year before. His two sons had left to work others crofts some years before. Roby now in his late forties worked the land on his own and prided himself in his efficiency and keeping his croft tidy and clean. He was an outspoken and self-opinioned man who often disapproved of Lord Ossin's running of the

Mark. Roby believed that more 'should be done' to help the ordinary folk of the glens.

"Ecta, what brings you here?" Roby looked rather quizzically at Ecta's companions.

"Bad news I'm afraid. The divines are having a census of the Mark."

"Why should that worry me? I'm too old to be of use to them." Roby didn't seem too concerned by the news and was quite ready to dismiss it as irrelevant.

"Maybe, but you're not too young to die. We've found evidence of crofters forcibly cleared from their land earlier today. We found no sign of them." Ecta carefully avoided mentioning the involvement of Lord Lowd. "Favir is out warning people even now."

"Aye, he's a good man is Favir. How Ossin has allowed this to happen is what I want to know. What's the fool thinking of, eh?"

"Ossin might not know anything about it yet. Cullin is heading up the glen road to warn him"

"Ahh, smart lad is Cullin, smarter than his father anyhow. I should warn my sons."

"We want everyone we warn to get to the great corrie below Ardkiran."

"Not sure that's the best place Ecta, it's hellish cold up there this time of year."

"True, but the divines are less likely to find them there. It's not wise to stay here Roby"

Roby let out an irritated sigh "True enough. I'll give Ossin a piece of my mind when I see him though."

Ecta had similar conversations with everyone he met along the narrow paths. He led a growing party of worried people that eventually arrived at the corrie in the late evening when it was almost dark.

69

Disorganised and frightened they made a rough makeshift camp in the deep snow.

---

Goram viewed the retreating figure with a dislike bordering on contempt, but the news Drandan had brought was as disturbing as it was unwelcome. The divines were conducting a census in the valley; one that would make the previous census appear benign. Despite his complaints to Lord Ossin, they hadn't replaced his sister yet. He had struggled to maintain his small croft for these last ten years on his own, but all they did was demand more grain production for the winter stores. Goram had fallen behind on his quota for the last four years. Thus, Goram knew he would be a prime candidate for reassignment in this census.

Goram was a small wiry man, well meaning, he wouldn't see harm to anyone. He liked peace and for people to get on with each other without bickering and endless arguments. Drandan had little liking for him he knew, but had been a childhood friend of his sister Zoan. He wrapped his battered and over patched old morcote tighter about his weathered and wrinkled old body to keep out the chill. The crop marks of his Mark and profession were long since worn and illegible. He'd asked the weavers for a new one some time back, but had lacked the credit. If he had maintained his grain quota, his credit would have been good. Despite the many hours of hard work Goram put into his croft he was always short of something. He sighed and went back indoors out of the cold.

In truth, Goram had not maintained his croft well. Again, he lacked the credit and needed to grow more crops to get the credit from Grega, the old 'Tightfist' himself. Lone crofters, like himself, needed a bit of extra help from the Lord. With a little bit of extra help Goram was sure he could improve his crofts output and tidy the place up. How they expected him to do it all on his own was beyond him, he couldn't understand their thinking.

Despite his disaffection with Lord Ossin and the way they ran the Mark, Goram knew that the divines would be much worse. Goram couldn't imagine himself working in mines, or on beet farms, or harvesting calp from storm battered seashores. He shivered at the thought of it. Grudgingly Goram came to a decision, the Lord was better than the divines. He looked about his croft and realised he had little worth keeping or saving. He had no family either; nothing to keep him here.

He packed up a few things he thought would be useful, a small, but sharp knife, some well-matured cheese and ham, bread and headed outside. As he walked up the narrow paths that wound up the valley toward Ardkiran's Great Corrie, he met others who, like himself had made the fateful decision to leave their homes. They too, were not happy and complained as they toiled uphill. They hoped that the Lord knew what he was doing. It all seemed very desperate, but there was little alternative.

---

As Yayler and Cullin trekked down the glen Cullin reminisced on the last census of Mark Ossin. He had been young then, only five in fact, but he still remembered those unpleasant days with freshness and clarity as if they had only recently happened.

Cullin had been very close to Dillis and Katrin who were his only source of support and affection in his early childhood. Cullin grew to be a reserved, reflective and introverted child always wary of the discipline administered by his father, more given to watching than to participating.

By the time he was five Cullin was an active and mischievous child who had learned to some extent to control his breathing, usually by sitting in a quiet corner until his breathing returned to normal.

One day in late summer of NE 1005, Cullin was in one of his favourite spots after a particularly exciting game of 'chasing the ball'. The game was very simple. It was played with a small leather ball that was thrown down a corridor, or steps or some other interesting place and chased after to retrieve it before someone else picked it up. The only rule of the game was that nothing must be broken nor must anybody get hurt. This latter included Cullin himself, who during one memorable chase had slipped on some steps, narrowly avoiding being brained on a stone wall and receiving several cuts and bruises before recovering his ball.

Cullin could hear an intense conversation between his father and the Divine Howe19 who kept all the records for the glen. Cullin's spot was behind the heavy drapes of the Great Window of the Great Hall of the dun. The Hall was one of the oldest parts of the dun, abutting onto the original round tower. Heavily buttressed walls supported a high roof. Two rows of mighty columns supported the wooden crossbeams that bore the weight of the slated roof. The Great Window overlooked the high mountain ridges to the north east. Whilst hidden here Cullin found he could overhear all sorts of interesting things, such as when the next feast day would be.

However the current conversation was not about such wonderful things. The Divine Howe19 was instructing Lord Ossin in his duties for a census that would be held the following day. Although Cullin didn't know what a census was, it couldn't be a good thing as his father was in the foulest temper young Cullin had ever witnessed, and he had witnessed many examples of his father's temper.

The census wasn't good news for Howe19 either as he had been somewhat lax in collating population data, one of his main functions for the aimu. In fact, a squad of divine soldiers had sealed off the lower end of the glen earlier that day before delivering their instructions to Howe19. Grega had become particularly grouchy and Cullin did his best to avoid him where ever possible. Grega's records would be under intense scrutiny before being transferred to the divine's lodge and forwarding to the Frame's data base.

Cullin sneaked away from his hiding place at an opportune moment and sought out Dillis, leaving the two men arguing over details of the census.

An unhappy Cullin was kept in his own chamber with Dillis while the census was conducted whilst his father Lord Ossin paced with agitated strides in the Great Hall when the white gowned Divine General Beck25 entered bearing his staff of office and followed meekly by Howe19 and a grizzled, grey haired Grega. The divine's staff also served as a communication device that kept him up to date with instructions from the Frame. Capable of energy bursts that could melt stone, a divine would never be in the company of muckers such as Ossin and the peoples of the glen without one.

''Lord Ossin, I have the list of those who are to be reassigned, you have until midday tomorrow to make the necessary arrangements'', the slender dark faced Beck25 handed over a list of some fifty names from various families of the glen.

Ossin glanced through the list noting with some relief that none of his own kin had been included. ''That is fine General, I will see to it directly''.

''There is another matter. Divine Howe19 has also been reassigned and I will now be taking over his duties''.

''May I enquire why? I believe Howe19 performed his duties quite adequately''. Ossin spoke softly, not wishing to irritate Beck25; it was never wise to irritate a divine. Lord Ossin knew he had little choice in the matter. The divines were his overlords, his masters, and the source of his authority and strength, such as he had. They could take that power away all too easily. Lord Ossin did not take the paltry control and influence that he had lightly; his main focus was survival, not for himself so much as for all the people of the glen. Lord Ossin was also very aware that he himself could be reassigned.

''He did not! Two families at the lower end of the glen had unregistered people living with them. They have been reassigned and the heads of their families executed. Their heads are to be placed on spikes outside the Dun entrance as an example to others. Your people must be registered. See to it or I will have your head on a spike beside them.''

Ossin glared at Beck25 in shock, aghast at the brutality of the man. ''I'll see to it,'' he finally choked ''but could they not have been punished in other ways?''

''No, I have followed the Laws as directed by the Mighty Frame. They sought to avoid their responsibilities toward the common good. Such slovenly laziness is the bane of decent civilised people. Do you not think so Lord Ossin?''

Lord Ossin held his tongue, seeing little benefit in arguing the point other than irritating the divine, a man he was going to have to work with and, if he could, manipulate to avoid more needless hardship for the people of the glen. ''Aye, it is so.'' He eventually grumbled in an unwilling acquiescence.

''Grega, would you see to the Divine General Beck25's accommodation and refreshment while I make the necessary arrangements. Is there anything else I can do for you Divine General?''

''No, that will be enough for now. Tomorrow we will discuss your new duties.'' Turning to Grega he said ''If you have mead, have a pitcher sent to my chambers. I doubt that anything else you have to offer will be remotely adequate. Now I shall retire to my chambers. Today's exertions amongst the squalid muckers of your glen have vexed me greatly why I even saw one scrabbling in the dirt with his bare hands. What he thought to find there I have no idea''

It should be recognised at this point that most divines are not taught, but trained to have a superior attitude. Children are born rarely and by orders derived from the aimu, usually to replace worn out or reassigned divines. They are taken into the care of the aimu when they are four years old and either adapt or are deleted. Survivors learn to be selfish and anti-social and become very insular caring only for their own success in the divine hierarchy. They forget their parents who are never told about the fate of their children. Most divines are only too happy to be rid of the unwanted burden of raising a child.

They are educated from a young age and are very knowledgeable. Failure to achieve the desired standards of their masters, the aimu results in severe punishment or death. All divines are connected via a subcutaneous com-chip inserted under the scalp to the Frames communication network. Information and instructions or even punishment is transmitted through the chip.

''If you would follow me Divine General, I will see to your comfort'' Grega bowed to the divine, his face stiff and flat with a cold hatred sparkling in his blue eyes.

As Grega and Beck25, the new ruler in fact of the glen, left the hall Ossin slumped shaking with an uncontrollable disgust into a nearby chair. Ossin was a hard man whose duty was to make difficult decisions. He knew what reassignment would mean for those fifty unfortunates. Labour on the Beet Farms or in the Mines, digging out the few remaining resources and minerals left available to the aimu. The mines were a certain death sentence, few down in those hellish pits survived more than a year. The Beet Farms were better, but not by much. The Beet produced a rich oily substance that could be processed for fuel. Poor sanitation and little food meant that workers soon became weak and ill. It made little sense to Ossin. Why would the aimu and their servants, the so-called divines, be so callous towards people; he could not understand it.

Life in the glen changed little over the coming months of winter, the Great Hall being the focus of activity. Deep drifts of snow, frequent snowfall and several blizzards made life very difficult. Only the most essential work could be done. That is, those essential to the welfare of livestock and the repair of storm damage. For the most part the main focus of daily activity was to stay warm, well fed and entertained.

The women's work was mostly involved in cooking, the care of children and repairing clothing. The men spent their time cleaning and repairing tackle, tools and equipment. Essentially, winter in Glen Ereged was one of enforced inactivity. The high mountains east and west diminished light throughout a significant portion of early morning and evening light significantly shortening the time available for most work to around four wairs. The drudgery and extended period of darkness caused many people to seek the warmth, light and social intercourse that could be found at the Great Hall. The women worked comfort and the company of friends and neighbours, performing needlework, embroidery and repairs to clothing and other essential tasks. The men mostly indulged in gaming with tiles, stones, dice or trying to impress any young maidens that they had an eye on.

A nudge from Yayler brought Cullin out of his reverie and back to the present. "Stop your woolgathering lad. We're nearly there."

"Sorry, I was remembering the last census. Father always refers to it as the 'Black Days', we lost many good people then."

"I dare say, and likely to lose a lot more this time unless we do something about it." Yayler replied sympathetically.

A curious thought crossed Cullin's mind, they had passed several divines on their way down Glen Ossin and then up Glen Ereged, but they hadn't been challenged.

''Ah that is a good point, but look how I'm dressed Cullin; am I not the very essence of a divine?''

Cullin considered Yayler, dressed in immaculate white clothes despite their journey of several days. Yayler even bore a staff. He on the other hand was dirty, scruffy and travel worn. ''I guess so. How are we going to get in?''

''Through the main gate of course. You will be my prisoner.''

''Oh. Won't your presence have been reported?''

''Why should it have been. I'm just another divine as far as they are concerned.'' Yayler appeared to be very calm and in control.

'' Won't they challenge you at the gates?''

''I expect so, but then I just ask to be taken to the administration, which is where I want to go first anyway. Oh, I almost forgot, I'll need your knife.''

Despite Yayler's implacable calmness, Cullin was worried, handing Yayler his utility knife. Two guards were at the gate as they approached who barred their way with staffs.

The older guard, a lean tall man with narrow features called out in a deep strident voice ''state your business!''

Yayler spoke to him a passive, but authoritative tone ''I have somewhat of importance to discuss with Beck25.''

The guards looked distastefully at the dishevelled Cullin making numerous biased assumptions about the young man.

''Take the mucker to Administration, they'll deal with him.'' The lean grey haired guard ordered.

Yayler strode across the outer courtyard of Dunossin shoving Cullin ahead of him roughly. Once in Grega's administration rooms they were ushered over to an overweight and pompous divine who was pouring over mounds of Grega's paperwork.

"State your business. Be quick, I am very busy with important work." The balding divine didn't even look up from the papers spread before him.

Yayler puffed himself up and replied in an irritated and superior manner "I am not acquainted with you boy. I am Victor8 and I don't care for your manner."

The divine looked up with surprise "I am Smythe14 and I am in charge here. Take that to the other muckers to be reassigned."

Yayler raised his eyebrows "I was under the impression that Beck25 was in charge here not some office flunky!"

A dark look of irritation crossed the soft, flushed features of the divine as he leaned forward in what he hoped was an impressive and authoritative manner "what do you want?"

Yayler leaned forward until he was nose to nose with Smythe14 and spoke very quietly "I need to search the servants quarters and storerooms for illegal weapons. This boy was carrying such. I believe a revolt has been stirring in these glens." Yayler took Cullin's knife out of his pocket and slammed it point first into the desktop severing through a small heap of papers and nicking Smythe14's hand in the process.

The startled divine gestured to one of the guards as he sucked on his hand and had Cullin taken roughly to the Great Hall. He shooed Yayler away allowing him into the servants quarters and calmed his nerves as he tried to re-order the desk.

As Cullin arrived in the Great Hall, a fierce argument raged between his father and Beck25. Three of his brothers were also in the hall along with many of the staff of the dun.

"Why are so many people missing Ossin? You are charged to keep the Mark in order. Preliminary reports show several hundred people short of your figures." Beck25 was scarlet with rage. He had ordered Lowd to remove twenty five people, not hundreds. It appeared that Lowd had overdone it.

"I am certain that those people will be located before the end of the census." Ossin was a worried man. Grega he knew would not have made a mistake, so what had happened to those people? With some relief, he had seen his son enter the Hall, but it appeared that he had failed in his task or that circumstances had overtaken him.

Beck25 gestured toward Cullin, "well that's one, you had better be right about the others, or I'll have you and all your kin reassigned."

Ossin knew that to be no idle threat.

"Tell me Ossin, what do you produce that is of any use to the Frame in these miserable glens of yours. What purpose do you muckers serve? Is there any reason I shouldn't have the whole population reassigned and put to proper useful work elsewhere?"

"You could do that, but when they die, and they will, who will replace them, surely not you superior divines or the Frames precious machines?"

"I see, so your only product is muckers to work for the Frame, is that it?" A chilling softness dripping with malice had entered Beck25's voice. "So you must understand my disappointment that you have lost so many of them?"

Beck25 turned his attention towards Cullin. "And who is this filthy mucker, does it speak?"

"I am Lord Ossin's son, Cullin, and I speak quite well" Cullin deliberately missed off any honorific when addressing the divine knowing that it would irritate the man.

Beck25 simply walked over to him and punched him full in the mouth splitting his lip. "Address me properly mucker or I'll have the skin flayed from your back."

Cullin spat blood onto the wooden board flooring "I am so sorry My Most Gracious Lord Divine; I failed to realise that you were so important. We don't see divines in these rude and poor glens very much, I failed to recognise you."

Beck25 glared at Cullin hardly believing the impudence and ignorance of the mucker. He delivered a kick toward Cullin's chest that caught him a glancing blow as Cullin attempted to turn aside. ''Tell me little mucker what you have been doing that makes you late for the census?''

''I am not late, I am here and available for the census that I understand from your conversation with my father is not concluded yet.'' Cullin had seen things in the glens that day that had upset him. Unnecessary things, horrible things; things that hinted at dark corners of the human psyche that he had previously only heard about in stories. He was determined that he was going to be heard and have his say. He had little to lose that wasn't already at risk due to the census.

''Oh, I see. Don't you understand; I am your superior. If I say you are late then you are late.'' Beck25 was by now a very irritated man. The wise mouthed youth before him was only a fraction away from reassignment. Beck25 generally tended to avoid reassigning members of a Lords family because it raised difficult questions from his aimu overseers. Not that he really cared in this instance as he intended to have the whole population reassigned anyhow. What he did need was enough evidence to justify a mass reassignment and this boy was doing that perfectly well. Let him blow off steam, it would just be added to the growing pile of documents that Beck25 intended to use as corroborative evidence.

''So you are making up rules as you go along. How can you possibly expect us to obey your rules if you change them without informing us first?'' Cullin thought he had a good question here.

''A decent question, you do surprise me, but had you been here as you should have been you would have known that I have already explained to your father the need for laws to evolve and reflect the current needs of the Frame. Now your father has told me that you have been away looking for lost sheep. I must say that there have been an awful lot of lost sheep lately. So tell me little mucker what you have been doing; you can't expect me to believe that you still have sheep that are unaccounted for''

Cullin explained that he had been to the borders of Mark Ossin investigating the movements of game and went on to explain that game was an important part of the diet of the people of the Mark.

''I see. Sheep and game and wild animals seem to be the sole value of these glens.''

''The people have value beyond the figures compiled for the records. People who have struggled hard to make a living in these glens. People who would not leave all they have built for themselves willingly.''

''Ahh, an ignorant mucker that thinks itself a philosopher. If they value their homes and lives in these wretched valleys why do they leave their homes?'' Beck25 was smiling, how easy it was to win arguments with these inferior creatures.

''Perhaps because they didn't leave by choice. I saw a croft earlier today where there was evidence of violence. Those people were certainly removed from their home by force.''

''What is this talk of violence? So they left their homes recently, what of it, it matters not'' Beck25 was getting tired of this debate and was angry at this turn in the conversation.

''It matters because there was blood on the floor. You can't claim that those people left by choice if there was blood on the floor.''

''Actually, it proves nothing; the blood may have been accidently spilt. Who would want to remove those people from their home anyway?''

''Lowd may do, but that would not explain this'' Cullin held up the locater disc. You are the only divine in this area that might have one of these.'' Cullin threw the disc to Beck25's feet as if in challenge. Beck25 merely glance at it, leaving the disc where it lay.

''That is not so, there are many divines in the Mark right now. One of them performing their duties for the census could have dropped that disc. You are accusing me of serious crimes without sufficient proof. That disc is meaningless, mucker, you can prove nothing with it.''

Yayler had been eavesdropping from the door to the kitchens recording the events using the cammic device and data dump on his staff. He thought Cullin had done well, but would never be able to prove

80

anything with the evidence he had. It was time for him to show himself and confront Beck25 directly. ''Keep the disc Cullin, Beck25 knows that it belongs to him.''

Yayler stepped out from his concealment with his staff directly in front of him.

''Who the hell is this. Will somebody tell me what is going on.'' Beck25 was now on the defensive; somehow, he had let events get out of his control.

''Yayler, my old friend, what are you doing hiding in the kitchens?'' Ossin was delighted to see the old man. Cullin, it seemed, had achieved his task after all.

''Evening old man, it is a joy to see you again.'' Yayler had a broad grin on his lined and wrinkled face, which died abruptly as he turned toward Beck25. ''I see you're up to your old tricks again. Beck25, a divine who wouldn't liberate his own sperm to save his life! It's been a long time since the mines has it not, eh?''

''Victor8, I thought you dead in that accident. Can't say that I'm happy to see you alive after all these years.'' Beck25 was feeling very nervous now.

''The locater disc is registered to you Beck25. It indicates its location to you and only you. That means you gave it to another so that they could give you a signal. Therefore, I accuse you of the abduction of the missing residents of Mark Ossin.'' Yayler smiled at Beck25.

''You can't accuse me of anything. There are no bodies.'' Beck25 was no longer thinking clearly. These dreadful sub-human muckers were revealing little bits of information and implicating him in the murder of the missing people. The situation was completely out of hand. How this old divine had found the bodies he did not know and why was the man consorting with muckers? He could not risk evidence getting to the aimu, but there was one thing he could do. With a twisted grin and a glint of sick pleasure in his eyes, he levelled his staff at Yayler and triggered a blast of energy toward him. A white stream of hot pulsating blue fire crackled and sizzled as it scorched the air between them. His aim was good and the blast struck the man squarely in the chest with a shockingly loud blast of crackling noise. As the blast struck, there was an explosion of light and a thunderous roar. Smaller bolts of energy radiated from the explosion that seared and burned the walls and furniture of the hall where they struck. The man who called himself Victor8 should have been a smoking corpse, but remained there, standing with that enigmatic and irritating grin. Everyone scrambled to find the best shelter they could as tendrils of acrid smoke eddied about the hall leaving Yayler and Beck25 facing each other.

Beck25 sent another, longer blast of energy towards Yayler. The resulting explosion of energy engulfed Yayler entirely and the secondary bolts caused devastation about the hall. The bolts blasted stone from the walls sending hails of rock flying about the hall. Hangings and soft furnishings were set alight. Groans and whimpers from injured and dying muckers made a dreadful counterpoint to the noise of the explosions. Again, Yayler remained, unharmed and passive.

The dying and injured did not matter to Beck25; they were just collateral damage and unimportant, but irrational hatred commanded his actions now. Victor8 should have died from his first blast and, certainly, the second, but Beck25 had more power at his command. Beck25 fired another blast of energy toward the old man. A narrow beam of harsh white light poured from his staff striking Yayler's chest. Pulses within the beam sent out powerful shockwaves that shook the walls of the Great Hall.

Yayler staggered and sank to his knees, but his grip on his own staff remained firm. Yayler forced himself back to his feet. The energy shield Dook had added to his staffs compliment of applications worked as well as he'd known it would, though it had never been used in anger before. Beck25's staff lacked such a device. Yayler stood with grim defiance, resolute and steadfast before Beck25.

Beck25 lost complete self-control, sending a blindingly bright blast toward Yayler, and continued the fire in an arc about the hall. It was his last mistake. Yayler sent a continuous blast of fire from his own staff that engulfed Beck25 and reduced him to a smoking heap of burnt flesh in only a few heartbeats. The smoke filled air tingled with residual energy and a burning acrid stench.

Yayler stepped further into the hall and levelled his staff toward the two divine guards who were now rushing forward toward him. Two blasts reduced the guards to smoking hulks on the floor.

For a few moments as the smoke cleared the room remained in shocked silence. Then the room erupted into a frenzy of noise and confused activity as everyone tried to figure out what had happened. The noise rumble into silence again as people noticed Yayler kneeling over the prostrate, still form of Lord Ossin. Beck25's sweeping blast had stuck Ossin and two of his aides.

''No, no, father, no!'' Hamadern was the first of Ossin's sons to their father's side. He gently cradled his father's head and shoulders in his powerful arms.

No words came from Ossin. His eyes stared sightlessly as Hamadern tenderly closed them for the last time. Ossin and the two aides were dead, killed by the blind rage and heartless action of Beck25.

''We need to leave this place.'' Yayler broke the silence handing Cullin Beck25's staff. ''Cullin take this and come with me.''

''We can't leave him here.'' Cullin looked in horror at Yayler, not quite believing what had just happened.

''Then carry him! We must go before more divines arrive'' Yayler's quick decisiveness galvanised the others into action. Yayler raced out of the hall toward the administration. He killed the guards with two swift strokes of Cullin's knife. The first slumped to his knees, blood pumping from a deep neck wound. The second died even as he stood, a back handed slash from Yayler had severed his throat and blood gushed from the gaping wound. Smythe14 looked up in shock, his soft fleshy mouth working silently as he stared at the staff levelled towards him. White fire blazed from Yayler's staff killing the officious divine. With an afterthought, he set the piles of papers alight, leaving less information for the inevitable investigation to recover.

As he stepped back out into the outer courtyard, the two gate guards were hurrying towards the Great Hall where people were now milling about in confusion. Orvalt was yelling and shouting at them, trying to restore some kind of order. Yayler's staff blazed once more turning the last two guards into flaming torches.

After a hasty and heated conference Orvalt, who had become the leader of the fifty or so staff of the dun. With Ossin dead and Cona still in Mark Lowd, he was effectively in charge of Mark Ossin. He led the group to the Great Corrie below Ardkiran Mor taking whatever food and supplies that could be gathered quickly. Cullin had insisted that it was the only place they could go. They buried Ossin on Brayfrowk so that he could be with his beloved Kuli again.

# Chapter Six

When they arrived at the corrie, they found that Ecta had done a competent job of organising the folk. Arranging shelter for the most vulnerable and stockpiling food to enable fair rationing. As Orvalt took control of the refugees, he left Ecta to carry on with the work he had started and sat with his brothers, deep in discussions until early morning.

They knew they were in a desperate situation, but were unsure about how the situation had occurred. They strongly felt that either Cullin or Yayler must be somehow to blame. They were certain that they had to move from the corrie as soon as possible, but where could they go?

A short, blond haired young man named Uska interrupted Orvalt's meeting with panic in his voice. His young wife, Freyna was in labour. Cullin found Katrin exhausted, worn out from the climb up to the corrie and told her of the impending birth. Katrin made her tired way to the young woman's side and in the cold midmorning, the woman gave birth to a baby boy. They named the boy Uskabeg after his father. News of the newborn spread quickly about the corrie and did much to raise the spirits of the corrie's population. Many people were saying that the boy deserved a free future without the rule of aimu or divines.

Goram huddled up with a group of others. They were all cold and worried. Many had seen the smoke rising from Dunossin earlier and there were rumours that the divines had killed Lord Ossin. Rough justice thought Goram. What had his Lordship ever done for him? Goram kept his thoughts to himself; he knew they were unpopular and voicing them now would only upset these good people further. Deep inside, however, Goram took pleasure in the news of Lord Ossin's death. One less Lord was one less problem.

Yayler had left by himself to spread the word of what had happened about the glens and advise them to head for the corrie. He rejoined the frightened group early in the morning looking tired and weary.

Morning light found them in charge of nearly a thousand people with more arriving in small groups. Orvalt still had no definite plan of action. He needed information. He knew they couldn't stay in the corrie or go back to the glens. Cullin's suggestion that they move the folk to the hidden valley east of Ardkiran was the only viable course of action to take that was currently on the table for discussion. Orvalt didn't like the idea as it only provided a temporary solution. The people needed somewhere permanent to live.

Yayler joined Orvalt and the discussions after only having had a couple of wairs of sleep. Cullin's brothers distrusted him, blaming him for the death of their father. He encouraged quick action, as the divines who were already starting their investigations would soon discover their presence in the corrie. Once the people were in the relative safety of the hidden valley Orvalt would then make further decisions. Orvalt reluctantly agreed and started to organise a group led by Ecta of the fittest and strongest to arrange shelter in their temporary home.

By the end of the second day the refugees had been transported up the rake and were safely in the hidden valley leaving only a handful in the corrie to help any stragglers and warn of discovery by the divines.

Cullin heard loud voices raised in anger. He found Orvalt, Hamadern and Ulbin surrounding Yayler, demanding to know who he was. They knew he was a divine and shouldn't be trusted.

To Goram's mind, this was utter madness. He watched a small crowd gathered higher up in the corrie the Lord's sons were amongst them and arguing heatedly with some old man in a white coat. Goram clearly saw them shoving and pushing each other and making aggressive hand gestures. The shouting and noise settled down after they made some sort of accommodation and decision. Was this how overstuffed Lords and leaders made decisions that affected the lives of ordinary folk? Somehow, Goram had expected more intelligence and thought from people in charge.

Reluctantly Yayler told Cullin's Brothers how he had left Divine Society and that he now spent his time in efforts to improve the lives of muckers. Yayler had formerly been a Divine Supervisor in one of the Frames copper mines. He had been ambitious back then, caring little for the mucker slaves he supervised. The Frames minions mined the copper ore despite severe depletion. Those traces that still survived were difficult and dangerous to extract.

The divines and their aimu masters expected good performance from the slaves, to achieve set productivity targets. When results met the targets, the slaves received their full ration. The designs of the targets left them always slightly out of reach, but achievable in the short term. The nutrition rationed to the slaves was not sufficient to maintain the health of a hard working slave. The slaves productivity would inevitably drop and with it, their rations. Their productivity would drop further and thus a vicious cycle would start that invariably resulted in the death of the slave.

The mucker slaves flogged and driven hard pushed to the limits of their endurance by their Supervisors. They had rations cut if they did not obey. divines considered slaves a cheap and replaceable commodity.

Yayler noted that one of the slaves continued to live, despite the appalling living conditions and pitiful rations. This was something Yayler knew to be impossible. Records showed that the man was forty-five years old; ten years older than the next oldest worker. Further research showed that he always fell behind quota, but not sufficiently to have his rations cut. He invariably hit the minimum productivity he could maintain without a cut of his rations. He was achieving an incredible balancing act.

Yayler got to know the man and found that his co-slaves had the highest productivity of any group of slaves in the mine. With subtle questions and instructions Yayler found that he had an incredibly high IQ for a mucker. Normally a bright mucker would have an IQ of about 120. This one had an IQ of over 140. Yayler found that he encouraged his co-workers to work as hard, but no harder than himself. Those who failed to follow his advice fell into the nutrition trap. The others who followed his advice had longer, healthier lives.

Over the years that Yayler observed the man, his attitude changed as he began to view them as people, not inferiors.

When Beck25 took over the running of the copper mine the mucker had been dead from an accidental cave in for some years. He had been fifty years old, very old for a slave miner. Beck25 changed the work ratios, increasing productivity targets and reducing rations. Inevitably, productivity dropped and so Beck25 had the entire work force killed and replaced with fresh slaves.

After a short period of training productivity went up to a record high, but began to drop again after less than a year. Beck25 had repeated the clearout procedure sparing only those slaves that had maintained the impossible targets for three months or more, the rest he had slaughtered and replaced by more fresh slaves.

The mine employed over three thousand slaves with a life expectancy of less than a year. That meant that over three thousand slaves died from accidents and starvation that needed replacing every year in order for Beck25 to achieve his targets. Yayler was surprised to discover that those targets were only fifteen percent higher than the productivity gained by the clever mucker.

Beck25 increased the targets again, by which time Yayler was a different man. He had seen enough unnecessary death, enough of the pointless waste of life. He had learned to respect the muckers whom he now regarded as people who might achieve so much more with better facilities and food.

Yayler organised an accident on a day chosen at random. Not willing to be the cause of more needless death, he altered work schedules and rotas. The mine suffered from a catastrophic explosion that destroyed half the mine and much of the infrastructure. The explosion killed many divines and destroyed a substantial number of aimu. Thankfully, few slaves lost their lives, largely due to his manipulation of the work schedules and partly chance.

Yayler had arranged to 'die' in the accident. He had found a place where he could hide and rebuild his life. The disaster ruined Beck25's reputation, as he was responsible for the running of the mine.

From his hiding place, Yayler had found one of the cables that transmitted power and data to divine residences. He had tapped into this and had been able to manipulate and alter data that helped to reduce the worst excesses of the divines.

Yayler had known Ossin when the Lord was younger and had helped him to avoid a census arranged by the divines. Ossin had always been grateful, as many people had retained their liberty and possibly even their lives.

Cullin's brothers were silent when Yayler finished relating his story.

The people, old, infirm and young alike had to climb up the mountain. Someone had found some ropes to help, but many people were unequal to the task of the climb. It was crazy, but over a thousand people made that climb without anyone getting hurt. More luck than judgment in Goram's opinion. He helped many people by pushing, pulling or hauling on ropes until they were through the most difficult parts of the climb. No one would ever say that Goram didn't pull his weight. They now had to find shelter in a frozen valley exposed to the worst elements of the weather.

When Goram arrived in the valley they gave him a rough hide, it was all that was available to him to make a shelter. It was another foul up he noted. Others were better equipped, but he made the best of what he had. He found a waist high boulder and used a few of the many large stones lying about under the snow to secure it. What he finished up with was an open-ended lean-to, it would be draughty, but would keep off the worst of the weather. He decided it was the best he could do with the equipment available. It was, of course, a failure on the part of the leadership not to provide better equipment.

The old man in the white coat had been arguing with Ossin's sons again, but peace soon settled over the valley again. The quiet was short lived as someone started to sing an old refrain. Goram remembered the old song from his childhood, but with new words. These people were singing a badly rhyming ode to Lord Ossin. They were out of tune and time. They sounded awful. Goram moved away downhill so that he didn't have to listen to the dreadful noise.

As Goram left the vicinity of the singing Cullin was talking to people, encouraging and fortifying their morale. He promised that things would get better. He heard singing; a sad and lilting lament was hanging and drifting gently on the breeze in poignant melancholy. He found Dillis and Katrin were singing before a small group of onlookers. Cullin found it compelling and beautiful. Tears welled up as he realised that it was a lament for his father.

Fare you well our one and only
Bright in life, in death had glory
Fare you well this final journey
Angels light shall guide you surely

We loved you so well
Kind in thought and deed
Vanity vanquished
You loved us so well

Now you roam beyond the skies
The shrouded veil between us lies
Humble, thoughtful and ever wise
You watch over our earthly guise

Beyond the veil you now reside
Now beauty bright the grey storm hides
Till joined again, the fates decide
Now you sit at angel's side

We loved you so well
Somehow your life's gift
Shall bring us the truth
You loved us so well

Light our days with memory bright
Your shade shall guard through restless night
And cruel darkness shall endless fight

*And keep us safe until dawns grey light*

*The sun for you shall be no longer*
*Your words so wise have made us stronger*
*Your wonderlight shall shine forever*
*Softly now in peace hereafter*

*We loved you so well*
*Words of great wisdom*
*Guidance and strength*
*You loved us so well*

Cullin couldn't help a lump rising in his throat as he listened to the music. Tears threatened to come, but he choked them back not wanting to show weakness in front of the people. He went in search for his brothers and brought them to hear the song. His brothers listened in silence as others joined the group. Before long, an Impromptu memorial service was being held in honour of the deceased Lord Ossin.

As the memorial ended Cullin, his brothers and Yayler went aside to discuss the future of the people. First on the agenda was the matter of trusting Yayler. Yayler asserts that it is his desire to relieve the Islands of Garvamore from the control of the Frame and its' minions, the aimu and divines. He thinks that the people should have self-determination, the freedom to make their own choices.

Grudgingly, with no lack of animosity and little genuine trust, the brothers accepted Yayler's word and offers of help. In the absence of Cona it was agreed that Orvalt should act as Lord for the refugees.

Orvalt's first comment as the temporary Lord Ossin was to make an obvious statement ''we cannot stay here; there is not enough food or shelter''.

Cullin replied ''there is plenty of game, but not enough to keep these people alive all winter''.

"Cullin is right. We have six and a half wairs of daylight, we'll have less than five soon. These people will not survive long unless they can be moved to somewhere with more food and shelter". Yayler had deep concern etched onto his lined, ancient face.

"I agree, we can't stay here, but we have nowhere else to go. We can't very well go back to Glen Ereged. You were far too aggressive Yayler" Orvalt's face was dark with anger.

"Don't blame me for the death of your father, Beck25 was set on taking a considerable number of people as slaves for the Frame, quite how many we'll never know, but life as one of the Frame's slaves is short and hard. They wouldn't live long I'm afraid.

"You need to move on Orvalt, I'm sorry your father is dead, but the people are alive and free. We need to keep them that way. The forests east of Bandrokit would be a good place to take them. There are people in Bandrokit I know who can help. It will be tough to get them there without the knowledge of the divines or aimu, but I believe it can be done."

"I'm not sure that we need your help; you haven't been much help so far." Orvalt's contorted face twisted with suppressed rage.

"Really? These people would now be slaves of the Frame, a couple of years from now and few if any of them would be alive." Yayler realised that Orvalt's anger was deep. The young man had watched his father murdered whilst being helpless to prevent it. Orvalt wasn't going to listen to reason; he was full of resentment and deep-rooted antipathy towards Yayler.

The arguments raged on, but eventually they reached a grudging consensus and despite disparate opinions, they formulated plans to move the refugees, both on foot through mountain passes and by wagon to Bandrokit. Orvalt would move the people to the lower end of the valley and organise a temporary village with shelters made of hide and other materials they could find.

The valley was full of game that could be dried and used to supplement the meagre supplies available to them. Many of the refugees had plentiful supplies stored for winter at their, now empty crofts that could be filched late at night and transported back up Cullin's rake. The food would need rationing, but they should be able to gain sufficient supplies to avoid starvation.

The brothers had agreed that Yayler should travel with Cullin to Bandrokit to arrange the transportation of the population. Time was running short. It was now early winter and many passes would soon become impassably choked with snow.

The brothers were busy organising the people and making arrangements to move them to the lower end of the valley.

During the intense preparations Cullin was left to organise the gear for the journey to Bandrokit while Yayler worked on Beck25's staff, reprogramming it so that it would work for Cullin. divine's staffs work by reading the DNA of the holder. It was a simple job for Yayler to delete Beck25's DNA profile and enter the data from Cullin's rune disc. The staff would then work for anyone with Cullin's Y DNA. Thus Cullin's brothers would also be able to use the staff although Yayler had no intention of telling them that.

Cullin and Yayler made an early start the following morning. Cullin was by now used to the travelling and was, in fact, very fit. He had noticed that Yayler although old and could even be described as ancient, was much faster and possessed a seemingly inhuman stamina. They made good time.

The ice in Furlok extended further north than it had when Cullin and Ecta had crossed previously and they were able to travel directly across the frozen water.

''Where was this com-post you told me about?'' the old man asked Cullin.

''Oh, a couple of wairs walking south from here I think.''

''Ah, then I expect we'll find another further north.''

Yayler set off along the frozen track at such a fast pace that Cullin struggled to keep up. Cullin was amazed at the old man's strength and fitness. Toward mid-afternoon they saw the typical pillar shape of a com-post ahead.

Yayler stopped by the post and turned to Cullin. ''What I am about to do is quite difficult and I may appear to behave oddly. This is normal, so don't be concerned about it''. Yayler turned to the post and was about to place a hand on it when he paused and turned back to Cullin. ''Please don't disturb me unless someone, especially an aimu, comes along the track.''

Yayler placed his hand on a slight depression on the face of the com-post and his face went blank the muscles slack as he connected with the com-posts software through sensitive communication pads in his fingertips. After a few brief moments his face started to twitch involuntarily as he connected with the device. A concerned, but fascinated Cullin watched as Yayler's face contorted and mouthed unusual words that Cullin couldn't understand. The process continued for about a quarter of a wair before Yayler's face relaxed and returned to normal.

''We have to move quickly, Cullin; there's a lot of aimu activity in this area, far more than normal.''

If Cullin had thought that they had been walking quickly earlier than the old man further surprised him by increasing the pace. At times Cullin found himself trotting to keep up. Late afternoon the following day they arrived in Bandrokit. Curiously, Yayler still appeared quite fresh whilst Cullin was on the verge of exhaustion, his feet dragging as he stumbled along.

The small town of Bandrokit nestled in a bay formed by two broad, rounded ridges that descended from the surrounding hills, giving the inhabitants protection from the worst of the winter weather. Occasionally, winter storms would roll in from the north and grip the town with an icy chill for weeks on end. A stone bridge spanned the swift flowing stream that flowed from the surrounding hills. The houses, packed along the harbour, were small with thick stone walls and small shuttered windows. Music, song and strong drink provided most of the winter entertainment for the long, dark winter days when it became too cold outside for anything but essential work.

As they walked into the town, the strong smell of seaweed and fish that seemed to permeate everything in the town overwhelmed Cullin's senses. An icy wind came off the narrow strait of Bancaol that separated the island of Ardyvinland from Anklayv Island.

Cullin had never seen the sea before even this thin strip of sea was the largest expanse of water he had ever seen. As they approached the quayside, Cullin could see a bare foot figure he recognised as Sara sat on the quay with her feet dangling over the edge. He realised that he quite liked her easy going, openhearted nature. He had found that he enjoyed her friendly company very much. A few other hardy folk wandered about the harbour, intent on their own business; otherwise, the town was quiet as the people settled into their winter routines.

Sara's feet had almost completely healed now with only faint purple and yellowing discolouration remaining. She liked her feet and appreciated their shape and form when she could. Still she couldn't understand how they had healed so quickly. Yayler's treatment appeared to have had a certain magic. They were still tender, but that wasn't a problem to someone accustomed to beatings from her former divine masters. Sara smiled broadly when she saw Yayler and Cullin walking towards her and jumped to her feet with a small squeal of delight and ran lightly to greet them and gave Cullin a big hug.

Dookerock was in the Fish and Hooks bar nursing a beer when Yayler and Cullin and a grinning Sara entered. Dook grinned broadly, grasping Yayler's hand firmly. This gesture may appear to be a friendly greeting, but in fact, they were exchanging large amounts of data.

When divines are still young they are taken from their parents by the aimu for education and training, they undergo surgery by aimu to insert implants into their brains and bodies. Powerful memory chips and miniature processors increase their cogitative and memory capacities. Implants in their fingertips allowing direct and discreet connections with aimu and other divines. They are trained over many years how to use them effectively.

Dook's expression changed ''It's a bit of a mess old friend. It's going to be difficult to move all those people under the aimu metal noses''.

''Yes I know, but I'm sure Beck25 had worse planned for them. You know that he had a knack of making even the worst excesses of other divines seem kindness in comparison. I was hoping they could be secreted into the resistance.'' Yayler had had time to think over the problem and had a course of action in mind. ''To make things more

95

awkward the Frame appears to have increased surveillance in this area''.

''We could slip a few through the mountains, but it's a huge number of people we're talking about; many of whom are not fit enough to make a journey like that anyway, especially at this time of year.''

''I thought that wagons could work. We could move large numbers that way without the metal minds seeing anything.''

''It's a bit late in the year for that, Yayler, and more than a little suspicious, but there isn't really any other way to move a lot of people.''

''I agree, Dook. So we move the least able by wagon and the rest on foot through the mountains. How many do you think we can move that way?''

''A couple of hundred on a decent wagon train and only the strongest through the trails at this time of year. So, a few hundred; four hundred at best. The rest will have to stay put for the winter.'' Dook looked mournfully at his empty beer mug.

Sara, sitting quietly by next to Cullin made a small little sigh and took the mug to the bar for a refill. The planning and conversation went on for several hours with Cullin and Sara only making occasional comments. It was quite late in the evening when Robert the Red joined giving Dook a brief handshake and barely glancing at the others.

''You have a problem for me Dook?'' the muscular red headed man asked.

''You might say that'' Dook replied lifting his empty mug to his mouth. Realising the lack of ale in the vessel he thumped it back on the table with an annoyed look of exasperation on his face.

Knowing Dook's habits well, Robert merely queried ''Top up?''.

After receiving his latest refill from Robert, Dook introduced the others.

''Ah, I've heard a lot about you Yayler'' Robert said with a curt nod toward the old man. ''What plans have you made so far?''

The discussions went on late into the night with the result that over the next few weeks the drovers road saw a couple of large wagon trains from Dunban roll into Bandrokit carrying 'vital' winter supplies.

To the east of Bandrokit lay an extensive forest that stretched around the mountains and as far south as Dunban. The forests and the coast were sparsely populated by the occasional fishing croft. Hidden in the dense woodland the resistance had bases where their activities could remain unnoticed by the aimu. Yayler and Dookerock intended for these bases to become the new home for the refugees. Over three hundred people had been moved to various locations in the forest, Hamadern among them, but eight hundred remained in the hidden valley where they would have to stay until spring.

Dook and Robert were in the bar of the Fish and hook talking over the progress of their covert operation. Icy winter winds ripped through Bandrokit effectively closing the town down for the winter months. Few ventured outside for long in the bitter weather.

''We should be thinking of moving Yayler's young friends into the forest, there isn't much else that can be done here.'' Dook was looking a bit miserable as he spoke. Even by his standards, he'd had a lot to drink the night before and was suffering the inevitable consequences.

''That's a good thought. I'll start the arrangements tomorrow; I've got a few things to tie up today. Though we are having difficulty finding places to put these people.'' Robert looked at Dook with a certain amusement. ''You know, you really should drink less; you look awful.''

''Thanks for the advice, but I suspect I'll recover as normal. Just make the arrangements.'' Dook wasn't in a good mood and didn't enjoy Roberts comments about his drinking.

''I'll move them in a couple of days, but I want to keep Varee here. She's a good organiser. She can work here as a cover''.

Two days later Robert introduced the guide Rollo to Yayler and the others. He was a small wiry man with the dark weathered skin of somebody who works outside all the time. Rollo's head was almost bald, only a narrow band of grey hair extended from behind his ears to the back of his head.

A thick evergreen canopy hid a complex series of narrow forest trails cut between the trunks. It was dark and forbidding under the trees, little light penetrating through the dense canopy. Therefore, there was almost no undergrowth; an environment seemingly without life other than the dark pine woodland. The trees formed an almost uniform blanket over the landscape with occasional clearings with leafy vegetation clinging to the edges connected by a web of narrow tracks. Rollo led them with the ease of long familiarity. Cullin soon lost his sense of direction and doubted he would be able to find his way back out of the forest without a guide. He felt completely lost in the oppressive gloom.

In one clearing there were vegetables were growing in random patterns that appeared to be naturally occurring. Rollo led them to a large outcrop of rock by a grassy mound in one of the clearings and pushed gently on the rock. The rock parted, revealing a small entrance. Rollo took a lamp stowed in a recess just inside the doorway and quickly lit. The pale light provided by the lamp revealed a wood lined room with several small, but comfortable sleeping dorms. Rollo explained the design of the dwelling as a home for a small family.

They found a plentiful supply of food in simple, but functional cupboards. As they settled in Rollo said that someone would come by later and give them some duties to pay for their keep.

It had been a tenday since the burning of the Dun when they started to move people further down the hidden valley. Goram was surprised, but happy to be chosen to be among the first moved. It was bitter cold in his shelter. The open ends allowed snow and wind into the shelter. Worse still, he had nothing to sleep on and had to lie directly on the frozen ground. It was of course unacceptable, a failure on the part of leadership.

A pleasant young mucker called Ecta, with none of the trappings of authority, had picked him out explaining that they were setting up new camps and needed people like Goram to set up fields to grow food.

''Are you keeping warm enough?'' the youth had asked.

''Hardly'' Goram had replied indicating his shelter.

''Ahh, we'll have to do better than that. You'll need to help build more shelters further down the valley so that we can start to move people.''

''Sounds good to me'' Goram had replied.

The next few days were hard work for Goram and not being skilled at building he had struggled, but his work was satisfactory. The shelters varied according to the materials available. The one Goram had just completed had started with a ring of stones round an open ended hollow and covered with slanting boards. He had then raised the floor level of the hollow with more rocks so that water could drain more efficiently and keep the occupants dry. He thatched the whole lot with heather that he cut from beneath the snow.

The following morning Goram was moved on again and stayed in a shelter on the shore of Furlok that Goram was horrified to see was a frozen jumble with slabs of ice at odd angles. He knew that part of their journey was to cross Furlok to a track on the far side. How they hoped to get some of these people across the contorted and twisted ice Goram couldn't imagine. Over the next few days Goram was kept busy building more shelters that were quickly filled with people from further up the valley.

He was introduced at this time, to a small group of elderly refugees that Goram noted were cold and tired. One of the women had a racking cough that needed the attention of a herbwoman. Another woman was surprisingly large and Goram wondered privately how she had managed to ascend the rake. Not without considerable assistance from others, Goram assumed.

One day about a wair before midday two large men arrived along the shore from the north. The idea was that Goram's group of refugees would walk north along the shore to the open water. It wasn't too far the men assured them. The group would then be rowed across Furlok to awaiting wagons that would take them to Bandrokit.

The whole process of crossing Furlok took several wairs, but toward dusk the entire group were loaded onto the wagons already loaded with wood and food. They made a short journey that first evening and pulled up after only a few strides at a camp where hot food and shelter was ready for the refugees. The efficiency and scale of the operation impressed Goram greatly.

He was woken early the following morning by Rona, a large woman of middle years, to help out with the breakfast chores. Several large earthenware pots had been set out and Goram was given a sack of oats and told to measure into each pot. He was then instructed to fetch water from a burn that tumbled down off the hillside beside the track.

''You need to speed up'' Rona called out ''we need to get the food cooking or we'll be here all day.''

Goram did his best to be quick, but it was awkward to transport the water. Rona had given him a large water skin that was difficult and heavy to move when it was full. The bung that sealed the skin appeared ill-fitting and Goram spilled a lot of water on each trip.

Rona, watching him, called out ''twist the bung into the neck.'' He did better on subsequent trips, but was still too slow for Rona. ''Will you hurry, you need to be slicing the meat by now.''

He tried to speed up, but it was another quarter wair before all the pots had sufficient water in to satisfy Rona

''You will have to be quicker this evening and tomorrow'' Rona scalded. It was clear to Goram that she was disgruntled and unimpressed with him.

She gave him a small wooden board and a number of large platters and a large ham. ''I want thin slices and I do mean thin. I don't want the meat wasting.''

''Is there a knife to slice with Rona?''

''On the wagon'' Rona indicated a wagon whilst fussing with the cook fires ''just behind the drivers bench.''

He quickly found the knife and was soon carving the ham into decent sized portions.

''Not like that! Rona barked and with great irritation showed Goram how she wanted the job done. ''And don't forget to stir the porridge, don't let it burn.''

''Aye Rona, I won't'' Goram managed, but soon found himself hard pressed to attend to several pots and slice the meat at the same time. Rona continued to nag and complain until the breakfast was complete and not too badly burned. Goram was relieved that the work was over for a while and was about to start his own breakfast.

''Goram'' Rona barked ''you need to clean the pots before eating. You can eat once we get under way. You really need to get a move on.''

Before he'd finished the last of the pots an assortment of dirty bowls and platters, spoons etc' appeared and piled up by his side. Goram got the message without being told by Rona and set to on the pots. Rona still scowled he noted, but was eventually satisfied that he had completed his chores adequately.

Once underway he remembered that he hadn't eaten himself and realised he'd now have to wait until evening before he got another chance to eat. He resigned himself to a bumpy, uncomfortable day of hunger and misery.

The woman with the cough was still bad that evening, though no worse. He asked Rona about getting some herbs to help her.

''You should have told me sooner Goram.'' Rona's scalding reply came. She scuttled off to one of the wagons, but not before having Goram fetch more water.

As Goram went through the same routine he had at breakfast Rona busied herself with a small pot, adding various dried herbs to the simmering brew. She eventually satisfied herself with her concoction and decanted it carefully into a flask, which she gave to Goram for the woman.

The evening varied from breakfast only in that dried fruit was added to the platters and a hard cheese melted into the porridge. Rona made no complaint when Goram helped himself to food and even smiled when he complimented her on the idea of adding cheese to the porridge.

''We have no time for sophistication on the road'' she had replied. ''Our food is basic, but wholesome.''

The following day followed the same routine and Goram found that he was more efficient and received less scalding from Rona. The wagon train rolled ponderously through the countryside with Furlok to one side and mountains to the other. The track constantly turning as it followed the coastline. They rolled through Bandrokit without stopping and pulled up in a clearing on the edge of a large forest. A large amount of wood in neat stacks lay scattered about the clearing.

Later Goram was talking to Kensi, the leader of the wagoners. He was a short man of huge girth and completely bald. He had a high-pitched voice that sounded somewhat feminine, but he was quick witted. ''Rona tells me she was quite pleased with your work. I hope she didn't bully you too much''

''Oh, no, not at all.'' Goram heard himself reply whilst inwardly cringing at the mention of Rona.

''Ah, that's good'' Kensi laughed with a broad smile and slapped Goram on the back.

Goram had settled into his new life in the forests, he had a comfortable weatherproof shelter provided for him. Food production was a serious problem for a thousand refugees. They had arrived at the end of the growing season and it would be late spring before reasonable quantities of food could be grown. This was something Goram had explained to Joz, his overseer when he had first arrived in the forest.

''But we have a thousand people to feed'' an indignant and shocked Joz had stressed to him.

''I'm sorry, it can't be done. You must have other growers saying the same thing.''

''But we can't let the people go hungry Goram.''

''Plants need the warmth of spring and summer to grow. Nothing will grow when the snow is on the ground.''

''We've got to do something'' Joz had protested.

''We can trap game, birds and deer must be in these forests.''

So Goram and many others had spent a hard winter foraging and hunting, making do with what they could get.

It was now late spring and Joz was not happy with the way he had organised his clearing, but otherwise she was encouraging and easy to work for. The people running things here seemed well organised, but had odd ideas on how to grow things. As a crofter, he had grown most of his food and had ample surplus that he could barter for what he couldn't grow. Here though, vegetables and grains had to be arranged in a certain way. The system had no logic that he could see.

Nips and cabbages might grow together, but to add patches of grains and even gorse bushes made little sense. Apparently he was being too orderly and that as unacceptable, even dangerous here.

Goram did as was asked, even though it felt wrong to him. Joz was a kindly young woman, not officious, but patient. ''It's a disguise'' she had explained ''It has to appear random'' and so on always touching her finger to her temple and smiling sweetly.

Joz even congratulated him on one occasion saying that his plants all appeared healthy and should provide a good crop. He'd 'disguised' the inevitable paths that developed with plant material and covered the more delicate plantings with straw or other grasses to provide protection from the frost.

# Chapter Seven

By the following spring a few of the refugees had succumbed to the cold, but most remained healthy. The resistance stealthily moved them the following spring and soon put them to work constructing weapons from manufactured parts. Where the parts came from or how they were manufactured they wouldn't say. How they worked was a complete mystery, but they had detailed instructions on what to do. Strangers from the resistance came and took the weapons to store them in camouflaged caches in locations known only to a few. Orvalt and his brothers were not entirely happy with the organisation because it left them with little access to their people. Never the less they were busy organising the movements of food, fuel, clothing and so on; utilising skills they had learned from their father.

Dookerock, Ecta and Sara left the forests as soon as the weather was mild enough. They were breaking camp on a chilly clear morning. A rude plaz shelter was drying spread over the branch of an old gnarled tree. Once folded the plaz was compact and light. They had little other equipment other than the walking poles that Ecta and Cullin had previously used.

The party had been following the course of a deep gorge with sheer craggy sides. Rivers were running in spate with snowmelt from the spring thaw. They could hear the water churning with a constant dull roar in the gorge below. The gorge carved a cleft that cut a path through rough moorland toward a distant peak with bright spring sunlight glinting off its snow-clad summit.

Dookerock pointed to the mountain ''that, my young friends, is my home, Rustick More.''

''Wow'' Sara looked impressed ''and you live there?'' Despite her slight build, Sara proved to be very tough with an amazing stamina. What she lacked in physical strength she compensated for with sheer force of character.

''Sometimes, I wander about a bit. You might have noticed that. It'll take about half a day to reach it from here.'' Dook spoke, half in a whisper, as if trying not to break the peaceful quiet of the morning.

Ecta was a little startled by Dook's statement ''really Dook; it looks a lot closer than that.''

Dook nodded ''Ah, true. It's bigger than it looks and separate from its neighbours. That makes it look nearer than it is; the distance is hard to judge.''

The route Dook took towards the mountain twisted and turned to the extent that it was obvious that Dook was intimate with the countryside. They crossed many turbulent streams that made their courses between rough hills and peat bogs. Dook navigated unerringly though there appeared to be no obvious path. Seemingly impassable ravines were negotiated via half hidden gullies and streams spanned by stepping-stones. By midday, Rustick More loomed high above them, brooding with immensity and pride.

Dook took them up a steep incline over a loose scree slope that narrowed to a gully, becoming rubble choked. Snowmelt ran over the rocks making their footing treacherous and difficult. Ecta noticed that the rock had a reddish hue he had never seen before.

''Dook'' Ecta asked ''why is the rock red? I don't think I've seen red rock before.''

''Ah, that, young man, is an interesting question. It's caused by iron in the rocks.''

''Oh'' Ecta was taken aback by the reply ''I thought there wasn't any more iron.''

''Hah! So the Frame says, but there is iron to be had. It's just hard to extract.''

Below them the moors and hills, surrounding Rustick More began to look insignificant and small. Even the deep gorge they had earlier followed lost its grandeur as they gained height.

They were still only about half way up the mountain with the sun beginning to dip low and casting a ruddy glow to the mountain tops. Dook called a halt and pointed out a distant snow-clad peak that was higher than its nearby neighbours were.

''That, Ecta, is Ardkiran Mor. I believe you are quite familiar with it.'' Dook scratched at his unkempt hair, idly teasing out a twisted knot.

''Really?'' Exclaimed a surprised Ecta ''you can see it from here?''

Ecta gazed at the mountain for long, spellbound silent moments, awed and humbled by the immensity of nature spread out before him. The majestic massiveness of the mountain scape caused Ecta to realise how insignificant he was when compared to the world beyond the orange tinted horizon.

''Where's my home Dook?'' Sara asked suddenly, breaking the silence. Her eyes were shining with excitement; this was a world far beyond her experience.

''Oh, I'm not sure. It's a long way off though.'' Dook indicated a south-westerly direction ''beyond those mountains over there, I think.''

A chilly breeze caused Ecta to shiver, shifting his attention from the magnificent spectacle. ''Where do we stay tonight Dook? I assume you have something in mind.''

''Aye, I do indeed young man.'' Dook grinned broadly ''Here, in fact!''

Ecta looked puzzled; so far, Dook's 'home' was nothing like what he had been expecting.

Dook reached behind a flange of rock and pressed down on a smooth flake that clicked quietly and gave way to the pressure, gently sliding inwards. A narrow doorway was revealed and a passageway beyond.

As they entered light flickered on, sections of the walls glowed with soft light illuminating a stairway that climbed upwards. Dook asked Ecta and Sara questions as they climbed. ''Ecta, do you think you could find this place again, if you had to?''

Ecta frowned as he thought, trying to picture the route in his mind. ''I think so, crossing those moors and streams might be a bit confusing, but as long as I knew my direction I would manage it.''

"Hmm, interesting, you sound confident; do you think you could do it at night?" Dook pressed.

"Possibly, I see quite well in the dark. It would be much harder though." Ecta didn't want to exaggerate his ability, but believed he had gained enough experience to navigate at night.

"And you Sara, what about you?" Dook stopped and faced the young woman.

"No, never" Sara was astounded that Dook might think she could navigate in the dark "I don't have the experience or knowledge Ecta does. I grew up on a farm."

The questioning continued as they climbed until after the last flight of steps stood a doorway. As Dook opened it he revealed a large cavern beyond filled with the bustle of men and women working on machines. Dook addressed Ecta and Sara as they entered. "You two are now in the heart of a resistance cell. All the machines you see are operable by muckers. We hope to use them eventually to fight against the Frame."

Ecta was stunned speechless by the spectacle before him. He knew about machines, but had little contact with them. He had never seen machines like these before, only the occasional hiu.

One of the mechanics saw them and stood up with a wide grin on her face "Welcome home Dook. Using the backdoor again?"

Dook looked embarrassed "Ah, hello Neev. Can you organise some food and drink for us. We're hungry and, er, very thirsty."

Neev laughed "you're always thirsty Dook." She rolled her eyes in mock despair.

Dook was leading Ecta and Sara across the cavern floor when Sara spotted a familiar machine and pointed to it. "That looks a bit like the fliers the divines had back home. It looks different though."

"Aye, different. Eventually, you may learn to fly one yourself."

"What, me?" Sara was incredulous.

''Aye, you'll both learn how to use some of this machinery. When the fighting against the Frame starts, we'll be using places like this as bases.''

Dook led them through another door and up another flight of stairs at the top of which was a large room with soft evening light streaming through a window at its far end. ''Welcome to my home, make yourself comfortable. We'll sort out rooms for you tomorrow.''

Ecta and Sara were given their rooms the next day; not as big as Dook's, but comfortable. For both of them it was a new experience as neither had ever had their own private chamber before. It was more profound for Sara as she had only ever known a communal life before and found the experience uncomfortable at first. Sleeping alone and privacy in general was a privilege for divines, not ordinary farm folk.

---

A cold breeze dried the sweat from Ecta's brow as he studied the ruins in the valley below. He had been negotiating his way through a snow clad mountain range called 'Feeaklan Deyaval' or the 'Devil's Teeth' that ran along a peninsula northeast of Rustick More. The range consisted of three distinct peaks interconnected by jagged, knife edged ridges that gave the mountains their toothed appearance.

Ice rimed rocks made travel along the range precarious and difficult, but over a number of days, Ecta had found routes below the snowline that avoided exposure on the precipitous crags. As he progressed along the ridges, he mapped the peninsula and entered the data into a compad given him by Dookerock.

Tomorrow would be the first day of Ooan, the fifth month of the year. The spring thaw had filled the rivers and streams with icy water. Fresh green spring growth covered the lower slopes contrasting with the harsh, near lifeless crags of the range.

Below him lay a small inlet surrounded by steep rock faces that made access to the valley only practical by sea. The inlet formed a natural harbour that had once served a cluster of now dilapidated stone buildings, some with tall chimneys the purpose of which Ecta couldn't fathom. He made detailed descriptions and pictures of them. Roofs had long since collapsed and walls crumbled. Decayed storage sheds, rotten and barely recognisable as buildings, bordered the edge of the site. One shed even had a large tree growing from it. What remained of the place was the skeleton of once impressive buildings.

Ecta shivered and drew his morcote close about him and leant back against the rocks. Dookerock had asked him to find a suitable landing site for boats and map a route from it to Rustick More. That route would be along the coastline of Lok Kruay, which he would check and map on his return to Rustick More.

Ecta continued his work with short breaks until mid-afternoon when he decided to descend into the small valley below. The only practical way down was to follow the ridge declivity as it dropped to Lok Kruay and swing back north and west into the valley.

The ridge was a sharp arête with steep or vertical slopes on either side with a series of towers that compounded the difficulties of negotiating the ridge. Ecta found the exposure on these towers daunting and struggled to control his fear. His progress was slow until a final steep drop down scree and craggy outcrops brought him to more gentle terrain.

I was dusk by the time Ecta arrived at the buildings and the mountains cut out much of the remaining evening light. He set up camp by one of the buildings by making a lean-to with a sheet of plaz.

The following morning the sun rose over the ridge he had climbed down the previous day and cast a ruddy glow that reflected off low clouds. It was a very beautiful sight that Ecta appreciated greatly, but he knew the signs and steeled himself for a wet day.

Down at the small harbour he found rusted metal rails. These he traced back to their source, a shaft that delved deep into the mountainside. What was mined here Ecta didn't know, but he entered as much detail as he could into the compad for the rest of the morning before starting his journey back to Rustick More.

Torrential rain soaked Ecta as the route twisted and turned around inlets along the rugged coastline. He arrived back at Rustick More in the dark tired and looking forward to some rest in a warm and comfortable bed.

The next few years saw Ecta given many similar jobs as well as hand to hand combat and machine operation. mapping, and so on. He excelled with mapping and learned to describe an area with a high degree of accuracy. He even found he was able to do so at night, maybe not with the same accuracy, but good enough for others to navigate by.

---

"Ah, Neev" Dookerock called out. "I have a job for you."

"Another one. I still have this one to complete." Neev indicated a work station scattered with bits of wood and part completed grenades.

"I know. Sara here can help you. Teach her what you can as you work."

Neev placed her hands on her hips and stared at Dook "Just that? What would you like me to teach her? Anything specific or just everything?"

"Oh, everything and anything will do fine Neev. I'll leave it in your hands then." Dook turned leaving Sara with an astonished Neev.

"Well, that's just typical. That's just like him you know." She said to a confused Sara. "He doesn't know what to do with you, so he's dumped you on me so he doesn't have to think about it."

"I'm sorry if I'm a nuisance" Sara whispered meekly.

Neev laughed "nay, not you, you're not the problem. It's just Dook being lazy. You can help me with these." Neev indicated the wood on the bench.

"What do I do?" Sara asked quietly.

"There's an instruction sheet there, just follow the instructions. Ask if you don't understand anything."

Sara looked at the indicated sheet blankly and at Neev helplessly.

"Is there a problem Sara?"

Sara frowned with frustration at the instruction sheet ''I can't read this. Slaves like me aren't allowed to read.''

''Ah'' Neev raised her eyes with surprise ''you're not slave now, so I guess you had better learn how.''

''How do I learn Neev?''

''I guess I will have to teach you. We'll start with making glue for the boxes and leave the letters till later. Mix small quantities of these containers in this bowl into a smooth paste. It goes off quickly so you have to work quickly with small amounts.''

Sara wondered how simple things like milk, beer and ash could make glue, but left that question for a later time. For now all she needed to know was that it worked. The glue was used to construct wooden boxes that were then packed with grenades. Sara quickly picked up the routine and the two women talked about their lives as they worked.

Neev had been orphaned when she was five years old and barely remembered her parents. Dook had taken her in when he'd found her wandering aimlessly along a track with a dirty tear streaked face clutching a doll made from twisted knots of wool. Dook had stunk, but Neev cared more for the comfort and being cared for than she disliked the smell. Her parents had been crofters working a sheep farm in a high valley providing wool for Mark Tymeum. They were taking washed and spun wool to the Mark when the accident happened.

A barking dog had spooked the ox harnessed to the cart. Neev had been thrown clear as a wheel shattered in a deep rut casting the cart down steep slopes and crushing Neev's parents.

Dook, unused to the care of a child had taken the easy option and hired Roz, a young woman from the local Mark to care for Neev. At the time Dook had only a handful of people that assisted him. This was the beginning of a remarkable expansion of Dook's mountain home to the fortress it was to become.

Neev started to teach Sara to read and write after their work was finished. Sara learned quickly and studied hard and was always thirsty for more knowledge. She always considered herself to be making up for lost time. For the first time in her life she felt valued.

111

---

Varee was working at the bar of the Fish and Hook and even had her name added to the local Marks population details. Her duties however were not exactly those expected of public house staff. She was able to pass on messages between Robert the Red and other resistance people. She spent a lot of time honing her fighting skills and practising marksmanship with a crossbow given to her by Robert.

The Frame strictly banned such weapons, but the Fish and Hook had a large and long cellar and a barrel could easily turned on its side and its base used as a target. Though the distance between shooter and target was still quite small, the crossbow was small and not powerful. Robert had said this wasn't really a problem because it was the target practice that was important, not the weapon.

Robert also trained her in hand-to-hand combat techniques, skills at which he was remarkably proficient. However, where he had gained those skills he was unwilling to say.

Fraze was a regular visitor to the bar. He was a tall, muscular man with icy blue eyes and a long mane of golden hair. He was quietly spoken and mild mannered. The gentle giant was generally considered to be a solid and reliable man.

Varee gave him a warm smile as he approached the bar ''what can I get you Fraze?''

''Just an ale Varee, and a couple of hams for our guests.'' Fraze handed her a sheet of paper ''can these be dropped off on Usklatha?''

''Next week? Usual place?'' Varee glanced at the sheet briefly as she pulled a large mug of foaming beer for Fraze.

''Aye, usual place.''

''Will Red be there, I have some notes to hand to him?''

''Who knows? He goes where he wills and appears when he wants. He is a law to himself, that man.'' Fraze laughed with easygoing light heartedness.

''Aye, he's an admirable enigma and no mistake.''

''Leave the notes with me and I'll make sure he gets them.'' Fraze took a long pull on his ale and smacked his lips appreciatively. ''Good ale Varee. Much better than the stuff we're used to here.''

''It's my Dad's recipe. It sells well at the Tavern.''

Life changed little over the next couple of years. People forgot about the hardship of that first winter and fleeing from the wrath of the Frame. Cona was instated as the new Lord of Mark Ossin with a much reduced population and frequent inspections and visits from a new and officious Divine General.

The refugees settled into new routines with little idea that the Frame had its own plans and they had no place in them.

# Chapter Eight

The Frame was unhappy, that is, if a machine could have emotions such as joy, fear or happiness, then recent data reports were making it unhappy. The reports the Frame was receiving from its hiu were unsettling. The Frame preferred order, questions that had answers not conundrums. The Frame found new situations and changes difficult to analyse, everything should be ordered and systematic to maximise efficiency.

The recent killing of a very trusted and capable divine in Dunossin apparently by another, yet unknown divine caused the Frame considerable distress. Detailed and diligent records on the movements of divines failed to enable the Frame to determine who the other divine was. In short, no one could possibly have killed the divine known as Beck25 and none had had the opportunity. Yet the crime had indeed been committed and for no reason that the Frame could understand. Data records showed that such a crime had only occurred twice in the last thousand years.

The disappearance of many inhabitants of the Mark was confusing. They had simply vanished. The destruction of the dun had also destroyed much of the intelligence concerning the inhabitants of the Mark and access to the dead Divine Generals data records were still unavailable. The Frame had no way of knowing how many people were missing until that data could be read and downloaded.

The Mark had been quiet, but efficient, providing a steady flow of fresh, but inefficient labour, but useful where automated systems were difficult to introduce. The humans were soft machines, weak and required a high level of maintenance. The Frame preferred its own dependable mechanical creations.

The Frame was also analysing reports from its hiu. The incoming data suggested unusual movements of the population in the Bandrokit area. The data supported reports from spies the Frame had planted in the mucker population. Yet, suggestions of a growing resistance movement in the area were unsubstantiated, but couldn't be discounted without further data.

There didn't appear to be any connection between the events in Mark Ossin and Bandrokit, but a probability analysis resulted in a strong correlation.

The Frame concluded that it needed more data and issued instructions to increase surveillance and vigilance and report any unusual occurrences.

An additional consideration was the consequences of not being prepared for an uprising. The Morven Rebellion of NE 876 had caused a lot of disruption and reduced productivity for many years. The Frame had introduced tighter controls on the population to prevent similar rebellions in the future.

In preparation for a possible uprising the Frame ordered the construction of weapons and updated its logistics software. Combat programs were designed that could be downloaded to the divines and provide them with the necessary skills and knowledge to fight the muckers. The Frame was determined that any conflict would be a very one-sided affair, after all the muckers had little to fight with.

Since the Frame had already concluded that, it no longer needed the human race and was already formulating plans to eliminate the creatures, preparations for conflict were entirely consistent and had a soothing and pleasing effect on the Frames processing.

---

It was three years on from the events that led to the death of his father as Cullin sat by the doorway to Yayler's bothy watching the changing moods of the valley as clouds drifted overhead. Occasionally he had seen a large eagle soaring above the high crags. Although he had seen eagles at home, the sight of one never failed to thrill him. A cool breeze dried the sweat from his recently finished workout. Yayler had insisted on regular workouts as part of his training regime. Cullin's body had filled out over the last three years. He was lean and muscular with the strength and stamina of the ancient warriors of myth and legend.

Cullin was mulling over the story of the Morven Rebellion; Yayler had recited the legend the day before adding details and colour

Cullin had not heard before. When Cullin had remarked on the remarkable depth of detail in the story Yayler had cryptically replied that they probably hadn't been there. The Great Halls of the past had become the performance stage of the bards who learned all the traditional lore by heart and performed stories and songs for the enjoyment of all. Holidays had become feast days and gatherings that would occur throughout the Marks. Laughter and entertainment filled with historical ballads, stories and dances that ensured the people would never forget their past, or the fact that they had once been free from the yolk of the Frame. Bards were highly skilled peripatetic waits that wandered the towns, glens and fields of Garvamore entertaining the folk of the Marks. Through this oral tradition handed down through the generations, history remained a living thing that became part of the soul of the people and the land. A waits fee was the food and clothing provided by their host.

The legend of the Morven Rebellion went that in NE 876 a Divine General selected a bard for reassignment to a labour camp near Fort Castle. The bard had made disparaging remarks about the divines character during an extended and vulgar passage in the Great Hall of Morven. The local population had been enraged to see a talented orator treated in such a manner and rebelled against the divine. The locals cornered the divine one evening and hacked him to death with farming implements.

The Frame had retaliated in vindictive style by sending a contingent of aimu to the village and executed the entire village down to the last child 'as a lesson'. A rebellion started destroying the aimu contingent. The Frame ruthlessly put down the rebellion and many thousands of muckers had been lost their lives before the restoration of 'peace'. Since the Morven Rebellion, however, no divine has dared to select a Bard for reassignment again. It was at this time that the Frame introduced the divines staff as a mark of office and authority as well as being a weapon.

Cullin's mind wandered as he relaxed and he wondered what had become of his friend, Ecta and the others. Ecta and Sara had gone with Dookerock the spring following the exodus to a mysterious place called Rustick More. Yayler refused to provide any details except to say that they were busy and happy enough and sent him their good wishes. Cullin felt that Yayler was being evasive and missed his friends.

Yayler gave Cullin a broader and deeper training than that of his friends. Apart from the physical training, Cullin learned a great deal about the history of the divines and the technology used by the Frame. Yayler explained about the neuro-chips placed in the brains of divines and that this technology pre-dated the Frame.

The invention of the technology increased the memory capacity of the rich and powerful. These people then became the ruling elite who called themselves the divines. They had also invented nanos composed of complex carbon molecules that once injected into their bodies strengthened their natural defences and slowed down the aging process. The divines derived their names from the original group of enhanced people.

The divines had invented the Frame as a central processing unit that was accessible to all the divines. Through successive developments, the Frame became more complex and eventually took control of human society at the beginning of the New Era. The Frame developed various automated units that stored and processed data and performed other specific tasks.

Yayler gave Cullin a small device he called a compad with a screen that lit up when he touched it. Using the compad, Cullin learned the Frames language and how to write programs that performed specific tasks. Yayler was convinced that these programs were the key to defeating the Frame.

Anroshin, the Balcleric of the kirk near Dunossin who was responsible for the spiritual welfare of the valleys populace had always maintained that the Frame that created such devices as compads and rune discs and the paraphernalia normally associated with divines. Cullin had been about ten years old when Anroshin had befriended him.

Cullin remembered one morning towards the end of winter. He had been playing skits in the kirks grounds with a handful of other boys and had been preparing to make his cast at the pile of ten stones within a circle two feet wide marked out in the dirt. A commotion near the dun gates had disrupted their game as a small party of crofters brought an injured man into the dun on a makeshift stretcher. The man, a shepherd from lower down the valley, had been attempting to retrieve a heavily pregnant ewe from high crags on the eastern side of the glen overlooking the dun when he had misplaced his footing on loose rocks and fallen some twenty paces onto rough ground below the crags. Sometime later searchers had found him suffering from hypothermia, dehydration and a broken arm and leg. The elderly Katrin had treated the poor man's injuries though he died from internal bleeding later that evening.

Sheep were an important resource in the glen, both for food and for their thick wool. The harsh environment meant that ewes had a short productive lifespan of around four years after which the shepherds slaughtered the animal for their meat. Shepherds went to considerable effort to avoid losing pregnant sheep and most would put themselves at risk to retrieve escaped and lost ewes. This particular ewe had developed the habit of escaping and lambing in the isolation of the crags above her fields. They'd buried the shepherd at the kirk with a short ceremony given by the ancient, thin, white haired Balcleric Anroshin, the minister in charge of the kirk.

After the ceremony, Anroshin called to Cullin and asked him why he spent so much time at the kirk wasting his time playing skits. Cullin replied saying that he had 'nothing better to do'. Anroshin responded by saying that it was about time that he did have something better to do. Taking the boy under his wing Anroshin, taught Cullin how to read and write using an old slate and had begun to teach the boy some of the basic doctrine and philosophy of the Unified Church of the Prophets. The aimu forced the religion on muckers through divines such as Anroshin. The religion was essentially an amalgamation of the major religions at the time of its creation, setting The Frame as the supreme head of the church. The church officials were in fact divines whose purpose was to teach the church philosophy and rules on social behaviour. At its core, this essentially meant obeying the authority of The Frame.

Cullin was startled by Yayler calling to him ''Finished your tasks have you?''

''Aye, I was just enjoying the sun.''

Yayler ignored that and asked ''how's the drum practice going?''

''Not so good I think, the story you gave me to play to doesn't make a lot of sense.''

''Ah, it's not supposed to. You're meant to convey the emotions of the different scenes.' Yayler approached Cullin and sat down amiably beside him. Cullin had once asked Yayler why his training was different to the others who had left Mark Ossin.

Yayler had replied that emotions largely rule the actions of most people, but some people have better self-control. Cullin was one of the latter, one of a rare breed that is able to control their logical thinking processes even whilst undergoing severe emotional stresses. Yayler claimed that he had determined Cullin's abilities by observing his reactions to his Yayl music three years previously. Yayler believed that Cullin was not a person easily swayed by his emotions.

Cullin looked at him directly ''How are you supposed to 'convey emotion' with a drum?''

''Ah, you need to alter the tones and rhythms to suit the moods of the story or music. Here, let me show you''

Yayler picked up the small drum that had lain disregarded on the heather during Cullin's reverie. The drum was about one and a half hand spans in width with an open back. Crossed sticks within the drum served as a handle that left fingers free to caress the skin and adjust the tone and pitch of the drum. He played a slow, shifting soft sequence that was almost arrhythmic in its cadences. The resulting sound had an uneasy sense of longing. ''How does that sound, happy, sad, jubilant?'' Yayler finished the question with querying raised eyebrows.

Cullin was thoughtful for a few moments trying to find a clever answer and failing provided the obvious ''well sad really.''

''Ah, good,'' Yayler played another brisker sequence that set Cullin's teeth on edge ''what about that one?''

Cullin was getting the idea now ''Oh, that one is harsh and brutal, like climbing mountains in bad weather.''

''Excellent, see what others you can come up with and we'll talk later.''

Cullin took the drum and spent a couple of wairs in practice before Yayler disturbed him again. In fact, Yayler had been listening to the rhythmic patterns Cullin devised for some time and was impressed at how quickly the young man had picked up the concept. Cullin was good enough to pull off a disguise as a journeyman bard. That meant less interference from divines or aimu. Yayler intended to gather information on aimu activity whilst disguised as the peripatetic bard Tyarly.

''That's good, Cullin'' Yayler handed the young man a platter of venison and dried fruits. ''I need to talk to you about what we'll be doing over the next few months.''

Cullin had been playing a rapid sequence of beats that he hoped depicted excitement and joy.

''What was that you were playing?'' Cullin's fast-paced rhythm within rhythm style impressed Yayler.

Slightly embarrassed, Cullin tried to explain what he was trying to do, but felt that his description was somehow inadequate. ''I was imagining myself on a mountain with the world spread out before me. I was trying to let my feelings make the music.''

''Ah, I see it now, well done.'' Yayler went on to explain his plans for a covert intelligence-gathering mission.

The aimu had been very quiet over the last few years, but Yayler had noticed an increase in communication activity whilst hacking into the Frames databases. While the information he could find in that manner was invaluable, it was also at risk of detection. The aimu recorded such data from their own perspective and as a result, it lacked personal details and the muckers viewpoint.

The following day Yayler and Cullin started their journey on foot. Cullin was a little sad to be leaving the bothy, though small and cramped, it had been his home for the previous three years. He was also excited with anticipation, glad to be doing something other than dry studies and physical training. Cullin felt alive and joyful as they stepped out along the track to Baylycraig.

They both bore stout wooden staves. Yayler had hollowed out a couple of normal walking staves he had then inserted the mechanics of the divines staves they had used previously. The result was a natural appearing bough that disguised a lethal surprise.

---

Pyta was in a bar somewhere, disgruntled, unhappy and drowning his sorrows in a mug of dark, slightly sour ale. The landlord didn't look after his ale very well, but Pyta didn't care, he was dwelling on his fate and be-groaning those that had caused him harm and getting very drunk. Pyta had fallen on hard times since the Mark Ossin debacle. He had always had a pouch full of tokens and good accounts with a number of Marks. Funds he had gained by performing various unpleasant jobs for those divines who liked to keep their activities quiet. His last source had been the now deceased Beck25.

Since he'd been arrested and detained for the incident at the Tavern, divines considered him indiscreet, a loose cannon, not to be trusted for those awkward little jobs that needed to be done now and then.

Events were turning Pyta's way again. He grinned maliciously into his ale at the thought for Pyta had a new employer. He had recently arranged with his new boss for a few particularly unpleasant and dirty jobs. Pyta's pouch was again full with the advance for his unique services.

Pyta liked the thought that Lord Ossin had died as well as Beck 25 snickering into his beer and taking a long pull on the foaming brew, draining the mug. He signalled the scrawny smelly barman for a refill.

Ossin's son, Cullin had trouble coming his way for stealing his tokens, but the brat had inconveniently disappeared forcing Pyta to wait for his vengeance. Pyta was a patient man and he was sure that he would soon find the boy. When they met, again the boy would suffer.

Pyta carried on muttering into his beer and thinking his dark thoughts until late in the evening. Pyta was about to order another ale when he noticed his hand. His right hand had what looked like six fingers. Funny, he thought, I've never noticed that before. Perhaps it is an optical illusion of some kind. Pyta shook his hand vigorously and looked at his hand again. The vision was true, but unreal. Pyta snorted loudly, turned his gaze to his left hand, and was astounded to see that it too had six fingers. He shook his head and looked again. He angrily thrust his mug away and stood rather unsteadily. He staggered home weaving an uncertain course along the tracks to the shack he currently called home.  He collapsed face down on his pallet.

The following morning when he woke up he again had five fingers on both hands. He grunted and sought out the bottle he always kept near his bed and downed most of the contents. The bitter spirit calmed him so he could focus on his work. He had to rendezvous with 'him' later.

# Chapter Nine

The steep sided gorge was stark and oppressive, even the mountain bred Cullin found the high, bleak crags forbidding and enclosing, claustrophobic. Steel grey cliffs rose on either side, struck through with gullies choked with compacted snow. He was following Yayler on a narrow, twisting and winding track that took an uncertain course around boulders and rock falls that had once been part of the massive cliffs.

''Why does anyone come this way, Yayler?'' He asked breathlessly due to the fast pace the old man was setting.

''Fastest way'' was Yayler's brief and unhelpful reply.

'Eh?''

''To travel between Dunban and Baylycraig.'' Yayler completed ''Goods have to be transported via Aldee.''

It had been a good days march from Yayler's bothy to the small town of Baylycraig. The town nestled amongst mountains, huddled on the flood plain of the River Aldee. The local Inn, surrounded by stone cottages with heather thatch, served the small community as the social meeting point. Despite the cold, children had been running about barefoot, playing hoops or skits with childish enthusiasm. Baylycraig was a town of sheep farmers, although a few miners scraped a living digging for ore and minerals such as copper. Such things could be traded in Aldee; the Frame always gave good tokens for raw materials. During the summer, the able-bodied drove the sheep up the glens and mountains where the sheep could graze the lush summer pasture. Small dwellings constructed from stone and wood served for the summer months. In late autumn, the sheep were brought back down to be pastured in fields on the flood plain of the Aldee River.

As Yayler entered the Inn he was greeted with welcoming calls of ''Tyarly, welcome back.''

''Ale for Bard'' called out another.

''Where have you been?'' and so on. It was very joyful, smiling faces beamed all about the room.

Enthusiastic customers ushered Yayler over to the fireplace where a hastily placed comfortable chair waited for him and a small wooden stool appeared next to it for Cullin. Jak, the short and rotund innkeeper handed both a large mug of foaming dark ale. Flush faced and business like, Jak wore a plain trousers and a woollen shirt with the designs of his Mark and trade, the square of Mark Kissom set above a brewers swirl embroidered into the sleeves.

''A song, a song, give us music'' went up the cry from Jak's eager customers.

''Ahh, let me tell you first about the blue nitch. Who knows about the blue nitch?'' Yayler paused to sample his beer and got blank stares from Jak's customers. ''Ahh, then let me tell you. The blue nitch is a faery spirit that attaches itself to people. Some people, some very rare people, like myself, have the ability to see them and tell of a beautiful blue furry creature that appears gentle and kindly.

''As I said it is a spirit creature, it does not belong in this world, but back in the land of faery, where it is closely related to the shee. The shee is a red scaly beast that sometimes slips into our world when it is unhappy. The shee has viscous sharp fangs and long claws.

''Now both the nitch and the shee feed off their hosts feelings, and both are entirely selfish beings, caring nothing for their host, just for the emotions off which they feed. The shee is surprisingly gentle, given its appearance, because it feeds off pleasure and so will caress and soothe its host.

''Many years ago I had a friend who had a blue nitch; it was very small and easily ignored when I first saw it. I warned him, I told him to ignore it and it would go away, but he didn't. I saw him a few weeks later and the blue nitch had grown huge, almost as big as a man. It followed my friend everywhere, constantly irritating him with sharp burning maliciousness.

''my friend was in great distress, not knowing what to do. I asked if he'd ignored the nitch and he admitted that he hadn't and so the nitch had fed off his misery.

''And so my friends'' Yayler concluded ''Don't scratch a nitch, for you will surely make it worse.''

Yayler settled himself into a comfortable position as a few chuckled and others cast their eyes heavenward at the joke. He leant over to Cullin ''Follow my lead, keep it simple''.

Suddenly nervous, Cullin realised that he was expected to entertain these people. Licking his lips apprehensively, he sampled the dark ale finding its rich full-bodied flavour not to his liking.

Yayler started with a bright and lively dance that Cullin found easy to follow and was greatly appreciated by all. ''Another, another please good Bard'' they called out as the piece ended.

Yayler played another lively tune and Cullin began to settle into the rhythm of the evening. He found that he could add a respectable accompaniment to Yayler's songs and tales even though many were unfamiliar to him, a result he realised, of his unusual musical education.

As the evening progressed, more instruments appeared, retrieved from homes or borrowed from neighbours. The tale telling, music and exchange of news continued throughout the evening. Yayler became particularly attentive when listening to the odd bits of news the locals provided.

Over a simple supper of mutton stew and coarse bread provided by Jak they heard rumours of increased aimu activity and more frequent 'reassignments' of the population. The coasts around Aldee produced masses of calp, seaweed that the Frame harvested in ever-increasing amounts.

Jak provided them with a room for what remained of the night after the last stragglers of the gathering had headed home. The following morning he gave them a package ''for the road'' he had said. Wrapped simply in an old cloth they found strips of dried meat, cheese, dried berries and fruits and hard biscuits. The basic foods required for a boring, but healthy and sustaining diet, ideal for travellers on foot.

Cullin reflected on the evening as he followed Yayler along the track. As usual, Yayler set a brisk pace causing Cullin to wonder how the old man kept himself so fit and vital. While Yayler appeared unaffected by tiredness, too much drink or lack of sleep, Yayler only allowed brief stops for water. Cullin was still jaded from the night before; his head was pounding even though he'd had little of Jak's dark ale.

It was thirty strides to Balcon through a narrow winding mountain pass. The track was wide enough for small carts and the mountains had a gentler more rounded character than those near Yayler's home. Time passed for Cullin in a steady, rhythmic trudging. He was only half-aware of his surroundings as the wairs passed. His mind turned inward as he thought about his life. He missed his family and friends. He even missed his father's explosive temper. Such thoughts brought a lump to his throat and he wiped his eye as a tear escaped.

Daylight was beginning to fade when Yayler called a halt. A little way from the track, a waist high heap of piled stones formed a rough wall. ''We camp over there tonight'' Yayler declared indicating the wall.

''Ahh, let's get settled down then. Looks like it will be cold tonight, Yayler, we could use a fire tonight.'' Cullin had good experience now with camping wild in cold and damp conditions, but that did not mean that he enjoyed it. He had learned to cope, but took no pleasure in the uncomfortable conditions.

A mischievous glint was in Yayler's eye when he showed Cullin the low entrance to a concealed cave. ''Enter young Master'' Yayler was grinning.

Inside the cave was spacious enough for several people and even boasted a small fireplace near the entrance. ''There are a few places like this, dotted about the mountains, known only to a few. I guess you're now one of those privileged few.''

Yayler continued ''the golden rule about using these places is that they must be left tidy and ready for the next visitor, including the fire.''

Yayler indicated the carefully arranged dried peat bricks laid ready in the fireplace. A pan sat beside the fireplace ''that can be used to collect water from the stream.''

Realising that he had been given an instruction, Cullin took the pan and their water skins to the little stream. When he returned, Yayler already had the fire burning a ruddy glow that was already warming the chill evening air.

''I wish I knew how you and Dook get a fire burning so quickly'' Cullin complained as he set the pan in the fireplace.

''Oh, that's easy. Dook likes to make a mystery of it, it amuses him. It is time you learned anyway. Get your staff, Cullin''

Cullin did so and stood uncertainly by the fire.

''Now thrust your staff into the peat and command 'Fire', hold the staff steady now.''

Cullin followed Yayler's instruction and energy poured from the end of the staff, heating the peat to a ruddy glow.

''Of course, you don't have to speak out loud, just in the mind, try again.''

Cullin did so, his face a study of concentration, and fire blazed from the staff end obliterating the fire. Burning peat flew about the cave and the pan shot from the fireplace spilling its contents in its flight and landed spinning at Yayler's feet.

Yayler flicked a piece of glowing peat from his shoulder and stared at the stupefied Cullin ''Cullin, you don't need to shout! Now, fetch some more water and I'll show you where to get more peat from.''

Cullin gathered his wits and refilled the pot and Yayler showed him a stash of dried peat bricks set on a wide shelf at the back of the cave. More peat bricks were cut and left to dry on the shelf.

Later, after their supper, Cullin remarked ''I see you haven't taught me everything about these staffs yet.''

''Ahh, well, you know enough, you just need to use your imagination. It's not just a walking stick or a stick to fight with. I've shown you a few tricks like the energy blast. The fire is just a variant of that feature.'' Yayler unexpectedly laughed ''I'm surprised you

127

haven't worked it out! Dook was a little more tentative when I first knew him, he doesn't like to show off.''

Cullin looked oddly at Yayler ''Dook doesn't use a staff.''

''No, too clumsy, he says. He had a knife fitted the same way.'' Yayler looked closely at Cullin, ''looks just like an ordinary knife doesn't it?''

''Aye, it does.''

''Not a very accurate weapon though, difficult to aim!'' Yayler was still regarding Cullin closely. He knew Cullin was clever, but in practical ways, not intellectual. muckers tended to be like that; a by-product of hard practical lives. Abstract ideas were of little use to most muckers.

''Good disguise though.''

''Not as good as a stick, I think young Cullin. A knife is a knife and still a weapon. Your staff appears benign, a knife doesn't. Divines use the staff as a symbol of office; that's probably why Dook changed his into a knife. He doesn't like anything that can be associated with divines. Our staffs are quite crude compared to one from a higher ranking divine.'' Yayler was watching Cullin's body language closely now.

Cullin's brow furrowed with thought as he tried to remember Beck25's staff; the one he'd been using before Yayler had fashioned the plainer staffs they now used. ''The grooves down the sides, I thought they were just for grip; your old staff doesn't have them. What do they show?''

Yayler smiled and exhibited no embarrassment as he said ''Beck25, your staffs true owner, was a rank above me. I was at Supervisors rank; he was a Coordinator, but he hated me from the moment we met, that is the nature of divines, they identify their competition quickly and eliminate it when the opportunity arises.''

''That doesn't sound very productive to me, My Father always told me that the Frame favours efficiency, he never considered me to be efficient; too whimsical he said!'

''The Frame is a machine and considers itself to be perfect. Humans, including divines are, by default, imperfect, At least to the Frame's perspective.''

The conversation continued, becoming less and less important and in the end just filled the silence. It was in fact, a human conversation; something the Frame could never understand. It didn't contain detailed facts or data, it didn't contain concise reports or statistics, or calculated conclusions based on such collated data and statistics. Yet it was more than words to fill the time. Indeed, data was conveyed, but in a human manner that included more than mere data or information, but descriptions and emotions specific to personal experience, witticisms and jokes that were beyond the Frames understanding. Eventually, they settled down to sleep, having by use of inefficient conversation reaffirmed their trust and friendship in each other.

They packed up early the following morning, leaving the cave clean and tidy and the fire laid ready for the next user. Little was said, just brief comments as they performed their tasks.

''We should reach Balcon this afternoon. I have a friend there who should be able to help us.''

A watery sun was high in the sky when Yayler called a halt. Some distance ahead at an awkward turn in the track where the track twisted beneath steep crags, Yayler could see an overturned aimu transport with its hiu driver trapped beneath. Water cascaded down the crags to a stream that ran beneath a stone bridge. The bridge had collapsed, tipping the transport and hiu into the stream.

Yayler smiled, a grim smile as he turned to Cullin ''now let's see if we can find out what that thing is doing here. We'll have to be divines for a while. I am Victor8 and you can be Beck25. Let me talk to it while you make yourself busy looking over that transport. Don't talk to it yourself or it'll realise that we're not divines.''

Cullin nodded. ''Why would it think we're divines anyway, we're dressed as muckers?''

''Ahh, magic Cullin, magic!'' Yayler grinned cheekily waving his hand in the air. ''Just remember; don't talk to it. Let's get this done.''

Yayler approached the hiu and hunkered down before it, knee deep in the icy water. ''May I be of service? I am Victor8.'' Yayler held his palm up, facing the machine as he addressed it.

The hiu replied with a surprisingly soft feminine voice, almost human in tone ''you may communicate.''

Yayler placed his hand on the machines breastplate and his face took on an unfocussed, twitching as he spoke with the machine. He remained motionless for several sents as he squatted in the stream 'talking' to the machine. He beckoned to Cullin when he finished and the two returned to the track.

''Achh, I'm all wet!'' He complained.

Cullin looked surprised ''shouldn't sit in streams talking to machines then!''

''That's not funny Cullin'' Yayler complained.

Cullin shrugged ''did you learn much?''

''Indeed, indeed I did. Come on, I'll tell you as we walk. I told it we couldn't move the TU, transport unit, so we are to send help when we reach Balcon.

''The hiu was going to Baylycraig to observe the local population, usually the job of divines, when the bridge collapsed. It was unable to reach any comsats because of the mountains and so we are to report the situation when we get to Balcon. We won't of course, it can rot there for all I care.''

''Rust, Yayler, it'll rust.'' Cullin had a straight faced when he spoke.

Yayler stared at him and muttered under his breath something about a 'smart mouth'.

''Rust then'' Yayler continued, ''I downloaded a report from it, which we are to pass on in Balcon. When it is missed, another machine will be sent out to locate it. Then our deception will be uncovered, because we won't have made a report.''

''How long will that take?'' Cullin asked.

''A couple of days perhaps. Then our descriptions will be circulated in Balcon.'' Yayler was worried about this turn of events; he wanted to keep a low profile whilst he gathered information. He also needed time in Balcon to make arrangements. He didn't need divines or aimu looking for him.

''What if we made that report, wouldn't that delay things further?'' Cullin asked thoughtfully.

''It might, if we're not discovered whilst making the report.'' Yayler considered, mulling over possibilities. ''Two dead divines appearing out of the wilds dressed as muckers is just a little obvious''

''Use a com-post then, that way, all they have is a report from a dead divine and we can disappear afterward.''

''Hmmm, and cause a bit of confusion as well. Good idea, Cullin. They'll piece it all together, of course, but that could take a few days.''

''Just need to find a com-post then'' Cullin continued as if a decision had been made.

''Hmmm, there is one on the road north of Balcon on the road to Dunban. It'll mean a bit of a detour.''

''And we'll arrive in Balcon coming from a different direction.'' Cullin pressed further.

''Indeed so, and cause confusion.'' Yayler smiled ''the plan has merit; I like it. It might just give us the time we need to conclude our business in Balcon and be on our way to Pirt before they realise we're even there.''

''So what is our business there?''

''Oh, to try to find out a bit more about what the aimu and divines are up to.'' Yayler supplied ''they appear to be becoming more active in these areas; I'd like to know why. I can pass the information on and try to protect people from harm the machines might cause.''

By early afternoon, the valley opened out with a broad flood plain divided into fields. The mountains gave way abruptly into broad flatlands. They could see occasional patches of trees. The landscape appeared ordered and cared for, unlike the wild and haphazard landscapes that Cullin had grown up with. The track widened into a road as wooden huts appeared by the roadside. An occasional passer-by would stare at them with intense curiosity. Yayler continued pass them in silence, ignoring their stares.

After little more than a wair Yayler turned down a narrow track ''I found this many years ago; it should take us onto the road north from Balcon. Then we need to find that com-post.''

The com-post was about five strides north of Balcon on a small rise in the road. Further north a great forest could be seen and distant mountains. To the east lay the mountains they had traversed through, with the afternoon sun glinting off their snowy peaks.

Yayler worked at the com-post for a surprising amount of time before turning to Cullin who was relaxing by the roadside. ''Come on young man, got to get on; don't want to be camping outside the town do we.'' At that, Yayler set off at a quick pace quietly humming a tune to himself and leaving Cullin struggling to catch up.

They reached Balcon as light was beginning to fade from an overcast sky that threatened rain. A road encircled the town and Yayler followed it south, ignoring the north gate, ''we're not allowed in that way'' had been his only explanation to Cullin. They entered the town from the east gate into a maze of narrow streets with central gutters.

The powerful smell of the town struck Cullin immediately, dogs wandered about, nosing into anything that might be edible. Muck and filth was everywhere. There were no walkways so everyone had to walk through all the muck and filth.

Wooden terraces lined the streets, blocking out the evening light, leaving the streets dark and dismal. Cullin watched as a dog defecated in the street. Everything appeared rundown and uncared for.

A cold, dispiriting rain began as they walked, quickly over running the inadequate drainage system.

Someone shouted "below" from an upper storey window and threw the contents of a wooden bucket into the street below. To his disgust, Cullin recognised human faeces as the contents that were added to the slime that coated the cobbled streets.

Yayler noticed Cullin's discomfort "not pleasant is it; you'd think they want to clean it up."

"Why do people live this way? Surely, this filth can be prevented."

"Of course it can, but this is the muckers half of the town. The Frame and, thus, the divines won't spend the time and effort to improve it. It makes the whip and lash of working in the fields almost preferable; even the mines are cleaner than this.

"The town is split into two halves divided by a wall. The divines live in the northern half, that's why we couldn't enter by the northern gate; the divines don't want muckers spoiling their streets and homes.

"The divines patrol this half of the town so if you meet one, call him or her 'Your Worship' and only speak if they speak to you. They probably won't; they don't like to talk to muckers."

Yayler continued, talking almost absently as his eyes scanned about him, constantly watchful. "The divines live in individual mansions separated by wide avenues lined with trees. There are walkways for pedestrians though most divines have personal transports. The streets are constantly kept clean so there is none of this filth. Towards the centre of the town is a central complex, Communication Offices controlled by the Frame. You can't see it from here, but there is a wall separating the two halves, with offices built into it. Any business between divines and muckers is conducted there."

The rain pelted down turning the streets slick with foul smelling slurry. Yayler stopped in his discourse suddenly exclaiming a happy "ah, here it is."

Yayler turned down a narrow passage that was almost invisible in the dingy light and pounded on a door. A grumbling voice could be heard from inside. Yayler pounded the door again, harder.

133

They heard a grudging creak of a bolt being drawn and the door creaked open. A short grey haired woman stared out. ''Yayler, you're wet'' she complained making no move to let them in. Dona wore a plain Beetick dress in need of repairs that hid a slight, but well-proportioned figure. She had a woollen shawl wrapped about her shoulders to ward off the evening chill.

''Dona, you're still alive! I thought they had fed you to the dogs years ago.''

''Your cute friend is wet too.'' Dona continued.

''It's a peculiarity of the climate, it's frequently wet.''

Dona began to close the door on them, but Yayler's foot prevented her.

''My friend is very partial to vegetable pie'' Yayler continued as Dona pushed harder on the door

''Good! He has better taste than you then.'' Dona remarked watching Cullin shuffle his feet uncomfortably in the muck.

''He heard all about your famous pie, all the way back in Dunossin.''

Dona had stopped trying to close the door and regarded Yayler warily. ''What do you want Yayler, you're not usually this polite.''

''Transport from Pirt to Aldee'' Yayler supplied.

''Not tonight, come back tomorrow'' Dona attempted to shut the door again, but it was still blocked by Yayler's boot.

''And some pie.''

Dona still looked unconvinced.

''And some information.''

Dona looked particularly sour and irritated at the last request ''No, tomorrow.''

''And this'' Yayler held up a small rectangular device that was clearly of divine origin.

Dona looked startled, held out her hand for the object, and inspected it closely. ''Come in.''

Yayler and Cullin were ushered into a small room that clearly served Dona as kitchen, lounge, dining room and bedroom. A small fire burned in the grate, but did little to warm up the room. There were several wooden comfortably padded chairs, that Dona used when entertaining guests and a single table. ''What's so important that it's worth a compad?''

''There's been an increase in aimu and divine communications; some of those I've been able to intercept are about mucker reassignments; a lot of reassignments, far more than normal. The Frame appears to be changing tactics and I'd like to find out how.'' Yayler stood in the middle of Dona's room, water dripping from his morcote and pooling around his feet.

''I see, you want to talk then. I didn't think you came all this way for pie.'' Dona looked in disgust at the water messing up her floorboards. ''Hang those morcotes up behind the door. You might as well stay now you're here.''

Dona busied herself making the pair supper whilst she and Yayler talked and made the introductions, pausing only when Yayler mentioned the aimu travelling to Baylycraig. When she served up the supper of ham and cheese, thick slices of buttered bread, pickles and large bowls of peppery carrot and turnip soup Yayler looked at the food with a crest fallen look on his face. Cullin, not realising how hungry he was before, set to with relish.

''No pie?'' Yayler complained.

''No pie'' confirmed Dona.

Cullin looked up at the two with a mouthful of buttered bread ''this is good, thank you Dona'' he said simply.

Dona smiled at that ''at least you have a few manners about you, not like this selfish old man.''

Yayler sighed, but said nothing. He did eat well though, continuing his discussion with Dona as he ate.

It was quite late and Cullin stifled a yawn. Dona noticed this and nodded ''Cullin is right, enough talk for tonight. The two of you can't stay in Balcon, they will have picked up that stranded aimu tomorrow, so they will have your descriptions. The identities will confuse them for a while, but they'll pick up the trail quickly enough.''

''Dook won't like it though, I used his identity at the com-post'' Yayler smirked with an amused glint in his eye.

Dona raised an eyebrow at Yayler's comment, but said only ''you two stay here tomorrow and I will ask a few discreet questions from people I know, then we have to see about getting the two of you out of Balcon.''

The following day Dona had left before the other two had woken. Confined to Dona's single room Cullin and Yayler had little they could do until she returned. Yayler set Cullin mathematical problems whilst he worked at his compad. Cullin did well with most of them but could make no headway on the last one; if $a+b=c$ prove that $a^2+b^2 \neq c^2$ for all integers. Although Cullin could demonstrate individual cases easily, he utterly failed to demonstrate that it was true in all cases, but also failed to find a case where it wasn't true.

Outside it was still raining and Cullin threw his compad on the table in frustration. Its holographic screen went blank and shut off. Yayler had been teaching Cullin how to use it for three years, though Cullin was now fairly competent in their use, he still had a lot of tricks to learn about them.

Dona returned mid-afternoon with fresh bread and vegetables. ''I have some wagoner friends who can get you out of Balcon tomorrow. They arrived here a few days ago with a couple of wagons of Beetick. They want to leave for Pirt tomorrow with tanned hides. We shall be going with them, I have herbs I can trade there and the wagoners are a man short.''

''No discussion Dona?'' Yayler looked at Dona with a wide eyed and annoyed expression and clearly wanted to say more.

''No, you need to get out of Balcon before the divines start looking for you and you want to go to Pirt. What is there to discuss?'' Dona puffed up her small diminutive frame and looked Yayler directly in the eye, challenging him.

''Plenty, I assume you know these people?''

''Of course.'' Dona placed her hands on her hips as if she wanted to provoke Yayler.

''Oh, and there have been rumours.''

''Rumours ---'' started Yayler, but was cut off by Dona.

''Oh yes, farms being destroyed by aimu. The wagon master tells me they passed a small farm near Pirt where they intended to pick up some beetick. There are no people there now, their homes are burned down.''

''Really?'' Yayler looked surprised ''That I would like to see for myself. That sounds a bit more aggressive than the normal reassignments.''

''Oh, so you do approve then?'' Dona's voice raised in pitch, penetrating and shrill.

''Dona, let's not start squabbling like children, this sounds important.''

''Me, a child am I?'' Dona raised her voice another octave, so that she was almost screeching.

''That's not what I meant'' Yayler threw his hands in the air in exasperation. With difficulty Yayler calmed himself, giving up on the unequal battle of words ''what time tomorrow?''

''Second quarter, so we need to be up by three wair.'' Sensing victory, Dona's voice returned to its normal tone.

''Aye, not too many divine patrols about at that time'' Yayler looked very unhappy.

''Ahh, poor baby; just behave and we'll get on fine.''

Yayler shook his head and wished he understood women better. "Do you want a hand with supper?" He asked Dona, resigned to defeat.

"I certainly do" Dona swished across the room to the work surface next to the sink "that is the most intelligent thing you've said in years!"

Watching silently from his chair, Cullin simply wished he could be somewhere else.

A couple of days later, mid-afternoon, two wagons led by Wagon Master Feeack were a few strides from Pirt. Yayler, Cullin and Dona were in the second wagon creaking along the track. Yayler and Dona were arguing. Cullin, who sat in the rear of the wagon on top of bundles of leather hide and sacks of Dona's herbs, found that their ability to find things to argue about was extraordinary. He could find no way to escape their bickering and so, ignoring them, immersed himself in that irritating mathematical problem Yayler had given him.

The current argument in a seemingly endless queue of trivial quarrels was that Dona wanted to detour to a farm where every few months she would deliver herbs for the muckers to use as medicines. Yayler was adamant that it would be too dangerous and a waste of time and they still had the burned out farm to check out as well. Dona repeatedly accused him of not caring about the muckers. The pitch of Dona's voice was steadily rising; this was usually the point where Yayler gave up the argument. This was no exception and Yayler an unnerving peace and quiet descended on the wagons occupants. The wagon creaked on.

---

"I'm sure this is the right track" Dona was saying ",but it was much rougher and narrower before."

"It's quiet too; there doesn't appear to be any people about." Yayler frowned.

They had left a disgruntled wagon Master behind to wait for them at the junction with the Pirt road.

138

Either side of the track, hedgerows had been removed revealing large empty fields. A large newly built store shed stood a little way ahead, glinting in the late afternoon sunlight. As they approached, they could see a large yard before it into which the track emerged. The yard also appeared new, constructed of a hard, smooth stone-like substance that Yayler called creet. Nowhere could they see any habitations or shelters for slave workers.

As they neared the yard they could see an aimu, standing as if on sentry duty by the store shed. Yayler halted the wagon and they watched in bewilderment as the store shed doors began to slide open. From the shed emerged automated farm machinery; a loaded metal wagon followed by a variety of other autonomous farm equipment.

By the entrance to the farm, Dona saw a rag of Beetick cloth half covered by overturned turf. She clambered down from the wagon and went over to look more closely. She dug out a small peg doll in a rag dress. Dona clutched the doll to her breast, shaking as tears appeared in her eyes. ''They've gone, they've all gone'' she was repeating to herself quietly, over and over.

Yayler put his arm around her shoulders as she returned to the wagon and tried to comfort her. ''I'm sorry Dona, but there's nothing we can do here.''

''The people, where are the people?'' Dona turned to face Yayler with a pleading look in her eyes.

''I don't know, but I can guess. They may well be beyond our help now.''

''They wouldn't have killed them? Surely not that?''

''I doubt it, too inefficient. They've probably been taken to mines, or calp harvesting. The Frame won't waste them.''

''Why doesn't the Frame care, they're people?''

''It's a machine, it can't care. It just analyses and computes. People are just a commodity to the Frame.''

''I hate it, hate it, hate it!'' Dona was shaking with vehemence and grief.

---

It was getting dark as the wagons crawled through the unusually quiet streets of Pirt. A strong smell of sea pervaded the air. Their brief visit to the second farm had confirmed that the machines had automated it and reassigned the slave workforce.

Pirt lying at the edge of the most productive land on Ardyvinland was a small crowded busy seaside town that owed its existence to a natural harbour on a rocky coastline. Fertile land called the Plains of Plenty ran east to Aldee between the mountains inland and the coast. Sea cliffs ran for several strides east and west. Pirt lay at the northern end of a thirty stride long sea loch. Calp collection, delivered to the divines in exchange for food, provided the main employment for the people of Pirt.

The wagon master stopped at a rundown inn that overlooked steep cliffs. A light breeze blew off the sea bringing with it a strong odour of fish and adding a chill to the evening. A few fishing boats lay moored in the harbour. They pulled into a small courtyard behind the inn. Inside the inn was unadorned, bare wooden floorboards bleached from many years of scrubbing creaked as the two young men entered. Likewise, wooden planking lined the walls. Heavy wooden tables and chairs served the inns customers.

The innkeeper, Pul, a friend of the wagon master, provided a supper of mussels collected by calp harvesters during their labour, served in liquor with bread and a light ale flavoured with seaweed. Cullin found it not to his liking, but he was hungry and ate in silence. Pul sat with the wagoners talking quietly. Other than the wagoners there were only a handful of customers. An air of despondency and depression pervaded the atmosphere.

Yayler nursed his ale, deep in thought. How had he not heard about what was going on here? Whole communities reassigned and replaced with automated machinery. The Frame had cleared the land to make way for machines and Yayler had no idea how far those clearances extended. They disrupted the structure of the local

140

community that was now breaking down. If the Frame was automating the production of oil beet the future of the people of Pirt looked bleak.

Dona sat quietly, lost in her own thoughts, picking at her food with little interest; the peg doll sat in her lap.

Yayler glanced at her ''we need to get these people moved.''

''Hmm?'' Dona looked at him blankly.

''These people, they can't stay here.'' Yayler took a long pull on his beer and grimaced at the unfamiliar sharpness. ''The Frame has no use for them here and if the farms are being cleared, how long will it be before the people here are also reassigned?''

''Oh, yes you're right.'' Dona roused herself from her morbid reverie. Tears glinted in the corners of her eyes.

''Where can they go?'' Cullin asked remembering the people of Mark Ossin as they left their homes for an uncertain future.

''Aldee, Willemsbree or possibly Garvin.''

Cullin looked at Yayler with surprise ''Garvin? That's a long way. How would they get there?''

''Well, not on wagons, that's for sure.'' Yayler looked intently at his beer as if deciding whether to continue drinking it or not.

''What about boats?'' Cullin asked.

''Aye, the fishermen's boats, I'll ask about the quayside tomorrow. I still want to find out what is happening around Aldee. After that we still have to get back to Bandrokit to meet up with Dook again.''

There was a scrape of wooden chair legs on wooden floor and Feeack came over to their table. He drew up a chair that protested loudly from Feeack's excessive weight as he sat. ''We have been talking with Pul, he says these clearances started about a month back.''

Yayler looked at Feeack.

Feeack leant forward and addressed Yayler quietly. ''We've been talking over what we've seen with Pul. We think the machines are taking over oil beet production and putting the people in the mines.''

''I agree'' Yayler nodded.

''There's nothing for us around here anymore. They used to allow passengers on ships bound for places like Willemsbree or Aldee, but they've stopped that now. Apparently, they're also tightening up on people using the roads.'' Guvin continued ''the only way out of the town now is on a fishing boat.''

''So what are you planning to do Feeack?''

''Pul's son is captain of a fishing boat. Pul can arrange for us passage to get passage to Aldee.''

''You won't be able to take the wagons.'' Yayler stated

''No'' Feeack agreed '', but we could take the hides and start fresh. Those hides are good quality.''

''Why are you telling me this Feeack?'' Yayler couldn't quite see the point in the conversation. Up to now, it had little relevance to Yayler and his friends.

''We think you should come with us.''

''Hmm, I've been thinking about Aldee, too. There are many beet farms around there, Willemsbree and Dundoon also. The Frame may clear those too.''

Feeack looked crestfallen at that thought ''Further north then. Tuaport or Kilgarv''

''Those towns are also surrounded by beet farms. I was thinking Garvin would be a better place to go.''

Feeack sighed; he was a practical man and knew that Yayler was right. ''There's nothing, but mountains there. We can't live there. I don't know what we're going to do, but I'll not transport fish guts for the machines''

"Fish guts? What does the Frame want with fish guts?" asked Cullin.

"It's taken to a factory unit in the divine sector; they do something with it there" Feeack told Cullin.

"They use it in cleaning and processing the oil beet" Yayler addressed Cullin. "I think Garvin is the best option for you, Feeack. Many small communities up that way get little interference from the Frame. They're too remote to be of any use to the machines. It'll be hard, but you'll be able to make a living."

Feeack, is head bowed in despair, looked up for a moment "I'll think on it then."

They spent the rest of the evening with Pul discussing various options. Pul had formerly been a fisherman and had retired to run the inn. When Yayler and Cullin described the events in Mark Ossin all agreed that moving people who wanted to go discreetly to Garvin was the best option available. Pul would take Yayler, Cullin and Dona (who now insisted on travelling with Yayler) to Aldee and from there to Bandrokit.

# Chapter Ten

Cullin stood at the stern of the fishing boat watching the sea as a chill wind blew spray into his face. He had found the design of the boat fascinating as it was so different to the small boats they'd had back home. The immensely tough wooden boat could withstand the storms of the open ocean. The wrights had completely decked over the double thick hull and sealed it against high seas. A large triangular lateen rigged sail billowed from the forward mast. The crew quartered in a basic, cramped cabin located between the mast and the bow, furnished with a single small cook-box for preparing food. Set toward the low stern of the boat was a second mast rigged with two booms from which the fishermen lowered nets.

A hatchway, central and flush with the deck, located before the second mast sealed the hold from the elements. The deck was dressed with removable baton sections that allowed water to flow between them back into the sea.

Cullin had tried practising on his drum, but Yayler had advised him that the salt water would damage it. He had also tried using a compad, but couldn't read the screen with the tossing of the boat; so he'd filled his time watching the sea for three days since leaving Pirt. A school of porpoise joined them seemingly enjoying following the boat. The creatures fascinated Cullin, but still found it hard to believe that they weren't just big fish.

Pul's crew, his son and two other large men with dark weather worn faces went about their duties with few instructions, so familiar were they with the work.

The sky had turned a steely grey and Cullin could see a darker smudge on the horizon. Despite his ignorance of the sea, Cullin knew what the smudge was having seen the phenomenon in the mountains of his home.

Cullin distracted Pul at the boats wheel, pointing out the smudge. ''Hey Pul, looks like we have some rain headed our way.''

Pul squinted toward the horizon ''hmm, you might be right. A bad squall headed our way by the look of it.''

Cullin, anxious for something useful to do asked Pul ''you want me to tell the others?''

''Nay, they'll find out soon enough, if they haven't seen it already. Don't worry about it.''

Disappointed, Cullin turned his attention back to the sea and its eternally shifting motion. As he watched, he thought the waves were higher than they had been. Pul didn't appear bothered. ''Pul, isn't the sea getting rougher?''

''Aye, it's not bad though. I told you don't worry about it. Anyhow, the boat can't sink.''

''Ahh, why not?''

''Double thick hull. It's a tough little boat''

''What about really big waves? Wouldn't they swamp the boat?''

''No, the water just runs back into the sea and the boat self-rights.''

''Self-rights?''

''Aye, if the boat is capsized, erm, turned over by the waves, the boat turns the right way up.''

Cullin was silent and thoughtful while he tried to picture the boats construction in his mind and thought he saw a flaw in Pul's logic. ''What would happen if you hit big rocks under the water?''

''Ahh, well, that would depend on the rock and how hard it was hit.'' Pul considered Cullin carefully, recognising thoughtful intelligence in the young man. ''Mostly, a boats Captain would know where such rocks are. Such knowledge has been passed on for generations. Such things do happen occasionally and boats can be driven onto rocks in bad weather. The hull of this boat is strengthened and double thick, so it can survive all, but the worst mishap. The 'Banree Na Mur' is a good boat Cullin.'

145

Cullin thanked Pul for the explanation and returned to contemplating the sea. The crew began to sing a simple shanty with repetitive words that Cullin found uplifting and cheerful.

The rain came later, light drizzle at first, but building swiftly into a chilly drenching downpour. The wind had picked up and the first of the rain began. Maybe the experienced seamen weren't bothered by 'a little rain' as Pul described the hard pelting squall. They appeared unconcerned as the boat pitched alarmingly in the deepening swell. Perhaps it wasn't bad weather to them, Cullin mused; just weather and quite normal.

After another wair, the squall had developed and rain lashed across the deck. They could now see the broad estuary of the Aldee River and would soon be entering its calmer waters. They continued passed the estuary before turning back towards it. Pul had explained that it was to do with tides and currents, but Cullin couldn't quite grasp the complexity of the seas movements, but watching the endless swell and movement of the sea fascinating. They would be at Aldee soon, late afternoon perhaps.

The boat slipped quietly into the harbour with the rain still lashing down. As soon as the crew had completed their duties, they made their way to an inn on the quayside. Yayler, Dona and Cullin joined them and paid tokens for a room for Dona. Everyone else would sleep on the boat. Yayler entertained in his guise of Tyarly and asked discreet questions about the beet farms, but gained little useful information.

For the next couple of nights Yayler and Cullin scouted the nearest beet farms, but they appeared to be running as normal. This at least eased some of the bickering between Yayler and Dona. On the third night, they were watching the movements of the divine enclave and saw machines unloaded from one of the Frames huge metal ocean vessels. Cullin had thought the fishing boat was big, but these massive ships dwarfed it.

This was enough information for Yayler to make a decision; they would sail on to Bandrokit. He left word with a contact he knew in Aldee that the people might be better off if they moved further north. This started an intense argument between Yayler and Dona. Yayler was adamant that they were unable to help the people on the beet farms and finally, after a long argument, demanded of Dona a way to move the slaves. Dona couldn't think of any viable means to help them and stormed off to her room in floods of tears to brood alone. There was a definite frostiness between them as they waited for the tide the following day.

The passage to Bandrokit from Aldee passed through narrows, a sea channel that was difficult to navigate due to strong currents and tides and hidden sandbanks, rocks etc'. Pul knew the dangers and the safe routes from a lifetime of sailing the waters, but was far from complacent. He had many stories of shipwrecks and disasters. At this time of the year, there was still ice in the channel clinging to the coast. Occasionally tides drew icebergs from the northern seas into the channel that caught many a seaman unawares.

After several days of tacking against a bitter, icy wind, they pulled into the small harbour at Bandrokit. Small icebergs passed through the narrow strait, carefully avoided by Pul. A glancing blow on one of these could cause great damage to a boat of any size as it could open up long gashes along the boat. It was better in such circumstances to hit an iceberg head-on as this only damaged the bow and the boat stood a greater chance of remaining seaworthy.

A wet sleety rain fell from a dismal grey sky as Pul's small fishing boat pulled into the tiny harbour at Bandrokit. There was little in the way of luggage to be unloaded as the passengers disembarked and huddled together on the quayside as the fishermen busied themselves on the deck. Presently Pul joined them and announced that he and the crew would remain aboard.

The Fish and Hook was close by and they could see a bored Dook sitting by a small window with a large mug of calp beer in hand, gazing at the sullen weather. Cullin and Yayler were soon warming themselves by a blazing wood fire while the innkeeper readied rooms for them. Dona had left with the innkeeper intent on finding a hot bath.

''Good journey?'' Dook asked Yayler.

''Aye, not bad. Pul tells us he's had much worse at this time of year.'' Yayler replied, a large drop of water clinging to the end of his nose.

147

"Good." Dook was silent for a while as Yayler and Cullin sat close to the fire, concentrating on reversing the effects of a damp and uncomfortable sea journey.

"Red should be here in a few days" Dook announced presently "we spoke over a compad a few days back."

"That was dangerous Dook. Those communications are monitored."

"I know, I don't make a habit of it" Dook answered after a long pause.

"I wish we had some way to communicate over distance without the Frame being able to monitor or intercept those communications."

"Aye. It's a problem."

"Do you know what he has been doing? We need to get our information together. I fear that the Frame is getting more aggressive. Whole farms are being reassigned."

Dook sat in stunned silence at Yayler's last piece of information, his mug held midway between table and mouth. Dook carefully returned the mug to the table and regarded Yayler in a long pause before answering. "Are you sure of that? I mean absolutely sure? The Frame has always taken a few here, a few there, but has always allowed the population to recover before taking more."

"We've seen it; whole farms with their people removed and replaced by machines."

Dook looked from Yayler to Cullin who nodded affirmation. "Yayler, we can't leave people on those farms and have them reassigned; it's certain death."

"I know, Dook, as Dona is constantly reminding me, but how do we move or hide them without risking our activities being discovered. We're not strong enough to survive a confrontation against the Frame."

"And yet we need more to join us if we are to have a chance of success."

''Thinking about it, we arrived here on a boat registered in Pirt. I think I'll go and talk to Pul.'' Yayler left for the harbour with a scrape of wooden chair legs on the floor.

Cullin took a short pull on his beer, grimaced and left it untouched whilst Dook returned to gazing at the scene out of the small window.

Yayler returned a little while later with a grim smile. ''Well, it seems our fisher friends are pretty smart.''

''Meaning?'' Dook replied lazily.

''They've been setting up bogus identities with the Harbour Master for years. We'll borrow some for a while. The boat that left Pirt will be presumed 'lost at sea'. The crew will carry on with new names as if nothing has happened.'' Yayler contemplated the empty mug at his place on the table and then at Cullin's almost full one and remarked quizzically. ''I thought that was full when I left?''

''No'' Dook muttered through a moustache of foam.

Cullin merely shrugged non-commitally.

Yayler snorted rudely and wandered over to the bar to replenish the mug. Returning he settled himself quietly ''Where's Dona?''

''Bath'' Cullin supplied.

''Still?'' Yayler raised his eyes with surprise.

''It's not been long for a bath; they've got to heat the water first'' Cullin added.

''Gahhh, she'll be all day and we have things to discuss'' Yayler retorted with disgust.

''Not here surely; too many ears'' Dook muttered staring into his now empty mug.

Yayler looked in mock astonishment about the empty bar ''I see what you mean!''

''Now it is, but it will be busy later. I'd suggest we talk on the boat. Pul can keep nosy ears away.''

''Nosy ears?'' Cullin looked up at Dook.

''Erm, nosy people with big ears looking into other peoples business'' Dook added unbothered by his verbal slip.

''Oh, nosy people with big ears and sharp eyes, then. I see.''

Dook gave Cullin a withering look as made his way to the bar for a refill.

Cullin grinned cheekily ''I want some fresh air so I'll see you on the boat later.'' Cullin's ale was left remained almost untouched on the table.

Later that evening Yayler, Dook, Dona and Cullin were in the cramped quarters of Pul's boat. Dook had a large jug of foaming ale that he used to top up a mug. He offered none to the others. A rough map of the Islands of Garvamore sat on the table of the small forequarters of Pul's boat. Pul was on the deck and the crew were spending their tokens in the Fish and Hook.

Yayler had been filling Dookerock in on recent discoveries on the Frames activities.

Dook then proceeded to describe his own activities and the progress of training and weapon production at Rustick More.

''The More is working at capacity'' Dook was saying ''there are over five hundred people working there now, making weapons and training. There is no room for further expansion.''

''To defeat the Frame we need to expand, we need more people training and more weapons. So what do we do?'' Yayler had become the unelected chairman of the group, guiding the discussions forward with quiet authority.

''I don't know; Rustick More was only ever intended for use as a base for investigating the Frames technology and develop it for our own purposes. As such, it serves well, but it was never meant to be used as a military base; it's too small to withstand an assault from the Frame.''

Dook took a long pull on his beer as if to say that the point was no longer up for discussion.

Yayler nodded slightly, introspectively as he thought, creases lining his face as he leant forward to study the map.

''So build another base'' Cullin spoke up brightly.

''Aye, somewhere the Frame won't find it'' Dona with a hint of sarcasm.

''They haven't found the refugees yet, so what about the woods here?''

Dook sorted derisively, but made no comment.

''With aimu in this location that would be unwise, we need to look farther away.'' Yayler gave Cullin a small smile of approval and returned to the studying the map before adding ''somewhere where no one lives.''

Dook suddenly leant forward, intent as he pointed on the map. ''Ardbanacker then, the forests there are extensive and hardly a soul lives there. All the communities are coastal. The land is so unproductive that the Frame doesn't bother with it''.

''That's good'' muttered Dona '', but who would run it?''

''What about my brothers, they know how to run things?'' Cullin added.

''Your brothers know little about technology Cullin and someone would have to run the military side.'' Yayler said thoughtfully. ''Any ideas Dook?''

''Aye, I could do that from the More initially and send a few people to set things up.''

''We could set up several bases'' Cullin added ''that way, if one base is discovered the others can still operate.''

Dona unexpectedly laughed derisively ''look at you guys; all ready to go to war against an enemy that is hugely more powerful than we can ever be.''

''Dona,'' Yayler explained ''we know more now than has ever been known about the Frame before. Though I agree that we cannot afford an all-out conflict, but we can build our strength and start to fight back.''

''With what?'' Dona pressed ''you need weapons, people; lots of people.''

Yayler scratched his head in thought ''Ahh, I think you're a little transparent there Dona; I suspect I know what people you're thinking about''.

''Aye, I am indeed; and are we to abandon so many to the cruelty of the Frame without some attempt to help them?''

''I'm tempted to agree; as ever Dona, your heart does you credit, but we can't risk being discovered through a desire to help those people. It grieves me, but I don't see how we can help.'' Sincere gravity of emotion crossed Yayler's face as he spoke and regarded Dona sadly.

Cullin interjected ''We might if the Frame or the divines didn't realise they were gone.

''Hah, not even the Mighty Rossein, the God of all thinking, could manage that miracle Cullin.'' Dook had been a Divine Ardclerick and had preached the gospel of the Frame before befriending Yayler and switching allegiance.

''Not so Dook, don't forget the divines don't see muckers as people. They read reports from Advocates like Grega and count heads. So as long as things don't change outwardly they won't inquire too closely into the affairs of muckers.'' Cullin pressed on with his argument.

''Who's Grega?'' Dona enquired.

''He was the Advocate from Cullin's former Mark; a good one and a clever man.'' Yayler supplied Dona. ''Sooner or later they would realise something was wrong. We couldn't do it anyhow because the slaves on the farms are far too closely watched and the idea achieves nothing in the Marks.''

''Don't go too fast old friend'' Dook leant forward with sudden interest. ''What if we took over a farm completely?''

''What? How'' a surprised looking Yayler exclaimed.

''By replacing the divines with our own people and carry on with the administration and reports as if nothing has happened.'' Dook continued.

Dona snorted with derision ''that's ridiculous Dook, the Frame would notice.''

''No, not if it was done properly, if the reports are consistent and output remains unchanged. If everything appears as it was, then why would the Frame notice? Take the divines out of the equation leaving aimu and the Frame itself. Both are machines lacking imagination. I think the idea is sound.''

''Hmm, it might work.'' Yayler was thoughtful ''We monitor a remote farm, take over and train the slaves. It's a bold move, Dook, and dangerous. It is the nature of things to go wrong at some point. Believe me, the Frame will find out that something is amiss; sooner or later.''

''Then let's make sure it's later and not sooner.'' Dook was quite earnest now.

''It's a workable idea, so let's find a small, remote farm and work out the details. A scheme like this will succeed or fail on the details. Make a start on this as soon as you can Dook, but for now we keep quiet about it.

''It's getting late, I think we should turn in and wait for Red and his report on the refugees and aimu activity.'' Yayler effectively adjourned further discussions for the evening.

Red arrived the next day, dirty and tired from trekking from deep within the Dunban Forest and cursing the weather. Chilling torrential rain descended from the sky and all about was a swirling grey fog

153

creating an ethereal quality to everything about Pul's small boat. ''Cursed rain, why can't we have some decent crisp snow, better than this muck!''

Dook greeted him as he boarded the boat and laughed; a deep rumbling sound that came from deep in his belly. ''At least the machines will find it hard to snoop on our activities. Here this should warm you up a bit.''

Red took the proffered flask suspiciously, sniffing at the contents. ''What is it; not alcohol I hope?''

Dook should his head ''No, just a herbal for the cold.''

Red removed his morcote and shivered and took a swig at Dook's cold cure. Red choked, gasping his face turned crimson as he swallowed the raw liquid. Between gasps Red spluttered ''what the hell is that?''

''Oh, just something one of the fishermen gave me.''

''Gave? I notice they didn't charge for it!'' Red returned the offending flask and its contents with a disgusted look. Suspicion crossed his face again ''it's not alcoholic is it, you know I don't drink?''

Dook, with a look of pure innocence replied ''Oh, I don't know, maybe; I didn't think about it.'' He sipped from the flask as if tasting it for the first time. ''You know I think it might be''

Red was annoyed ''Dook, you're an evil man!''

The group again used the boat as its meeting place. Red was tucking into a plate of fish stew and drinking herb tea. Red never drank alcohol, but Dook was more than happy to make up for his abstinence.

Between bites Red muttered ''The aimu are very vigilant around Bandrokit now, we have one stationed here permanently now. They've also built a Divine Hall. The Frame is keeping a very close watch on activity here.''

''I don't like this development, the Frame has never bothered with remote communities before.'' Yayler replied.

Dook coughed and took a long pull on his ale and looked mournfully into his empty jug. Belching loudly and farting he stood up and stomped from the cabin.

Over the next wair Red outlined the progress of the refugees and agreed that they should be moved to somewhere more secure and permanent and suggested Rustick More as a suitable location. They formulated how groups of the refugees would be moved to a secluded bay known to Pul. Newly built boats would speed up the process overseen by Dona. Red would continue his current activities and run the evacuation to the bay. Yayler, Dook and Cullin would expand the operations at Rustick More.

Yayler shook his head in mock despair ''you'd think he'd wait until he was outside before doing that. Open the door Cullin and let some fresh air in.''

Dook returned shortly with a fresh jug of ale and Red gave him a disgusted look ''Dook, you stink, you are uncouth and not over bright I fear. You have a talent for trouble and little skill.''

Dook, unperturbed settled himself back in his seat and gave Red a hard look ''bye Red.''

Red gazed steadily at Dook '' Don't mess up your part in this!'' and left the cabin.

Dook turned to Yayler ''Keep that man away from me; he's not right somehow. I might have to hurt him.'' He returned to his communion with his ale without further comment.

# Chapter Eleven

Goram was being moved again; one of the first. They needed his help to set up new camps in another forest. He had settled into a comfortable routine and felt that the overseers appreciated his work. They had listened patiently to his requests for better equipment, a larger shelter, somewhere to store his tools, this or that to help protect the plants.

Goram had taken time to settled into his new life, but now felt a part of the things that were going on about him. He was part of society and valued, he knew his place. He'd had his place in Mark Ossin, of course, but that had all ended rather suddenly.

It was typical of the leaders, Lord Ossin and Tightfist Grega to meddle in the affairs of the divines. The divines had always left them alone, other than a rare census. Goram was convinced, having given much time and thought to the subject, that meddling by the Lord in affairs that didn't concern him is what had triggered those traumatic events.

Now he had a different set of leaders who made equally ridiculous decisions. Why they had to move people from these established clearings, these homes, was beyond Goram. He would have to help to set up and supervise a group of clearings like his in another forest, further away and safer from the machines. It was ridiculous of course, the machines would never find them this deep in the forests.

Goram scoffed at the idea of danger from 'machines'. In his long life, he had never seen a machine, or heard of one causing any harm at all. The idea of danger from machines was preposterous.

So now, so that they could all be safer from machines that caused no harm anyway, they all had to move and start up again. Others would harvest his carefully tended home; then nature would take over and the lands return to a natural state and all his hard work would turn to dust and be wasted.

Goram knew he was a simple person with simple aims in life, not for him the desire to issue orders and make decisions on people's lives.

He loved to make things grow and a good healthy crop was his greatest pleasure. He didn't ask for much.

He had walked with a small group of others, Joz among them, to a small beach where an old woman who had organised some basic shelter for them greeted them. Many had never travelled at night and had needed lights. This caused upset among the leaders, 'too visible' Goram had heard them say.

People were unhappy, like Goram because no one had taken time to explain why they all had to move. There was a lot of resentment and anger as they felt their lives turned upside down again.

A boat would arrive soon to move them on. They must not reveal their presence and must not, at any time, walk on the beach.

---

Ecta marked the position of the clearing deep in the heart of the Ardbanacker Forest on the chart displayed on the compads holoscreen. He added a couple of streams that fed the river he'd been navigating. This was the second such clearing he'd recorded today and light was beginning to fade from an overcast sky. It had been a hot day and a light breeze brought the promise of a cool evening. Booen was the eighth month of the year and this year it was one of the wettest that Ecta could remember. Ecta preferred the crisp cold of late autumn, before the winter storms blanketed the earth with snow.

He turned his attention to the top of the clearing where his assistant was busy making a shelter for the night. ''How is it going Roz?'' Ecta bellowed toward the distant figure.

Roz was in her mid-thirties, but as fit and agile as anyone Ecta had ever met. She wore her hair long and neatly braided. They worked well as a team, dovetailing skills and weaknesses and learning from each other.

''About done here; how about you?''

''I'm done, I'll come and give you a hand.''

Ecta made his way up the slope, occasionally disappearing in deep vegetation. Bracken grew high in these forests, the moist climate suited the bracken well. The fresh green vegetation caught at his feet causing him to stumble. He cursed loudly as he stepped knee deep into a hollow filled with stagnant muddy water.

He looked up to see Roz laughing ''that way dummy'' she shouted indicating ground to Ecta's left ''it's drier!''

Embarrassed he followed the indicated direction finding it much drier and easier to walk through. Looking back, he failed to see any difference in the appearance of the two routes. Green vegetation covered both routes equally as far as he could tell.

Roz and Ecta were one of many teams Dook had sent out to scout the forests for paths and clearings intended for the new training camps. They had been plotting and recording these clearings for three months now and had a well-practised routine.

They knew that clearings plotted earlier in the year were now working. Crops growing, former refugees being trained and even micro-factories set up to make tools and weapons all added up to the forest becoming a hive of human industry and activity.

Ecta busied himself making a fire. Roz had trained him in the subtleties of fire making. The following morning they would clear away the fire leaving no trace of their passage. Tomorrow they would return downstream and meet up with a runner. The runners job was to collect compads from scouting parties and deliver fresh ones with more up to date data patches. Back at Rustick More the fresh data was analysed and added to an ever growing database.

Ecta mused on the activities of Cullin's brothers; Ulbin he knew was now running one of the first waves of new camps. Orvalt, as the apparent Lord of the Mark, found himself tied up with the logistics of moving large populations discreetly. Hamadern was busy on the eastern coast near Creelan, stuck on the wild coast of the Varamor Sea.

The following day Roz and Ecta started their return to Rustick More. The nights were distinctly cold now and autumn rains would soon be turning wintry. Their portable, lightweight shelter was fine for summer, but would be inadequate for the winter. The following three tendays saw them return along thin tracks and paths that connected clearings they had plotted earlier in the summer.

The clearings appeared, superficially at least, much as they had last seen them, but looking closer revealed growing crops. Cabbages, carrots, turnips and other winter hardy vegetables grew on well-drained mounds fertilised with calp brought up from the coast. The seaweed helped to neutralise the acidic peaty soil of the forest. Beans and other pulses grew, twined about trees at the edges of the clearings. To protect the crop from deer, high fences meandered from tree to tree, forming a cordon that was all, but invisible from the air.

When he had first started working in the forest, Ecta had assumed that one would be much the same as another. Roz, with much amusement, had explained how different trees preferred different environments. Hazel and Willow grew close to streams in pockets of open woodland. The giant Alben and the quick growing softwood Surwane vied for space on the rolling hillsides. Broom and Juniper were also common. The whole produced surprisingly varied woodland that Ecta was only beginning to understand and appreciate.

They had arrived at a large clearing surmounted by a rocky outcrop that gave them views of distant peaks and the long stretch of Marlok that separated Ardbanacker from Anklayv Island. The 'workers', former refugees, resistance and staff from Rustick More, used heather to disguise weapons stashes. Some of these, a precious few, were energy weapons that utilised the same technology as a divines staff. The components were difficult to obtain and they were not as efficient as a staff. Ecta had heard that these people now called themselves aneksa, or free people.

Projectile weapons were more prolific, being easier for the aneksa to manufacture. Under the trees Ecta could see squads of people training for combat both with and without weapons.

''Ecta! I see you're back from the forest.''

The deep voice belonged to Ulbin who now ran a number of these clearings, organising training and the logistics of feeding large numbers of people.

''Ulbin, you look like you've been very busy.''

159

''Aye, very. Welcome to Ossin's place. There are many hereabouts now from our old Mark.''

''You look like you're building an army''

''Aye, about five hundred aneksa trained up now. With more camps being developed, we're looking stronger all the time.''

The last few years, since the burning of Dunossin, had seen a change in Ulbin. He was no longer the course, rude man of his youth. A deep-seated hatred of divines and the Frame replaced his youthful rudeness and basic nature though he was still often ill mannered. He now lived for the day when he could avenge his father's death and focused entirely on that goal.

Ecta knew Ulbin's impulsive nature of old. Once Ulbin had an idea he believed in he rarely thought it out thoroughly. He often tended to act on half an idea and frequently forgot to consider consequences. ''Five hundred; that's amazing. There could be thousands by spring.''

''Five thousand under my orders by the month of Kerev, is the plan'' Ulbin puffed himself up, showing his pride. Five thousand people would make up a small Mark under divine governance. By spring, Ulbin would effectively be a Lord, independent of the Frame.

''That's a lot of people. I presume others like yourself will be building similar forces'' Ecta grinned broadly, expressing enthusiasm.

''Aye, but this is the first to start up. Others, deeper in the forest and out towards the east will have different functions.'' Ulbin went on, eager to demonstrate his importance. ''Hamadern is developing production camps, so more weapons can be made more quickly. Others are finding ways to produce more food.''

''So, how many troops do the machines have? They must have a big army?''

Ulbin nodded ''Aye, but not out here. Between Willemsbree, Aldee and Pirt they may have a few thousand, maybe the same again in Port Main. Then they have to start drawing their army from the mainland. They have relatively few trained troops and weapons compared to the population of Garvamore. We are stronger than they would like to think and getting stronger.''

''Surely you're not thinking of fighting them?''

''Nay, My lieutenant Yaren runs the military side of things. I run the logistics side of operations.''

''This all looks very impressive Ulbin, I'm sure your father would be very proud of you.'' Ecta knew Ulbin would appreciate such a comment; a bit of gentle ego stroking was always useful with people like Ulbin.

Ulbin made no answer other than smiling, broad open smile that, somehow, conveyed honesty.

''so, what weapons has the army have to fight with against machines; not bows and arrows surely?''

''Ahh, they were used in the Morven Rebellion. We have learnt and moved on. Yarin tells me that Dook has been working for years on better weapons.''

Ulbin took them over to a nearby stash of weapons. The mound appeared to be a simple hummock covered with heather with a peat groughs on either side. Once he was closer, Ecta could see that the whole mound, constructed of a wooden frame had storage racks inside. A lowered floor with drainage back to the peat groughs to prevent flooding allowed the three of them to stand upright inside the mound.

''Ahh, these,'' a delighted Ulbin enthused ''these are based on the divines staff such as Yayler used to kill the Bastard Beck25. We call them short staffs.''

Ecta raised a surprised eye at Ulbin's addition to the divines name, but remained quiet. Ulbin held up a short, stumpy object about the length of a man's forearm. The weapon moulded itself to the forearm and fired with a simple clenching of the fist.

Another rack stored metal tubes with an arrangement at one end.

''What are these?'' queried Roz holding one up and inspecting it.

''Ahh, those are 'gunna'; it's an ancient weapon Dook found designs for in archives. It fires a small pellet with great speed. I'm told they can kill a man from a great distance'' Ulbin was happily warming up to the job of explaining the various weapons at his disposal.

Deep in the driest part of the mound, thick cylinders wrapped in layers of beetick lay in neat rows on racks. ''Those are plazboma'' Ulbin supplied ''Dook is very proud of those. He hopes to use them to destroy machines. I don't understand how they work myself, but I know they are very dangerous and great care has to be taken with them at all times.''

''This is all very impressive, Ulbin; where do you get all the metal and so on to make these weapons?'' Ecta asked.

To his surprise Roz answered the question ''Dook has been building up stores at Rustick More for many years. Even so, supplies are always short and difficult to find.''

''Aye, we always need more. Demand outstrips supply all the time. It slows down the expansion of our forces'' a momentary flicker of irritation crossed Ulbin's face.

Ecta was inspecting a short staff and a thought crossed his mind. From Cullin's description of events at Dunossin, he knew that Yayler's staff had an energy shield for defence, whereas this short staff appeared to be offensive only. ''How would you defend against energy weapons, without defence your troops could be torn to pieces?''

Ulbin was quiet for a moment. His brow wrinkled with thought as he cast his mind back to that fateful day when Beck25 had killed his Father. He remembered the devastation about the Great Hall after only a few blasts from Beck25. Then he imagined what such weapons would do to his troops and his face suffused with anger. It was unacceptable.

Ulbin took a moment to regain his composure and then turned to Roz and Ecta. ''Someone will be with you shortly.'' With no more said, Ulbin stomped off angrily in search of Yarin.

A few days later Roz and Ecta were on Pul's boat the 'Banree Na Mur' sailing eastward through Marlok. The weather had turned cold over the last few days and Ecta had noticed the snowline on the mountains, both north and south, had descended their flanks. Their trip so far had been one of intermittent snow-squalls and cold brittle sunshine.

They all wore finely woven waxed morcotes adapted to have hoods with heavy woollens underneath. Ecta noticed that once damp the woollens did little to keep out the cold and did everything he could to stop damp getting under his morcote. This generally meant keeping his morcote wrapped whenever on deck. Pul and the crew just laughed when he complained, saying that the weather was normal for the time of year.

Ecta was on deck watching mountains and forest slip past as the boat sailed on an eastward tide. He found his eye drawn naturally northward to the mountains, though not as magnificent as the peaks of Mark Ossin, they were mountains and gave him a peaceful longing for his childhood home.

Although not strong, the wind caught the tops of the waves sending fine plumes of spray into the air. Ecta was not a seaman by any means and knew his level of ignorance, which was considerable. He did, however like to ask questions and found that the crew were happy to answer them.

A short distance ahead of them, Ecta noticed a disturbance in the water, splashes and spray that looked different to the spindrift about them. Then he saw a larger plume of spray and he was certain it wasn't ordinary.

''Pul, what's that?'' Ecta indicated with a pointed finger. ''Is that rocks over there?''

Pul glanced at the disturbance and frowned. ''I'm not sure. There are rocks, but they should be a little further to the north or closer to the shore.''

The Banree Na Mur made steady progress brought them closer to the disturbance and Pul lowered the sail. Noticing the change in the boats headway the two crew and Roz came on deck. The strange phenomena fascinated them as the boat bobbed in the swell.

163

"Finnan" Pul called to one of his crew "fetch me the charts, please."

Finnan, a grizzled old man with more wrinkles than a wizened apple, disappeared into the cabin and returned a few moments later with a roll of parchment. Pul studied the chart for a few moments as he verified their position. He frowned, double checked the chart and returned it to Finnan.

"Well" he said at last "there are no rocks marked there on the chart, but there are some nearer to that rocky island, Aylinron." Another large plume of spray shot high into the air as he spoke.

As they watched spellbound, drifting on the tide, a small dark shape leaped briefly from the sea, the disappeared again. Finnan spoke to his Captain "I think that was a seal, Pul."

"I think, maybe you're right." Pul replied. "The position has moved as well."

They watched the spectacle for a short while longer. Pul was about to re-hoist the sail when there was another large plume shot several paces into the air.

"Pul," Ecta called out "all those plumes seem to be happening on the same spot."

"Aye, I think your right young Ecta." Pul nodded his approval

As they spoke, the tip of a large fin was visible for a brief moment, racing swiftly away from the foaming disturbance.

"Guvin," Pul raised his voice to be heard "hoist sail, we've stayed here long enough."

Pul's son was quick hoist the sail and the small boat quickly made headway. "Where are we stopping for the night, Pul?"

"There is a good little bay a few strides east. I've used it before."

Ecta asked Finnan quietly a little later "why did Pul decide to move on so suddenly, we were still some distance from that disturbance?"

164

''Did you see that fin? That was an orca; they feed on seals. There were probably rocks just under the surface that the seals were trying to use as protection from the Orca. It was fun watching, in all my years at sea, I've never seen that before, I don't think Pul has either!''

Pyta sat high on a peninsula with his back resting comfortably on rounded wind worn rocks. He had found this place a few months earlier when his boss had sent him here. Pyta called him 'The Man' or more often just 'Boss' as he did not know his real name, or any name to call him. His job was simply to record all boats that passed his position.

For this easy work he got a comfortable croft to lodge in, all his food cooked for him by a large and considerably overweight woman called Pibeg. Pibeg was a bad tempered woman who was unpopular in the local village as a result. She was grateful for the tokens that Pyta's lodging brought in and they managed to tolerate each other. Pyta cared little for her, or she for him.

Pyta watched the small fishing boat as it sailed east along the north coast of Marlok. He added the appropriate tallies on a slate; Pibeg would send the data to The Boss later. As he watched, the boat appeared to stop for no reason that Pyta could see. Then, awhile later, the boat set sail again. The Boss had asked him to watch out for just this kind of unusual occurrence. He marked it down on the slate and reached inside his morcote for his flask.

The whisky was rough, but Pyta drank in anyway. He peered into the flask and sighed regretfully as the flask was half-empty. Pibeg only allowed him to take the one flask and she would beat him if he tried to take more.

The following morning was dismal, grey and cold with a bitter north wind. Pul said he could smell snow in the air and was eager to be away from their small overnight harbourage.

By the first wair of the morning, Pul determined that there was sufficient water in the bays entrance for them to depart. The Banree Na Mur was soon making steady eastward progress into the Varamor Sea. Frequent squalls of hail made the voyage a miserable affair for Ecta and Roz. They huddled in the cabin wrapped in blankets to ward off the cold. The crew made regular brews of a herbal infusion sweetened with honey.

165

In the late afternoon Ecta made a foray onto the deck to escape from the claustrophobic cabin. He had always had open spaces about him, mountains and wild moors and distant views. Once on the deck he felt the calming effect of the open ocean. After a short while, he noticed that the sea was behaving oddly, sluggishly. ''Guvin, why is the sea so flat? I thought it would be rougher farther out.''

Guvin, who was at the helm while Pul took a break, was slow to answer. ''It normally is this time of year, but I think the north wind is bringing colder water down from the north.''

''Ahh'' replied Ecta, not really understanding.

Seeing Ecta's blank incomprehension Guvin added ''this water comes down from the Wild Sea on currents. Those currents often bring icebergs with them. The cold makes the water sluggish, it will begin to freeze if the weather gets much colder.''

Ecta returned his attention back to the sea, but then a thought occurred to him ''Guvin, are we likely to see any icebergs?''

''Hope not, but it's possible.''

Ecta shivered involuntarily ''I'm going for a brew, did you want one Guvin?''

''Aye; good plan and my thanks.''

That night was a sleepless one as the Banree headed deeper into the Varamor Sea. Squalls of snow and hail blended into each other and coating the Banree in a thick rime of ice. The crew regularly had to remove fingers of ice that hung from the rigging to prevent fowling. About midnight Pul, who sat grim and enigmatic at the tiller, announced a new bearing that brought cheer to Guvin and Finnan who redoubled their efforts on their tasks.

Pul had given Ecta and Roz oil lamps that they shone out over the sea, searching for icebergs. They both sensed the relief in the crew. The night dragged on as the Banree made good headway on a south-easterly heading chased now by the weather rather than heading directly into it.

Toward dawn, they all felt drawn, worn down and gritty eyed. Pul, who had remained steadfastly by the helm all night, looked grim and determined, but was clearly very tired.

The wind direction had changed overnight to a westerly direction, bringing warmer air from off the land causing a thick fog to form about the frosted Banree. A fine crystalline rime formed on the Banree as the fog froze onto every surface. The visibility was appalling. They were no longer looking out for icebergs, but rocks or land. Pul reefed the sail and their headway reduced to a dead slow creep.

Finnan, Ecta and Roz peered intently forward into the murk with Guvin at the helm. Pul was intent with his charts making careful calculations. By his reckoning, they were approaching the mouth of Marvlok, a broad fjord that cut deep into Anklayv Island.

Pul came back onto the deck and spoke to Finnan ''drop the sea anchor, then go below and get some rest. I daren't go further in this murk.''

He turned to Ecta and Roz ''Thank you both for your vigilance. You must be done in. Go get some rest; you've earned it. Guvin and me will look after the boat for now.''

A loud grinding, rending noise, as if something was tearing the boat apart, woke Ecta a couple of wairs later. Alarmed he went onto the deck. It was still thick with fog with snow falling from a black sky. The others were all peering over the sides intently.

''There!'' Finnan called out pointing at something in the water toward the bow.

Pul joined him and saw it, a large rock just under the surface. ''ahh, for the love of Hesoos!''

With each swell, Pul could see tearing at the hull, enlarging an ugly looking hole below the waterline. Pul grabbed a boat hook from its home beneath the gunwale and gently pushed at the rock. The point of the boat hook repeatedly slid from the rock. The Banree continued to grind against the rock causing more damage with every movement. The attempts continued for some time without success.

Pul was on the verge of despair when Ecta asked ''are we not on the wrong side of the rock? The waves and the wind just push us back on to it.''

''Aye, we know that Ecta.'' Pul was short tempered and irritated and Ecta's comment didn't help.

''Ahh, but what if we could get the rock to the other side of the bow? Then the wind and waves would work in our favour'' Ecta continued.

Pul considered and asked ''how would you do that, Ecta?''

''Inch the rock along the hull rather than pushing it away.''

''We could damage a much greater section of the hull by doing that, Ecta.''

''The hull is being torn to pieces anyway.''

Guvin joined them at that moment and reported ''No sign of leakage below, Pul. The inner hull appears to be intact.''

Pul nodded his thanks, deep in thought. After awhile he clapped Ecta on the shoulder ''we'll try it your way young man! Everyone listen, this is how we're going to do this.''

Guvin was at the tiller, Finnan was a freehand, ready to hoist the sail or fend off as ordered, Ecta and Roz manned boat hooks whilst Pul stood precariously on the snowy bow with one hand holding the forward cabin grab rail and directing Ecta and Roz with shouts and hand-signals.

''Push!'' Pul hollered at the peak of each swell.

Ecta and Roz shoved hard against the rock at each command. Progress was small, but Pul kept up the rhythm, push, pause, push, pause, push. At each pause, they could hear the rock grinding into the hull.

The Banree wallowed more heavily in the water making the job of the pushers more difficult. However, from his precarious vantage point, Pul could see progress and kept up the relentless rhythm.

Push, grind, push, grind, push, grind, pause.

"Hold" came the command at last. Exhausted and sweating despite the freezing weather stopped, watching Pul intently for further commands.

Pul leaned over the bow, looking intently at the rock and the sea, current, wind direction and using his years of experience on the sea, he made a conclusion. "Guvin, steer hard port, let's see if she'll swing round."

"Push, push, push!" came the command and Ecta and Roz bent their backs to the task again. "Keep it up, she's moving!"

Finnan joined Ecta and Roz, using an oar for lack of a third boat hook.

Gradually they felt the boat turn and with each effort against the rock, she turned a little more. Then with one last rending, grind the Banree tore free from the rock.

Two days later, a battered, ice rimed, Banree limped into the Creelan Harbour. Tarred sail-cloth covered the gaping hole in the hull. Dawn after the incident with the rock had revealed a gash below the waterline, about two paces in length. Investigation had revealed that the inner hull had remained intact and this, Pul was certain, is what had allowed them to stay afloat.

# Chapter Twelve

Cullin was feeling moody, reflecting on the eight months since the meeting on Pul's boat. Ecta had joked about this moodiness saying that Cullin was grumpy and becoming more like his Father Ossin. Cullin had returned to Rustick More with Dookerock and Yayler Poddick, which quickly became hectic with activity.

They were currently surveying Drimneev, a mountain that Dook had located from an old map out of archives at Rustick More. Dook wanted three-dimensional images of the area with a view to building a new base similar to Rustick More.

A deep sigh escaped from Cullin as he nibbled on a slice of venison sausage. He thought about Sara, who had been overjoyed at seeing him again and managed to find any excuse to spend time with him. Cullin was surprised at how easily the relationship had developed and found he cherished the time they spent together. Cullin had no idea why Sara had such feelings for him, but his feelings for her had grown. He missed her when she wasn't there, but couldn't quite understand why, so he simply accepted the situation. He found that he admired her tremendous, quiet strength, positive character and the way she could always find the most comfortable position when she snuggled up next to him.

---

When he had arrived at Rustick More Yayler had organised training routines for Cullin, both physical combat exercises and technical. Yayler had given Cullin a large compad with holographic controls to work on. He learned how to dig into the Frames low security level data files and close his activities down without leaving a trace. Yayler would then check his work to ensure that no trace of Cullin's activities remained in the Frames data files.

On one of these sessions had found in a report that was hundreds of years old, a reference to Victor8 and knew this to be Yayler's former divine name. Though much of the short report went far beyond Cullin's current knowledge, he knew enough to discern that it confirmed completion of enhancement. Reading between the lines Cullin understood that Yayler was not entirely human anymore, but part machine.

Yayler had been very upset when he reviewed Cullin's work, quizzing Cullin extensively on his understanding of the report.

''Well, you are a bright lad, Cullin, so I should have expected you to find out eventually. I need to talk to Dook about this, but I need you to remain silent about this until I do.'' Yayler had then left Cullin as he went to search for Dook.

Dook had been equally perturbed, but had concluded that Cullin needed to go through the 'procedure'. The next few days were a nightmare for Cullin. He was immediately taken to a small room, deep within Rustick More and known to only a few.

The room was full of strange equipment, the nature of which Cullin could only guess. At the centre of the room was a silver coloured table that stood on a crystalline plinth. A slender curved white beam supported a clear glasslike hood arrayed with blinking lights. More equipment lined the walls. Holoscreens projected three-dimensional displays of a subject into the room that the operator could then examine. Ranks of cabinets and desks with buttons and dials lined the walls.

It was an alien room, completely outside of Cullin's previous experience. To see it here at Rustick More in the heart of the resistance movement against the Frame was profoundly shocking and, oddly, hopeful.

Yayler went to one of the cabinets and removed a few items placing them on a tray. He carefully laid out slivers and needles of a shining material and a dark capsule all set in a protective gel and wrapped in film. A drawer set within one of the cabinets held equipment, sharp small knives, pincers and manipulating devices of unknown purpose to Cullin. Another cabinet held vials and bottles the contents of which Cullin could only guess.

An apprehensive Cullin was worried seeing the unusual equipment and had a strong urge to escape from this room. Only his trust in Dook and Yayler, built over the last few years stopped him from running.

"Don't look so worried Cullin, we're not going to do anything to hurt you." Yayler spoke gently. "You've made a remarkable discovery about Dook and myself. We've gone through this procedure and now you know about it, Dook and I think you should go through it yourself."

"Firstly we will give you interfaces that allow you to communicate directly with computers and machines, even aimu, but we don't recommend that, of course" Dook added.

"The second process is to give you Nanos; these are tiny devices that help to repair your body and allow you to live longer." Yayler went on "divines have these procedures completed when they are about five years old. Both Dook and I have had this done; it is a memorable day for a young divine as it is the first step toward becoming a divine. Those children who don't go through the process, sadly, don't make it to adulthood. They are considered inferior and no better than muckers.

"This operation won't make you a divine, you will still be yourself because this technology is independent of the Frame and the machines, but you will find that you are better at some things than you were before.

"There are more procedures and operations that will improve your eyesight and other physical attributes that we'll complete over the next few weeks. You must remember though, that you cannot talk to anyone about this. That is very important Cullin, because you will have abilities that will be very useful to us that we don't want others to know about; abilities that will be very useful in the fight against the Frame as it intensifies, which it will."

Dook interrupted Yayler at this point, adding "Cullin, you must realise that the technology we are about to give you is very difficult to get hold of and even more difficult to manufacture. We have to be sure about a person before we even consider giving it to them. You should consider yourself very privileged Cullin, we are putting a lot of trust in you."

The first procedure was simple and relatively painless. An odd-looking device was loaded with one of the gel wrapped needles and slipped over each finger and thumb in turn. The operator squeezed the handle of the device inserting the needle into the pad of the finger. Releasing the device handle withdrew the needle leaving a web of

172

microfilaments under the skin. A different attachment allowed the operator to insert a silver sliver under the scalp. It was explained to Cullin that the inserts worked in concert through the scalp implant and Cullin would be trained how to use them.

The black capsule contained nanos that Cullin simply swallowed. The stomach enzymes quickly digested the capsule casing, releasing the nanos, which the body then absorbed as they passed through the intestines.

Yayler continued to explain the procedures to Cullin ''There are in fact several different types of nano and all are automatic. They carry on doing their job without instruction and replicate themselves as needed.

''When first introduced they have a blank template which they take from your DNA. That information is stored in the scalp implant. Your body adjusts to a symbiotic equilibrium with your new technology. The process takes a few days and you will feel a little unwell as a result. This is nothing to worry about; it's just the nanos working on your body and will subside in time''.

Cullin had returned to his quarters and for several days was indeed unwell and not just a little unwell. He was feverish, feeling cold one minute and flushed and sweating the next. His stomach churned at the mere thought of food and he ached all over. A constant headache added to his misery.

Sara tended him, constantly at his side and making sure that he drank a few mouthfuls of water at regular intervals. If he hadn't felt so dreadful Cullin would have enjoyed the fuss.

Ecta made a few visits to see his old friend, but Sara barely left his side and even went without meals, such was her concern for his welfare. Yayler and Dook made a couple of visits to check on his progress and muttered between themselves, but announced to the others that he was fine and would get better. On these visits Yayler merely held Cullin's hand and frowned, he was in fact downloading data through his own implants and those newly given to Cullin.

Yayler was, of course busy, an endless round of discussions and planning with Dook and his Lieutenants, reviewing collated data and maintaining communications with other groups of resistance; small pockets of local Lords, fishermen, woodsmen and stonemason and many other skilled craftsmen that Yayler felt could be utilised. Yayler knew that the Resistance would not beat the Frame without violence and battle for which the vast majority of muckers were completely unprepared. Rustick More held a small arsenal of weapons, but was woefully short of the strength needed. More of such places were needed and many, many more weapons.

Cullin soon recovered from his 'illness' and went back to his training schedules. He underwent more procedures in Dook's operation room that included more skull implants to improve his memory and speed of thought, cornea implants to improve eyesight and so on. Although these operations caused him relatively mild discomfort, none of them made him feel ill. Learning how to use the implants was difficult and caused Cullin a great deal of stress. He was suffering from a sensory overload that caused him to become bad tempered. Only the short periods of intimate relaxation with Sara helped to calm his mood. Although the way she ran her fingers through his hair or her gentle caresses and soft kisses that normally he found wonderful on these occasions were almost unbearably intense.

Over time, Cullin became used to the amount of data his enhanced senses were giving him. His brain learned to filter out unnecessary data as he found the trick of focusing on details that interested him.

When Yayler had become satisfied that Cullin had grown used to the implants he took Cullin to a room darkened to pitch black, deep in the bowels of Rustick More. Within the room was a hidden panel with some items that Yayler wanted. It was a test, Cullin had believed, to determine his ability to use his enhanced senses.

First, he had tried touch and found the walls all bare and smooth. He had then tried tapping the walls and found them all to be solid. He had lost track of time and became disoriented. His brain had begun to play tricks on him. Ethereal images would appear before him, but he couldn't quite touch them.

He saw his mother, young and beautiful in a meadow of spring flowers. She smiled at him, but how could it be? Kuli had died when he was born. He saw a monstrous metal creature, huge and soulless, behind her, poised to strike. He urged his mother to run, shouted, but she couldn't hear him.

The ground beneath his mother's feet moved, thousands of metal spiders crawled along the ground in sinuous waves, devouring everything in their path. They were almost upon her, but he couldn't help her. He screamed.

The image vanished and he was plunged back into the pitch black room. Suddenly he felt a hand on his shoulder and yelped from startled fear.

''Come on lad, that's enough for today.'' Yayler's familiar, calm voice brought him to his senses, back to the real world.

Yayler had spent the entire time waiting, patiently outside the room and brought the wide eyed and disoriented Cullin out of the room without showing surprise or upset by the failure. He had simply told Cullin to use his 'other' senses, though what was meant by 'other' senses Cullin had no idea.

The next day was another failure. On the third attempt, Yayler had suggested making 'clicking' noises and moving about the room using the clicks.

Cullin had thought it a crazy idea, but went along with the suggestion and for the next several days tried the unusual 'seeing' technique'. At first there was the inevitable walking into the walls and losing any sense of direction. Only once after several days of stumbling about the room did frustration cause him to blurt out in exasperation ''Yayler, it can't be done!''

Yayler had placidly replied ''keep trying, you're doing well. At least you're not bumping into the walls anymore.''

Cullin persisted and had soon found he could walk about the room with ease. Yayler gave up the practice of waiting outside the room, simply saying that he had other things to do and had urged Cullin to continue his efforts.

Eventually Cullin found the trick of seeing in the dark and found the hidden panel. Inside, once he has worked out how to open the panel, he found a small tablet in a recess. This is a small compad shaped to fit the palm of a hand comfortably. When he shows this to Yayler, he is urged to keep it as a 'reward'. Yayler explained that would perform all the functions of the larger compad he was currently using, but his new implants would allow him to connect with it directly rather than manually through holoscreens.

Cullin continued his practice in private and was surprised to find his 'new sense' developed, giving him more detailed and precise 'visual' image that overlay his normal sight, even in broad daylight.

When Cullin had started to use the compad from the darkened room, he found it operated a little differently from compads he had used before. Rather than operate the compad manually through a holoscreen he found that he had only to hold the compad with his hand on its shaped surface, his fingers lightly touching the surface for it to operate. He operated the device with his mind working through the implants in his fingers. He was soon able to use the compad faster and more efficiently than with previous compads.

---

An icy gust blew spindrift into Cullin's face bringing him out of his reverie. Cullin sighed again and turned his attention back to the valley below. Dook had spent days poring over maps at Rustick More looking for defensible and remote valleys to expand the operations of Rustick More, which had now reach its maximum capacity. Dook had thought one of these two neighbouring valleys would be suitable.

''Welcome back'' quipped Ecta when he noticed his friend stir ''the weather's still rotten and its going to start getting dark fairly soon and you'll see Sara soon; when we've done this job.''

''Aye'' Cullin stretched, ignoring the mention of Sara, though he blushed slightly, unnoticed by Ecta. He looked at the section of rock they had been recording ''of course, ideally, we should have done this job in the spring.''

''True, but we were both busy with other things then.'' Cullin turned his face to the sky and sniffed gently ''Hmm, I reckon we could get some snow later.''

176

"Certainly cold enough" replied Ecta "Do you reckon that flat bit over there could serve as a landing pad for a flier?"

Cullin looked to where Ecta indicated and frowned at its obvious shortcomings "it's too narrow and that overhang would make a landing difficult."

"It might be extended though and that overhang reduced" Ecta defended his idea.

"It's a lot of work Ecta, but we could plot that section and mark it as a possibility. That whole mountainside would need excavating and that ledge would have to be extended and made to look natural."

"--, But the ledge continues all the way to the notch and the path down we found the other day" Ecta pressed his enthusiasm for his idea, finishing Cullin's sentence.

"That's true, an army of aimu or divines would fight all day against a handful of defenders and get nowhere."

"Ha ha, Dook would love that idea." Laughed Ecta

"Aye, but Yayler would scoff, 'we're not ready to fight such battles against the Frame."

"Hey," exclaimed Ecta pointing to the crags above the ledge "picture that bit while the light's on it."

Cullin used his small compad to take manipulate images of the area and then fused about with the device for a few moments. He played with the image briefly making small adjustments and added it to a three dimensional form of the mountain held in the compads memory. This form Cullin now viewed and announced "We're almost done on this side of the mountain now; there's just a few gaps left. We can finish those off tomorrow".

"Aye, let's get back to camp then."

The following day started out bright with clear skies allowing Cullin and Ecta to complete the job of recording the mountainside. They decided to have a closer look at the ledge.

After a simple traverse over a broad rocky escarpment and along an eroded dyke, they started their way towards the ledge. The traverse to the ledge proved to be a little trickier, but after a few failed attempts where ledges became too thin, or disappeared completely, they found an 'easier' route from below the notch. A broad fissure in the rock-face led onto a wide buttress, which they negotiated with an easy scramble. From there a narrow ledge clung to the mountainside with a narrow crack running along its length between it and the vertical rock wall.

Powdery snow and ice choked crevices and gullies on the south facing massif. Ecta had to clear every step and handhold of snow and ice before proceeding to the next hold.

''Where are you taking us, Cullin?'' shouted an unhappy Ecta. His heels were protruding over the edge of the ledge as he clung onto damp and slimy handholds.

''Just take your time, Ecta, it gets easier'' Cullin shouted back.

''I hope so; this is truarly, stupid, utter cac!'' After a pause to regain his breath Ecta shouted again ''It must be a thousand paces straight down!''

Ecta missed Cullin's reply, but thought it sounded like 'so don't fall'. There was little else he could do, but continue his slow, tentative progress along the ledge. Loose grit and gravel made his footing precarious, as did handholds of small cracks, hollows and raised sections of the irregular rock wall.

Ecta's chest tightened with fear and his breath came faster as adrenaline pumped about his body. His mouth was dry and his thoughts became panicked. He was desperate for an escape from the terror that had gripped his racing mind. With his face pressed hard against unforgiving rock, Ecta prayed. ''Dearest Mozog, don't let me fall; dearest Mozog, don't let me fall.'' His prayer was a mantra and little by little it helped to calm him and allow him to focus.

'Slow down' he told himself. 'One bit at a time.' Inch by inch, move by move, Ecta progressed along the ledge, always making sure of a hold before moving to the next one. Slowly he crept along the ledge until as he rounded a corner, he could see a very relieved Cullin ahead, standing on a much broader section of the ledge.

He sat down besides Cullin, resting his back against the rock wall that loomed above them and realised that he was shaking quite violently. Slowly he recovered, restoring his equilibrium and spoke quietly to Cullin. ''That was terrifying, we can't go back that way Cull, it's suicide.''

''Aye, I thought about going back, but realised we were committed'' Cullin was quiet for a moment and then added ''I didn't realise you were struggling so much; I'm sorry.''

Ecta nodded to himself; knew Cullin wouldn't have risked his life deliberately. He told himself to drop the subject and not mention it again; Cullin, he knew, was probably tearing himself apart inside. Instead he simply remarked ''you know, we could've used a rope! We have one back at the camp.''

''Ahh, if one of us had fallen he would have pulled the other one off the ledge as well''.

The comment shocked Ecta and he was silent for long, profound moments. Eventually he broke the silence between them ''Cullin, please don't ever do that to me again''.

''I won't. Look, stay here for now, I'm going to look ahead. I'll be back soon.'' Cullin left Ecta and started to look at the ledge, recording as many details as he could on the small compad.

The ledge was broad enough for a flier, but not deep enough. It was also remarkably level, dipping slightly towards the cliffs above and composed of a smooth dark, almost black, rock. 'Not bad' thought Cullin,'but not quite good enough.'

He noticed a small cleft between the rock wall and the ledge where the two rock forms didn't seem to connect. In places, he could place a couple a fingers into the gap. He began to dig out small rocks and ice and found that the cleft extended further into the rock-face. Intrigued, he continued to investigate, moving toward a buttress that marked the farthest end of the ledge.

When he looked closer, he realised that the buttress was a fin of fractured rock that didn't connect with the cliffs above. Jamming his hand behind the crags, he pulled himself up. He levered himself up further with another handhold and looked into gap in front of him and opened his eyes wider with surprise. ''Oh, Ecta, what have we got here'' he whispered even though Ecta was still resting back on the ledge.

Cullin clicked and tut-tuted for a few moments listening intently to the response he got ''Ahh, interesting''.

Cullin worked himself further up until he could sit comfortably in the gap. He then recorded as much of his discovery on the compad before zooming the image back out to view the results. He looked at the narrow ledge they had traversed and knew that it would be foolish to try that route again.

How to get back? That then was the question. Looking closely at his model of the mountainside, he noticed that the gradients were much less acute away from the notch. Was it possible, then, to work their way up further away from the notch and then come back around? He could see that it was, indeed, possible and decided to return to Ecta with the good news.

Back on the ledge, Cullin could see that Ecta was looking at bit glum.

''What's up?'' Cullin tried to exude cheerfulness and lighten his friend's mood.

''I think you've lost it, Cull. How can you be so cheerful? We're stuck here unless we use that ledge again''

''Ahh, erm, no! I thought so too, but let me show you something.'' Cullin activated the compad and brought up the image of the mountain.

''That's where we are now.'' Cullin indicated their position with a grubby finger and then traced a line through the image. ''Here's the other end of the ledge. If we follow this crack up the slope lessens and we can climb onto the summit ridge by following this diagonal line.''

Ecta frowned, but followed the route, studying it in minute detail. ''Well'' he said at last ''it certainly looks possible and is a far better option than retracing our steps along that ledge, but how do we get down the other side? How do we get to our camp?''

"On the natua-side, north as the divines say, the rocks are more broken and easier to negotiate."

Ecta grudgingly conceded the point and with distinct reservation in his tone said "Well let's get on with it then."

Whilst jamming his way up the crack by the fin of rock Cullin stopped and shouted down to Ecta "there's something I want to show you!"

Cursing slightly Ecta scrambled up to his friends side "what" he said simply and looked in the direction of Cullin's pointed finger. "What? I don't see anything, just rock!"

"No, look there" the finger still indicated.

Baffled Ecta gave up on the game and shrugged "I don't see anything, Cull, just a hole with rocks in it. What are you trying to show me?"

"Aye, a hole, but not just a hole. It's huge. It extends deep into the mountain."

Cullin suddenly grabbed Ecta by his morcote and looked him in the face, excitement in his eyes. "Don't you see Ecta, this place is perfect for Dook to build his new base and you found it!"

Stupefied, Ecta looked blankly at the insignificant hole. "How do you know how far it extends?"

"Ah, magic!" Cullin waved the compad by way of explanation for a still confused Ecta.

"All right, Cull, I believe you, but I think you must have had some of Donal's spiced spirits, your wits are clearly addled!"

Cullin was looking at the sky "nay, but I think we had best get on; it's getting late and we don't want to get stuck up here overnight".

The ascent up onto the ridge proved to be a relatively easy scramble without the exposure of large drops. They found themselves on the crest of the mountain ridge as the late afternoon sun obscured by dark clouds dipped below the horizon. Light drizzle dampened the rock making it greasy and slippery.

They were still some distance from their campsite and descending gullies and clambering round large craggy buttresses as the light faded to darkness. Ecta, following Cullin was stumbling about and their progress became slow.

Snow flurries reduced what visibility there was still further until Ecta could manage no more. ''Cull'' he hollered toward the vague shadow ahead that he believed to be Cullin. ''don't go so far ahead, I can't see you.''

No reply.

''Cull!''

Ecta stopped and listened, but all he could hear was the wind whistling through the rocks. ''Cull, where are you?''

Ecta had momentary feelings of panic as he realised he didn't know how to get back to the camp. He only had a rough idea where he was or where their camp was in relation to their current position.

''Cull!'

Where was he? Ecta thought about his options. Did he carry on and completely loose his position or possibly have a fall and break something. He could stay put wrapped up in his morcote.

''Cull!''

Still no answer.

''Ahh, cac!'' Ecta realised that his position was hopeless. He looked about for a suitably sheltered nook or cranny where he could hunker down for an uncomfortable night. Ecta spoke into the wind though he knew no one would hear him ''well Cull, I shall see you tomorrow, I hope.''

Ecta rummaged about in the morcotes deep pockets and found some venison sausage and a few oat biscuits. At least he wouldn't be hungry, lost, but not hungry, and the cold wouldn't bother him too much.

The weather got worse, the wind gaining force so that it was difficult to stand up in it. Snow turned to hail that stung exposed skin. A black freezing void was all Ecta could see beyond the confines of his rudimentary shelter. It was a swirling hell of bitter, freezing wind and hail into which only a fool would venture. Ecta pulled his morcotes hood further down, closed his eyes and tried to rest; tried to sleep whilst the storm raged about him.

At one point Ecta thought, he heard a soft thump nearby; it wasn't the crash of rocks, but of something soft and alien to this environment. He strained to listen, would it occur again? He began to doze, tired after a long and, stressful day. His head drooped and he yawned as sleep took hold of his mind and he fell under its blissful spell.

Crump.

His mind was confused, halfway between the waking and sleeping worlds, but he had heard that sound again. Was it in his mind? Was it real? Ecta didn't know. A part of his waking mind tried to listen; tried to fathom out this odd noise. His sleeping mind still had a powerful grip and added unreal details, the roar of Ferlas Mor, the spirit that roamed the mountains in search of souls to steal.

Ecta let his mind wander; musing on what creatures would live amongst the rocks and corries of these barren mountains. Was there a creature like Ferlas Mor that lived off things other than flesh and bone? He remembered an old poem he'd heard from a travelling wait who'd spent a few ten-days at Dunossin. He muttered the poem aloud, still half asleep, in a dreamland where the mind plays tricks; were reality becomes a dream and dreams are reality.

*Strange spirits abound this time of year*

*Of Rayanam season, beware*

*If you should dare to wander, near*

*Ferlas Mor's mountain lair*

*A primeval beast of Faery*

*Cast out by a righteous Queen*
*A warning for all to be wary*
*The depths of his dark soul she had seen*

*This Old Grey Man is natures' bane*
*By frozen Ice Moor lies his lair*
*Souls of the living his aim to gain*
*A poisoned mind, with madness there*

*Don't go out tonight*
*Stay warm and close by the fire*
*Ferlas Mor hungers this dismal night*
*Heed a warning should you tire*

*His hollow shade seeks life force*
*Black of heart and foul of breath*
*To take your soul is his course*
*This night creature seeking death*

*If you hear him tonight*
*He'll taste your fear*
*Stay close to the light*
*Pray for your life when he's near*

*For Ferlas Mor's icy mind preys*
*As he creeps down the glen*
*A tortured mind in bloodlust craze*
*To slaughter an unwary denizen*

*Blood on the ground*

*Shattered bone and shredded skin*

*Life and soul taken without sound*

*Dawns cleansing light reveals his sin*


Then he suddenly heard some scrabbling sounds a little below him. Again, Ecta strained his ears, but all he could hear was silence and the wind. He rubbed his eyes and tried to force himself awake.

Then he felt something land on top of him. It wasn't heavy, but he drew his hood back to look. There was nothing, but blackness about him. His half-asleep mind was confused and couldn't make sense of his surroundings. Ecta shook his head, stretched out his hand, and felt a cold smooth surface only a handbreadth from his face. His fuddled mind tried to recognise it, but the information came slowly, grudgingly. Plaz? Was that a sheet of Plaz?

Then he felt himself shaken roughly and came fully awake. ''Cull? Is that you?''

''Aye'' came a cheerful reply ''how do you expect me to find you if you hide behind the rocks?''

Wrapping the plaz sheet about him, Ecta looked in stupefaction at his friend. Then he laughed out loud with relief ''I thought I was in for a bitterly cold and miserable night. How did you find me? And in this weather too?''

''Ahh, well, you couldn't get to the camp, so I brought it to you.''

''What happened Cull? You were just ahead of and then you disappeared. I couldn't see you anymore.''

''I know, I thought you were just behind me, but then I couldn't see you anymore. You've found a good spot to bivvy though.''

Within a short space of time, the pair had set up their camp again and had a broth of dried pulses and venison sausage brewing.

The following day they woke early, it was still night, but they could see the distant glow of pre-dawn on the horizon. The air was still, freezing, but with no trace of the previous night's storm, just the occasional breath from a lazy breeze.

Cullin had leant his staff against the rocks and set it to emit a soft glow of light. As they busied themselves packing up camp Ecta stopped to look about him. A strange phenomenon, caused by the light from Cullin's staff struck him as beautiful, even mysterious.

''Aye, it's going to be a beautiful day, and we're off back home to Rustick More.''

''Aye,'' replied Ecta ''a beautiful day, but look!'' Ecta gestured vaguely at the air before him.

Not understanding Cullin looked about him, but saw nothing. He shrugged and returned to his packing.

''No, Cull, look! In the air, like stars in the night sky, but in the air!''

Cullin stopped and looked again. The air about them was full of fine ice crystals that floated gently in the lazy air currents. Tiny pinpoints of light that made the very air about them sparkle with ethereal splendour.

''Oh, wow, Ecta that is amazing. I've never seen anything like that before!'' A broad, cheerful smile lit up Cullin's face ''it is beautiful isn't it?''

''Aye.''

''Ecta, I've never realised it before, but you have the soul of a bard, like that poem you recited last night. Sorry, I couldn't help listening.''

''Aye, I love those old tales; there's so much humanity in them. They're wonderful.''

''Hmm, true. I've done the packing, shall we get off this hill?''

''Aye, we shall, I miss home.''

186

# Chapter Thirteen

Keem, a lean, slightly built athletic redhead with many years of experience within the resistance, led her small team of three aneksa in two bark canoes towards Dundoon's harbour under cover of darkness. They carried no weapons, as they believed that harm to any divines would bring reprisals against the local population. Their paddles made barely a sound as they neared the harbour in a slow deliberate manner. Lights ahead shone brightly, illuminating the harbour with barely a shadow. A bend in the harbour wall caused a large enough shadow that one member of the raiding group could use to hide the canoes whilst the remaining two carried out the raid.

Recent expansion of aneksa activities had caused a severe shortage of resources including metals and technological components needed to continue weapon and equipment development. The aneksa constructed the majority of their weapons and equipment using ancient technologies; technologies that included wood, natural substances and whatever they could manufacture with their limited resources. More sophisticated weapons required the use of stolen technological parts that were in short supply, hence the need for this raid.

Keem assumed the raid had been with the full knowledge of the leadership at Rustick More because they had never allowed such raids before. She shook her head putting such thoughts behind her as she focused her blue eyes on the harbour. Get in and get out quickly, before the divines knew what was happening.

Dundoon was not a large town though it had a large divine complex appended to the harbour. Its location made it useful to the Frame as a storage facility for raw resources that arrived from other islands. Muckers conducted their administration from a wooden Great Hall just outside the town walls. Muckers themselves tended to be scattered, building their small farms and crofts so that they had protection from the weather by natural topography. Dundoon lay in a valley between broad rounded hills that lacked pride or grandeur. Further south of Dundoon's range of hills lay broad grassy plains with a few small hills breaking the horizontal monotony of the landscape.

The canoes slipped quietly into the harbour towards the deserted quay. The divines felt secure in their superiority and were complacent. The few muckers in the area were no threat to them and caused no trouble, so the divines felt no need for much in the way of security. Keem turned the canoes and headed for the shadows.

They remained silent, speaking no words, as they slid up against the harbour wall. Keem and the youngest of the three raiders, Isla, slipped up a flight of stone steps onto the harbour wall and headed for the quay. Their target lay just beyond; the large steel and plaz warehouses filled with the resource materials the aneksa desperately needed.

They used a small side entrance to the warehouse that was unlocked. Keem couldn't believe their luck; the fat, lazy divines of Dundoon didn't bother to secure their valuables against theft! Idiots!

Inside were rows shelving stacked with containers of different sizes and shapes. They soon find useful devices, and loaded leather backpacks with computer hardware. They ignored bulky items, but chose small items difficult for them to manufacture, but essential if the aneksa were to build on their technology and fight effectively against the Frame.

Both women were nervous and fearful of discovery, fighting a feeling of nakedness, of unseen eyes watching their every move. They wanted to scream, to run, and to find safety back in the shadows. Keem ignored her nervous tension with a struggle focusing on their search for useful items.

They had soon filled three of their four backpacks, with which Keem sent Isla took back to the canoes with whispered instructions not to wait for her. Keem would follow shortly.

She found a container of motherboards and swiftly loaded her sack and made her way back to the side entrance. A shadow stood in the doorway. A divine.

''Halt! Do not move!'' A shout broke the fragile silence.

The divine levelled his staff at Keem's chest and fired. Searing pain stunned Keem as the blast threw her off her feet. Her muscles

189

twitched as she gasped for breath. The divine stood over her, smiling coldly, with his staff pointing at her heart.

---

Keem woke to pain; pain from the cuts and bruises delivered by the beatings the divines had given her. How many times had she woken and lost consciousness again from the beatings administered by the divines? She had lost count. Her mind was a fog, she could not think clearly. A feeling of panic threatened to overwhelm her; she knew she was in a desperate situation.

Bright lights burned her eyes when she opened them causing them to water profusely. They had her strapped into a chair, bound with over tightened plaz cords that cut off blood supply to her hands and feet. Would they care if caused her more injuries? Keem thought not; they seemed to enjoy her pain, relishing in her suffering.

Questions, endless repeated questions, over and over again, without end. Who was she? Where was she from? Why was she stealing from them? What did she know about a resistance movement? Who were their leaders? Where were their bases? Who was she? On and on they went, breaking down her defences little by little.

Keem wanted to die, to end the pain. The torment would be over then. The divines wouldn't let her die; they wanted information. Who was she? Where were the resistance bases?

The fat one sat in front of her now, silhouetted against the bright lights. The questions would start again soon. Who was she? Why was she stealing? What was her name? Surely, she could answer that. They would make the pain go away if only she answered a few simple questions. Who was she? What was her name?

---

Yaren picked at his food without appetite or enjoyment. Pickled vegetables and salted venison were standard fare for the time of year. There was little fresh food available, but with spring approaching, everyone was looking forward to fresh greens. He took a bite from a dried apple ring and glanced at Ulbin.

''How soon will we be getting fresh food again?''

''Well, we still have turnips and onions in the ground and good food stores. I understand though, that fresh vegetables are still a couple of tendays away. It's the frost of course, but our diet should brighten up a bit fairly soon.'' Ulbin was not a man to worry too much, personally, about such things. He ate to live and ate in big quantities when he could. The finer qualities, textures and subtleties of the food he ate went unnoticed by Ulbin.

They sat in a shelter made to resemble a mound lying on the edge of the clearing the aneksa used for a headquarters. Duncan, a young lieutenant who showed much promise entered the shelter with a sheet of paper in his hand. Yaren frowned at the paper as he usually received reports verbally. Paper was difficult and time consuming to make and always in short supply.

Yaren read the report with care as he always did with written reports. One of the aneksa cells, against standing orders, had attacked Dundoon. Such foolhardy attacks revealed their presence on Ardbanacker to the divines and the Frame. He thought he had made this point clear to his officers. It now appeared that he had failed in this respect and would now have to deal with the inevitable problems that would arise. There would be a rise in scouting drones, investigations, questions asked of Mark Lords and a tighter grip on mucker activity.

The report continued to list the components brought back from the raid. They were useful, very useful in fact, something that went a little way to alleviating his annoyance at the raid. He read on through details of how the raid had been organised. Yaren was surprised at how easily they had avoided security.

Then the report went on to detail Keem's capture. Yaren's heart skipped a beat. Keem? They'd captured Keem! Divines held his daughter captive!

Cold shock struck Yaren, his only child would probably lose her life at the hands of the divines. His hands were shaking as he stared at that last paragraph of the report. He slid the sheet of paper over to Ulbin who was looking at him quizzically, without saying a word.

Ulbin glanced at Yaren after reading the report ''what do you want to do?''

''I don't know, they all knew the risks of course, but there is a problem.''

''Oh?''

''Keem, the one who was captured knows who I am.''

''What? How would she know that?'' Ulbin demanded.

''She's my daughter!'' There, one of Yaren's closest personal secrets was out.

''Daughter? You don't have any children Yaren; how can she be your daughter''

''I had had an affair and Keem was the result. The family have been keeping quiet about her ever since.''

''How much does she know, Yaren? How much could she tell the divines?''

Yaren looked troubled ''I don't know. I tell her as little as possible of course, but she is bright. She may well know more than I think.''

''Is she likely to know anything about our numbers and base locations, weapons capabilities?''

''She is well trained in weapons and she certainly will have a good idea of our strengths. If she talks, she could cause a great deal of trouble for our operations.'' Yaren was silent; his brow furrowed as he thought hard for a few moments and glanced up at Duncan who was waiting patiently for further orders. ''Duncan, can you bring us whatever maps and plans we have available for the Dundoon area, then I'll need an up to date breakdown of our current weapons stocks.''

''Yes, Sir.'' Duncan dipped his head slightly as an informal salute and left to perform his duties. At well over two paces in height and broad chested, Duncan was an intimidating man with short-cropped black hair. Broad, strong features, a prominent brow, and an intense stare did nothing to dispel his demeanour.

''You arse Yaren!'' Ulbin glared at Yaren. ''You're not thinking of a rescue are you?''

Yaren chose his words carefully ''it's an option, certainly. We need to talk about all our options. We can't let her talk and I will not abandon her to the divines.''

''Cac!'' Ulbin bunched his fists in an attempt to control his temper. ''If you attack that town again you'll cause even more harm. Dookerock will rip your guts out and use them to string you up on the nearest tree!''

''Don't threaten me Ulbin! We need to discuss this.''

''You're talking cowshit Yaren. I can see what you're thinking. If you go in there with gunna blazing, I'll rip your guts out myself and present them on a platter when Dook howls for your blood!''

Ulbin pushed himself back in his chair furiously staring back at Yaren.

''I understand that Ulbin.'' Yaren regained his composure with difficulty; withstanding a verbal assault from a physically daunting man like Ulbin was never easy. ''If it was the only option available, would you consider it?''

Silence, broken only by the sound of the wind beyond the door answered the question.

''We need to act quickly Ulbin.''

Sensing a trap Ulbin coughed and thought. ''If it was the very last option, the very, very last option, perhaps.''

''Perhaps?''

Another cough ''I guess I would consider it if there was no other option.''

''Well, let's look at those other options then.''

''Aye, let's look at the other options.'' Ulbin was dissatisfied, he felt defeated, but failed to see where he had lost the argument.

---

The last session had been a living nightmare for Keem. ''It's not your fault that you were caught, just tell us your name and we can stop the pain.''

Pain, she hurt everywhere. She wanted to escape from the torment and ignored their pleas to talk, to express her name. They lied she was certain. If she uttered one word, they would demand another, then another and then she wouldn't be able to stop telling then everything she knew.

She withdrew inside herself, hiding in memories, places they couldn't go or find her. Not one word would she utter, or she would be lost.

She remembered her Mother and her childhood; collecting shellfish for supper.

---

Ulbin was at a loss. He wasn't quite sure how he had done it, but Yaren had convinced him that a rescue was the only viable option. He had realised that he had little understanding of military strategy sometime during their discussions. Every proposal he put forward was greeted with a variant of 'you can't do that because –'.

Yaren had proposed a distraction whilst a separate raid extracted Keem. If the raid came from the sea, then the divines would have no idea of where the raid came from. In addition, if the raid appeared to be a follow up from the previous raid then it would downgrade Keem's apparent importance to the resistance. Confusion was the key, keeping the divines guessing.

The plan was to make a larger scale attack on the quay, breaking into more of Dundoons industrial units. Once the distraction was underway, a stealth unit would scale the perimeter wall, extracting Keem and leaving the divines none the wiser as to the means of her escape.

The plans of Dundoon Duncan had brought were old. Isla's debriefing report had added few details about the town. As a result, the stealth unit would have to split up to locate Keem causing an unavoidable delay in her extraction.

Ulbin wondered if they'd made the right choices as he watched a company of one hundred strong set out on the march to Dundoon. They had a rendezvous down the coast from Dundoon where they would embark on fishing boats for the raid into the harbour.

---

Keem was sitting on a rock with a very scruffy Terran, her little white terrier. Terran wasn't very old and was still very excitable. She'd been playing in the rock pools near the croft trying to catch crabs that always seemed a little too fast for her little fingers.

The sun had come out from behind large fluffy clouds, warming her back as she idly watched the wave's crash against the rocks. Out on the rocky islands she could see the seals lazing in the warm sunshine.

Overhead the gulls cavorted with cacophonous screeching, she didn't like them much, always so noisy and rude. Terran didn't like them much either. He was intently watching them now. In a moment, he would chase one. It was a hopeless task for the little dog, but Terran didn't seem to mind and it always made Keem laugh with delight as he splashed through the pools.

''Keem'' Mother called ''come in now.''

Keem sighed, called Terran and went indoors. Terran ignored her, intent on something he'd seen in a rock pool.

''wake up!'' A sharp insistent call this time.

Terran suddenly looked up at her and barked his high-pitched yap. Something was wrong, Keem didn't understand.

"WAKE UP!"

Suddenly there was pain from a rough smack. Bright lights burned her closed bleary eyes.

Terran was gone. The sea, her Mother, all gone. All she had was pain and them.

Keem was exhausted. When had she last slept? She couldn't remember. They wouldn't let her sleep.

"Your name, tell us your name."

They always started with that.

---

Five fishing boats carried the aneksa attack unit toward the Harbour. The setting sun cast a languid orange light as it dipped below distant mountains across the expanse of Marlok. Duncan led the attack from the bow of the lead boat, directing with hand signals. They entered the harbour swiftly without any resistance. A luckless divine standing on the quay, his mouth open with surprise, crumpled in pain as he received a blast from a short staff.

An aimu transport moored to the harbour wall with surprised divines staring at the fishing boats swarming into the harbour. A fire arrow fired from the nearest boat arced toward the transports central communication array. Several more followed, engulfing the array in flames as the attached plazboma exploded into fireballs.

Isla and her squad rushed along the quay towards the armoury that abutted the southern town wall where a defence was being organised. They needed pinning down. A divine with his staff levelled, emerged from the blockish armoury looking wildly about. Isla stunned him with a quick blast from her short staff. She guessed there were about four of five divines within the building.

The divines were reacting now, but too slowly and too late. Their shock and disbelief at the attack was palpable to the attackers who pressed home their advantage of surprise. Twitching stunned bodies lay on the quayside as the fighters burst into the town.

A few divines returned fire from the armoury. Isla's squad returned fire with arrows. Short staffs and gunna were still in very short supply so most of the aneksa still had traditional weapons.

"Grenade!" Isla ordered.

No response came from her squad. She turned, irritated, to them. "You" pointing at one randomly "I need grenades now!" The young man, Jonti, scuttled off, head down.

'You and you, find something to make a barricade."

All she could do for the moment was to keep the divines busy and hope they didn't use grenades or plazboma themselves. Just keep them off balance, she told herself. Don't give them time to think. Keep them busy.

Sporadic staff fire came from the door and windows of the armoury. "How many fire arrows do we have?"

"four each" came the reply "we need those for signalling."

"Keep two in reserve. I want four through that door and those windows right now."

"Sir."

The arrows arced through the air. Two skittered and bounced through the open door, one through the window and the last one caught a divine through the throat. Isla saw his clothing burst into flame as incendiary fluid spread over his clothes. She could hear his screams, high pitched and piercing, cutting through other sounds of battle.

A dull explosion boomed off to Isla's left somewhere above other screams and noise of battle. Where were those grenades? She fired off a round of staff fire every time she saw movement within the building, all the time imagining them opening boxes of explosives.

Isla checked the charge on the short staff and noted that a quarter of the charge had gone. 'So quickly' she thought 'they need to be better than that.' She glanced back, hoping to see Jonti returning with grenades, but there was no sign of him.

She turned her attention back to the armoury. The end of a staff had appeared in the window, pointing in their direction. ''Arrows on the window, NOW!'' she snapped and a volley flew followed by a blast from her short staff.

A burst of energy crackled blue fire from the window. The aim was poor, striking the roof of the warehouse that provided Isla's squad shelter and bringing down debris about them. She replied with another burst from her short staff.

After a pause, a longer, sustained discharge from the armoury struck the roof of the warehouse again. Steel and plaz showered about them forcing them against the warehouse wall. ''Ahh, for the love of Mozog! Where're those Grenades?''

In answer to her prayer, there was a scuffle of footsteps behind her. She glanced back and saw Jonti returning with another squad of aneksa, a broad grin on his face. He carried a small sack with him.

''Thought you could use a bit more help'' he quipped in greeting.

''Good man, Jonti.''

Isla faced the leader of the other squad ''I want to rush that armoury. Can you guys provide cover fire?''

''Aye, no problem there'' came the deep bass reply.

Isla shouted at her squad above the rising noise of the battle. She distributed grenades among them as she gave her orders. ''Two grenades, door and window. Then we go. Two more grenades inside, then we enter.''

''Aye, Sir'' they responded.

The two grenades flew towards their targets, missing slightly exploding away from the building. As the squad charged across the gap toward to armoury Isla sent blue fire from her short staff toward the window in a long continuous blaze. She screamed in rage as she ran ''truargan barsick, truargan barsick!''

Isla maintained her fire as two of the squad threw grenades through the window and door. A massive boom shook the building and

198

Isla charged through the door. The smoke filled annex inside was a mess, but Isla could make out three prone still figures on the floor.

A heavy door ahead marked the entrance to the main armoury beyond. Isla bolted for cover behind it and screamed to her comrades ''Grenades NOW!''

Two of the pebble-filled explosives bounced swiftly into the armoury followed by incendiaries and Isla threw her weight against the heavy door, slamming it shut and sealing the fate of the occupants.

She felt herself shaking, her back to the heavy door. She could hear dull booms, cracks and reports as small explosions started in the armoury. A louder eruption punched at the door, moving it despite its weight.

''Out, let's get out of here!'' She noted with grim satisfaction during the swift withdrawal that the bodies in the annex now had arrows protruding from them.

They raced back to the warehouse as the armoury shook with blasts and huge detonations from within. Suddenly there was one almighty thunderous roar as the armoury erupted in a massive conflagration of flame, noise and flying debris. Gouts of flame streamed from the building as it disintegrated, collapsing in on itself.

Isla starred in shock and awe as smaller eruptions continued. ''Holy Hesoos, what in Irin did they have in there?''

A touch on her shoulder followed by a coarse ''just be grateful it's not there anymore'' had her nodding in dumb agreement.

The sounds of battle were more distant now. Isla could see the security block not far ahead. There was activity by its doorway as a group of divines began a hasty exit, dragging a flaccid body with them. Keem.

As Isla's squad fired upon them, they dropped Keem's limp body and fled. Keem was barely conscious when they got to her, breathing shallowly and caked in blood and filth.

''Keem, Keem'' Isla urged a response from her. There was the barest flicker of the eyelids at the sound of her name. Isla cradled Keem's head protectively. ''We need to get her to the boats, now''

The leader of the second squad squatted down next to Isla and spoke gruffly ''Aye.''

He lifted her gently, Keem looking like a child in his massive arms. ''Grozet's the name'' grated the giant squad leader with surprising gentleness. ''Let's go then.''

A boat by the quayside had a number of injured on the deck; some still bearing arms, and ready to defend the boat at need. As Grozet laid Keem on the deck the boats skipper quickly looked her over.

''Ahh, by my barnacled arse, what a mess. Get her inside'' the skipper indicated the boats cabin with a tip of his head.

Moments later, he had the small, but highly manoeuvrable boat heading out of the harbour. Isla and Grozet's stood on the quay watching the boat depart. Grozet grated to Isla ''feel like bashing a few divine heads?''

''Good plan'' she nodded and headed back into Dundoon.

The aimu transport on the opposite side of the harbour now lay quiet with several aneksa standing guard or taking defensive positions. The dispirited crew were lined up on the quay under guard of menacing aneksa.

The two squads headed for the now somewhat muted sounds of battle coming from the Divine Generals Demesne and adjoining administration complex. A number of squads surrounded the buildings sending volleys of arrows towards the entrance.

A number of aneksa had edged closer to the entrance and lobbed grenades and incendiaries through the doorway. An eerie silence followed the booms of the explosions. Aneksa flooded into the complex and quelled the remaining, ineffectual resistance.

Shortly afterward aneksa escorted the Divine General roughly from the building. The Battle of Dundoon was over. A mocking cry rose from the victors. ''Truargan barsick, truargan barsick, die evil ones.''

# Chapter Fourteen

Yayler was tired after an evening of entertaining the people of Mark Brus. Mark Brus rarely had such visitors due to its remote location. He had arrived as Tyarly the Bard a few days earlier and quickly became popular in the Great Hall, which now heaved with people drinking and laughing.

''Tonight my friends is the 'Night of the Spirits' or 'Oyki na Spirad' in the true tongue. Tonight the wild spirits of Faery roam free in the world of men.''

Yayler took a mouthful of the local ale and then projected his voice above the general hubbub and noise of the Hall.

''The tale of the tempting of Agrin'' he began ''of Queensbane and the murder of the Prince of Faery.''

He struck a chord on his yayl followed by a run of plucked notes and the noise of the room settled down.

*''Haughty Agrin, full of pride*
*Sought the Prince of Faery*
*For to be his Bride*

*But angry was the Queen*
*Not for her son*
*Was the arrogant Agrin*

*Other suitors she created*
*From the beasts of Faery*
*Made fair and noble*

*First was Tuseek*

*Pious and true*

*Wise in the heart*


*Second was Dara*

*Handsome and brave*

*But not so very wise*


*Third was Tres*

*Clever, but weak*

*Shallow and base*


*Forth was Anak*

*Vain and callous*

*And selfish indeed*


*Tuseek saw her soul*

*But gave the Queen's enchantment*

*Then made his own way*


*Then Dara plied his troth*

*But little skill he knew*

*And Agrin's heart could not gain*


*Then Tres fared no better*

*Scorned for being frail*

*And Agrin's heart remained unbound*


*Anak, Agrin rejected also*

*In him saw a soul reflected*

*One that matched her own*

*Unbowed Anak chose trickery*
*And guised as the Faery Prince*
*He won the maidens heart*

*Nature blessed them with child*
*But Anak's heart was an empty vessel*
*And abandoned wife and child*

*So Agrin sought the Queen of Faery*
*Travelled to the 'source of three'*
*Where three mighty rivers rose*

*Agrin called on the Queen of Faery*
*For to ask her favour*
*For her love to find*

*''I cannot help you*
*For he is not my son''*
*The queen scorned Agrin's plea*

*To Dara and Tres Agrin returned*
*Telling of the Queen's falsehood*
*Enchanted they sought Agrin's revenge*

*Murdered was the Prince of Faery*
*Vowed vengeance did the Queen*
*Such was her mighty fury*

*On the 'night of the spirits'*
*At full moon with aurora bright*
*The Queen entered the world of men*

*Vain Agrin she found*
*And bound her soul*
*To an old rowan tree*

*Forever called the cursing tree*
*Forever was it groaning*
*And cursed fates bemoaning*

*A single blood stained white flower*
*Is all that would bear that tree*
*A flower forever named Queensbane''*

Later, after the entertainment was finished, Lord Brus was talking to Yayler. ''The divines don't bother us much here. The Divine General is a tenday away from here and the valleys are rough and difficult to travel through. Of course, we make sure they stay difficult to discourage the divines from coming here. We produce little for them. They'll check population records and collect what resources and produce we can spare and leave.''

''Hmm, I think there is much we can do for you.'' Yayler suggested ''we can provide metals, wood and food. Anything you need that will make your lives a bit easier.''

''As long as you can build your base up on Drimneev.'' Brus added. ''I don't want these people being militarised. That would be inevitable, I think, if you proceed with your plans.''

''Aye, I'm afraid it would, but conflict will come anyway, whether you're prepared for it or not.''

"It is quiet here, I don't anticipate any problems." Brus commented bluntly secure in the belief that the Marks isolation would protect it.

"I quite understand that, but let me tell you about some of the things I've seen recently. I'm afraid that the Frame is becoming more aggressive." Yayler went on to describe the farms now empty of people and run by machines. He described increasing reassignments of populations and increasing difficulties with divines. He backed himself up with reports he'd hacked from the Frames data bases on a compad. By the time he'd finished talking Brus was looking concerned.

"I had no idea these things were going on. How did you find out these things were happening?"

"I make it my job to find out. I am part of a group that is trying to build up strength to combat the Frame. If we don't succeed, I don't think our peoples will survive."

Brus took a deep breath. "You make a convincing case Tyarly, or should I call you Yayler?"

"Yayler is fine."

"Yayler, then. I need to think about this. I would want to see minimal impact on the Mark. There must be no apparent change or the divines may get wind of something happening." Brus gave Yayler a long steady look. He knew it would take time to build trust between them, but also knew that his options were limited.

I took Yayler several days to conclude his negotiations, but he got the agreement from Lord Brus that he wanted. Engineers from Rustick More would arrive and start the new base on Drimneev.

---

Pibeg gazed with profound shock at Pyta. "What in Garvamore are you doing?"

"Sewin' me dear." Pyta downed a large slug of whisky.

"You moronic numbwit, you can't sew!"

''Can, there'' he showed off his handiwork with drunken pride. He'd been embroidering new 'Runes of Office' down the sleeves of a new morcote.

Pibeg looked at the proffered work and scoffed. ''That is the worst stitching I have ever seen. The stitches are uneven and disproportioned. It's scruffy Pyta.''

Pyta bridled, shifting his weight on the old wooden chair that supported his slight weight. ''Yer a mean wifman Pibeg. Nuffin wrong wiv it. Me mam wer' a stitcher, did all the wuk fa the Lord.''

''I guess I'll soon be rid of you then and not before time either'' grunted Pibeg unimpressed. ''What's that rune, I don't know that one?''

The rune was course and clumsily formed, looking like a diagonal slash in a roughly realised rectangle. ''That's me job, recordin' data.''

''Oh, is that meant to be a feather?  It looks like I don't know what. I hope your data is scripted better, but knowing you, I doubt it!''

''Yer jus bein' a nasty fat blubberwitch Pibeg.''

''I may be fat Pyta, but I know you'll come to a bad end. Your sort always do.''

''Ha, so much yer know.'' Pyta returned to his whisky and embroidery. He was going places, he was important and the work he was doing for his boss would make his life so much better.

---

Ulbin thumped down the ships corridor with Yasga, the squad leader who had captured the aimu transport. ''Where is this machine? Can it still communicate?''

He was quite ignorant where the Frames machines were concerned having had little experience or education on them in his former life in Mark Ossin.

''It's just along here. We don't think it can communicate with the Frame because the array was destroyed in the attack. It is still active though'' replied Yasga.

207

''Ahh, let's make it de-active then. Where is this array?''

''Oh, on the deck above us'' Yasga thought a bit more explanation was needed. ''We hit the array with grenades and incendiaries. It's all delicate equipment, discs, aerials, spheroids and so on. It's completely destroyed. Ahh, here we are.''

Yasga showed Ulbin into a stark brightly lit room. Luminescence glowed from the walls and ceiling, creating an uncomfortable flat shadeless light. The rectangular block of the aimu sat one and a half paces high, enigmatic and silent against the back wall projecting at three-dimensional display into the centre of the room. A black, sloping panel sat on top. Otherwise, the room was bare of furnishings or equipment.

''There was a technician working on the machine when we got here. We have her held separately to the other divines. We thought she might be able to provide some useful intelligence about these machines.'' Yasga laughed a long burbling rumble of contempt for the captive forced through a vicious smile. ''I think she crapped herself when she saw us heathen muckers.''

Ulbin smiled in response as he stared at the aimu, not knowing what to do.

Yasga disturbed Ulbin's thoughts ''I have other duties I need to attend to. I'll leave you to sort this out then. If you need anything there's a guard outside the door.''

''Right, thank you. I think I can deal with this'' Ulbin replied.

As Yasga, left Ulbin waved an experimental hand through the display and watched his hand disappear. Snatching it back, he frowned. There was no response from the machine.

He tentatively tried again, more slowly this time and saw a virtual hand appear in the display that mimicked his movements.

''Ahh'' he exclaimed with delight.

Ulbin move his hand about experimentally, but nothing further happened. The thing was ignoring him!

"Hmm" he frowned again. Ulbin decided to ignore the display and walked directly through the display, causing it to shimmer briefly and stopped in front of the aimu. He prodded a stumpy finger at the black panel. Nothing, the machine remained stubbornly unresponsive.

"Oh, for Hesoos sake!" he exclaimed in exasperation and grabbed the aimu in a powerful bear hug.

Wrenching the solidly fixed aimu from side to side made the plaz structure protest, yielding to forces with snapping groans and creaks. Much encouraged by the sound of breaking struts and fixings Ulbin continued wresting it back and forth until he'd ripped the entire unit from the floor disgorging a confusing mass of cables, wires and conduits.

Studying the exposed contents gave Ulbin no better idea of how to deactivate the aimu. He chose a direct and simple solution and started to pull out important looking cables. Pulling hard on one cable produced quick results. The cable came free with a satisfying spray of sparks as circuits shorted out. The three dimensional display winked out.

Ulbin continued to work on cables in similar fashion, but found the largest and thickest cable resisted his efforts. He grunted and removed his knife from his belt, placed the cable flat on the floor and started to carve through the outer sheath with brutal determination. After a few moments, he exposed gleaming metal wires. Suddenly there was a crack and fountain of sparks flew into Ulbin's face. His hand jerked, gripping his knife harder as sparks continued to spray over him. He couldn't let go.

He jerked himself backward, forcing himself away from the aimu. His knife slid free from the cable and Ulbin landed with an unceremonious thump on his behind. He sat stupefied rubbing his hair vigorously, looking at the aimu that was quickly becoming his nemesis.

When he had recovered his composure, he returned to the machine and grabbed the cable with both hands. He pulled for all he was worth and he cable began to yield slowly, then it suddenly tore free with another shower of sparks. Ulbin found himself dumped on his backside again holding the free end of the cable as some kind of trophy.

"Ahh, ah hah, got you" he proclaimed in triumph.

209

Ulbin continued yanking and hacking at cables until he could find no more and announced to no one that he'd deactivated the aimu. The aimu lay on its side in defeat, dead to all intents and purposes.

---

Dona sat quietly on a small rocky island lying just off a small stony beach. The air was still and cold and scattered patches of snow still lay on the ground. It would be spring soon, she mused; life was threatening to burst forth, just waiting for the current cold snap to end. Dona looked forward in anticipation to the bright fresh greens and the bright vibrant colours of spring flowers.

She shivered; she disliked the cold and yearned to be back in her little hut warming herself by the fire sipping hot herbal tea. Dona glanced at the sun, bright in the clear blue sky. It was getting late she judged. The refugees should be here by now she thought. Two fishing boats lay off the shore waiting patiently to pick them up.

She stretched herself, stiff old joints protesting from the movement. Were they just late? They had never been late before, so why would they be late this time? The resistance were well organised and liked refugee movement completed efficiently. They wouldn't allow delays she decided. So something was wrong, something they couldn't control. Dona didn't like the situation; it felt dangerous. A feeling of disquiet settled over her as she thought about what she should do.

She glanced toward the trees noting the shadows and undergrowth beneath their branches.

''Damn'' she muttered to herself. ''I bet it'll be cold under there.''

With a decision made, she wasted no time and made her way gingerly across wet boulders, rocks and seaweed to the trees. Casting her eyes about, she searched for a suitable hideout. Snow made it difficult, if she disturbed any she would leave clues to her presence, but there, by that fallen alben, that looked promising. A bit more undergrowth would cover her tracks.

Dona made herself busy choosing her camouflage carefully and being wary of making footprints. She arranged her trigs and branches into the semblance of a bush, hunkered down beneath the trunk next to the vertical roots and settled down to wait. Her morcote kept most of the cold out, but warmth was elusive.

Where were those refugees? She was convinced now that there as a problem and determined to wait in chance of finding out what that problem was.

She waited, judging the time by the passage of the sun as it slanted across the sky. Soon, though she heard voices, low hushed tones that barely carried to her in the still afternoon air.

Dona shifted her position, silently cursing a foot that had gone to sleep and now irritated her with pins and needles. The voices were nearer, arguing. She could hear twigs and undergrowth crack under clumsy feet. Moments later two men stepped out of the trees onto the beach bearing staffs. Divines! A cold shiver ran through Dona; what, how had divines found them?

The divines in bright white plaz suits started searching the beach, making their way slowly from end to end.

Dona peered through a narrow slit between the albens trunk and the earth. She glanced quickly to where the boats should be waiting, but they were now distant specks on the still waters of Marlok. Looking back at the divines, she saw one of them hold up a device and scan the area.

''She's gone now'' the divine with the device reported 'there are no heat traces.''

''The fighting delayed us. We had them trapped, but still they decided to fight. Heathen fools that they are.''

''They killed Tatcher16, slit his throat with one of those blades they carry'' the first divine added.

''Tatch was an idiot, dying was the best thing he ever did!''

''We'd better go. There is nothing more we can do here.''

211

"Yes, let's go"

The divines departed, talking quietly, their voices fading into the distance. Dona remained in her hiding place, shocked and worried by the turn of events.

---

Dook and Yayler were reviewing reports and catching up on recent events. Yayler had just returned from Mark Brus.

Dook was chose a report from Robert the Red that he was unhappy with. An expanded Divine Hall at Bandrokit now housed an unknown number of hiu that now controlled divines activities. Aimu construction units were currently building a new complex, the purpose of which was still not known.

"Yayler, read this. What do you think? This came in a few days ago."

Yayler began reading through the report raising an eyebrow. "Interesting, this hasn't happened overnight. I wonder why this wasn't reported sooner."

"I agree. All the same, it suggests that the Frame is becoming more active in the area. I wonder if Red has been careful enough."

"How many refugees are left in those forests?" Yayler asked.

"Not many, a few hundred I think. They are being moved over the next few tendays. By Kerev, next month, they should be gone. Some are now active within the resistance group and will remain there."

"Good, It's taken a year to move them, that's long enough."

There was a disturbance at the door to the chamber. Grega stopped at the threshold, his old face looking more haggard than usual. Grega had decided to stay at Rustick More rather than move to the forests due to his advancing years. He found Dook difficult to work with and avoided him if possible, but he was happy enough.

"Come in Grega, what's the problem?"

Grega wasted no time getting to the point ''There's a woman here to see you. It's urgent.''

Dona stood behind Grega looking very tired and agitated.

''Oh, Yayler, they didn't come. The people, they didn't come.'' Dona just stood, her emotions taking over as tears began to course down her cheeks.

Yayler shot up from his seat and gave her a warm gentle embrace ''Come in Dona. Tell us what's happened. Take your time.''

Over the next wair, Dona recounted the story tearfully adding her own ideas and theories. Somebody had thoughtfully brought some food and refreshment, which she picked at without interest despite not having eaten since the events on the beach.

When she was finished, she leaned against Yayler for emotional support and closed her eyes. With surprising sensitivity, Yayler told her not to worry, that he would go and help Red sort out the problems with the Bandrokit resistance cell. The captured people might get rough treatment, but would not be harmed.

---

Yaren's report on the Dundoon raid had just arrived at Rustick More. Dook's hands trembled as a riotous mixture of emotions warred within him. He didn't understand how the man could have been so stupid. The fact that he had taken control of the town was nothing short of astonishing, but the repercussions were something he was loath to contemplate. He needed a clearer picture of the events.

How a lightly armed force had taken over well trained and armed divines needed detailed analysis and explanation and the sooner he started the job the better.

He headed down to the cavern, the workshop floor of Rustick More and found it almost deserted. Sara was the vast room's only occupant. She had her head down as she bent in concentration at her workstation. A short staff lay on the bench next to a tray of parts. Sara selected a small oblong strip with a flange at one end from the tray and delicately inserted the flange in a locating slot on the short staff. She was completely oblivious to Dook standing behind her.

''Where is everyone?'' Dook asked her.

''Oh, hello Dook.'' Sara looked up ''they're taking their downtime.''

''Ah, I need the flier. Is there anybody who can nav' or pilot it?''

Sara thought for a moment before replying. ''Only Fil, he's with his family on his break, but I don't think he's any flight experience.''

''I need someone to help me fly that thing.'' Dook indicated a flier parked nearby.

''I'll check the flight logs, hang on.'' It only took Sara a few sents to check the logs. ''Oh, he was only done simulations, no flights recorded. I've done more simulations myself and I can navigate a flier quite well.''

Dook compared their logs with delight. Sara frequently surprised people by doing the unexpected. This was a case in point. He had noticed that as soon as her confidence in technical equipment had grown, she had learned very quickly.

Rustick More only had one flier available through engineers were building more that would be ready in a few months. Technical problems had delayed the builds, but Dook was confident that future fliers would progress more quickly.

The only other operational flier was at Ecta's Ledge with many of the technical and engineering staff of Rustick More developing the new site. Thus, Rustick More was short of manpower with those that remained working long hours. Dook had insisted that they have a long break during the day as downtime so that they would have, at least some time with family.

Of the two hundred and fifty people at Rustick More, there were about twenty children of fourteen years or less at Rustick More. After fourteen, they had a combination of work and education.

Dook quizzed Sara on basic navigation and found that she could answer promptly and accurately without hesitation. ''Looks like you're going to get some practical experience to add to your log Sara.''

Sara grinned broadly, fluttering her eyelashes outrageously ''Ahh, Dook you're such a nice man!''

She took the navigators seat of the flier without hesitation, turned expectantly to Dook as he settled into the pilot's seat, and started the pre-flight checks. Green lights appeared on various displays confirming that each system was functional.

Fliers were a general purpose aircraft intended for transport. Short retractable legs extended from stumpy wings housing variable thrusters. The wing provided little lift, but had multiple control surfaces. The thrusters were an adaptation of a divine's staff's power source that Dook had designed many years previously. He had crafted his utility knife to test the technology much to Yayler's amusement and occasional joking.

Two large rounded canopies, above and below, formed the front of the flier. Sleek vertical control surfaces rose along the length of the blockish body.

''How's your night navigation Sara?''

''I've only done a couple of sim's, but I'll manage if I have to.''

''That's fine Sara; you know Cullin is a very lucky man to have you.''

Sara went a bit misty eyed when she thought about Cullin. ''Hmm, he's smart, clever and nice. I like that in him.''

''You're smart too Sara, very smart and you keep proving it to people. We'll have to get you some proper training.''

Somehow, Sara managed to keep her face straight as she replied. ''Ahh, thanks Dook, you're such an angel. Er, I'm all ready to go here, I just need a destination.''

''Oh, Dundoon, just tap the icon on the navmap.''

''I know how Dook.''

As the flier's legs left the ground, the nose bucked up, pointing at the ceiling of the cavern. Dook cursed and brought the nose back down with a heavy thump.

Startled Sara quipped ''you do know how to fly don't you Dook?''

Embarrassed Dook replied coolly ''Of course, I designed the controls. I just haven't flown it in a while.''

''Oh, good, but do you know how to fly?''

''Sara, please, I –'' irritated and rattled, Dook decided on a bit of face saving. ''I just had too much front elevation, that's all. I just need to make a few adjustments.''

''Oh? All right Dook.'' Sara managed to sound sweet and innocent, but not really convinced by Dook's explanation.

Dook lifted the flier again and made a ragged, bumpy course to the hangar doors.

''Smooth, Dook.'' Quipped Sara.

Dook muttered something unintelligible under his breath.

Sara became serious and professional the moment the flight was underway. ''Once clear of the hangar, steer course 115° and maintain an altitude of one hundred and fifty paces. Follow the valley for ten strides.''

''Thank you Sara'' pleased at the efficient tone Sara had adopted.

Their flight plan took them down a deep valley that broadened out into low hills and moors and a wide flood plain that flowed into Marvlok where Sara ordered a changed of course.

''Steer course 78° for twenty-five strides maintaining an altitude of fifty paces.''

''That's rather low Sara.''

''Aye, it is. I want to mask our flight as much as possible. Occasionally drones monitor the area for heat traces.''

Dook thought for a moment ''Good idea Sara, but it's more than occasionally. I'll drop the speed a bit to reduce our heat signature, but we're sure to be picked up somewhere along the route.''

The flier skipped along above the waves leaving a wake behind as the thrusters churned up the water. Another change of course took them down a narrow gorge that twisted, turned and had Dook cursing at the controls. Rocks and crags raced past the cockpit at alarming speed. He banked to avoid crashing into a rock face on a particularly sharp bend.

''Sure we don't want to go a little higher, it's a little tight in here?''

''Keep low Dook. Another stride and the gorge will open up and widen.''

''Fine, thank you.''

''Ahead you should see the Banklayv Mountains. Keep them to starboard and rise to three hundred paces. Most of the hills are below that height.''

The Banklayv Mountains were a small and relatively isolated group of peaks surrounded by low foothills that formed rolling moors. Deer, goats, wolves and other wildlife roamed the moors. The central peaks were a series of acute interlocking peaks and ridges. From a distance, the mountains had the appearance of pointed canine teeth in serried rows. The highest peaks still had a substantial winter blanket of snow that glinted in the sunlight, enhancing the appearance of teeth.

''Sara, wouldn't it have been easier to use a direct route?'' Dook asked.

''Oh, no Dook. Some of us have been plotting the flights of drones in our spare time. We've noticed a pattern.''

Dook thought about this and realised that few of the staff at Rustick More had any spare time. He suspected that Sara had done a lot of the work herself. The idea might have been hers in the first place.

''The drones'' continued Sara ''tend to fly a west to east pattern, so I'm keeping high ground west of our position. Turn to 180° just beyond those small peaks ahead.''

''Thank you, why haven't I heard of this, it's good intelligence?''

''We're still working on the details. There appears to be two drones over Ardyvinland during most of the day and they only come over Anklayv Island in the late afternoon. So I'm hoping that by following a convoluted route the topography will hide our signature. Take a new course of 210° after those pinnacles in the distance. That will take us across Marlok and then east of the Wicksills. We approach Dundoon from the east.''

The Wicksills were an extensive range of high moors and rounded hills. Flashes of green amongst the dark brown of winter vegetation were a sign of spring arriving to the hills. As Dook flew south, the hills gave way to broad grasslands and Sara directed Dook to Dundoon.

The landscape changed again to extensive dense forest with rocky outcrops with small lakes interspersed by small clearings. Streams and rivers cut through the forest as they tumbled and meandered their way to the sea. Finally the landscape changed again as they flew east to grasslands that extended across wide plains. Soon they could see Dundoon ahead.

Dook landed the flier by the wooden Great Hall. Dundoon was by far the largest town Sara had ever seen, appearing huge and uninviting. The town had a surrounding wall and set out with ugly block buildings in rigid rows. It was unnatural to Sara's eyes.

Dook left her in charge of the flier after thanking her for an 'interesting' flight. Yaren and Ulbin stood nearby, waiting for them and convened a meeting in the Great Hall so that Dook could debrief them. The Hall was almost entirely wooden with only the fireplaces and chimneys at either end built of stone. Heavy beams supported a vaulted roof where the little warmth provided by the fires became lost. Dook shivered, unimpressed by the building.

''So gentlemen, tell me why Dundoon was raided in the first place. Who authorised it and why wasn't I informed?'' Dook asked.

Yaren replied ''Keem was part of a new stealth unit. I'm still waiting on a full report on the planning details, but it seems that a young lieutenant overstepped himself and authorised the raid in an attempt to gain replacement parts for compads and other technology. Dook we are desperately short of such items and need parts urgently if we are to keep up with the expansion and training programmes you're putting in place. There is a lot of pressure to find shortcuts.''

''I understand that Yaren, but these programmes have to be accelerated. Did you know anything about the raid?''

Yaren replied with conviction and sincerity. ''Dook, no. I would have cancelled it if I had known. I'm sure we can source what we need through other means. There are always divines who can be duped.''

''Hmm, maybe. So why did you authorise this extraordinary rescue mission?''

''Because Keem could have divulged information about the aneksa, the resistance. I wanted her out of there to limit the amount of information she could reveal about our operations.''

''And revealed in doing so that we are strong enough to capture a fortified divine town.'' Dook added.

Yaren was uncomfortable; he knew his explanation was lame and unconvincing. ''I assessed the risks and thought they were worth taking.''

''Hmm. How much did Keem know?''

''Enough, she has a good idea of our numbers; she knew what weaponry we have available. She's more limited on our locations, but knows we are scattered throughout the forests –''

''In other words'' Dook cut in ''less than the attack on Dundoon revealed.''

Yaren knew that Dook was right; he also knew his reasoning sounded weak. Better judgement was expected of him. ''Keem is my daughter!''

Astonishment caused Dook to pause his questioning. He had known Yaren for many years and had never heard about any children. ''Yaren, you don't have a daughter. How can she be your daughter?''

Tears appeared in the corner of Yaren's eyes. He had difficulty breathing as emotion took the better of him. ''She's not my wife's child'' he started hesitantly. ''I had a dalliance with a young woman and Keem was the result. It's been a family secret for all of her life.''

Dook remained silent, giving Yaren time to compose himself. He knew Yaren had never been a man to exhibit his emotions, that this was a difficult revelation for him. Dook respected Yaren's candour and his feelings.

Dook spoke gently ''Ahh, for the love of Hesoos Yaren, you've kept this secret for all these years. That must have been hard.''

Tears still coursed down Yaren's cheeks as he spoke still shaking ''She's my only child Dook and I love her very much. What else was I supposed to do? What else could I have done? There wasn't time to think about following rules.''

''It's done now Yaren, we need to move on. We need to re-assess our plans. I want you to do that for me.''

Yaren nodded absently, his focus broken. ''I can do that. We have the ship of course.''

''Ship? What ship? I didn't see a report about a ship.''

Dook looked aghast at the wrecked aimu. He was keen to ensure that it had sent no communications before being prior to Ulbin's aggressive deactivation. He began by searching for backup power sources noting power cables wrenched from sockets. He shook his head in despair at Ulbin's 'direct' method.

This was not a sophisticated aimu requiring little communication ability. It navigated the ship and operated the equipment aboard.

Instructions for the divine crew came from the Interface, the computer system that coordinated human affairs with the Frame. This aimu had functional design only.

Ulbin's attentions to the machine had loosened a faceplate that came away easily and revealed drives and circuit boards and a backup power source, which Dook quickly reconnected. The aimu emitted a series of beeps, but otherwise remained inert. After a few more cables had been, reconnected Dook was rewarded with the black screen flickering into life.

''Ahh, it lives!'' Dook was delighted and was soon searching through history files, memory dumps and other data. He found the aimu reduced to basic functions only, higher functions including its artificial intelligence programs remained inoperable. This suited Dook perfectly as he only wanted to find out what jobs the aimu had performed prior to and up until deactivation.

Searching through endless files was a tedious task, but Dook eventually satisfied himself that the aimu had sent no communications. Happy that the Frame would remain ignorant of the attack for some time Dook had a couple of aneksa take the aimu to the flier. The machine could be studied in detail back at Rustick More.

Back at the Great Hall Lord Kissom wrapped in a heavy morcote and mane sat in conversation with Ulbin and Yaren. He was a small elderly man with a shock of white hair and spoke in hesitant slow sentences that belied a keen intelligence.

A large wooden table now stood in the centre of the hall, scattered with maps and reports. Dook joined them and spent the next wair deep in discussions.

''Gentleman'' he started ''there is much to talk about and decide. I'd like to know your thoughts on the current situation.''

Kissom coughed a rasping sickly cough that suggested serious ill health. ''Dookerock, I know you expect to take charge here, but this is not your Mark. I have administrated this Mark for a very long time and I know my people and I will remain in charge.''

Dook nodded ''Good, that is as it should be.''

Kissom smiled in response before replying. ''We thought Ulbin superfluous here. He should be back performing his normal duties.''

It was Dook's turn to smile ''I agree, he is needed to maintain supply lines and logistics.''

As talk and negotiations progressed, it became apparent that Kissom was annoyed about the current situation. The thought of repercussions worried him. He did not believe that the Frame would leave them alone. There would be reprisals.

By the end of their talks, they had decided that Yaren would remain at Dundoon to improve the town's defences. A force of aneksa would garrison the town.

Tuaport became a major subject of discussion. Tuaport was a purely divine town in a large natural harbour. Its function for the Frame was one of warehousing and storage of resources from the northern islands and eastern Ardyvinland. The town was almost defenceless having only a perimeter fence. Even so, it now represented a major threat to the aneksa as a focus for a counter attack from the Frame.

Retreating back into the forest was a poor option that would lead to eventual defeat. Therefore, Tuaport had to be taken as soon as possible, while the divines were still in a state of confusion. The aneksa needed to hold what they had gained.

# Chapter Fifteen

Garvin didn't impress Pyta. Perhaps that was because he was tired and wanted a drink. It had taken him nine days to reach the village from Pibeg's hut. The fishing village spread out along a single rutted and pot-holed track by the shore with some buildings nestled in sheltered spots behind them. The grey wooden buildings that predominated had long seen their best days; many had rotten boards or wood split with age. The few stone buildings also showed signs of neglect. 'Garvin is falling apart' thought Pyta.

The people of Garvin lived off the twenty stride sea inlet they called Lokru. Small boats lay dotted about on the water, but Pyta had no interest in such things. He was looking for the ''house'' ran by his new landlady, a young widow called Linn. The Boss, who would arrive later, had assured him that Linn would be more amenable and less shrew-like than Pibeg. Since her husband had drowned in a freak fishing accident Linn had run the house, brewing ale to make ends meet.

A small scruffy white haired dog charged down the track toward Pyta yapping madly with enthusiasm. 'Terrors' he thought the type of dog called, used in some types of hunting. The dog growled and nipped at his ankle, but he shoved it away roughly with his boot. It seemed unbothered and followed him closely with tongue lolling out as he continued up the track.

There was a larger building ahead with a faded and split wooden sign, now illegible with age, creaking in the breeze. As he entered, the dog followed and settled down in a corner. The room was comfortable with stout wooden tables and chairs, some of which even had cushions. A few old men sat around a table playing tiles looked up with curiosity and a hint of suspicion.

Pyta looked about the room, but could see no bar or service hatch of any kind, so after a lengthy pause he spoke to the old folk who were now busy at their game again.

''Linn abaht?''

The old folk gave him odd looks. One of them shrugged.

Pyta tried again ''Linn?''

''Aye'' replied the white haired old man who had shrugged and then returned his attention to his game.

Pyta gave up with the old men and sat down on a cushioned chair by the room's only window. 'Fings 'appen slow 'ere' he thought.

After a while, one of the old folk got up, crossed the room to a table standing behind the door, and rang the bell sitting on it. A few moments later an attractive young woman entered the room, glanced briefly at Pyta and spoke to the old folks.

''Same again gents?''

''Aye'' came the brief reply from the white haired man who unexpectedly laughed and slapped a tile on the table and put it in position. The other two leant forward to inspect the move and redoubled their concentration on the game.

''I'll be back in a moment'' the young woman said to Pyta as she left the room. She returned with three foaming mugs of ale ''you must be Pyta?'' she queried.

''It is.''

''Good, come this way, I see you met Kurra'' she indicated the dog which now followed them.

Linn's home was a pleasant place with a separate lounge with comfortable chairs that Pyta was 'welcome to use'. A number of bedchambers were at the rear of the house. Pyta had the smallest of them for himself he noted, but it had a good solid sleeping pallet rather than a mat. He also had a chair and table for his 'writing' and a few wooden pegs on the door for his clothes.

''Yer gotta nice place'' commented Pyta.

''Aye, the Boss has been good to me since my husband died. I don't know how I would have managed without his help.''

''E's a gud un fer sure.''

"I'll serve your food back here Pyta." Linn took Pyta through to the kitchen. It was quite a large room that Linn also used for dining. There was an adjoining larder well stocked with preserved foods and a number of ale barrels ready for tapping.

"Help yourself to the ale; it's not too strong or bitter, but I get compliments on its flavour."

"Ah'll do that me duk."

Linn ignored the familiarity "the Boss is bringing some hams and venison later; beef too. I sell it in the village for a few tokens."

"Gud plan that. Gotta mek a few tokens when yer can."

Pyta proved true to his word and wasted no time in helping himself to Linn's ale and by the time the Boss arrived some wairs later, he had consumed a substantial amount. Pyta had taken a comfortable chair outside the front of the 'house' to enjoy the bright spring sunshine and watch the people of Garvin wander about their daily activities.

Suddenly Kurra bolted out of the door and chased up the track yapping excitedly. The dog came back following a cart and horse driven by a lean redheaded man.

"Wukin' already Pyta?" The Boss commented from the seat of the cart.

"Ah am."

"Gud, tek this in ta Linn." The Boss indicated a haunch of venison to Pyta.

Pyta took the meat into the kitchen returning with a fresh mug of ale. If the Boss noticed that Pyta didn't help much with the unloading, he didn't comment. The two conversed in their peculiar, coarse accent whilst the Boss did most of the unloading.

When finished the Boss gave Pyta a small compad. "Use this ta mek yer reports. Jus spik inta it 'ere an' it'll send a report daily via da over'ead drones."

"Ah ken do that."

225

''Ah'll need ta know 'bout all da traffic 'tween 'ere an' Tymeum. Wot people luk like an' wot they transport.''

''Yer wan' stuff on boats an' all?''

''Ya, that'll be gud.'' The Boss kept instruction as simple as he could for Pyta, never giving him complications.

Linn joined them after all the food had been stored. ''Will you be eating before you go Boss?''

''Na, Ah be stayin' in Innish, ah'll eat there.'' The Boss wasted no time and climbed back onto the cart. Noting another full mug in Pyta's fist, he spoke to Linn. ''Ah'll bring mur malted barley nex' time.''

''Aye, good idea.'' She replied.

---

Isla sat with her squad relaxing and eating an early breakfast. A glow on the horizon showed the first hints of dawn. About them, the detritus of battle lay scattered about. Smoke rose from the divine Generals demesne, which had been the only real point of resistance during the battle. Most of the divines had been asleep with only token security around the quay and administration buildings.

Lieutenant Cam was not a happy man despite taking control of the town so easily. His orders were to hold Tuaport, but he found that the town was virtually un-defendable. Dookerock had stressed to him that they were playing for time so that they could devise new strategies. Time, it seemed, was in short supply.

Tuaport had about a stride of perimeter fencing and nothing else. With only a hundred aneksa to provide defence, he would only be able to defend a small area. The harbour and the quay were the most important areas of the town that he could defend if they had some earthworks. The captured divines would have to do the work.

Cam headed over to where he could see Isla sitting. ''I have a job for you Isla. I want you to get a group of divines and use them to start

226

building earthworks and a ditch.'' He sketched out the plan in the dirt on the ground.

Isla nodded ''Aye, It'll take a while, depending on how high you want the earthworks. How many guards can I use?''

''No more than twenty.'' Cam left Isla to get on with the job while he looked for someone to inventory warehouse stocks for items useful for defence.

Isla turned to her squad grinning with a hint of malice. ''Well, this day just keeps getting better! Now get to see divines to do something useful!''

---

Much of the snow had melted from the summit plateau of Rustick More, revealing the browns of dead vegetation. Here and there bright greens hinted at fresh new growth of spring. Snow patches remained in dips, gullies and sheltered spots.

Cullin was practising with his sling, finding his aim still good. He'd had the idea of turning slinger stones into small grenades and was working on the casing. He was using creet because he could produce a consistent case with a known thickness.

He wanted to get the thickness of the casing right. He was trying to find the best compromise between strength and fracture on impact. He had settled on a knobbed design that broke into pieces well. The 'grenades' contained a powerful explosive that, after priming, would ignite on exposure to the air.

A large boulder with a roughly flat vertical face had a target scratched onto it. Sara had contrived to be with him though she was supposed to have other duties. She claimed that it was so that she could keep score for him and record the data. Cullin wasn't convinced, believing that she just wanted a bit of downtime with him. He certainly wasn't going to complain.

He selected a new box of trial 'stones'. ''Thick, grade one'' he announced.

Sara giggled "Aye, boss."

As he let the first stone fly, he felt a nudge behind his knee. The stone sailed wide of the target and disappeared over the edge of Rustick More. He glared at Sara, who feigned innocence.

The next stone shared the same fate and Sara still pretended innocence. Cullin tried again, but palmed an extra couple of stones he then held in his left hand. The first stone missed again, but the second and third flew true in quick succession. Both hit the target dead centre.

"Hey, not fair!" exclaimed a pouting Sara.

Cullin grinned at her "moderate shatter I think. Shall we get this done, then we can have more time to relax?"

"And waste the afternoon sun lounging?"

Cullin shrugged without enthusiasm "I guess"

"Oh, how dull." Sara sounded profoundly disappointed.

"Well, unless you have better ideas?" Cullin added lamely.

Sara giggled again, grinning mischievously "of course I have better ideas."

Later that evening Cullin found himself in a philosophical mood. The recent events at Dundoon and then Tuaport had made him think, about not only his own future, but also the future of Garvamore and its people. He had realised for a long time that Yayler had been grooming him and training him in different skills needed in the fight against the Frame. He was part of the process of developing the means to fight back.

'Am I just a tool then?' he thought to himself, considering the idea carefully before concluding 'no, I'm not a tool, I am a person. We strive so that people can be themselves both as part of society and as individuals.'

The implications of his conclusion set his mind racing. 'Thus we all should have the freedom to make our own choices. I am a man and I am free to do so as should all people be.'

What choices did Sara have in her life as a slave? He glanced at her slim back as she sat quietly at the desk in their chamber working on a compad. Though she didn't talk much about that part of her life, Cullin knew her choices had been very limited. Essentially her life was reduced to 'do as you are told or not and suffer the consequences'. Yet she had an extraordinary focus and desire to defeat the Frame. Something within her character had disavowed the requirement to obey without thought.

As if by some sixth sense Sara knew Cullin was thinking about her. ''You're very quiet.'' She queried.

''Aye, I was just thinking how beautiful you are.''

''Liar'' she accused, but smiled as she joined on the bed and cuddling up to him. She kissed him gently on the cheek and rested her head on his shoulder.

Cullin laughed softly ''guilty, but you are beautiful''.

Sara rewarded him with another kiss.

The following morning Cullin was working on his compad, digging into the Frames data files, snooping as Yayler called it. He'd found a reference to 'The Interface' from a file on the captured aimu and didn't know what it was. It wasn't just an interface, but 'The Interface' and something greatly more important. He wanted to find out how important and what it did.

After two wairs he'd found several more references to The Interface and all references were associated with divines. He wondered if disrupting the function of this Interface would damage communications between the Frame and the divines. He needed to discuss the idea with Yayler and collated the material he'd found.

Yayler was chatting with Dook in Dook's eternally messy quarters. A large wooden shield and parts of a short staff sat on the table on top of piles papers left in disarray. ''Come in Cullin.''

Dook was speaking quietly lounging in a chair and a half finished ale in his hand. ''Well, as you know I don't believe in laws or rules as such. They only exist to control populations.''

"Yet without rules there would be chaos."

Dook shook his head "but if Yaren had obeyed the rules, we wouldn't now be in control of Ardbanacker Island. We have real territory for the first time. Of course, the Frame will want it back, we know that, but we have gained many resources in the process. We are now in a much stronger position now because Yaren broke the rules."

Yayler was profoundly sceptical of Dook's theory "but without those rules people would do as they please without fear of repercussions."

Cullin commented "Sara wouldn't be here if she had followed rules and orders."

"Precisely, Sara is another example of what I'm saying." Dook continued his argument "we teach children the difference between good and bad behaviour by rewarding the good with love and attention and withdrawing that attention in response to bad behaviour. Thus, good or positive behaviour is encouraged from an early age."

"Yet, there are still those who grow up to become anti-social." Yayler argued.

"True, but they do so, often, despite good parenting. It is the nature of chaos. No matter how you control a system, new patterns of behaviour will emerge." Dook continued.

Yayler looked irritated by this argument and shook his head in despair. "You can't just accept that negative things will happen. There has to be some form of control."

Dook smiled as if he'd won some point in the debate. "Of course not, but there is control, something I call the 'philosophy of consequence.' "

Yayler buried his head in his hands. He didn't have time for this. They were supposed to be discussing their plans for the future, but Dook had headed off on a tangent. "I never had you as a 'great thinker' Dook. Intelligent, yes very, but not one of history's great thinkers."

''Well, it's an easy enough theory. There is really only one rule and that is that every action has its consequence. It causes an effect. Of course, it's not possible to know precisely what that effect might be.''

Yayler shrugged without commitment. ''That seems simple enough.''

''It therefore follows that rules and laws are artificial concepts made to counteract the negative consequences of peoples actions.'' Dook continued his arguments, enjoying Yayler's discomfort.

Dook thought for a moment. ''In real terms then, look at the Frames governance of humans. The laws the Frame enforced through the divines are not the laws that govern the universe; they can be changed. What is acceptable one day is can be unacceptable the next.''

''Well, that I can believe. I've witness it enough times.'' Yayler agreed.

''The Frame promotes the positive effects of its governance and laws through religious dogma and other propaganda. It hides or distorts negative effects and thus creates a false positive image of its effectiveness. The Frame wants us to believe that it is good for society as a whole.'' Dook added.

Yayler scratched his head ''great, so this whole conversation was just to demonstrate that you know how to lead people?''

Dook shrugged ''it's important to understand things. Did you want something Cull?''

Cullin, who had been waiting patiently, nodded. ''What can you tell me about 'The Interface'?''

Dook looked blank ''what's The Interface?''

Yayler answered Cullin ''I thought you knew about interfaces. Essentially they are programs that translate data from one format to another and ---.''

''I know about those.'' Cullin cut in. ''No, I mean 'The Interface.''

Yayler was perplexed and gave Cullin a quizzical look.

Seeing that he was getting nowhere, Cullin continued. ''It appears to be a major software program, but separate from the Frame. It could be second in hierarchy only to the Frame itself.''

Yayler's eyebrows shot up in surprise. ''If that was the case, we would certainly know about it.''

''Here's the data.'' Cullin gave Yayler the collated data. ''It seems to prepare instructions and protocols for hiu, which are then used to instruct the divines.''

Dook studied Cullin's data and turned to Yayler. ''Looks as if the lad might be right. Just think what it would mean if we could disrupt communications and protocols, or even orders given to the divines. This is a very interesting discovery.''

Their discussions continued for over a wair before they decided that a great deal more needed learning about the Interface, before any attempt to disrupt its functions.

---

In the wake of the capture of the beach, party former refugees and resistance members were abandoning their forest dwellings. Fraze led a tired group that had strung out along the trail. The sun was low in the west, dipping below ridges and casting an orange hue to low dark clouds. He wanted to press on despite the lateness of the day.

They had travelled deep into the Dunban Mountains heading for a remote Mark. The rough trail twisted and turned through heather, rock and across streams as it rose toward Belak Doo. Their destination beyond the broad pass dominated by black peat hags heavy and sticky with snow melt.

Fraze had witnessed the capture of the refugees near the beach and narrowly avoided capture himself. He had been assisting an elderly couple who were struggling with the pace and had realised that they would not make the rendezvous in time. After taking care of their comfort he'd gone ahead to catch up with the main group and report that, he would be returning to base with the elderly couple. He'd virtually stumbled into the divines while they rested in a small clearing.

The party passed a number of shepherds' summer shiels. Each small shiel that provided shelter for a single person was constructed with a low stonewall base embedded with branches that formed a framework for the roof. Heather thatch roofed the shiels, which had roughly stitched rawhide to cover the entrance.

A booming voice barked from one of the shiels ''you're a bit late Fraze. It'll be dark by the time you get to the huts.''

A tall rangy figure ducked out of a shiel and greeted Fraze with a grin and powerful hug.

''Aye, Shanks. I don't suppose there's a couple of spare lanterns about are there?''

Fraze indicated a shiel with a nonchalant gesture ''Down on the left. I'll join you as I'm done for the day here.''

Fraze noted a few other keen eyed figures alert and scattered about sitting on hummocks or squatting in a shiel. ''Busy up here for the time of year Shanks''

''Aye, we keep a few men up here all the time now to lookout for visitors.''

Fraze grinned broadly ''like us you mean.''

''Nay, you were expected. I mean visitors of the unexpected and unwanted kind.''

''Ahh'' Fraze nodded with understanding.

''Mark Konzie spreads over most of the valley, down to Mark Glaskarn and the large lake you see in the distance. Red has been negotiating with the Mark Lord of Glaskarn to get them to join us. The more the better Red says. Here we are.'' Shanks said crouched into a shiel, flicking the hide aside and resting it on the thatch.

Inside the shiel was stacked with weapons, crossbows and short hunting bows. ''Expecting a war Shanks.''

''Aye, seems that way. We have other weapons in other shiels and in scattered locations about the Mark. Ahh, here we are.'' He said as he found a couple of lanterns.

''It might be a very short war fighting with this lot.'' Fraze was not impressed with what he saw. He knew the firepower the divines had available to them.

Shanks misunderstood Fraze's meaning and glanced at the group milling about. ''Aye, but we'll soon train them.''

''Nay, not them, the weapons. You can't fight divines and machines with bows and arrows.''

''That's true, I agree. Red tells us that we will be getting better weapons soon, ones that we can realistically fight with.''

Fraze shook his head ''I hope he knows what he is doing.''

''Aye, he tells us that good weapons are in very short supply.''

The party made reasonable time on the last leg of their journey, but it was still dark by the time they reached the huts. The roughly made wooden affairs were sound and weatherproof. Fraze got the impression that Mark Konzie was very poor in resources. Everything he had seen so far had the impression of making do.

They had not forgotten the comfort of the party and laid a rough wooden table with wooden platters and drinking vessels fashioned from deer antlers. Oatcakes and a smooth creamy cheese had been prepared for them. Jugs of fresh water and a bottle of pale whisky also sat on the table.

---

The Frame was getting confused reports about Ardbanacker. There had been no reports directly from Dundoon for over seven days and now Tuaport fail to produce reports. The Transport T-109-NT-A due to deliver calp, wood and minerals from Dundoon had failed to report also.

Data from drones suggested that muckers now ran the port town of Dundoon, but that couldn't be the case. Yet photographic data showed that there had been violence, explosions and fire in Dundoon suggestive of a violent takeover of the town.

Statistics, population behavioural studies and probability studies showed less than one in ten thousand chances of assaults or aggressive actions by muckers in any given year. Reports from its growing spy network among the muckers suggested that the resistance groups had become more sophisticated, but still employed primitive technology. The Frame was pleased with recent successes in this area.

Yet the Frame found that it was forced to conclude that uneducated, unintelligent muckers had done the impossible and conquered the town through military assault. The Frame needed more information and needed it fast.

The Frame had been monitoring Ardyvinland for several years, but had less information about Ardbanacker Island due the sparse population. Reintegration of the population of Ardyvinland proceeded at intended rates and the people put to good use.

The training of divines to counter resistant or insurgent groups went well. The North Temperate Zone A, of which Garvamore was a part, now had fifty thousand combat ready divines with newly designed weapons. Staffs, used primarily as a symbol of divine authority over muckers, were now easily carried hand weapons. New aimu combat units able to negotiate the difficult terrain of Garvamore were near completion.

A force of one thousand combat divines would be able to take control of the island again and the flow of resources restored. Thus, the Frame made plans for the retaking of Ardbanacker. Orders were drawn up, processed and issued. The Frames long-term plans for the muckers would proceed as intended.

---

Goram was working his home clearing, which was untidy from the long winter, but green shoots and spring growth were now showing.

He had cleared away dead material and was putting down a mulch of small twigs and heather sprigs as his guests arrived.

"I must say Goram, that was the best meal I've had in a long while." Cabar said round a mouthful of bread.

"Thank you, it's all grown here of course. I get meat from traps. Most of the food is taken for use elsewhere." Goram maintained several clearings, spending a few days at each.

The aneksa had devised a transportation system where a squad would travel down trails collecting produce every few days and return with any items required on the trip back up the trail. They then used wagons in more densely forested areas. Each clearing had its own collection point. The system worked, but was inefficient because they needed to keep the population in the forests hidden.

Such groups used the huts of people such as Goram for lodging. The current group were trainee troops heading for the aneksa headquarters.

"What was the meat in the stew?"

"Calman, they're not bright birds and are easy to catch. I thought about having a few chickens, but they would destroy the crops unless they were kept in a separate area."

Idle talk continued for a while. Goram produced a bottle of whisky after he'd cleared away the plates from their meal, bringing cheers from his guests.

"So where are you going to?" Goram asked.

"Headquarters then probably Tuaport, They're short of troops there."

Goram frowned darkly. He had heard about the attacks on Dundoon and Tuaport and failed to understand why. "Good luck then. I expect there'll be more fighting there."

Cabar made a face " who knows. We just go where we're told and do what we're told. The whys aren't usually explained."

Goram laughed ''perhaps they should be. After all these years hiding from the Frame and divines our leaders suddenly decide to reveal themselves with these attacks.''

''It was certainly a surprise, maybe they think they're ready to kick some divine arse.''

''It's brilliant. A few dead divines. The only good divine is a dead divine if you ask me.'' One of the other guests added.

Goram snorted ''Personally, I think it was reckless warmongering.''

''That's what we trained for. Give the high 'n' mighties a good beating'' Cabar sipped from one of Goram's antler horn mugs.

Goram realised that this group were not going to be receptive to his thoughts on the matter. They were in fact spoiling for a fight. He hoped for their sakes that it didn't come to that. Fighting and wars killed people; Goram believed that there was always a better way.

The talking went on until late becoming trivial, banal, but Goram was glad of the company.

# Chapter Sixteen

Anders39 watched as a thousand divines disembarked from the aimu transport ship anchored in the broad estuary below his position and set up camp on a grassy hill thirty strides south of Dundoon. An impressive amount of equipment now lay stacked by the shore, ready for loading into land transport aimu. Two hiu were with him, passive and silent, but no doubt recording everything.

A series of cliffs formed the coast both north and south of Dundoon and made landing an army difficult. The Frames analysis software had ruled out a direct assault and determined this river estuary as the best location for a landing. Beyond the estuary lay seemingly endless rolling plains and low hills, but few tracks that the army could use.

It would take two days to complete the march to Dundoon, by which time the aimu ship would lie off the harbour. Anders39 was confident that the fighting would be short and quick. Victory was certain.

---

The fishing boat tied up in Dundoons harbour, closely watched by a squad of aneksa. It was late, near dark and a very unusual time for a fishing boat to be making port. The skipper of the small boat shouted up to the troops. ''I need to talk to someone in charge.''

''What is the problem?'' came the reply.

''An army of divines has landed to the south of here.''

There was a pause while the group on the quay discussed this. ''You had better come up.''

Yaren greeted the skipper warmly ''thank you for reporting this quickly. Now, can you show me on the map where they have landed.''

The two men were soon deep in talks with his lieutenants who thought a direct assault would be suicide.

''We can't allow them to march without a challenge'' Yaren commented.

''A small force could attack their supply lines, that would at least slow them down while we get word to Rustick More'' Grozet suggested.

''Not a bad idea, how many troops would you need?''

''Oh, no more than twenty. We would have to travel fast and light. Hit and run with light weapons. Those short staffs would be ideal.''

Yaren thought for a moment before agreeing. ''Good, how soon can you be ready?''

''A couple of wairs, no more than that.''

''Good get going then, but no direct contact with that army'' Yaren instructed.

The following day, late in the afternoon Grozet's troops found a lone transport and manoeuvred to the northwest. Around twenty-five divines escorted dispersed separately about the transport, presenting only individual targets.

The attack was swift and brutal, concentrating on the escort first. The divines used the transport as cover as it lumbered on. Those unlucky enough to be too far away from the transport to use it for cover were despatched with short staff fire.

Grozet's company received return fire, hampered by the low sun to their backs. A young man to Grozet's left had the top of his head blown off by blue fire as it spewed from the defending divines.

''Grenades!'' shouted Grozet.

The grenades landed behind the transport cutting the divines to pieces. Still the transport lumbered on. Grozet pressed the attack on the transport, disabling it.

After forcing their way into the transports hold, they found food and heavy weapons. Taking what they could carry, they threw several grenades into the hold and withdrew. Fire and smoke erupted in gouts from the transport. After burying the dead Grozet marched his troops back north, the transport a burning wreck behind them.

---

''Hey, Dook, you know we really should have somewhere to test this stuff properly. I mean, isn't it risky testing energy weapons up here where the drones will see the heat trace?'' Cullin was strapping a wooden shield to his target boulder.

''Ahh, Sara tells me that at this time of day the drones will be over Ardyvinland. You are right though, we do need proper weapons testing facilities, but this will have to do for now.

''It's secure now Dook'' Cullin called out.

''Good, turn on the repulse shield.''

The repulse shield was two feet in diameter and constructed from seasoned oak. Thick rawhide leather glued with a mixture of ash, milk and Dook's best ale protected the wood. A metal boss and spike adorned its centre.

After the attacks on Dundoon and Tuaport, Dook had realised that the aneksa troops needed a defence against the divines' energy weapons. Many years earlier Dook had reverse engineered the technology of the divine staff and discovered that a force shield was possible. Once he had developed a practical shield, he installed it into Yayler's own staff. Now Dook took the idea a step further and installed into an ancient design of shield.

Cullin, who's strength belied his slender frame, complained to Dook ''does this thing have to be so heavy? It could prove to be a clumsy defence in battle.''

''Hmm, possibly, but imagine being hit by it.''

''Ahh, painful, broken bones or worse with that spike. I hadn't thought of it as an offensive weapon.''

Dook laughed ''Aye, it's easy to make too. The force shield is harder to make, of course, but that's an addition to the shield.''

''Shall we test it then?''

'''Aye.''

Dook took aim with the short staff and let loose a short burst of energy. Blue fire spewed from the weapon and struck the shield dead centre. The shield instantly glowed with iridescent blue light that extended beyond the diameter of the shield as the fire from the short staff sank and melded into the force shield.

''It seems different from the force shield on Yayler's staff, Dook.''

Dook looked pleased with the test.'' Aye, there have been a few developments since then. The unit itself only creates a very small field. Any energy that strikes the shield feeds back into the unit and powers the field. Thus, the more energy that strikes the force shield, the stronger the shield becomes.''

Cullin scratched his head ''I'm not sure I understand that. How does the energy feedback on itself?''

''Good question; the force unit produces two fields of energy. One positive and one negative. The result is a loop of force that radiates outward. When the energy from the staff strikes the force loop it follows the direction of the field. That energy then gets used to strengthen the field.''

''So how much energy can it absorb? There must be a maximum.''

Dook grinned ''Aye there is, this one would take about five times the maximum output from a staff. I'd like it higher, but time is short. Troops need them as soon as possible.''

Cullin nodded ''should put some on fliers as well''.

''Hmm, good idea Cull. Let's try this again.'' Dook indicated the shield ''more energy this time.''

Tests and idle conversation continued for about a wair before Cullin turned to more serious matters again. ''I found a possible location for the Interface in Desert Zone A; a place called Tyber.''

''How in Garvamore did you find that out? Both myself and Yayler have been hunting for its location.''

''It was in a food requisition I found in a data dump. Once I made a more specific search, I ended up with surprisingly few locations. After that, it was a process of elimination.''

''Interesting, well done Cull. What made you think to search food requisitions?''

''Ahh, easy really; the Interface must have human operators.''

''Clever; I've been digging myself and found that the Interface uses different algorithms to the Frame. The Interface software design appears to approximate the human mind.''

''How did you work that out, Dook?''

''I analysed old reports found in the data dumps. Simply put, the Interface works differently to the Frame.''

''So it was probably designed for communication with humans then.''

Dook began packing up bits of equipment as he talked ''Aye, I think so. I think we're done here.''

Cullin unstrapped the shield from the boulder ''Hey Dook, it's almost completely undamaged!''

Dook frowned ''it shouldn't have any damage at all. Let's see.''

''That last blast has scorched the leather on the rim.''

Dook looked carefully at the browned leather and concluded that it was heat damage.

''Dook, just a thought. If the Interface is more human like in the way it works, then maybe we can make it ill?''

Dook paused to mull the idea over ''not sure how we could do that. I'd need examples of its software and operating system. It's an intriguing thought though. I'll talk to Yayler and see if he has any ideas. I think for now we need to keep digging.''

---

It had been big responsibility for Briga to oversee the transformation of Ecta's Ledge, but most of the heavy work had now been completed. A large hanger had been excavated behind the ledge with smaller caverns and corridors following fissures and natural weaknesses in the rock mapped out by Cullin and Ecta's original survey. The geologist and engineers were frequently asking how that had been done.

Briga was loading extracted slabs of granite onto a flier that would be added to the ever growing heap of rock at the base of Drimneev. The hustle and bustle about the hanger as people went about their work was deafening. She needed to get those noise levels reduced somehow. The new base was, however, operational and Briga would be reporting it as such to Dookerock later at Rustick More.

Designs for rockets that fliers could launch from wing pods were almost complete. Excited about the meeting and wanting to be away, Briga hopped down from the loader and went in search of the pilot.

Robert the Red and Ulbin sat in the back of a flier on their way to Rustick More. Red had requested a meeting between the Commanders of the aneksa to discuss what they would all be doing in the near future. He wanted to raise his concerns about increased activity from the Frame in his area and the recent attacks on Dundoon and Tuaport. It would be late when they arrived, but that suited Red as he wanted to talk to some of the other leaders before the meeting.

Yayler had wanted to start the meeting early, but the brothers and Red had insisted on a tour of Rustick More. Three operational fliers including one from Ecta's Ledge now sat in the hanger area. Near the workbenches stood a rack with completed short staffs stacked on the shelves.

Dook saw that Ulbin and Red were particularly interested in the weapons. "We'll get some of those loaded for you Ulbin along with grenades. Have a look about for anything else you might find useful. You should take some as well, Red."

"That's kind of you Dook." Red muttered sarcastically.

The morning dragged on for Dook. He wanted to get the meeting done and over with so that he could get on with some of his projects. He took a cask of ale into the meeting and invited the others to help themselves. Ulbin accepted, but the others declined, Red with noticeable ill humour.

Dook only paid half attention as the meeting got underway and let his mind idle over the Interface enigma. He was puzzled that he could find no software for the machine, yet it must have some. There must be software for it backed up somewhere. He needed that software if he was going to write a virus for the Interface.

"I realise we need iron Hamadern, but it would require a great deal of effort to mine and process. We really need to know how much ore there is before we commit people and resources." Yayler was saying; Dook refocused on the meeting. The Interface problem would have to wait.

Hamadern frowned, it was not the answer he wanted "I realised that, but I don't have anybody available to me that knows anything about rocks."

Briga replied "It's a geologist you need. I have one, but she is very busy with the development of Ecta's Ledge."

"I don't suppose I could borrow her sometime?" Hamadern asked, expecting a flat refusal.

"Not at the moment." Briga shook her head.

Yayler, who had become the unelected chairman of the meeting, agreed." Briga is right. Ecta's Ledge is a priority. I'm sorry Hamadern, but you will have to be patient for the time being."

Briga shook her head again. "There may be a way. Whoever did the original study could do the job. It was quite impressive. The fissures in the rock had been mapped accurately to an astonishing depth."

"Who was that?" Hamadern queried.

"Cullin, your brother, and his friend Ecta." Supplied Yayler.

Hamadern's eyebrows shot up with surprise "really?"

"Unfortunately, Cullin is needed here, but we could let you have Ecta. He could send samples and data to Ecta's Ledge for analysis."

Briga grinned "I'd be happy with that."

Hamadern nodded his agreement also and added "how much has been done at Ecta's Ledge?"

"Well, as most of you know, we have been building the base for just over a month, but we are ready to go operational. I was going to ask for parts for fliers. I think that would be our best function for the time being. We will certainly need more fliers if we have to fight the Frame."

Dook looked up from his ale "Parts are in short supply, but I will make sure you get what you need."

"Thank you."

Robert the Red shifted his position on his chair, leaning forward towards Dook. "I'm impressed, a new base. I'm wondering if it's the best idea though. It divides resources and forces, our strike power."

Dook looked at Red with distaste. "As you know, Rustick More has been operating at capacity. Replacements for the staff sent to Ecta's Ledge are being trained so we will be back to capacity soon."

"My point is that you are splitting your forces, that's never a good idea."

Yayler cut into the conversation, sensing tension between the two men. "Red, I have full confidence in Dook. I believe it is the right thing to do to develop Ecta's Ledge as quickly as possible.'

A number of heads nodded about the table in agreement.

Red shook his head in irritation. ''A weak, unfinished, base is a liability. I think there are more pressing concerns, better uses for our scarce resources and manpower.''

Yayler gave Red a steady look wanting to change the subject ''I suspect you're thinking about your own groups. We will come to those shortly. Orvalt, how are your groups progressing?''

''Don't freeze me out Yayler!'' Red struck the table angrily with a clenched fist. ''The matter of Ecta's Ledge is not decided. Those resources are needed elsewhere.''

Dook spoke coldly, looking Red directly in the eye. ''Actually, my dear friend, Briga works for me. Those are my resources you are talking about and Ecta's Ledge is part of my group. I don't need your agreement, approval or anything else. Unless you'd find it acceptable for me to tell you how to run your own group.''

Dook drained his ale mug and slammed it on the table.

''Absolutely'' Ulbin agreed, albeit a bit meaninglessly, and drained his own mug and added ''good ale Dook.''

Red gave Dook a long poisonous stare and threw his hands in the air. ''I see.''

Ulbin in typical blunt manner commented ''be nice Red, you might need some of my resources or troops before long.''

''I don't need your troops Ulbin, thanks all the same.''

Yayler raised his voice slightly ''this is getting us nowhere Red, Dook is right. It is his decision to expand Ecta's Ledge. Will we get to discuss your problems.''

Red shrugged, clearly not happy, but willing to let the matter drop for the time being.

Yayler continued in a normal tone ''Ulbin, how have your group been getting on?''

''Very well, we have good food production now. It's still inefficient due to the manner of its production, but we should have a good surplus this year. Training is going well; we have fresh troops going to both Dundoon and Tuaport. Yaren reports that Tuaport is particularly vulnerable at the moment.''

''I understand a defensive pocket has been set up about the harbour?'' Dook asked.

''That's right. The biggest problem at Tuaport is the lack of a defensive perimeter. Earthworks are being constructed, but they won't last long in any kind of assault.'' Ulbin said after taking a long pull of ale.

''We were very lucky with the attacks on both Dundoon and Tuaport with the divines being so unprepared for assault. They were complacent, but won't be in the future.'' Yayler pointed out.

''I have a mountain full of granite slabs that might be useful for you Ulbin.'' Briga offered. The excavated rock from Drimneev caused a problem for him as it was very visible and he wanted to make the new base as invisible as possible.

Ulbin clapped Briga on the shoulder. ''That would be helpful.''

''Anything else you need Ulbin?'' Yayler said.

''When do you think to expand onto the plains? Food production would be a lot more efficient if we could do that.''

Dook replied ''in the long term, it would be a good idea it would be wise for the time being to keep our numbers quiet.''

Yayler turned to Red. ''You are in the most awkward position. Can you give me an overview of your problems?''

Red answered ''since the divines discovered our activities and some of our locations in the forests, we've had to abandon many of our facilities. Our network has been badly disrupted and has become disjointed and scattered.

We have friendly Marks that we are developing, but facilities are poor. We have few decent weapons, poor communications and poorly trained people. It will take a while to sort out.''

''You've had those people for many years now. Why are they poorly trained?'' Dook asked quietly.

Red bristled ''they are widely scattered and there are too few to train them, especially for fighting. We have been and still are over stretched.''

''That may have been the case initially, but most of those people are now in Ardbanacker.'' Ulbin pointed out.

''With new Marks under my control I have many additional people to train. There are as many as fifty thousand to feed, train and defend. How many do you have Ulbin.'' Red replied.

Ulbin raised an eyebrow with interest ''under ten thousand currently, but we have a slow trickle from Willemsbree and Aldee who arrive steadily on fishing boats.''

''How are your people distributed Red?'' Yayler asked.

''There are seven isolated Marks that still make reports to Divine Generals who are none the wiser for our involvement; so far. Populations range from two thousand up to about six thousand. We can't manufacture or produce anything other than basics in those Marks. The rest of the people are in scattered pockets deep in the forest. The logistics are very difficult.''

''Keeping in mind that we still want the divines to think they have control, what do you realistically need?'' Yayler queried.

''Good weapons. They need to build up their defences.''

Dook leant forward and spoke sharply. ''Those weapons are needed at Dundoon and Tuaport. They have barely enough for their needs as it is.''

''That doesn't surprise me '' retorted Red sarcastically.

Orvalt asked ''is there a key position that can be defended?''

Red smiled at the question. ''Indeed, there is a strong position on the western edge of the forest, bounded by rough mountains.''

''Make a start developing that position into a defensive pocket then. Make a list of your requirements.''

''I'll do that Yayler, but it won't be a short list.''

The talking went on for a while longer and they eventually agreed that another meeting should be arranged in a few months to discuss progress.

---

The divine army were about five strides from Dundoon on a grey and dull, windy afternoon with low clouds threatening rain. Anders39 was confident that they would reach the town within the next two wairs.

Navigation had been difficult due to the rolling nature of the topography north of the plains. The hiu would order a course only to find that it was overgrown and un-navigable. Route changes needed reporting to the transports that made their slow way from the south with food and more weapons. A transport loaded with heavy weapons travelled with the army.

An unusual high-pitched drone was audible to the south. Anders39 turned to the nearest of the aimu ''HIUt2157, are you able to identify that noise?''

The hiu grated an unnatural sounding response ''it is moving towards us at one hundred and thirty five strides a wair, approximately. It does not conform to any sound patterns in databases available to me and so it cannot be identified. There is a 92% probability that it is a flier though it is unlikely to be of the Frames design parameters.''

Anders39 gave the hiu a startled look ''it's not from the Frame?''

''No'' came the grated response.

The noise was clearly audible now. Anders39 scanned the sky trying to spot the craft and realising at the same time that the entire army was exposed. Then he saw it, a single speck just below the clouds.

For precious moments Anders39 was at a loss for what to do then he gave the order. ''Spread out. Defensive groups. Return fire if fired upon.''

The flier stayed high circling overhead beyond the range of their side arms. The side arm, the stol, held in the hand was a shortened version of a divine's staff. The ground began to erupt with violent explosions amongst the troops who began running to escape. Anders39 saw the leg of a man ripped off as he ran. The blast tore one to pieces with shrapnel and blew another off his feet with half his chest missing.

The flier moved off, climbing into the clouds leaving a pall of thin hazy smoke drifting in the air. The whine of the engines still audible as the flier loitered. One of the aimu had been damaged in the attack, it's body scarred and blackened.

Dead and wounded lay about the hill crying out in pain and anguish. Anders39 saw a man, who looked at him imploringly. A pool of blood lay about him and he realised there was nothing that could be done for him. As he knelt by the dying man he he the man whisper hoarsely ''kill me''. Anders39 placed the dying man's hand on his stol. A short burst of blue fire seared, punching a ragged hole through the skull.

The flier came at them again, this time at low level over the brow of the hill heading directly for the aimu transport. A few divine troops managed to return fire, some desperately trying to access the heavier weapons in the transport. A series of explosions engulfed he transport. The flier banked and started another run dropping incendiaries this time and then receding unharmed leaving the transport a fiercely burning wreck.

The flier returned and attacked again, this time targeting the aimu. Blue fire from stols was arcing up from the troops, but the aim was poor and caused no harm to the flier. The attack was swift leaving both aimu destroyed.

As the flier flew north, Anders39 pushed the troops forward, heading for a shallow tree lined valley thick with undergrowth. The flier came at them again picking off small groups of troops who hadn't reached the shelter of the valley. One group stopped and returned fire striking one of the wings.

For a fleeting moment, Anders39 thought the flier seriously damaged as it rolled alarmingly before correcting its flight and flying north again. For the next two wairs the flier loitered and attacking, if they tried to break cover.

A head count revealed eighty-seven troops dead or wounded, some of whom would certainly be dead before it was dark enough for them to be attended to. The divine army was in a poor state, without heavy weapons or support. Retreat was unthinkable. Anders39 would have to wait for a transport to reach them with more weapons. Once dark he could send a squad back down the supply chain and resume the march on Dundoon in the morning.

---

The flier landed close by the armoury in Dundoon in the grey early evening light. A raised feminine voice emerged from the rear of the flier ''why did you have to take us so low? You could have got us killed.''

''Had to get those aimu; they may have been able to report to wherever their base is.''

The female voice continued stridently ''it was stupid. I didn't realise you were such an idiot.''

''Sara, we here safe now, so can we let it go?''

Ulbin emerged from the flier carrying a box of grenades, which he placed on the ground. ''Cullin is right Sara, we couldn't leave that army.''

''But we nearly crashed!''

''Cac, Cullin controlled the flier very well, I thought.''

''Right now, we need to find Yaren, and report that army to him. They've been delayed, but they will attack soon.''

Robert the Red strolled casually off the flier, placing another box next to Ulbin's. ''Ulbin'' he called out ''I'm going to wander about a bit to stretch my legs. I hope you don't mind.''

251

Ulbin nodded his approval. ''Come on Cullin, let's find Yaren.''

Sara was studying the stumpy wing carefully and ignoring the brothers, tension and anger still evident on her features. She made detailed notes on a compad.

The leading edge of the wing appeared to have taken the force of the staff fire and had an arm length hole. A repair would have to be made before they could safely fly again. The leading edge strut was missing and needed replacing.

# Chapter Seventeen

It was a drizzly dark night as a frustrated Anders39 watched the flier land in Dundoon. He no weapons available to him with enough range to attack the flier and until that happened it would remain a thorn in the side of the divine army.

The army had passed a number of small crofts after resuming their march north in darkness. Even though the enemy now knew about their presence, Ander39 wanted no further information about the size and strength of the army getting to them. That meant leaving no witnesses to their passage.

At each croft Anders39 sent in a squad of troops who dragged out the occupants. Anders39 personally questioned each mucker before having them summarily executed. He gained little information and had the bodies dumped among the peat hags where they were unlikely to be found.

The last few strides to the town completed in darkness had been marched in a continuous wet drizzle that soaked man and equipment, permeating everything to dank dampness. After the flier attack earlier that day and light had faded, Anders39 resumed the march on Dundoon following the course of a river north of their position. The Doo River had been unpleasant, living up to its name, even the water discoloured with a brownish hue. The sticky peat stained most of his troops from the waist down.

Anders39 himself had found himself mired waist deep in the bog as he had stepped on apparently firm ground only to find that is was semi-liquid. It had taken several sents for a couple of troops to pull him out.

Now he looked down on the town he intended to surround by morning. The bulk of the army was still circumnavigating the valley to a low hill north of Dundoon. Anders39 wasn't happy about splitting his army, but had little choice due to the broad Dundoon River protecting the southern flank of the town.

Two hundred troops on the southern hill Gelkarn protected his supply line and the next transport, hopefully arriving soon. Another one hundred and fifty troops guarded the Tuaport road. The remaining five hundred had yet to reach their positions on the northern hill Begarn. They would make the main assault. He could do little about the harbour until he had better ranged weapons.

Daylight would see Dundoon in a divine fist and he would begin to squeeze and crush the life out of the muckers.

---

An exhausted Cullin set the flier down in the dark in Dundoon. After attacking the divine army and dropping Ulbin with the weapons off in Dundoon earlier in the day, Cullin and Sara had flown to Tuaport to warn them about the divine army and ask for reinforcements before taking Robert the Red back to his base in the Dunban Forest.

They had then slept in the flier wrapped in morcotes so they could be ready at short notice if the divine army attacked the town. It was a cold and damp as pre-dawn gloaming bathed the town with a diffuse dusky light.

''Grizzly morning Cull'' grumbled Sara.

''Aye, I reckon it'll be soggy all day.'' Cullin was feeling a bit grizzly himself and doubtless Sara was as well. ''I think we should get to Rustick More.''

''Nay, we have to stay here and do what we can. They'll send a message to Rustick More from Tuaport.'' Sara stretched and yawned.

''Ah, aye, you're right. I just wish we could get the flier repaired.''

''and the parts are at Rustick More'' Sara finished the thought for Cullin.

''Aye.''

''But we really are needed here Cull''

''I know. I guess we'll just have to keep an eye on it and keep away from those divine weapons.'' Cullin rubbed his chin feeling the course growth. He had picked up the habit of shaving some years before after getting disparaging comments from Yayler about his scraggy and pathetic beard. His brothers, themselves sporting full beards thought his clean-shaven face amusing.

Sara yawned again ''I suppose we ought to get up there and see what those divines are doing?''

''Still too dark. Let's grab some food first and wait for better light.''

The flier took off about a wair later, heading over the harbour and the Canut Strait gaining altitude to avoid fire from the divines. Sara piloted whilst Cullin lay prone in the nose peering through the lower canopy plotting troop positions on his compad. Sara made a few crude comments about his backside that Cullin chose to ignore.

The divine troops were fairly difficult to find from height at first until Cullin found that he could take detailed images with the compad and zoom into the image to view troop positions. His finger implants connected remotely with the compad when he held it. He then thought to take an image. The compad clicked away as Cullin pointed it in the direction he needed.

It took Sara about half a wair to fly over the area surrounding Dundoon. ''Have you seen enough Cull?'' she asked.

''Nay, I've got a good idea of numbers and positions, but I want to get another look at that southern group.''

Sara turned the nose of the flier to the south and flew over Gelkarn, the rounded hill south of Dundoon whilst Cullin took several more images.

''Let's get this lot to Yaren'' he said as he sat up and started to review the images.

Sara landed next to the Mucker Hall that Yaren was still using as a Headquarters. Cullin 'stitched' the images together to create a three dimensional holographic image of the terrain around Dundoon. He worked quickly, highlighting troops in red.

''This is brilliant'' Yaren complimented as he peered intently at the image.

Finally Cullin processed the final group of images taken overlaying them on the main image and thus could show troop movement. Yaren cursed loudly when he saw the result. The divines were moving forward, about a quarter wair march from the town.

A small wooden bridge was the only crossing of the Dundoon River lying between the hall and the town. A small group of twenty aneksa took up defensive positions near the bridge and Hall.

Inan was a small wiry man who'd grown up in Glen Ereged. Five long years had passed since that life had irrevocably ended with the fighting and burning of Dunossin. Now he faced that same enemy as they came slowly, spread out across the hill toward the hall.

Inan waited lying on the ground by the hall, for the signal from the squad leader Iner. He sighted on the nearest divine with his short staff. He could see the divines grouping behind a mound for cover about three hundred paces away. They would rush from the position soon, he guessed, and then the fighting and the dying would start.

Iner raised his arm, the palm of his hand held down, signalling to hold fire. He would clench his fist in a moment; that would be the signal to open fire.

A roar came from the divines and then another, then they charged. Iner brought has hand down suddenly and the two sides opened fire on each other. The divines charged. Inan missed with his first blast, blue fire scorching the ground. His next fared better, blasting the ground in front of the charging man. He went down as the blast whipped the feet from beneath him. Inan fired again and struck the man full in the chest as he struggled to regain his feet. Divine fire hissed passed Inan's ear, the bright light blinding him temporarily. Inan blinked, trying to ignore the after image of the blast on his retina.

''Withdraw'' Iner shouted. There must be a hundred troops bearing down on them, too many for the small squad to withstand.

Inan wasted no time and ran. Keeping his head low, he dodged and weaved to the hall and over the bridge. Aneksa pounded across the bridge seeking the relative safety of the north bank of the river.

Inan felt a tap on his shoulder. It was Iner ''keep your head down next time. Get back into the town; we can do no more here. I'll set the charges on the bridge.''

''Aye, will do.'' Inan replied still blinking.

From Dundoons wall, Cullin watched the handful of defenders scamper back from the bridge thinking they were lucky not to lose any men. Had it only been two days since he and Dook had tested the force shields on the top of Rustick More. It seemed longer somehow.

The divines were more cautious as they approached the bridge. Cullin took aim with his staff. He knew it outranged the short staffs and was more accurate. He waited.

The first of the divines stepped onto the bridge, slowly edging his way forward. He was halfway across before a handful of divines stepped onto the bridge. The first reached the northern end of the bridge and Cullin opened fire. The divine hunkered down looking for cover, but Cullin wasn't aiming at him. Charges laid on the bridge earlier had failed to go off. Cullin fired again, but still the charges didn't explode.

The handful of divines was halfway across the bridge now. Short staff fire from the wall falling short of the bridge. Suddenly the bridge erupted in fire. Wood and sods of earth blasted into the air as the north end of the bridge collapsed into the river. The current took hold of the bridge, swinging it round as it broke into pieces and sweeping it downstream.

One of the divines lay prone on the northern bank and Cullin opened fire on him hitting his upper torso with a long blast of blue fire. The smoking and mangled corpse slid into the river, turning lazily in the current with dead eyes staring heavenward. As smoke hung over the ground a profound mournful silence remained, marking the passage of the living to duvick namarv, the eternal realm of the dead.

---

257

Dundoon lay four strides away, hidden by the lower slopes of Begarn. Isla knew it might as well be four hundred strides. The grey misty murk of fine rain reduced visibility, but couldn't hide the thin pall of smoke over the town. The fighting, it seemed, had already begun.

Two hundred aneksa had marched under Isla's command for three wairs to reinforce Dundoon, but were too late. The divines already surrounded the town. Long ago, the road from Tuaport to Dundoon had been gravelled, but was now a rough and rutted track from lack of maintenance by the divines.

She set up her defences by the bridge that spanned the River Beg. Fifty troops set up defences south of the river and started to build a barricade with rocks dragged from the river. Isla waited for reports from her scouts while the troops found cover as best they could among the peat and heather moorland beside the track. They were isolated, vulnerable and outmatched by the greater number of the enemy on the high ground.

Retreat was possible for her lightly armed command and Isla was satisfied that she had options available to her. For now, she wanted to ensure that no army marched on Tuaport.

A runner approached from the mist bringing a report from one of the scouts. It was a young woman Isla realised, as she pulled up breathless.

''Take your time and catch your breath'' Isla instructed.

Between gasps the young woman managed ''about one fifty divine heading this way. They're only about a stride away.''

Isla positioned fifty of her troops north of the bridge in plain sight. The rest she hid in the peat groughs and hags on either side of the track. There was little more she do now, but wait.

They waited as the rain got heavier, soaking into clothing and the hills disappeared into the murk.

'The divines should be visible by now' Isla thought to herself 'what were they doing?'

Then she saw them, spread out across the moorland. The heavy, soggy ground and deep heather made their progress slow, but they advanced inexorably. At less than thirty paces, they opened fire with stols.

The air was suddenly alive with arcing blue light as the two sides discharged their weapons against each other. Outnumbered the aneksa retreated through the peat groughs and to the hastily built barrier. Still the divines came on.

The divines intense fire from behind the barrier forced the aneksa to retreat over the bridge with cover fire from north of the bridge. Isla cursed to herself as she realised that the barrier her troops had built now protected the divines. They still had to come over the bridge however, and then she would have them.

The aneksa continued their retreat using the peat groughs for cover, tempting the divines to cross the river. Isla's tactics relied heavily on the divines' self-confidence to cause an error of judgement and after a period of intense stolfire, they did just that.

The divines rushed the bridge despite a withering storm of return fire from the aneksa, many of them perishing and falling in crumpled heaps on the bridge. Still the divines pushed on as the aneksa fell further back. Step by step, grough by grough, the divine force advanced whittling away at the aneksa.

In the distance, Isla could hear the whine of the flier. Suddenly the craft was overhead. Isla was delighted as she sprang her trap, clenching her raised fist to signal the troops dispersed among the peat groughs.

The flier banked and flew low back along the track toward the divine troops. Stolfire struck the flier, but as it passed over the divines grenades and plazboma were flung from its rear by troops within the flier.

The divines were dismayed as explosions ripped along the track and forced them into the relative safety of the peat groughs. The flier banked again and made another pass, strafing the divines with short staff fire.

The fighting that followed was brutal and bloody, involving a lot of knife work. The aneksa had trained without the benefit of technology, but not so the divines who relied heavily on their stols, trusting in the technology. The divines also had poor training in stealth tactics.

The flier loitered overhead in the fading late afternoon light, but made no more attacks. Many of the divines succumbed to a knife in the back or a slit throat in those peat groughs, or they might turn round to find the trooper near them dead. Their shock and fear would last only moments as they found a knife in their own back.

The aneksa began to win the battle of attrition, paring down the divine force and forced them back onto the track. The divines retreated over the bridge and back toward Dundoon having suffered heavy losses. They had to hold the track or risk the divine army being split in two.

Isla consolidated the position at the bridge, but advanced no further. A quick head count revealed thirty eight of her troops dead or injured. She was upset to lose so many, too many, but guessed also that the divines had worse losses.

As the light failed and the rain became torrential, the aneksa tended their wounded. They had almost exclusively burns injuries from stolfire. Isla sent a trooper forward to the divines' position under a flag of truce offering the divines the chance to collect and treat their wounded. The divines fired upon and killed the trooper before he could even speak to them. So much for 'Divine Honour' thought Isla bitterly.

On Begarn Anders39 read the reports on the fighting at the bridge. He was at a loss. The reports made little sense. The trooper who'd brought the reports talked of magic devils in the peat hags killing their comrades. Anders39 couldn't abide such nonsense. He needed precise information.

He knew that the divines had outnumbered the muckers, but somehow half their numbers were killed. The attack by the flier had killed relatively few. He had to assume that more muckers were hidden in the moors. Anders39 noted something else; fear. Fear, not of the flier, which was a big problem, but of the unseen death lurking in the moors.

Otherwise the day had gone well. While the fighting at the Tuaport Bridge was waged, his troops on Begarn had attacked and taken the waterworks facility north of the town. There had been little fighting as the muckers retreated to Dundoon rather than defend the buildings. Despite the setback at the bridge, the divines grip on Dundoon grew tighter.

As darkness fell over the town Anders39 watched the flier take off again and streak off toward the east.

# Chapter Eighteen

Grozet and Jonti were on duty on the north perimeter wall of Dundoon approaching the end of their shift of two wairs. The rain hadn't stopped all night and both men were now soaked, the rain having penetrated morcotes through to their pullover tops and shirts. Jonti sneezed and shivered. ''It's been a grim night.''

''Aye, I just hope that lot out there are wetter than we are, but I doubt it. I don't think I could be wetter if I jumped in the river.''

Both men felt the chill air biting deep despite having wrapped up in morcotes and mains. Grozet's trousers chafed in places he didn't want to talk about. He knew those nether regions would be red with sores and walked with an oddly stiff gait as he patrolled the walkway atop the wall.

''I'll bet most of them are sheltered in those waterworks'' Jonti commented.

''Ahh, true. What a miserable night.''

''Any movement out there?'' Jonti queried sneezing again.

Grozet leaned on the parapet looking up toward Begarn. ''I don't see anything.''

Both men paused in their patrol, gazing intently over the wall into the black murk of the night. Bright lights caused night blindness for Grozet and Jonti. Anything beyond the pools of light cast by the security lights was black. It was Jonti who saw them first, just a slight movement easily missed. Deep heather and the black night had made the divines all, but invisible.

Grozet cursed under his breath, then noticed Jonti about to call out an alarm. ''No wait'' he urged. ''Quietly; let them think they still have the element of surprise. We have a few sents yet.''

Jonti grinned his understanding and sped off to raise the alarm. Grozet tried to estimate the numbers, but found himself unable to do so due to the darkness. The divines were still stealthily approaching the wall when Jonti returned with a grizzled, rough looking Yaren by his side.

"Any idea of numbers?" Yaren inevitably asked.

"Impossible to say, but enough" came Grozet's reply.

Yaren Frowned, thinking. More aneksa were quietly slipping onto the walkway.

"Ladders" hissed Jonti "where'd they get those from?"

"From the waterworks, I guess" grunted Grozet.

"Quiet now" ordered Yaren. "Let them get to the walls then open fire on those ladders."

They waited.

Many of the divines paused in their advance whilst still within the concealing darkness beyond the security lights. Then they rushed the wall in silence, still believing they had the element of surprise.

Yaren had been watching them intently gave the signal to open fire. Suddenly the night was full of flashing blue light as short staffs blazed upon the divines.

The divines responded with stols and the defenders had to duck below the parapet.

"It's getting dangerous up here" quipped Grozet.

"Aye, just keep your head" laughed Yaren.

A few unlucky aneksa had been caught out by the first volley from the divines and were struck by the blue fire. One bolt hit the man next to Grozet directly in the face. As he died, he turned a blackened visage to Grozet with an apologetic look of surprise. The unfortunate man collapsed to his knees before falling from the wall.

"Cac" groaned Grozet.

Ladders crashed against the wall and the divines started up. Yaren and Grozet pressed their backs against the parapet and moments later divines came over the wall. Grozet blasted them and then fumbled for a grenade. A shocked Yaren saw him lean dangerously over the wall and fire down on the divines climbing the ladder. Grozet dropped the grenade before ducking back behind the parapet.

Yaren grabbed him by the shoulders and shouted into his face ''don't do that again. I need you alive!''

A knot of divines had gained the walkway firing stols along the walkway. More divines gained the wall behind them. Yaren and Grozet fired short staffs and one of the attackers went down. Then Grozet's short staff failed. He fired again, but his short staff refused to work.

Grozet charged the divines, caring nothing for himself he bowled into them. Yaren and a few other aneksa sent a continuous barrage of fire over the head of the sprawled Grozet cutting the knot of attackers to shreds.

Grozet, his knife in hand quickly dispatched the divines he had knocked over, their blood quickly pooling on the ground. Grozet then reached into a pocket for another grenade, which he threw over the wall. Moments later a dull boom, almost lost in the din of the fighting, indicated the explosion of the grenade. The defenders threw more grenades over the parapet, destroying the remaining ladders.

Yaren sat down beside Grozet ''I said don't do that again'' he exclaimed.

Grozet moaned an incoherent reply. During his charge along the wall, he had been hit with stolfire and now blood was spreading alarmingly across his left arm and chest.

---

All Sara could see through the fliers canopy was thick cloud. Cullin followed close behind her in a second flier. They had tried to climb above the clouds and weather, but had been unable to do so due to the depth of the cloud layer. Sara was using all her skill to fly through the turbulence as updraft followed downdraft and wind shear threw the

264

craft about. She fixed her gaze on the instruments and hoped her navigator, Fil, knew his job.

Fil was one of the most experienced flier navigators and pilots, but none of them had flown for real in these conditions before. Reality was different as there was no room for error and a mistake could easily be fatal.

Cullin in the second flier had the worst job, that of trying to keep visual contact on Sara's flier ahead. If it hadn't of been for the pressing need to get back to Dundoon neither Sara or Cullin would have risked flying.

Sara knew they must be near to Dundoon by now, but waited for instruction from her navigator. A sudden and severe gust threw the flier sideways.

''Hesoos'' she cursed as the flier pitched and yawed wildly as she tried regain control. ''How much longer Fil? We need to get out of this soup.''

''A few sents, don't worry, I have our position.''

''I'm not worried about your navigation Fil, I just want to get out of this filth!''

''Not long Sara.''

''Ahh, cac! I can't see Cullin.''

''He's a good pilot Sara, he'll find his own way if he doesn't find us again.''

''I hope so Fil, I really hope so.'' Her concern for Cullin was profound, threatening to break her concentration.

The flier dropped without warning, the nose dipping and forcing the flier into an unexpected and dangerous dive. It took Sara long precious moments to level out.

''Steady Sara'' cautioned Fil. ''Descend to a hundred paces.''

''What about Cullin?''

"He'll have to make his own way now. He has his own navigator, Ela. He'll get down. Worry about us."

They failed to drop below the clouds as Sara descended.

"How high are the hills Fil?" Sara asked.

"Oh, no more than seventy five paces."

"Good, because we still can't see."

Fil, who had been concentrating on his instruments, glanced out of the canopy. "Ahh, that's awkward. Steer two sixty five degrees and drop to seventy five paces, but keep an eye out for those hills."

As Sara started to drop another gust threw the sideways and she fought to control the craft. "A gust like that could crash us into the hills Fil." She warned "we're at seventy five paces now."

"Stay at this height then, and keep this course. We'll fly over the Canut Strait and then come back towards Dundoon at a lower altitude."

Sara jerked the flier upwards, narrowly missing heather and rock looming abruptly out of the clouds ahead. She caught a glimpse of a machine as the flier flashed passed.

"Deetah! That was close!" Sara cried out.

"Sorry Sara, that must have been Gelkarn."

"Thanks" replied Sara sourly.

"Stay on this course Sara and drop to fifty paces. We're over the Canut Strait now."

"Fine" said Sara unhappily as she reduced altitude still further, but still they failed to drop below the clouds

"Cac!" Fil blurted. "Try twenty five paces. We're getting a bit desperate."

Gingerly Sara dropped the flier down and broke free of the clouds at under forty paces. White crests streaming spindrift and a rough sea raced past as wind buffeted the flier.

''Thank Hesoos for that!'' cheered Sara.

They turned back to Dundoon and the town soon came into view. Cullin was standing next to his flier looking anxiously toward the east as Sara landed. She didn't care how he'd managed to get down first, she was just grateful to see him down safe. As she exited the flier she doubled over and threw up.

Cullin raced over to her and put his arm about her shoulders. ''Sara, are you all right?''

''I'll be fine, it was a bit rough up there.''

''Aye, it was unpleasant. I was getting worried.''

A handful of aneksa began to unload short staffs, plazboma and Dook's wooden repulse shields from Sara's flier. Food and other supplies had been loaded into Cullin's flier.

''I've just had a thought Sara. Do you think those shields would work on the fliers?'' Cullin asked.

Sara, still recovering from her bout of sickness, was sitting on the fliers tailgate. She looked quizzically at the heavy and clumsy shields before answering. ''They might be a bit awkward and would affect the stability of the fliers.''

''We don't need the wooden part, the repulse bit is separate. If we attach those to the fliers, we'll have some protection from staff fire.''

Sara nodded interest in the idea. ''How many would we need?''

Cullin pondered for a moment. ''I'm not sure, maybe six on each flier.''

''Twelve shields Cullin. The troops need them and we haven't brought that many.''

''Forty seven, I counted. You're right, we'd best talk to Yaren.''

Yaren surprised them. He felt that the safety of the fliers was more valuable than the benefit of a few more shields for troops. If a flier got shot down then it would be difficult to get more supplies and weapons into Dundoon. He felt the fliers too valuable an asset to risk unnecessarily. He pointed out that Sara's sighting of machinery on Gelkarn was important intelligence they wouldn't have without the fliers.

Cullin and Sara spent the rest of the morning fitting the shields to the fliers before heading off to the canteen. The wooden shields minus Dook's repulse shield were quickly snapped up by nearby aneksa troops. The canteen was a converted warehouse on the quayside where the aneksa had their meals. Sara leaned against Cullin as they ate a cold meal of oatcakes and cheese with fruit compote. They were cold and tired, but then so was everyone else. Conversation in the canteen was muted.

There had been speculation on the nature of Sara's sighting of machinery earlier in the day. The lack of detail led to wild ideas and assumptions. Some aneksa were saying that another army had arrived under cover of the bad weather. Others said that it must be an aimu army of gunna and siege weapons. All that they knew was that there was something out there. Yaren assumed that it was a supply transport for the divine army. That assumption was correct, but not in the nature of the supplies.

There was a huge boom from outside. People started rushing from the building, leaving food half eaten. More booming followed. The area around the towns gates was being hit by plazboma shells. Black smoke rose from the explosions and drifted over the town.

''We've got to get the fliers out of here'' shouted Sara to Cullin.

Cullin grabbed a handful of oatcakes from his plate and stuffed one into his mouth.

''I don't believe you; how can you think of food now?''

Cullin replied around a mouthful of crumbs ''got to eat! Let's go and get those fliers to the bridge east of here.''

''I'll be there Cull, let's just get moving.''

The targeting of the divines was slightly off due to the cloud cover, but it was still only a matter of time before they destroyed the gates. Shells landed inside and outside the gates, many hitting buildings not designed to withstand such an assault.

Cullin and Sara had their fliers airborne and raced over the town gates, courting fate with plazboma shells. A mass of troops grouped beyond the gates, waiting for the chance to enter the town.

The fliers landed near the bridge and Cullin and Sara exited to raised short staffs and an assortment of spears, bows and arrows. It appeared that Dundoon got the main share of weapons and support from Rustick More, not Tuaport.

A tall, severe faced woman called out ''who are you?''

''We're from Dundoon, we're on your side'' Cullin called out, aware that the reinforcement group would be unaware of the situation in Dundoon.

''What's happening over there?''

Cullin noted that she carried herself with a certain degree of authority and assumed that the broad chested and heavily muscled woman was in charge. They're being bombarded with plazboma. We had to leave.''

''Come on over.'' As they approached she added ''well met, I'm Isla. I'm in charge of this bunch of salak.''

The troops about her roared with mock menace.

''Cullin and Sara'' Cullin introduced himself and Sara. ''I've heard of you. Keem tells me that you took Dundoon almost single handed!''

Isla laughed ''wonderful, she was out of it for the entire battle''.

''And now the divines want the town back. We need to stop that bombardment or the town will fall.'' Sara cut through the niceties.

Still smiling ''Well we can't have that, it would upset Keem.''

"Aye" agreed Isla.

Sara continued "visibility is awful up there, so we can't do much. We can see about twenty paces in the fog at best."

"We could drop some of you guys behind their position on the hill." Cullin added thoughtfully.

"I think we'd need some sort of cover, otherwise we'd be cut to pieces by stols." Isla adjusted her mane and morcote. Both were damp and the chill worked its way under the skin somehow, despite her best efforts to keep warm. They were all cold, damp and tired, but had to keep going.

"Hey Cull" Sara interjected. "Don't forget we've got those shields now. We can fly really low."

"True, but I'd really like forward facing short staffs, we still have nothing to fight with otherwise."

Isla looked quizzically between Cullin and Sara "what shields?"

Cullin explained to Isla about the repulse shields, that they were making more for troop use. The conversation continued and a plan began to take shape.

The fliers took off separately several sents apart. Sara was first, flying along the southern branch of the Dundoon River, and then following the wooded south east ridge of Gelkarn where six aneksa disembarked on a small bare knoll at the end of the ridge. Cullin then joined her in the second flier.

It would take the aneksa about two thirds of a wair to reach the guns. During that time, Cullin and Sara kept the divine troops on Gelkarn busy. Sara began with a low level circuit of the summit plateau with Cullin close behind. The noise from the open tailgate was deafening.

Sara turned toward the flash of the plazboma guns flying over scattered groups of divine troops. Stolfire scythed through the fog, groping for the fliers. The first few volleys missed Sara's flier, flashing across the nose.

''That was close'' Sara shouted to Fil in the navigators seat beside her.

Another volley struck the flier, raking down the side. The repulse shields instantly glowed with intense blue, combining to form a continuous arc as the stolfire dissipated harmlessly.

''That one was a direct hit. I can't see any damage though'' shouted Fil.

Encouraged Sara powered over the plazgunna and banked to her left. Aneksa strapped in with makeshift rope harnesses firing upon the divines.

''Is that all they have; three plazgunna?'' Fil shouted in Sara's ear.

''It's enough to destroy those gates.'' Sara shouted back.

Cullin's flier followed Sara's with its underside flaring intense blue from stolfire as he attempted to draw fire. The gunna crews ran for cover as Sara attacked with Cullin weaving a course behind her.

''Sara'' bawled Fil ''if we keep attacking the ground team won't be able to get near.''

''Aye, I know, but we need to stop them firing on the gates.''

''You've done that! Let's harass the troops.''

Sara thought quickly before replying ''Let's try that.''

Sara concentrated on the northern slopes of Gelkarn, strafing at small pockets of divine troops. She lost sight of Cullin behind her, but caught a glimpse of blue flashes from higher up the hill.

''Looks like Cullin's showing off!'' she bellowed at Fil.

''He's attacking the plazgunna, we should back him up.''

Sara changed course, heading for the flickering blue light of stols and short staffs. ''Drop some grenades as we pass over'' Sara shouted to the aneksa in the rear of her flier.

271

The grenades straddled the central platform and Sara climbed out of range of stols. Cullin appeared out of the fog and hovered on thrusters. Aneksa heaved grenades out of the flier before Cullin climbed up into the murk.

The plazgunna had a simple design, built for easy transportation and assembly in the field. Four legs supported a platform upon which the weapon was mounted and could swivel about three hundred and sixty degrees. There was no protection for the crews.

The grenades from Cullin's flier exploded about the central weapon blasting the legs from underneath. The muzzle toppled, digging into the ground and pointing skyward.

A plaz structure about fifteen paces from the plazgunna served as a magazine. Overconfidence led the divine gunners to stack shells outside of the magazine, not believing they could be located in the fog. One of Cullin's grenades bounced, rolled and came to rest against the stacked shells. The shells erupted in a huge fireball ripping open the plaz walls of the magazine. Burning shell fragments flew in all directions some landing in the now unprotected magazine. A massive conflagration of fire ensued as shells exploded and flew in different directions.

From a distance, the commando troops gaped at the orange glow flecked with blue in the distance. The uproar from explosion echoed about the hills. ''So much for stealth'' Atashin groaned to his squad.

He continued the approach, more cautious now. As they neared their target, they began to crawl through the heather and sodden black peat. The water saturated muck soaked through their clothing staining it black.

As they neared the plazgunna they split up into three groups of two troops each. They dropped grenades into the muzzles of each one and then made a hasty retreat. Atashin could hear the sound of the fliers thrusters through the fog.

As soon as the grenades went up the fliers would depart and meet them by the Doo River to the south. Dull metallic booms announced the destruction of the plazgunna as the fog closed in about them.

---

Anders39 stood watching the glow on the top of Gelkarn and felt desperation grip him. His heavy weapons had again been destroyed and couldn't be replaced. At least the transport had brought replacement communication equipment and he'd been able to send off a report. The Frame was now aware of the existence of the mucker fliers and their impervious nature to stolfire.

He felt he now had no choice but to commit to an all-out assault on the gates of Dundoon, with or without air support. That is what he wanted more than anything else; something to keep those fliers off his troops.

There was a good chance that the bombardment had weakened the gates. He had about two hundred troops near the gates and ordered them to attack.

As they approached the gates, the divines threw grenades hoping to weaken the gates further. The defenders sent a wave of withering fire on the divine troops. A small squad got close enough to deposit a small heap of grenades against the gates. They detonated and shook the gates, but failed to breach them.

In the distance could be heard the buzz of the fliers. Anders39 cursed. ''Get those troops out of there'' he barked at one of his lieutenants. ''We'll try and get close tonight and get some more grenades by those gates.''

''Yes Sir'' came the response from the lieutenants. He knew they would do as he ordered, but secretly each one hoped that he would fail to take Dundoon. Failure resulted in demotion or even execution and one of his lieutenants would gain promotion. They were forever ambitious for advancement and were jealous of his command.

The returning troops reported significant damage to the gates and a similar attack would likely be breach them. The news cheered Anders39, but he considered another daylight attack foolhardy. He would wait until dark.

Overnight he brought virtually all his troops north of the Dundoon River and placed them on the Tuaport Road. It would not be a subtle or clever attack, simply brutal.

# Chapter Nineteen

Kay47 was not the strongest or most talented of divines, he had always known that, but had always pushed himself to the limit. As ever, with divines, life was a struggle for survival and Kay47 was a survivor. He based his entire philosophy on the idea of being stronger than your neighbour. Word had it that a handful of troops had taken Dundoon. That didn't say much for the divines in charge of the town at the time in Kay47's opinion.

He carried a large sack of grenades and explosives that he had to place by the gates. He waited for the signal with almost the entire divine army behind him. A cold wind presaging dawn blew off the sea into his face. At least it was no longer raining.

A single whistle sounded and Kay47 started his charge over the undulating ground. His knees threatened to buckle at every stride. Blue fire from the mucker's short staffs licked at the ground and arrows whizzed past his head. The man nearest to him went down with an arrow protruding through his neck. Fifty paces to go.

'Distractions' he thought to himself 'ignore them'. He focused on the gates, with his legs pounding out a steady rhythm. Last evening he'd overheard others making bets on how long he'd survive. Not, he'd noted sourly, if he survived, but how long.

Twenty-five paces to go, not far now. His legs were getting tired and leaden. He was carrying more than half his bodyweight and it was sapping his strength. Kay47 stumbled and almost fell. He regained his footing, but had lost momentum. As an arrow whipped into the ground by his foot, he grimaced. He ignored it and stumbled on at a walking pace.

Ten paces to go. The army was sending a barrage of stolfire at the defenders on the walls. Kay47 felt very vulnerable as he stumbled up to the gates. He noted absent-mindedly the damage caused by the previous attacks. 'Too late guys' he thought to himself as an arrow whizzed past his ear 'I'm here now'.

With relief, he dropped the pack, set a grenade and slipped along the wall away from the gates. A huge boom reverberated behind him. The ground shook as the explosion rumbled in the air. Sods of earth and rocks flew into the air leaving a crater in front of the gates. Still the gates stood.

Kay47 gave the gates a hateful stare; all that effort and risk and the gates still stood. Then he heard a creak, a metallic groan came from the gates as the tortured structure failed. Slowly the gates toppled outward with a resounding crash.

Within moments, the divine army was rushing the breach in the town's defences and flooding into the town.

---

Sara was airborne again. Isla had asked her to provide support for the aneksa troops as they advanced down the Tuaport Road towards Dundoon. Cullin was still on the ground trying to fit a couple of short staffs to his flier. He had been up most of the night and was still working on the trigger mechanism when they heard the large explosion of Dundoon's gates being breached.

Isla had around one hundred and fifty able-bodied troops of her original two hundred and she now committed them to march on the town. She had split the army into four squads. One remained at the bridge guarding the captured divines. She commanded a central group and marched along the track. The other two groups guarded her flanks, moving swiftly through the moorland either side of the track.

Ahead to the left lay a small open deciduous wood. Isla halted her advance as she waited for her left flank to flush out any divines waiting in ambush. Sara's flier buzzed overhead with its tailgate open, but she was of limited use for the woodland because foliage limited her view below.

The track ahead was clear of enemy troops and so Isla assumed that there must be troops waiting in ambush in the woods. It didn't take long for her fears to be justified. As she advanced along the track the sound of battle emerged from the woods. No attacks came from the north and she trusted her right flank group to maintain that situation.

The familiar figure of Atashin appeared from the woods. Jonti quickly located Isla and breathlessly reported. ''there's a lot of troops hiding in those woods. Reckon as many as a hundred, but it's hard to say.''

Isla grimaced, she had hoped on fewer as she had earlier been forced to leave troops behind at the bridge. ''Cac'' she muttered ''Atashin, get to the right flank. Tell them to move ahead to the west end of these woods and prevent a breakout there. I want to surround these divines.''

Atashin set off at a jog, quickly disappearing into the peat hags. Isla was still apprehensive about troops from Begarn attacking from the north. If that happened, then her force would be split in two and chewed to pieces. Also, the forty or so troops she had in the woods were inadequate to face the much larger force. She needed to be decisive and act fast. She had little choice, but to take her own group into the woods.

Isla picked a handful of her best marksmen ''you guys need to stop any divines that emerge from those woods. No one gets out.''

''Aye'' they replied and set off at a slow run.

The remainder of the troops headed into the woods with herself in the lead. The wood had become strangely silent. Isla didn't trust the silence.

Isla's squad crawled through the undergrowth making slow progress. For an uncomfortable period that set her teeth on edge the quiet prevailed and they made no contact with the enemy. Then she saw a divine ahead using a tree for cover. His stol was not pointing in their direction, but toward her left flank.

She set her sights on him, but paused. There were others out there. Quickly she scanned the woods ahead and picked up another handful of divines lying in ambush. She indicated their positions to her troops with hand signals. By placing her finger to her lips and miming a bow and arrow, she indicated a silent attack; then she ordered them to fire.

The divines died quickly making only a dull thud as their bodies fell to the ground.

The aneksa crawled on. As she passed the divine she'd seen with an arrow protruding from his neck severing his windpipe, she looked over to her left and saw one of her troops indicating another divine. She also saw some of her left flank troops walking upright directly toward the indicated divine.

'Fools' she thought angrily, but couldn't indicate to the aneksa without giving away her own position. She fired her short staff on the divine who died with a hole punched in his chest.

Moments later the air was alive with stol and short staff fire, the tracks of the blue fire criss-crossing in a lethal web. Killing the divine had given her left flank troops barely enough time to react. For some there was insufficient warning and stolfire cut them to ribbons.

Isla moved forward to a moss covered fallen tree trunk. Ahead of her the positions of the divines were revealed by their stols. Urgently she grabbed a young lad near her ''Pass the word along; use arrows not short staffs. Don't reveal your positions to the divines.''

The boy who he wasn't old enough to be considered a man, nodded and sneaked off through the woods. It was a battle of attrition and it was difficult for Isla to tell who was winning. The fighting continued with the three aneksa groups linking up and surrounding the divines. They crept forward, tightening their grip until only a small knot of divines remained.

They spurned her offer of surrender even though their position was clearly hopeless. Isla repeated the offer a number of times, but they refused to accept surrender to muckers. ''Utter stupidity'' she muttered and ordered her troops ''send them to Duvick Namarv!''

Short staffs blazed cutting a swathe through the divines. The firing continued until the last of the defenders fell. Then silence fell in the woods. The fight had cost many lives on both sides. Isla knew it was an appalling waste of life, but what options were there?

In the aftermath of the fighting Isla saw the boy again. He was leaning over the blackened and twisted corpse of an aneksa. His distraught face streaked with tears as he sobbed, touching the face of the corpse tenderly.

"What's your name lad?" she asked gently, kneeling down beside him.

It took a long moment for him to reply, but eventually he looked up "Gensi" he muttered.

"Who is this?" she asked Gensi as softly and respectfully as she could.

"Dad, he's all I have." Fresh tears flooded down his cheeks.

Isla noticed Atashin standing close by and indicated for him to come over. "Gensi, this is Atashin; he is going to look after you. What's your father's name?"

"Garag."

"He was a good man Gensi" Isla turned to Atashin "look after him. I don't want him hurt. He's too young for this."

Atashin nodded his agreement and knelt down by the lad.

---

The short staffs under-slung from the fliers stumpy wings protruded in front of the leading edge. The system was now tested and worked though firing mechanism was still quite rudimentary and required a couple of troops to operate it. Cullin would've extended the wiring to the pilots' console, but had lacked sufficient time.

As he flew towards Dundoon he passed Sara's flier loitering above a wood. Ahead he saw the ruined gates of the town and fearing that Dundoon was completely over-run made a couple of circuits to reconnoitre the town.

He could see that the initial rush of the divines halted by a series of barricades Yaren had built over the eighteen days since they'd captured Dundoon. Cullin landed near the quay and searched for the command post where he found Yaren and his lieutenant Dundoon bent over a map of the town.

"What's the situation Yaren?" he called out.

Yaren looked up and frowned, for a moment not recognising the drawn and ragged figure of Cullin. ''Ah, Cullin. Come in. It's pretty desperate. The divines hold the gates. They're pushing into the south of the town. We hold the north and warehouse areas.''

''Is there anything I can do?''

''Not at the moment. I think I'd like you here while we work a few things out.''

---

An arrow flicked past Kay47's ear and skittered along the walkway. He was on point again, he was always on point he thought bitterly. One day his luck would run out and that day could easily be this day.

He was with a group of divines that were advancing along the south wall. The muckers ahead had built a barricade and had him pinned down behind one of the walls steel ribs. The other divines strung out behind him using other ribs for cover.

---

Jonti ducked his head down as he saw the divines rush the barricade. The other two aneksa troops fired upon the divines, but Jonti knew it was hopeless. They would be over-run in moments. The next barricade was too far behind them to make a dash. They would be cut down halfway.

A door to an office block was their only option. Jonti indicated the door the other two and made a dash for it. He crashed through the door even as stolfire licked the air about him. He provided cover fire for the other two as they made a dashed for the doorway. One of them made the distance, but the other was cut down halfway as the divines reached the barricade.

---

The plan of the town and the progress of the divines lay scratched out in the dirt in front of Anders39. He reckoned on half the town now under his control. The wall to the south was a problem. There was no progress there. If he controlled that wall then he would be able to push into the northern half of the town and squeeze the mucker defenders.

---

Grozet was hunkering down behind a wall in a small office. He'd been patched up and now had his left arm strapped up in a rough sling. He'd been badly burned by stolfire the day before. It hurt like hell, but the medic assured him that it felt worse than it really was. At least he still had an arm to fight with.

He should have had a hole blasted in his chest by the stolfire, but the power settings on the divine weapon must have been poorly adjusted. The aneksa's short staffs could be adjusted, but only had two basic settings, stun and kill. They had captured a stol from a dead divine earlier and now knew that the weapon had a variable power adjustment as well as the spread of the discharge.

Duncan had placed Grozet in charge of a group of aneksa with minor injuries. Out of a broken window, there was a good view over barricades controlled by divines of the gates. Both ends of the block of small offices had barricades controlled by the aneksa.

If Grozet had a mind to the divines were near enough to talk. They were too close for comfort in Grozet's view. He would have pulled out his lightly injured charges to a safer place, but Yaren needed everybody able to fight on the front line.

The fight was delicately balanced, with both sides fully committed. As long as Grozet held these offices the divines had to go around them and attack the barricades.

---

There was activity behind Kay47. A number of divines were moving onto the wall. Kay47 couldn't tell how many as more were continuously joining the group, but he knew they were ready for a push.

281

Twenty or more divines sent a barrage of concentrated stolfire raging along the parapet over Kay47's head. A handful started to move along the wall under the protective fire-power and then continued the barrage as another squad moved up behind them. The divines progressed along the wall despite the best efforts of the aneksa to repel them.

"Grief" muttered Kay47 to himself as some of the stolfire barely missed him, striking the metalwork just above his head. He ducked down further, trying to make himself as small a target as possible.

As the first wave of divine troops drew level one of them shoved roughly at Kay47. "Get up there. Move it. We've got to risk our lives because you can't do your job."

Kay47 didn't reply, he simply got on with it and joined his stolfire to the already considerable onslaught. He was still point and knew what they expected of him. The wave of troops forced the defending aneksa to withdraw down a flight of steps to the quayside as they neared the far end of the wall.

---

The two aneksa sat on the tailgate of the flier with Cullin quizzing them on the newly installed short staff firing mechanism. Grenades could still be dropped out of the back of the flier as they had been previously. Cullin wanted to work on that problem, but currently lacked the time and facilities to do so.

He'd been instructed by Yaren to wait for orders and be ready to fly at a moment's notice. He could do little else now, but wait.

---

The door rebounded into the path of the aneksa behind Jonti. Jonti heard the man curse, but cared little about that. He was more worried about the divines following them.

The door crashed behind them. Jonti could hear the frizz of stolfire; the divines were much too close. They crashed through another door and then came upon another that was locked. Jonti shot the lock,

282

but found the way ahead blocked by two more divines entering the building ahead.

Jonti shot the first divine before doubling back. ''Not that way!'' he shouted to the aneksa trooper with him and turned up a flight of stairs. The startled trooper followed, just quickly enough as stolfire struck the entrance to the stairs moments after his passing.

''Grenades'' Jonti said to the trooper as he joined him at the top of the first flight. The trooper shrugged and presented his hands palms up to indicate that he had no more grenades. ''Sorry'' he said.

''Cac, nor I'' complained Jonti.

They raced down a corridor and double stepped up the stairs and shot the lock at the top. They emerged onto a flat roof that was empty apart from a lighting tower built of steel girders.

Jonti made a strangled noise as he leant over the edge of the building. A barricade manned by divines lay below. ''Not that way. The tower, quick'' he called to the trooper and charged across the roof.

The disconcerted trooper tried to follow, but ran headlong into one of the lighting tower struts and collapsed unconscious to the ground. ''Oh, for the love of Hesoos'' cried Jonti quickly checking to trooper over. ''Sorry my friend, I have to go.''

A couple of divines emerged onto the roof cautiously and Jonti wasted no more time on the fallen trooper and raced across the roof closely followed by the fizz of stolfire. He didn't look as he leaped from the roof.

He landed heavily, twisting his knee in the process. Groaning with pain, he opened his eyes to an assortment of weapons pointing at him. ''Not me you retarded amadan, them!'' he cried pointing to the divines on the roof above.

Aneksa loosed arrows and short staffs blazed for a moment forcing the divines away from the edge. A divine fell from the roof, landing beside Jonti who stared at the corpse. An arrow had penetrated his chest and protruded from the back of his neck.

''Nice shot'' commented Jonti.

The large bulk of a man with an arm in a sling loomed over Jonti extending a hand. As Jonti struggled to his feet the man said ''look before you jump next time'' and indicated a pile of sharpened stakes heaped near where he had landed.

''Ah, I'm alive though, that suits me. The divines control this building now so it's probably a good idea to move.''

Grozet merely nodded.

---

Buoyed with the success of the push along the wall Anders39 decided to make a push along the quay. That would cut off any possible escape for the muckers and effectively surround them.

He was still unhappy with the general achievements of his troops. They were highly trained, but were struggling to overcome a few uneducated heathen muckers. Even with the fliers, they shouldn't have been able to defend the town for this long. Anders39 put this failure down to a lack of drive on the part of the troops and not any failure or weakness on his part.

---

One of the troops assigned to Cullin had managed to get some biscuits and dried meat from the canteen. They were eating when a runner came jogging from Yaren's headquarters. The man looked enviously at the food as he delivered orders from Yaren. ''Yaren wants you to get a message to the Tuaport troops. He wants to make a counter attack'' the trooper panted.

''Good, have you eaten lad?'' Cullin replied.

''Nay, not since yesterday.''

''Grab some food then and eat while we go through the plans.''

It was now mid-afternoon so there was still enough time for the counter attack, but Cullin reckoned that they may well be fighting at sunset and Cullin certainly didn't want to be flying in the dark.

''Yaren will signal with a series of three incendiary rockets to start the attack'' the lad said through a mouthful of biscuit.

''That's fine. When does he want the attack to happen?''

''In about two wairs.'' The lad shoved another biscuit into his mouth.

''Right, come on lads. Rest over, time to earn our keep.'' He grinned at his two troopers who shook their heads with mock despair and clambered into the back of the flier. Cullin noted with amusement that they took the food with them.

When they landed near Isla's troop, she was already there. She listened to the plans without comment, but said afterward that she would have preferred later because the sun would be in their eyes.

''It might be useful in Sara and myself could put up some crossfire, but we can only do that in daylight'' Cullin suggested.

''Aye, it's a good idea, I'll talk to her when she wakes.''

Cullin looked at Isla quizzically, not quite understanding.

''Oh, I'm having everyone sleep in shifts. I want them as fresh as possible when the fighting starts.''

''Ahh, I'll not disturb her then. It's a good idea'' Cullin replied. As Cullin was thinking about heading back to the flier Isla stopped him. ''I have a status report for Yaren, if you wait for a few sents, Cullin.''

With the report in his hand, Cullin jogged back to the flier for the short hop back to Dundoon. Back at Dundoon, he could see that there was a lot of activity on the quayside. It took him a moment before he realised that it was fighting.

The aneksa had built a large barricade across the quay and were putting up a strong defence. Some troops were on the flat roofs of the warehouses on the quayside giving them the height advantage. The

285

divines could only counter this from the south wall. Cullin thought to himself 'I've got the best vantage point of all'.

He brought the flier in low above the south wall, ignoring the stolfire that bracketed the flier. He gave a loud 'fire' command to his troopers and sent flickering blue bolts of short staff fire along the wall.

Cullin decided the forward pointing short staffs were better as he had more control of the direction of fire, but he still needed to get the firing mechanism sorted out. As he lifted away from the wall, he surveyed the scene below. The divines were scurrying about looking for cover. Cullin realised that a wall designed to keep people out worked less well for attacks coming from within the town. He wondered why the town needed a wall at all and decided to look into the question when he got back to Rustick More.

Cullin lifted away from the wall and made a circuit of Dundoon. He then came in slowly along the quay from the north, hovering on thrusters. As he approached the attacking divines, he pointed the nose of the flier toward the closest group of divines. The shields flared an angry and intense blue as multiple bolts of stolfire struck the flier.

''Gods'' he complained hoping the short staffs weren't hit. To prevent the repulse shields affecting the short staff he'd attached them outside of the blue nimbus created by the shields. ''Fire'' he shouted and blue fire licked through the group of attacking divines. The divines had a hastily built barrier of their own made from rubble taken from the destroyed armoury.

''Grenades'' shouted Cullin ''six, now''.

The two troopers partially lowered the tailgate and threw out the grenades, which landed scattered haphazardly. Two landed by the barrier and exploded with enough force to blast the heaped rubble apart. A couple of divines lay dead by the resulting rubble heaps.

The divines made a rapid and desperate retreat, but Cullin found himself unable to follow up the attack as the troopers were still busy at the tailgate.

''Cac'' he moaned as he lifted away.

The repulse shield flared a brighter more intense blue as the divines concentrated stolfire on the flier. As Cullin turned to head over the harbour the shields flared white, flickered and then failed. Cullin accelerated over the harbour, lifting out of range of the stols.

''Ah, not good'' he muttered to himself, grateful that the rear shields had held. ''Grenades'' he ordered as he flew back over the divines.

Cullin exhausted his supply of grenades, harassing any exposed divines. He found the short staff still worked when he tested them, but timing them was a problem. He was as likely to hit the aneksa as the divines.

There was nowhere safe to land now in Dundoon as the quay was off limits due to the divines attack. Cullin returned to Isla's troops landing neatly next to Sara's flier.

Sara was sitting on the tailgate and looked questioningly at Cullin as he approached. ''Oh, Cull! You weren't expected back here.''

''I know, I need to talk to Isla. There have been a few developments.''

Isla was frustrated ''If we go in without support we'll be cut to pieces. There aren't enough troops left who are fit enough to fight.''

''Me and Sara can cover you from the air, but Yaren will need to know what to expect.''

''Nay, he knows what he's doing. He'll do what he can, if he can.''

Isla was shaking her head with frustration, thinking hard.

''If he can?'' questioned Sara.

''Aye, if Cullin's assessment is correct, Yaren may not be able to meet us if we attack blind'' Isla explained. ''Your two fliers, useful as they are, won't give enough support.''

''I'll need to make repairs first. I got shot up a bit earlier. My shields failed.'' Cullin reported.

"What? Didn't they work?" Sara remarked with a startled voice.

"They failed while I was attacking. Overload, I think. I need to check them before flying again."

"Get that done then Cullin. Let me know when you can fly again. All we can do for now is wait. Oh, Sara, just a thought. Can you fly over the town a few times? Remind them we're still here." Isla looked stressed and tired.

---

Yaren had brought the shields delivered by Cullin and Sara to the quayside. Duncan looked horrified when he saw the heavy wooden objects.

"Yaren these are no good. They're too small, we'll be cut down before we get close enough to use those spikes." The spikes protruded from a boss at the centre of the shield.

"I know, but I'm told Dookerock developed them himself and Cullin verifies that they work." Yaren hefted one of the shields "not too heavy to be unwieldy. I wouldn't want to be hit by one."

"What's to develop, it's just a wooden shield."

"Nay, put one over there." Yaren indicated the wall to a warehouse.

When Duncan had done so he said "now turn on the device on the back and stand away".

Yaren shot the shield with his short staff and the energy bolt splashed against the repulse shield. "Now Duncan, get these shields turned on and set up a shield wall across the quay. You have ten sents. I want these amadan sent to Duvick Namarv."

"Aye."

Duncan quickly had the shield wall set up, but still had concerns. None of the aneksa had trained with the shields. "I want" he bawled at the troopers ''a line of shields across the quay and a line behind that with short staffs''

The men shuffled to obey the command, confused by its unusual nature. ''We are going to advance own the quay and kick these truargan to Irin.''

The men cheered, but were still uncertain.

Duncan marched in front of the line carrying a shield of his own and ordered ''shields up''.

The men obeyed, interlocking their shields. Duncan fired his short staff at the shield wall. The wall flared blue briefly as the energy bolt dissipated harmlessly. ''Remember this. The wood against physical attack; repulse shield against energy attack.''

Duncan joined the right flank of the shield wall and shouted ''Let's go. Advance!''

They advanced slowly, irresistibly chanting 'barsick, barsick' and hammering on their shields as they went. Despite a withering storm of stolfire, the repulse shields held. As the distance between the two sides closed, some of the divines began to edge away as nervousness crept into their minds.

A divine who didn't moved quickly enough was impaled on a boss spike. Others were simply bludgeoned to death with the heavy wooden shields. All the while short staffs kept up a steady rate of fire, cutting down any divines that broke cover.

A group of divines charged hammering into the aneksa line, which buckled and wavered for a moment.

''Hold that line'' hollered Duncan ''Don't let them through.''

The front line used their long utility knives to stab at the divines over the top of their shields. The Divines, lacking any hand weapons tried to shoot their stols over the top of the shields. Some had their stol ripped from their hands, but some made good shots and a hole appeared in the aneksa line.

A huge divine, towering over his comrades broke the shield wall, grabbing the shields from out of nerveless hands and roaring with bestial savagery. A wedge of divines filled the gap, splitting the line in two.

''Push those muckers into the water'' Duncan heard the divine order as the line began to fail.

The huge divine swung a shield around, clasped in a big hand, battering at aneksa troops.

''Get that man'' screamed Duncan shooting bolts from his short staff.

The divine seemed blessed as attackers failed to get near him. Duncan fired again, scoring a glancing hit that barely slowed the mammoth man. Duncan saw with desperation the hole in the shield wall grow into a mêlée. He charged down the back of the line, heavy shield held in front of him crashing into the big divine with brutal force.

The two men crashed to the ground and Duncan found himself pinned down by the big divine with the boss spike of his shield punched through the divines shoulder. The man grinned maliciously down at Duncan squeezing his throat with one massive hand.

Duncan found his left arm pinned by his own shield. He could barely move or breathe. He felt his head being pulled up, then bashed to the ground. Then again, and again and stars appeared in his eyes.

Desperately Duncan tried to get his right arm around the shield and could just reach the big divine's head. He jammed his thumb into the divine's eye, ramming it home with as much force as he could.

Again, Duncan's head was smashed to the ground and he tasted blood in his mouth. He pushed again with his thumb and felt the weight of the big man shift. He managed to force his right leg between the big mans and affected a rolling motion. Suddenly he found himself atop the divine.

He kneed the man in the groin, but the man appeared impervious to pain and merely laughed. Duncan pulled back on the shield and finally rolled away from the man onto his feet. He now had no weapon, but hit the man with the shield. The boss spike scored the man's face and chest as he began to rise to his feet.

The divine hesitated, surprised and Duncan took advantage, thrusting the shield into the man's head. The boss spike punched through the man's skull. Duncan ripped the shield back and repeatedly battered the divine with it, even as the man collapsed dead at his feet. Parts of smashed brain and skull fragments clung to his shield.

The fight between Duncan and the huge divine had not lasted long, though it seemed like an age to Duncan. Duncan struggled to re-focus for a moment, and then roared. The bellow was purely animal and absolutely terrifying.

Duncan ploughed into the mêlée, smashing at divines with his shield. ''Re-form the line'' he screamed. The aneksa tried to do so as Duncan went berserk in the breach. He whirled, twisted and turned, using the shield as a bludgeon.

A last twist and thrust saw the final divine die with Duncan's boss spike rammed through his chest. As the man collapsed to his knees, Duncan saw that he was the divine who had been giving orders earlier.

The line had been re-formed behind Duncan and now resumed the advance down the quay. Resistance to the aneksa advance failed as divines deserted their posts either singly or in groups. The barrier at the south end of the quay was retaken for little cost of aneksa life and there Duncan halted the advance.

---

The fighting had returned to a stalemate. Anders39 was very tired and he was beginning to lose his concentration. He'd not slept for two days and it now looked like it might be another day before he could get some rest. Deep down he felt he dared not let one of his lieutenants take charge while he got a few wairs sleep. He knew they were capable, but knew also that they would love to see him fail. It was even possible that they would deliberately let him fail in order to discredit him. Anders39 saw no option, but to stay awake.

The situation was balanced on a knife-edge. He had to stay focused. His vision blurred as he stared at the map of Dundoon in front of him as sleep threatened to overwhelm him despite his best efforts. He shook himself awake.

If he could control the centre of the town, he would be more able to take some of the warehouses and take the town piecemeal. He drew up his instructions and called for Hamil36.

"Hamil36, you failed to take the quay as ordered. Why is that?"

"It was the flier my Divine Commander." Hamil36 replied.

Anger contorted Anders39's face "that is not true. The reports clearly show that the flier made a sustained attack on the south wall, but we still hold there. All the flier really did on the quay was to drop a few little bombs and I'm told was badly damaged. Your troops should have been able to take the quay."

Hamil36 was abashed "My Divine Commander, we had to retreat from the muckers. They had shields that stopped our stols. We are still trying to take the lost ground." It was a lie, but it was the best answer that Hamil36 could give. It was true that there was still some fighting on the quayside, so the lie should hold, but Hamil36 had no intention of making another attack.

"I see. Hold your ground there. What I want from you is to take these buildings in the centre of the town." Anders39 indicated the buildings on the map. "Do you think you can manage that?"

"The situation is complicated there, but we should manage my Divine Commander."

Anders39 stared at Hamil36 for a long moment. "Don't manage. Take those buildings and don't fail me again."

Hamil36 winced, but bowed his head in salute and made a hasty exit. Anders39 watched him leave wishing the man was more capable. In truth, Hamil36 might not be at fault as Anders39 realised that the muckers fought with great tenacity and ferocity.

---

292

Light was fading. Isla wondered what was happening inside the town, but could do nothing without communication. As she stood watching the sun set over Dundoon an arrow arched up over the walls. As it landed, it barely missed the head of a resting trooper.

Attached to the arrow fired from extreme range was a message that read 'attack at dawn, will signal then. Y.'

---

Grozet was snoring loudly, snorting and breathing heavily. Jonti thought the man capable of sleeping through anything. Jonti returned his attention to the barrier outside on the other side of the street held by divines. The setting sun behind the building held by the aneksa, cast an orange light over the barrier. The window Jonti peered through was in dark shadow making the aneksa position difficult for the divines to see.

Jonti was taking pot shots at any movement he saw on the barrier. It amused Jonti to think that he might even hit a divine by random chance rather than skill. The point was that it would keep them awake, unless they were all like Grozet, which Jonti doubted.

Other wounded scattered about the building were doing the same. There would be a change of shifts soon and Jonti would wake Grozet.

Jonti caught sight of a divine as he moved behind the barrier and made a single shot with his short staff. He then moved position to the left of the window to prevent the divines sighting on the flash.

There was movement out there, almost concealed by the angle of the wall. By peering dangerously out of the window Jonti could see divines advancing up the street. 'These guys don't quit' he thought to himself and aimed at the most exposed. His shot was good and the man fell face down in the street.

''Attack, right flank'' he shouted.

Jonti turned, wincing with pain as he jarred his damaged knee. Strips of beetick found in a warehouse strapped up the badly swollen knee. There might be something broken, Jonti mused, but there was nothing he could do about that yet.

293

A young man stood on the threshold of the room expecting further information from Jonti.

''Divines, coming up the street. Get some guys on the roof and take out those child killers.''

The young man nodded and rushed off. Jonti shuffled over to Grozet and shook him awake.

''Uh, wah?'' Grozet mumbled ''is it time already?''

''Nay, but we are under attack.''

''Great, just when I was having a nice dream.'' Grozet mimicked having sex graphically. ''Show me.''

''Against the wall on the right.''

''Really, what were you doing with your head stuck out the window?'' Grozet looked surprised, but didn't attempt to look out the window. ''These slootar aren't happy with killing women and children, they want to kill the whole world.''

# Chapter Twenty

It was early morning, just before dawn and Isla and her small army were waiting for the signal from Dundoon. Cullin and Sara sat in their fliers, also waiting.

Cullin had spent the previous evening stripping out wire from non-essential systems to make improvements to the flier's short staff firing system, which now worked from a button on the pilot's joystick.

He had finished making the modifications to Sara's flier less than two wairs before dawn. He was tired, but felt alert enough to fly. Sara, on the other hand, had got a decent night sleep. They had decided not to take grenades as these were now in very short supply and Isla needed everything she had for the coming battle.

The orange glow of pre-dawn started as a ribbon between the eastern hills, reflected off a cloud base that promised rain. A cold breeze came off the Canut Strait bringing with it a chilling damp mist.

Cullin shivered and adjusted his mane. He disliked this waiting game, wanting to be doing something useful. At last, even as a thin arc of the sun rose above the hills, three incendiaries ascended into the sky over Dundoon. A roar erupted from Isla's troops, giving Cullin goose-bumps. Both he and Sara started their fliers' thrusters and climbed into the air.

---

He had been covered with so much blood after the brawl on the quayside that they were now calling him Bloody Duncan. He watched the sun rising in the east. As the signal went up, he heard the responding roar from the Tuaport troops. He found the sound somehow comforting, knowing they had friends out there.

'Time to go' he thought grimly and waved his troops forward. Silently they crept toward the barracks. It was Duncan's job to create a corridor through the divine army, splitting it in two. Duncan hoped that by occupying the three rows of barracks that lay between their position and the gates he could achieve this.

Duncan had the shields that had been so effective on the quayside arranged in a semi-circle with the bulk of his troops protected within. He squinted into the rising sun, trying to discern activity ahead.

---

Iner was at the front of the army as they charged the barricade the divines had built where the gates had been. The fliers overhead raked the divine position with short staff fire, resulting in little stolfire defending the barricade.

As Isla's army entered the town, they came under heavy fire from barracks either side of the street ahead. The two fliers make repeated attack runs on the first barracks to their right.

Iner lobbed a grenade, one of the few he had, left handed through the first window of the barracks and charged toward it. There was a dull boom and smoke escaped from the window and Iner clambered through into the barracks. Other troops followed.

The barracks was a long two story building divided into small dormitories connected by a central corridor. It had stairs at each end leading to the upper story. At the far end to Iner was a large common room. As Iner exited the room the aneksa had entered, stolfire ripped down the corridor tearing into his body. Iner was dead before he hit the ground.

Inan sent two grenades skittering down the corridor and fired his short staff after. The boom of the grenades as they exploded sent a wall of debris and smoke billowing back down the corridor. A number of aneksa rushed into the corridor and started to advance toward the common room after Inan whilst another group started up the stairs.

A divine emerging from a dormitory was shot before he could raise his weapon. The other dormitories were cleared in rapid succession with grenades.

The few troops on the first floor put up little resistance.

''What do we do with this lot?'' asked a young trooper of Isla as the last of the divines in the building were brought under guard.

Six dejected and tired looking divines stood in the corner of the common room with short staff and arrows pointing at them. "Tie them. Bind their hands and take their boots off them. Just don't let them cause any trouble" Isla replied.

---

Ela shifted her position in the navigator's seat next to Cullin as she watched Duncan's troops advance across the street protected by their wall of shields.

"I hope they don't have grenades in that barracks, Cull. It could be messy for our guys if they do."

"Aye, Let's discourage them a bit then."

As Duncan's troops crept across the street like some giant beetle, Cullin and Sara raked the barracks with his short staff. Halfway across the street Duncan's troops broke into a run and stormed the barracks.

Cullin pulled away and turned his attention to the first floor as the aneksa clambered through windows into the barracks and started to clear the building of enemy troops room by room.

The barracks between Duncan's troops and Isla's troops soon found themselves caught in a lethal crossfire.

Ela yelped as two unusual craft streaked across the sky above the town. They were sleek broad delta winged aimu fighter drone aircraft. Sunlight glinted off the silver-skinned craft as they banked around in perfect synchronisation. Cullin and Sara had to break off their support of Duncan and Isla's troops to attack them. Cullin and Sara climbed swiftly towards the low clouds.

Even as the Drones closed in to attack, Cullin and Sara Duncan had set up another, smaller, beetle formation to assault the next barracks. Cullin banked sharply with an instinctive jerk on the controls as a stream of blue fire missed the unprotected upper nose of the flier by less than a pace.

"Deetah! Feeaklackne irin, that was too close Cull!" Ela cried

Cullin pulled the nose of the flier up and climbed into the clouds. Sara followed.

---

The boy Gensi was lost. 'Stay here' the man Atashin had said, and then gone away. They'd all gone away leaving him alone. Gensi was confused, bewildered and frightened. He wanted someone there to tell him everything would be fine and make the fear go away, but there was nobody.

Gensi wandered aimlessly with tears flowing unchecked and un-regarded down his cheeks. Fear ruled his mind, freezing all thought and purpose.

Soon he came to the gates of Dundoon. The noise of battle and the screaming didn't bother Gensi, it had become familiar too him as he'd followed his father Garag in the training camps deep in the forests. It meant that people were near and someone that could give him comfort.

There were heaps of rubble and rocks piled on top of the fallen gates with men crouched behind. Most of them ignored him, but there, wasn't that the man Atashin? He was sure it was and walked up to the man who had his back pressed against the heaps of rubble.

''What in irin are you doing here boy?'' Atashin grabbed the boy, pulling him down behind the rubble. ''I told you to stay where you were.''

The words were meaningless to the fragile mind of Gensi, but brought him a measure of comfort. He said nothing, but sat mute in the filth and debris, shaking almost imperceptibly.

---

The fliers were no match for the fast and manoeuvrable drones. Again, stolfire raked across the nose of Cullin's flier causing the shields to flare.

"Cac" exclaimed Cullion as he pushed the nose forward putting the flier into a dive. "Ela, keep an eye on Sara."

"Aye, these drones are all over us. How'd they see us in the clouds?"

"I don't know. They can and that's all we need to know" Cullin replied.

Sara's flier dropped out of the clouds and pulled in behind Cullin. Moments later the drones hurtled past dropping below the fliers and then pulling up into a vertical climb. In perfect synchronisation, they stopped dead in the air ahead of Cullin and Sara and turned to face them. Stols blazed even as the fliers dived beneath the drones. Cullin escaped by a hairs breadth, but Sara was hit on a rear stabiliser where the flier had no shield protection.

Sara's flier went into an uncontrolled roll and dipped toward the ground. She regained control of the flier with moments to spare before crashing. The rear of her flier smacked into the ground heavily and the flier slid along the ground sending plumes and sods of peaty soil into the air. The flier came to rest only paces away from a large outcrop of boulders and there remained motionless.

"Note their position Ela" Cullin bawled. "See if they're all right."

"Aye, we're north of the River Beg. I don't see any movement."

Jinking about as he circled Sara's flier, Cullin looked for any sign of life. After what seemed like an age, the tailgate dropped and two figures stumbled out. Fil had his arm about Sara as she limped, clearly unable to support her weight on one leg.

"They're out Cull, get out of here." There was a hint of panic in Ela's voice.

Cullin's mind raced as stolfire repeatedly hit the flier. He needed to focus on flying and not on Sara. He continued the jinking and dropped almost to ground level, desperate to escape from the drones. He rolled and pulled the flier in the tightest turn he dared, but the drones remained on his tail. A rocket missed the flier by less than a pace and

Cullin jerked the nose of the flier up, breaking as he did so. The drones streaked past.

Instinctively, Cullin fired the short staffs. ''You hit it!'' Ela screamed ''By Mozog, you hit the damn thing.''

As the drones banked around to attack again, Cullin dipped and accelerated away. The flier raced above heather moors with the drones in close pursuit.

---

Duncan and Isla stood in the common room of the middle barracks discussing what they would do next.

''What were those things?'' Isla asked.

''Fliers of some kind. Unmanned by the look of them.'' Duncan replied.

''I hope Cullin and Sara can deal with them. We can do without those things up there making our jobs more difficult.''

''Hmm, having fliers has given us an edge. We could be in trouble if Cullin and Sara don't beat them.''

''About all we can do is station some troops on the roofs with short staffs and hope we can shoot the things out of the sky.'' Isla shrugged, feeling helpless and short on ideas.

''Aye, do that. Four or five on the top of each of these barracks will have to do for now. Get them to take a couple of those shields as well. At least they'll have a bit of protection then.''

''What about the injured?''

Duncan shrugged. ''If they can fire a weapon use them on the roofs; if not then get them over to the warehouses.''

---

Stolfire flashed past the cockpit as Cullin pulled the flier into a sharp turn, presenting the shields to the drones as best he could. He had noticed that the drones could turn much more sharply than he could, but couldn't hover or adjust speed as quickly. It was a slim tactical advantage for Cullin to use and he lost speed every time he used it.

Cullin slammed the thrusters into full forward and the drones zipped past presenting a reflex shot. He let off a burst from the short staffs and scored a hit on the rear most drone. He accelerated again and turned toward Dundoon.

As he flew over the town, he dipped below wall height and slammed the thrusters back into forward. Again, the drones flew past and Cullin got another shot, missing this time.

He twisted and turned the flier, weaving about the streets being hit by stolfire as he found himself unable to escape the drones. In a desperate attempt to shake them, he accelerated toward a building flying as low as he dared. The shields were flaring to an alarming blue-white as he pushed the thrusters into forward again. The drones flashed past narrowly missing the building.

As Cullin manoeuvred behind another building, he caught a glimpse of short staff fire from people on the roofs of the buildings. Cullin grinned, they were shooting at the drones.

---

Yaren entered the common room where Duncan and Isla were talking. It had been a dangerous trip as divines from the north pocket had shot at him. Anyone on the streets of Dundoon alone from either side was an easy target for snipers. ''I need an update on what's happening. Nice of you to join us Isla.''

''Sorry I couldn't get here sooner.'' Isla replied.

''We can expect a counter attack at any time, but with those drones up there it could be difficult to make our own attack'' Duncan reported.

''I think now is the best time to make another push. Those drones won't be shooting at our troops whilst they're attacking our fliers. Take the next row of barracks north. I'll attack from the west and we'll squeeze that pocket of divines." Yaren walked over to a window and added "we need to act quickly."

"It was costly taking these buildings, Yaren. We have quite a few dead and injured." Isla advised. Of her original two hundred troops, she now had only sixty two left fit to fight.

"I know" Yaren nodded "but if I guess right, they have lost more troops. They are weaker than we are. We must keep the pressure up."

---

The drones were banking again for another attack. The drones also appeared to be unable to hover in level flight. Cullin realised that gave him an advantage in the town where the speed of the drones counted for nothing.

Cullin dropped behind a building, forcing the drones to slow down to his speed. He caught a glimpse of short staff fire from a nearby roof as the drones overshot and flew overhead. As the underbelly of the rearmost drone passed overhead, he released a long blast of his own short staffs and scored a hit.

The drones lifted away with the rearmost trailing a thin vapour trail. They banked again and made another attack run with stolfire ripping through the town.

Cullin flew below the rooftops using the buildings to protect him and made one hundred and eighty degree turn. The drones appeared directly ahead of him and he fired again at the damaged drone, striking it from head to tail.

Both drones flashed overhead, the first continued its flight, but the second with damaged control surfaces flew directly into the south wall of Dundoon.

"You got it!" screamed Ela "you bloody well got it!"

"Where's the other one, Ela?"

"I can't see it." Ela looked frantically about.

Cullin rounded the corner of a building heading west toward the Canut Strait.

''I see him!''

''Where, Ela, where?''

''Vapour trail behind you. Its going north, I think.''

Cullin turned the flier about heading back toward where he'd seen the short staff fire coming from the roofs and lifted the flier making himself an easier target.

''He's coming round again Cullin.''

''I see him.''

As the drone attacked Cullin lifted the nose, presenting the belly of the flier. He was unsighted for a few sents, but dipped the nose and spiralled, spinning in an apparently uncontrolled flight.

''Hesoos! Cullin!'' Ela yelped as she was thrown about in her seat.

The drone attacked again, slower this time and less certain. Cullin's erratic flight path had brought him over the roofs of the buildings where he'd previously seen short staff fire coming from. As the drone attacked, Cullin faced it directly, holding his position above the building.

The drone flew into a wall of short staff fire, its long wings wavering as it passed over the building. It crashed into the street beyond, cart-wheeling, scattering broken parts about the street.

---

Grozet with his chest heavily bandaged and arm in a sling was retreating with a squad of other ambulant injured and non-combatants to the warehouses. He looked back to make a headcount and noticed Atashin and the boy Gensi were missing. Atashin had joined the squad with the boy's safety as his main concern. He would return to the fighting as soon as he could.

A completely bewildered Gensi emerged from around the corner of a building closely followed by Atashin. Grozet waved urgently to them to hurry up. Atashin shrugged, grinned and pointed Gensi in the direction to go.

To his horror, Grozet saw stolfire tear through Atashin's shoulder as two divines rounded the corner.

''Cac'' exclaimed Grozet, vaulting a barricade and raced over to the stricken Atashin. ''Get that divine'' he screamed to Jonti and the realised that Jonti was not there. The others had moved on, heading towards the relative safety of the warehouses, leaving Grozet alone without back up.

Gensi wandered away aimlessly, sobbing and completely disoriented by his mental torment. The boy pulled his morcote tight about him and sat down in the middle of the street.

Atashin knew he was dying. The stol had ripped a hole in his chest and his right arm was missing. His heart beat rapidly, pounding heavily in his chest. He thought that was ironic when he had so little time left. Atashin's mind raced with adrenaline shock and he was surprised to find the initial pain ebbing away.

The noise of battle about him seemed unreal, otherworldly, 'fitting' he thought as he now belonged to another world. The boy, what was his name, was sobbing nearby. Atashin felt sad for him, it must be hard to lose everyone and everything you knew and cared about. What must that do to a young person?

A divine stood over Atashin, gloating, even as his vision began to fade, shrinking to a tunnel of light. 'Not much time left' Atashin thought to himself. He thought he could hear singing, a beautiful feminine tone softly diminishing. Was that real? He wasn't sure, but it still fascinated him.

Now even his sight failed, paling into blank oblivion. 'No time' thought Atashin even as he died.

Grozet saw the dying man and two enemy standing over him. The look on the face of the one who had shot the dying man was the look of a man who enjoyed killing. Grozet fumbling for his short staff found it

304

snagged in his sling. He was sure the divine enjoyed killing and watched helplessly as the divine pointed his stol at the sobbing boy and shot him in the chest.

Grozet's hackles raised as cold rage suffused his mind. The divine's laughing over their prizes had not noticed Grozet approach. Grozet punched the nearest in the face.

The surprised man jerked his head back into the face of the other and laughed. They both roared at Grozet and started to raise their stols.

Grozet punched the divine in the face again, but the divine just grinned.

''No pain where there's no sense'' Grozet said to himself even as the divines pointed their stols at him. ''Too late'' he said pointing to the ground. ''Grenade!''

Self-preservation is engrained into the divine psyche throughout their lives and both of the divines looked at the grenade and then each other in shock and then bolted back around the corner. Something metallic clanged onto the ground as one of the retreating divines dropped it.

Grozet chuckled evilly and picked up the grenade, dropping it into a pocket. ''Er guys'' he said to the retreating divines ''it's not lit!''

On the ground lay a large shining meat cleaver with a blade half a pace long and a handle of deer antler. Waving lines ran along the blades length showing great care and pride in its crafting. Tradition stated that the blades soul created the lines.

''Nice'' Grozet whispered to himself as he admired the blade ''I didn't think you guys used these things''.

He knelt down by the dead boy's corpse and crossed the arms across the ruined chest in the symbol of peace he had learned as a boy.

As he was rising to leave, a divine turned the corner and stopped dead in his tracks. The man clearly had not expected to find enemy troops on this street. The sight of the enemy enraged Grozet and he grabbed his short staff.

The weapon was still entangled in bandages, but Grozet shoved at it until it protruded through them between his arm and chest. He fired and watched the divine crumple to the ground, groaning. Grozet leaned over the man who whispered, repeating a phrase, over and over. Grozet realised the man was speaking in the 'true tongue'. Knowing that he was dying the divine was asking for 'deranack byenact', a final blessing.

Grozet knew what he wanted and chanted the 'words of peace' as written in the gospels of the four prophets. ''May Rossein take you and bless your passage to the other world''. Then Grozet spoke gently to the dying man ''I'm not sure if you deserve a blessing, but it's not my place to make judgement.''

Grozet wasn't sure if he could give the words, but without a Balcleric present, it was the best the dying man was going to get.

---

''I'm sure you've got a death wish, Grozet'' Yaren was saying. ''You seem to have found the fighting even though you're injured and supposed to be non-combatant.''

''Not by my choice, I can assure you. I'd rather be back home on my parents' croft.''

''I do have a job for you. I want you to go through these warehouses and look for anything we can use for weapons. I want to crush that north pocket as quickly as possible now.''

Grozet nodded his agreement ''Good idea, enough people have died already; too many.''

''Are you thinking about that boy? That wasn't you're fault.''

''Aye, I know that, but it's not just the boy, but those crofters as well and all the troops we've lost.''

Yaren grinned, not an open and friendly grin, but something that was half way towards being a grimace.

As the day progressed, the aneksa took more buildings, often with little resistance. Cullin patrolled above the town making it difficult for the divines to move their troops. In many cases, there were only a handful of troops defending a building.

By the fourth quarter of the day, the northern pocket had retreated to the Divine Generals Residence. The Residence was a complex of austere buildings set behind its own wall. From there the divines of the northern pocket made their last stand.

Grozet was searching a warehouse by the quayside and had found an odd lumpy shape covered by sheet coverings tucked away in a gloomy corner. When he lifted the coverings he softly exclaimed happily ''Ohh nice, very nice!''

What he had found was a launcher for large gauge plazboma. He immediately set about looking for the ammunition and soon found it in large crates nearby. He then went in search of help moving it.

''I want it taking to Yaren now'' Grozet was saying.

''We can't, it doesn't fit through the doors.'' Replied the young man who was the leader of a squad he had found nearby.

''It must do, it got in here!''

''There are large double doors at the south of the warehouse, directly opposite the divines.''

''Cac!'' muttered Grozet in exasperation.

''The only other doors we might get it through are jammed.''

''Well un-jam them or I'll make my own door.'' Grozet patted the plazgunna.

Within half a wair, the large warehouse doors had been opened and the squad were moving the plazgunna towards the frontline in the northern section of Dundoon. Grozet enlisted another squad to move the plazboma shells.

Yaren was overjoyed at the sight of the weapon and immediately set about reducing the walls of the Divine Generals Residence. When the divines refused to surrender Yaren ordered the building reduced to rubble. Not a single trooper came out of the building alive.

The southern pocket continued to fight for the rest of the day. They, like the divines of the northern pocket refused offers of surrender as Yaren pressed the attack overnight.

# Chapter Twenty One

It was before dawn on the fifth day of the battle for Dundoon and the two moons Atha and Matha were visible in the sky casting a pale, cold light over the hills east of Dundoon.

Anders39 had summoned Hamil36 to explain why there had been no progress with the fighting. He sat behind a large desk in one of the offices in southern Dundoon. Laid out on the desk was a plan of the town with markers to indicate which side occupied a particular building.

A band of blue markers across the south of the town showed the extent of divine held buildings. Anders39 was beginning to get desperate as the position of the divine army looked increasingly weak.

''Why have you not moved forward?'' asked a stiff and exhausted Hamil36.

''We are doing our best, but we have suffered heavy losses'' Hamil36 replied defensively.

Anders39 stared at the man and waited before bluntly making his point. ''The muckers have had heavy losses also. You didn't push hard enough. You have failed again.''

A desperate Hamil36 started to protest. ''We have done everything possible –''

''Liar!'' screamed Anders39. ''If you had done everything possible, you would have advanced.'' When Hamil36 failed to answer Anders39 continued ''Am I wrong?''

''They used their dead to extend the barriers. My Divine Commander, even their dead fight against us!''

''That is defeatist talk! It gives me an idea though, perhaps you would be more useful as part of a barrier.''

An astonished Hamil36 watched Anders39 lift the stol from the desk. Cold fear froze Hamil36's heart as he realised he was a dead man. Anders39 shot him in the head moments later.

---

The flier was making another attack run along the wall. A heavy iron girder was all Kay47 had for protection. He hoped it would suffice. Short staff fire licked along the parapet as the flier slowed to a halt and hovered at the eastern end of the wall.

The return fire from the divines was poor and ineffective against the fliers shielding. Kay47 kept his body pressed hard against the wall and made a few half-hearted shots at the flier.

From his position, he could see the tailgate begin to drop and troops exit from the flier. There were perhaps twenty or so, all with those wooden shields that the muckers had used so effectively on the quayside.

The flier lifted away to reveal a wall of troops who roared a challenge and started a slow and deliberate advance along the wall. Kay47 fired his stol, concentrating on the feet of the muckers.

The shield wall glowed as it repulsed the divines' fire. Kay47 found himself pinned down, unable to advance or withdraw. He realised he was in a hopeless position and abandoned his stol. He held hands forward, palms up in a gesture of surrender and closed his eyes, hoping that the muckers wouldn't shoot him out of hand.

Suddenly he felt a burning sensation down his right side. He gasped from the intense pain. It was painful to draw a breath. He felt another burning jolt as he was shot again, but not by the muckers. His own side had shot him.

Kay47 collapsed forward and was dead before he hit the ground.

As the morning progressed, the divines lost more and more ground, finding themselves squeezed into a small pocket of a handful of buildings in the south east of Dundoon.

The plazgunna found by Grozet and Cullin's flier combined their firepower by bombarding each building in turn until its defenders either gave up the fight or retreated to the next building.

The endless pounding, the boom and whine of the plazgunna preceding a thunderous explosion had finally rattled Anders39's nerves. He was still without sleep since the beginning of the battle and this desperate lack now clearly affected his judgement. His lieutenants knew this as they confronted Anders39.

''The position is hopeless. We cannot hope to win.'' Rabin27 was saying.

''We must move forward and re-take the gates.'' Anders39 was quite adamant that the divine army keep fighting. ''Then if we are unable to fight on, we can escape into the hills.''

''We have lost the battle, Anders39.'' Rabin27 insisted.

''I refuse to accept that the muckers have not lost as many troops as we have. They are weaker then they appear to be.''

''That plazgunna is going to destroy each building in turn. This building is likely to be next.'' Rabin27 couldn't believe the stubborn stupidity of Anders39. Why could the man not accept defeat?

As if in answer to Rabin27's thoughts, there was a boom from outside. A loud crashing followed as the building collapsed.

''You will do as you are ordered and succeed or die trying.'' Anders39 had his stol levelled at Rabin27.

Rabin27 ignored the stol and looked out the window at the cloud of dust that billowed in the breeze where the building once stood. ''We had over twenty troops in that building, they refused to surrender. There is no chance of success Anders39.''

''You will do as ordered!'' Anders39 screamed, squeezing the handle of the stol.

Rabin27 fell with a large hole blasted in his chest muttering a last word ''idiot!'' It was unclear whether he meant Anders39 or himself. He was dead before he hit the ground.

The building shook with the impact of a plazboma shell.

Anders39 faced his lieutenants shaking with rage. ''Now get out there and fight!''

As one they replied ''no!'' They shot Anders39 before the commander could lift his own weapon.

For several moments Anders39 remained standing, long enough for him to deliver a last reprimand to his lieutenants. ''Cowards!'' he managed as his body failed. Even as his body gave way, he attempted to lift his stol and aim at the nearest lieutenant.

He never completed the action as his lieutenants with a last act of contempt shot him again. Anders39's body twisted and jerked with each impact as his body collapsed to the ground.

Yaren supervised the shelling of each building. There were limited numbers of plazboma and he wanted each shell to count. He glanced up into the air at the flier. Cullin had been in constant support since the air battle the day before. Cullin must be utterly exhausted, but still appeared relatively fresh and alert.

Yaren was about to order another round fired at the building when the main door opened. A single stol clattered and bounced out of the doorway and was followed by a single divine with his palms raised in surrender.

Duncan stepped forward warily with his shield solidly in front of him. He stopped in front of the divine and asked ''what is your purpose?''

''Our position is hopeless. We wish to surrender and avoid further bloodshed.''

''What is your name? What authority do you have to offer surrender?'' Duncan asked shifting his shield slightly to point the boss spike at the divine.

''I am Payg25; our Commander is dead. I have temporary command of the army.''

''I see. Your men must give up their weapons and come out palms up.''

The surrender went smoothly and within half a wair, the aneksa had about a hundred divines held in a single building under guard. Many of the divines wept openly with profound shock at captivity by inferior muckers, many of whom brandished bows and arrows rather than proper energy weapons. They were beaten people, their egos crushed by the ignominy of their defeat.

---

Sara and Cullin were sitting in bright warm sunshine of late afternoon on Gelkarn. It was still only spring for Garvamore, but the warmth in the sun was pleasant. They were eating the first proper meals they'd had in days from the depleted stores of Dundoon.

Before departing Dundoon, Yaren had thanked them for their parts in the defence of the town and dismissed them with big friendly hugs, knowing that they both had other duties at Rustick More.

Sara had commented that they probably needed a couple of fliers stationed at Dundoon permanently and promised to talk to Dookerock about it. Cullin added that there was divine technology on Gelkarn and probably Begarn as well available to scavenge.

Sara's flier needed repairs made if it was to fly again. Sara had done her best since the air battle to make the craft airworthy again, but had found a number of essential parts could not be bypassed or repaired. Cullin had suggested that they fly up to Gelkarn and have a look for them. After the stresses of the last few days, Sara had readily agreed.

They'd found transport cases neatly deposited by transports and started hunting through them for the items they needed. The aimu transports had faithfully followed their programming arranging containers in concentric rings about a central point and then returned to the aimu transport ship.

''Hey Sara'' Cullin disturbed her as she moved to a large transport container and started to open it. ''There must be a ship harboured down the coast. We really ought to talk to Yaren about it before we go back to Rustick More.''

Sara thought for a moment before replying. ''Aye, do you think they'll send another army?''

''Not from that ship, but there may be divines still on it and they will certainly be able to communicate with the Frame.''

''Well, there's nothing we can do about it just now.''

''Nay, not just now'' Cullin agreed. ''What's that one?''

''Ooh, I don't know. It looks nice, some sort of fruit I think.''

The container was full of small food packages labelled in a language Sara couldn't read and an image of the contents. Each container had a green spot in the middle of the label with no decorative or apparent practical purpose.

''Open one, see what it's like.''

Sara tried to prise the lid off with a knife, but found it too firmly attached.

Cullin laughed ''try pressing that green spot.''

When Sara did so, the spot turned a livid dark red and the edges of the lid pulled away from the rest of the container. Sara lifted the lid gingerly, expecting to find sweet fruit as shown on the label. Instead she grimaced ''that looks horrid!'' she complained.

She showed the contents, a dried husk of material on the base of the container, to Cullin.

''I don't expect they eat it like that'' Cullin mused. He looked at the label and added ''I don't know the language, but I do know this symbol. It means water. Try adding some water and see what happens.''

When Sara did so there was an immediate reaction. The container emitted small popping sounds and within a few sents the husk swelled

314

to produce a pulpy mass that smelt distinctly fruity, but appeared nothing like its depiction on the label.

Sara dipped her finger into the mass and took a cautious taste. ''Ooh'' she smacked her lips with distaste ''that's a bit strange.''

Cullin tried some and said ''It's not sour or anything. I'm sure it's supposed to be like that.''

Sara continued to eat the pulp, a habit of her past when you ate what you got without complaint or went hungry.

''I guess we should pack some of this stuff and get it to Dundoon.'' Cullin was looking at the different containers.

Sara was perplexed ''what I don't understand is why the divines just left it here. They must have been hungry without food.''

''Hungry and thirsty if they needed water to make the food.'' Cullin depressed the released mechanism on a larger container and peered at the contents. ''And they would certainly not have left this here if they had known about it.''

''Oh, what is it?'' Sara looked into the container herself, still spooning fruit pulp into her mouth. ''Oh, they certainly wouldn't!''

Cullin scratched his head ''why do you think they would leave a plazgunna here?''

''I guess they didn't know it was here. We should take it to Dundoon.''

''Aye'' Cullin sighed ''and we still need to get your flier repaired.''

''And it's nice not to be busy for a while.''

''Aye, but it would be even nicer to sleep in a proper bed tonight, back at Rustick More I mean.''

''Ooh, now there's a nice thought'' Sara gave Cullin a meaningful look.

---

The sun was high in the sky and Pyta judged it to be about midday. It had been quite a busy day at the road junction and he had a long list of activity to report to the Boss. A wagon train heading north to either Creelan or Balgeel from Kilgarv was the most interesting. Pyta could tell that the wagons had a heavy load from the way in which they lurched and creaked, but they had been far from fully laden. Whatever the load had been, it had been heavy and therefore interesting.

Pyta watched as an old wagon pulled by a donkey fit for the knackers made its slow way down the rutted track from Innish. It was drawing quite close before he recognised the hunched figure holding the reins as his Boss.

''Hey Boss, dint expec' yer back 'ere so soon.'' He called out. Pyta took a drink from a large water bottle and offered the bottle to the Boss as he drew up.

''Ta, Pyta.'' The Boss took a swig from the bottle and gagged on the contents, spitting them back out as he choked. ''Tha'll kill yer.''

Pyta ignored the comment and took the water bottle back, twisted the top and offered the bottle to the Boss again.

The Boss looked suspiciously at the bottle and took a precautionary sniff before having a long drink of water from it. ''In'erestin' bo'le Pyta. Ah 'ope yer doin' yer job proper, not ge'in drunk.''

''Where yer gan?''

''Got 'ams fer Linn.''

''Ah, 'ear's me compad, yer ken check me wuk.'' Pyta handed over the small device.

''Tha'll be fine.'' The Boss spent several sents checking over Pyta's data before handing the compad back. ''Be mur descriptive, Pyta. Wot did them people luk like in them wagons?''

''Jus' or'n'ry folk.''

''Ah need detail Pyta. Yer need ta put everything down an' drink less whisky.''

''Ah'm doin' me job fine Boss.''

''Da whisky'll kill yer 'fore long.'' The Boss shook the reins and the donkey heaved the wagon into slow ponderous motion.

Pyta laughed, not caring what his Boss thought about his drinking and called out to the retreating figure of his Boss. ''Hey, Red, Ah bet Ah outlive ya!''

''Tha's a bet yer ken't win Pyta''

---

Two days after leaving Dundoon, Cullin and Sara found their world returning to normal. They were relaxing in their quarters at Rustick More when Sara commented ''so what happens next?'' Sara asked. ''Surely that isn't it?''

''Hmm? Isn't what?'' replied Cullin sleepily.

''The battle at Dundoon, surely the Frame won't just give up. It will attack again.''

''Aye, I expect so. Yayler does too. There's going to a meeting later in Dookerock's quarters. Get some rest, we don't have to get up yet.''

''Hmm. I've got a better idea'' whispered Sara in Cullin's ear.

Later Cullin was looking for Dook and found him relaxing with a kitten in his lap by the target rock on Rustick More's flat summit. Dookerock had saved a scruffy looking mongrel cat from savaging by dogs a few days earlier. I was the cats' remaining kitten that he was absently stroking.

''Hey Dook, that meeting is about to start.'' Cullin reminded Dook.

"My apologies young friend, but I have other commitments right now." Dook continued to stroke the animal looking at the distant mountains.

"I don't understand. You are not busy at the moment."

"Ah, but I am. You see the kitten's mother has given this, her sole remaining kitten, into my care" Dook replied.

"I still don't follow" Cullin was perplexed, not understanding Dook's point.

"I need to be here with the kitten when she returns with food. She should be back soon." Dook explained as if it was perfectly normal.

"Isn't our situation a little more important than a kittens dinner?" Cullin found Dook's casual attitude irritating and failed to hide it well.

Dook shrugged "not to the kittens mother it isn't. It's a question of trust."

"You think a cat's trust is more important than a man's trust? We're in a very difficult situation here, my friend, and I see that the cat has already collected a couple of mice."

"Ahh, no, I caught those, but the cat has its' pride. You know how females are!" Dook laughed, disturbing the kitten, which mewed and yawned, stretching and then digging its claws into Dook's leg.

Cullin found Dook's inexplicable behaviour absurd, but realised that he wouldn't win. Dook would go to the meeting when he felt like it and not before. "Don't be too long then."

"Stay a while Cull, you're too impatient."

Cullin gave up and sat down next to Dook "what?" he said with ill-disguised frustration.

"You know what they're calling Isla's troops?"

"No!"

"Sheedoo, the black spirits. It's in a number of the reports."

Cullin laughed suddenly at the memory of Isla's troops plastered with peat ''they were very black''.

''I heard they're calling Dundoons troops the Bloody Duncans.''

''Aye, Duncan did make quite an impressive mess of the divines with one of your shields.''

''It was quite a fight down there. A lot of people got hurt, but you prevailed. It's quite impressive.''

Cullin nodded sadly ''aye, a lot of dead too. Too many.''

''There'll be another battle before too long that'll make Dundoon appear like a mere scrap. Ahh, here she is.''

''who? Oh, the cat.''

Dook was silent for a while watching the cat as it sniffed at the mice and made a tentative bite. He made no effort to go to the meeting and if anything appeared as if he would remain, where he was for the rest of the day.

''Dook, are you going to stay here all day?''

''Probably.''

Cullin stared at Dook, unable to believe what he was hearing. It was too uncharacteristic. ''Look Dook, I've got to go. I hope you and the cat will be very happy.''

''Sarcasm Cullin. That's beneath you.''

As Cullin stood up and started to leave, Yayler arrived. ''Ahh, here you are.''

''There's no point talking about it. You know how I feel about the idea.'' Dook didn't even turn to look at Yayler.

''I've been working on this for a long time Dook. The time is right.''

''I can't help you.''

''I could use your help, but I will go alone if I have to.''

''Am I missing something?'' Cullin interjected.

''Oh, not much.'' Dook gazed for a moment at Cullin as if trying to assess his feelings. ''Yayler is attempting to get aid from the divines.''

''That's a crazy idea'' Cullin regarded Yayler with shock.

''I want to build our strength here, getting aid from the divines is an impossible task'' Dook continued.

''It is only a matter of leverage, Dook.'' Yayler had the look of someone who had already been through the argument.

''It won't happen Yayler'' Dook added and turned his attention back to Cullin. ''Yayler has been talking to these divines for years. He thinks they'll come here to help us fight against the Frame.''

''What? Here? How would you stop one of them giving the location of Rustick More to the Frame?'' The thought of divines at Rustick More was profoundly disturbing to Cullin. He could only imagine what Dook must be thinking.

''I'll be leaving later today Dook. Make sure Cullin knows what he has to do.'' Yayler left without goodbyes, walking sadly towards a cleft in the rim of Rustick Mores summit plateau that hid an entrance to the complex within the mountain.

Dook didn't look, but Cullin could see that he was very unhappy. ''So, what do I have to do?''

''Oh, nothing much. Find the Interface and deactivate it.''

# Appendix

## Time

The day is divided into quarters. Night Morning Afternoon and Evening as might be expected. The quarters are then divided into quarters again to give sixteen sectors or Wairs per day that are further divided into a hundred Sents.

A Sent is 9/10ths of a minute.

2/3 wair = 1 hour = 60 minute = 66.6 sents

1 wair = 1.5 hours = 100 sents = 90 minutes

## Months of the Year

The year is divided into ten months of 36 and 37 days alternately.

The months are;

Tuseek 36 days

Darna 37 days

Tres 36 days

Kerev 37 days

Ooan 36 days

Savrah 37 days

Orach 36 days

Booen 37 days

Nuygev 36 days

Blenakriak 36 days

New Year Holiday 1 day

Days of the Week

Day 1 earth day

Day 2 moon day

Day3 water day

Day 4 fire day

Day 5 midweek

Day 6 hameed day

Day 7 Mozog day

Day 8 rossein day

Day 9 hesoos day

Day 10 tenday

## Money

Transactions made using paper promissory notes called Notes of Account or Notes for short. The Marks Treasurer or Advocate keeps these notes or records.

A barter system is used where 1 horse = 2 cows

= 10 pigs

= 20 sheep

= 200 fowls

= 4000 Tokens

## Distances

1000 pace = one Stride

1 pace = 3 feet

12 inch = 1 foot

## Measures

1 cubic inch = 1 fluid oonsa

20 fluid oonsa = 1 muga

100 fluid oonsa = 1 kead

1 fluid oonsa = 1 oonsa

## Weights

100 oonsa = 1 kudram (6.25 lb)

1000 oonsa = 1 jaykudram (62.5 lb)

10 000 oonsa = 1 keakudram

20 000 oonsa = 1 morkudram(129 kg)

# Characters

Atashin – One of Isla's aneksa; fought on Gelkarn in the Battle of Dundoon.

Big Jon – Cook at Dunossin.

Cabar – aneksa, talking with Goram.

Cona – Cullin's eldest brother

Dav – man from ruined croft in Glen Ereged.

Donal – Old man who makes his own hooch whisky in Mark Ossin.

Drandan (nag) – Goram's neighbour's wife.

Duncan – Yaren's lieutenant.

Ecta – Cullin's boyhood friend.

Ela – Cullin's female navigator.

Favir – crofter in Glen Ereged.

Fil – Sara's navigator.

Freyna – wife of Uska, mother of Uskabeg.

Garath – potter at Dunossin.

Grega – Advocate at Dunossin.

Goram – a crofter from Mark Ossin.

Guvin – fisherman, son of Pul.

Guvin – Wagon Master.

Hamadern – Cullin's third eldest brother.

Hameed – the Latter Prophet

Hamil36 – Divine lieutenant in battle of Dundoon

Hesoos – One of the four faces of God, the child prophet in whose name all children are blessed.

Inan – troop in battle at Dundoon.

Iner – troop leader in battle at Dundoon.

Isla – aneksa trooper.

Jak – Landlord of inn in Baylycraig.

Jonti – Young man, aneksa fighter in Dundoon attack.

Kensi – Wagon master

Kuli – Lord Ossin's wife, mother of Cullin.

Linn – Pyta's landlady in Garvin.

Mozog – the first prophet.

Neev – female mechanic at Rustick More.

Orvalt – Cullin's second eldest brother.

Pibeg – fat woman near Marlok who lodges Pyta.

Pul – innkeeper at Pirt and former fisherman.

Pyta – Tavern drunk, a thug.

Roby – A crofter in Glen Ereged.

Rollo – Resistance guide in the Bandrockit area.

Rona – Large female wagoner who Goram assisted.

Rorga – The Tavern landlord.

Rossein – God of thought and enlightenment.

Roz – Ecta's scouting assistant.

Shona – Roby's wife.

Terran – Keem's childhood dog.

Toby – A shepherd at Atalok.

Ulbin – Cullin's fourth older brother.

Uska – Father of Uskabeg in refugee corrie

Wagon Master Guvin – friend of Dona who assists Yayler and Cullin on their journey to Pirt.

Yaren – Ulbin's lieutenant.

Yasga – squad leader who captured the aimu transport ship in Dundoon.

Yayler Poddick – Old man who befriends and trains Cullin. Also known as Victor 8

# Glossary of Terms

Amadan – idiots.

Atha – Inalsol's first moon

Aneksa – free people.

Aimu – Artificial intelligent mechanoid units.

Alben – Scots Pine

Atalok – Lake to the south west of Mark Ossin.

Ar- east or eastern

Ardcleric – a clans head priest.

Ardyvinland – main island in the group called Garvamore.

Aylinron – small rocky island, northeast Marlok.

Balcleric – a local priest.

Bancaol – the narrow sea strait north Bandrokit.

Banree Na Mur – Pul's boat.

Barsick – die.

Beetick – the cloth made from Beet fibres.

Begarn – hill north of Dundoon.

Bivvy - bivouac

Brayvik Straits – a narrow sea passage that separates the Island of Brayvik from Anklayv Island.

Breergara – a liar.

Cac – faeces, shit

Calman – pigeon or dove.

Calp – kelp.

Cammic - A device that both records sound and visual data.

Compad – a small computer about the size of a modern credit card.

Com-posts – communication device of the Frame for use by aimu.

Comsat – communication satellite.

Canut Strait – small sea between Willemsbree and Dundoon.

Creet – hard artificial stone used by the Frame to construct buildings.

Darna – second month of the year

Deetah – damn.

Des – south or southern

Divines – the ruling elite in human culture who are overseen by aimu and ultimately the Frame.

Divine's staff – communication and energy transfer device.

Drimneev (poison ridge) – mountain that Cullin and Ecta survey

Dun – an extensive stone dwelling, frequently fortified.

Duvick Namarv – the realm of the dead.

Feeaklack – teeth.

Flier – a small flying machine, originally designed by the Frame, but adapted for manual flight by the resistance.

Furlok – Long sea inlet east of Mark Ossin.

Garvamore – a group of mountainous islands lying north of the main continent.

Gelkarn – hill south of Dundoon.

Gunna – gun.

Hiu – human interface unit.

Holoscreen – display unit for computers.

Inalsol – the world in which lies Garvamore.

Irin – hell.

Kerev – fourth month of the year

Kilree – head of the church – archbishop.

Locater disc – device registered to a specific person that signals its position to a specific receiver.

Lok Kruay – sea inlet east of Rustick More.

Mane – a fur or woollen wrap used to keep out bad weather.

Mark – an administrative unit of Garvamore.

Mark Brus – located near Drimneev.

Mark Glaskarn – Mark in Dunban Mountains

Mark Kissom – Mark that includes Dundoon.

Mark Konzie – Mark in Dunban Mountains

Mark Lowd – neighbouring Mark to Mark Ossin.

Mark Ossin – Cullin's home Mark.

Marlok – stretch of seawater separating Ardbanacker from Anklayv.

Matha – Inalsol's second moon.

Morcote – heavy densely woven knee length woollen coat that keeps out most bad weather and cold.

Morven Rebellion – rebellion against the divines and Frame.

Nano - Nanos improve mitochondrial efficiency. Different nanos improve muscular output increasing speed and strength. Further implants improve memory and can process data accurately as fast as computer speeds. The brain shortcuts by making comparisons allowing ultrafast human computation.

Natua – north or northern

Neuro-chips – miniature computers inserted into divines brains.

Nuygev – ninth month of the year.

Oyki na Spirad – Night of the Spirits

Oil Beet – a root vegetable that produces a heavy oily sap.

Plaz – A durable light material made from refined oil beet sap.

Plazgunna – plazboma gun, fires plazboma shells.

Plazboma – plastic explosive.

Rayanam – season of souls, runs from the winter equinox for three months (tuseek, Darna and tres)

Rune disc – indentification device that is programmed to recognise specific genes.

Salak - dirt

Sents – one hundredth of a wair.

Sheedoo – black spirits.

Skits – childs game played with stones.

Slootar – villains, person of low honour.

Stol - hand held energy weapon.

Surwane - spruce

Tendays – ten days, equates to a metric week.

Tres – third month of the year

Truarly – expletive - nasty, evil

Truargan – evil ones, a wretch.

Tuaport – divine town on Ardbanacker Island.

Tuseek – first month of the year

Tyber – possible location of the Interface in Desert Zone A.

Varamor Sea – lies east of the Islands of Garvamore.

Wagon Master Guvin – friend of Dona who assists Yayler and Cullin on their journey to Pirt.

Wagoner/s – traders in heavy goods requiring transport.

Wair – 1/16 th of a day. 90 minutes.

Wicks – sheep.

Wifman – woman.

Yaren – Ulbin's lieutenant.

Yasga – squad leader who captured the aimu transport ship in Dundoon.

Yayl – a six stringed fiddle.

Yer – west or western

CPSIA information can be obtained
at www.ICGtesting.com
Printed in the USA
JSHW041356300123
36808JS00006B/15